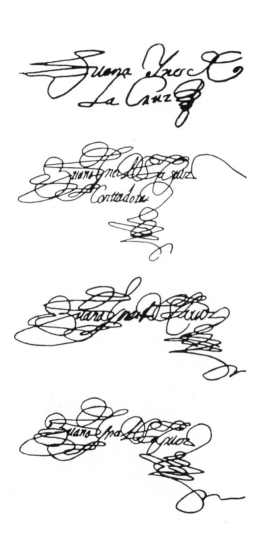

Sor Juana's Second Dream

Joana ynes dela cruz Monja nobisia de
este comb.to de n̄ro P.e S. ger.mo Digo que es-
toy Dentro Del term.o Dela año de aproba.on
En el Conforme alo Dispuesto Por el s.to
Conz.o Puedo Hazer testam.to y Renum
Sias.on Dequalesquier Vienes que me
Pertenescan y Para poderlo Hazer

A V.m Pido y Sup.co Se sirba de Concederme
Lis.a Para otorgar Testam.to y Renum
Sias.on ante qualquier Seriu.o &.a en el
Resebire m.rd Con Jus.t.a y en lo nes.o &.o—

Juana ynes dela Cruz

Sor Juana's Second Dream

A NOVEL BY

Alicia Gaspar de Alba

The University of New Mexico Press

Albuquerque

First edition

Library of Congress Cataloging-in-Publication Data

Gaspar de Alba, Alicia, 1958–

   Sor Juana's second dream : a novel / by Alicia Gaspar de Alba.
   —1st ed.

   p.   cm.

   ISBN 0-8263-2091-0 (alk. paper)

   ISBN 0-8263-2092-9 (pbk. : alk. paper)

   1. Juana Ines de la Cruz, Sister, 1651–1695—Fiction. 2. Mexico—Church
history—17th century—Fiction. I. Title.

PS3557.A8449 S67 1999

813'.54—dc21   98-58093
                                                                       CIP

On page i, Sor Juana's signatures are from the following years, from top to bottom: 1689, 1691, 1692, and 1695.

Selections of "The Poet's Answer to the Most Illustrious Sister Filotea de la Cruz" were reprinted by permission of The Feminist Press at the City University of New York, from Sor Juana Inés de la Cruz, *The Answer / La Respuesta*. Critical edition and translation by Electa Arenal and Amanda Powell. Translation copyright © 1994 by Electa Arenal and Amanda Powell.

Selections of "She Assures That She Will Hold a Secret in Confidence," Fragment of Doña Leonor's monologue, and "In a Reply to a Gentleman from Peru" by *Sor Juana Inés de la Cruz: Poems* (1985), translated by Margaret Sayers Peden reprinted by permission of Bilingual Press/ Editorial Bilingüe.

Section of "Vicarious Love" and "Convent and the Court" reprinted by permission of the publisher from *A Sor Juana Anthology* by Alan S. Trueblood (trans.), Cambridge, Mass.: Harvard University Press, Copyright © 1988 by the President and Fellows of Harvard College.

Selections reprinted by permission of the publisher from *Sor Juana: or, the Traps of Faith* by Octavio Paz, translated by Margaret Syers Peden, Cambridge, Mass.: Harvard University Press, Copyright © 1988 by the President and Fellows of Harvard College.

Selections of *Symposium: Plato,* translated by Benjamin Jowett, Upper Saddle River, NJ: Prentice Hall, Inc. © 1996 reprinted by permission of the publisher.

No soy yo la que pensaís,
sino es que allá me habeís dado
otro ser en vuestras plumas
y otro aliento en vuestros labios,
y diversa de mí misma
entre vuestras plumas ando,
no como soy, sino como
quisisteis imaginarlo.

I am not the one you think,
your old world quills
have given me another life,
your lips have breathed another spirit into me,
and diverse from myself
I exist between your plumes,
not as I am, but as you
have wanted to imagine me.
    —JUANA INÉS DE LA CRUZ, "TO THE
MATCHLESS PEN OF EUROPE," UNFINISHED POEM

To know is to dream, but that dream is everything we know of ourselves, and in that dream resides our greatness.
    —OCTAVIO PAZ

para Deena
única musa

and in loving memory
of my Honey,
Carmen Gaspar de Alba,
1946–1994

Contents

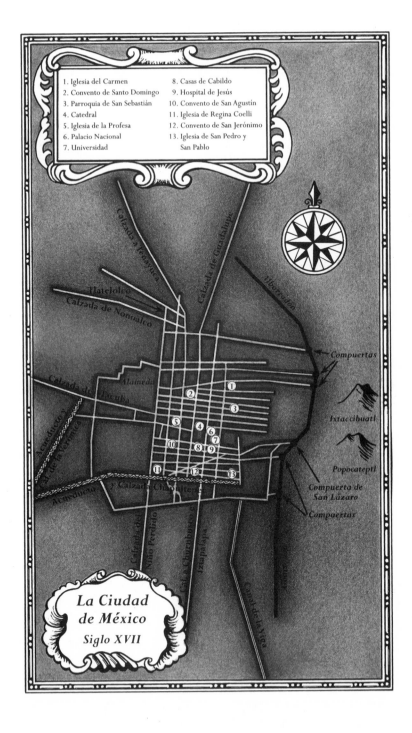

La Ciudad de México

Siglo XVII

1. Iglesia del Carmen
2. Convento de Santo Domingo
3. Parroquia de San Sebastián
4. Catedral
5. Iglesia de la Profesa
6. Palacio Nacional
7. Universidad
8. Casas de Cabildo
9. Hospital de Jesús
10. Convento de San Agustín
11. Iglesia de Regina Coelli
12. Convento de San Jerónimo
13. Iglesia de San Pedro y San Pablo

Fianchetto

JUNE 1693

Bishop's Pawn

"Get out of my sight, you brazen harlot!" thundered His Ilustrísima, Archbishop Aguiar y Seijas, his blue eyes blazing in horror. He hurled his cup at the girl walking through the door with a pot of chocolate. Startled, the girl dropped the pot on the bare flagstones of the library, and Don Manuel Fernández de Santa Cruz, Bishop of Puebla, covered his ears against the sound of shattering porcelain.

The Archbishop got to his feet. "This is a disgrace! How many times need I tell you, Padre Antonio, that no woman is ever to attend me? I'll not stay here a minute longer."

Padre Antonio rose, but Don Manuel remained seated, cleaning his nails with a fork tine. "Forgive me, Ilustrísima," Padre Antonio said. "I forgot to ring for the steward instead of the maid. It was an old man's mistake. No harm was done."

"You allowed the room to be defiled by a woman's presence. You know that causes irreparable damage to my liver."

"Forgive me, Ilustrísima," Padre Antonio repeated. "It will never happen again. I shall have that girl flogged for coming in here, but I beg you not to leave yet. We must discuss the chronicle that Sor Juana's Superior has proposed. Mother Andrea has been waiting for an answer since before Lent, and it's already Pentecost. I find it awkward, Ilustrísima, to continue rendering my services at San Jerónimo without broaching the subject with her."

"Nothing could force me to stay in this room," the Archbishop insisted.

"Why don't we move to your private patio, Antonio?" suggested the Bishop. "I know you allow no servants access to that inner sanctum of yours. And perhaps we could lunch on something salty after this—" He gestured disdainfully at the platter of apricot empanadas, of which he had already consumed half. "All this soft, sweet food makes my teeth hurt."

The patio's rose garden had been the only thing motivating Padre Antonio during the long weeks of his illness. He rose for the holy Offices as was his obligation, not even bothering to slip on his shoes or comb the wisps of his hair, disciplined himself three times a day, and even managed to write lectures for the weekly meeting of the Brotherhood of Mary, although it was Sigüenza who delivered them in his place. But he offered no Masses, heard no confessions, gave no sermons, prepared no lessons for his pupils, and ministered to none of his charities, preferring to stay indoors reading the lives of the saints or sweeping the church and the friary. He knew the city needed him after the devastations of the previous summer, but he had lost the strength to care about anything. Only the thought of his roses withering in the drought after all those years of cultivating them, pruning them, talking to God through them, experimenting with different strains brought from Valencia and Castile, kept him from submitting to the illness altogether, clippers or watering pail dutifully in hand.

It was his one and only luxury, for which he scourged himself almost as vehemently as for his pride. Here he liked to sit with his rosary every morning, here he liked to take his lunch, here he liked to visit with his closest friends and pupils. He winced at the thought of sharing his private sanctuary with the Archbishop, expecting to be criticized for his indulgence in roses. To his surprise, the Archbishop was a great admirer of well-grown blooms and cultivated a few rose trees of his own.

"What surprises me about Sor Juana's offer to write a new chronicle," Don Manuel called out from the bench on which he installed himself with the plate of bread and sliced sausage that the cook had prepared for their midday repast, "is that she knows it will be used against her. After the *Carta aténagorica*, how could she not?" He held out the plate. "Will you have some, Ilustrísima?"

The Archbishop grimaced at the smell of the sausage and shook his head, settling himself on the bench across from the Bishop, in the shade of a fig tree. Padre Antonio sat between them on the ledge of the fountain, trailing one hand in the water.

"Do you not see, Padre Antonio, how that woman is trying to trick us into regaining her writing privileges with that chronicle?" asked the Archbishop.

"Undoubtedly, that is her ploy, Ilustrísima. But I trust Mother Andrea implicitly, and know that she would make sure Juana did not stray from the margin. Besides, I think she will seal her own fate with this document. I don't see how it could hurt the Church for her to write down her sins."

"Must we read another document?" asked the Bishop. "Haven't we collected enough testimonies from the other sisters that may be submitted for the Tribunal's review? Along with her books and those letters, we have plenty of evidence of Juana's sins, Antonio."

"Am I mistaken," said Padre Antonio, "or did you once have a friendship with Juana, Don Manuel?"

"An intellectual understanding, perhaps, but never a friendship," said the Bishop, sopping his crust in the oil. "She used to be a favorite of mine, that is true, and I remain an admirer of some of her early work, but more and more I am repulsed by her insolence with the written word. And I daresay she hates men. I found even myself being swayed by her logic against my own kind. The woman's rhetoric is dangerous, Padre Antonio. She could persuade the Pope himself."

"And what could she persuade us of if she writes a chronicle of her sins? We already know that she is a sinner."

"As the recipient of one of her chronicles," said the Bishop, "I can assure you that she will most expertly twist logic and history around to her own benefit. She has the power of the verb, and is a master rhetorician. She might even sway the Inquisition. Not to mention the fact that she has a publisher in Spain."

"Since when is the Holy Office easily swayed? Master rhetorician or not, she's nothing but a woman and a nun. Only someone with a weak will can be persuaded by what she says."

"Are you suggesting that a Spaniard's will like mine is weaker than a criollo's?"

"I didn't dress myself up in a nun's identity to reprimand her," retorted Padre Antonio.

"You're the one who took her back after she renounced you over a decade ago. If she had sent the petition to me, I would have returned it immediately without bothering to break the seal."

"Don Manuel, por favor, we all know that you were her friend, and you just called yourself her admirer. You couldn't have been a very objective audience."

"I beg to differ. It was I, after all, who drew her out."

"You were playing games with her, assuming the persona of this Sor Filotea, chastising her through a veiled identity only to see your words in print. You had no intention of drawing her out."

"Brothers, please," interrupted the Archbishop, "let us not resort to the unmanly practice of bickering. The question is, Padre Antonio, what are *you* going to do to help us straighten out the infamous Juana Inés de la Cruz?"

"You may trust me completely to guide her back to the straight and narrow, Ilustrísima."

"Don't be a fool! I don't want you to save her. You have to bring her down. Why waste your time on that infidel? Once she is stripped of the sacraments she'll be none of your concern."

"I beg your pardon, Señores," said Padre Antonio, "but are we attempting here to purify or crucify Mary Magdalene? It was my understanding from discussing this matter at some length with my colleagues in the Holy Office that what they want is a recantation, not an excommunication. That is why I have gone to the trouble of getting her on the roster of penitents for the *octava*—"

The Bishop was chuckling behind his napkin. "Crucify Mary Magdalene? You do mix your metaphors, Antonio!"

Padre Antonio clenched his fist in the water of the fountain, quelling the instinct to douse the Bishop's face. How dare he stuff himself with my food and insult me in my own garden, he thought. He felt trickles of sweat slip under his hair shirt, and his skin began to itch, for which he was thankful.

"I am talking about a woman's soul, sir, not a primer on rhetoric!"

The Archbishop threw a fig at him, and it splattered on his cassock. "Padre Antonio, you will do me the kindness of never putting those two words together again in my presence. Women have no souls. But this one has a brain, and I will not allow the possibility of her publishing yet another treatise that she will use to our disadvantage. It would be the final drop in the cup of bile she has been serving me since I arrived in New Spain. Every word she writes is fodder for my enemies. Don't be a fool!"

"But, Ilustrísima, why must we complicate matters to such a degree? This is a simple case of a nun's renewal of her vows. A Silver Jubilee."

"What it is, Padre Antonio," said the Archbishop, "is our only opportunity to make her pay for the offenses she has committed against the faith and against mankind. The Bishop has already taken the first step with the publication of that blasphemous *Carta*. Now I want her library expurgated and every single text she owns compared against the Index. As a censor for the Inquisition, Padre Antonio, you must weed out all her banned books. I shall take care of dispossessing her of all she values. Can I trust you to be our ally in this endeavor?"

But my eyes, Padre Antonio wanted to say, I can't see anything with these eyes. "I don't see the need to go to all this trouble when all that's necessary is a rigorous confession and a complete renunciation of her past. I can achieve that, Eminence, I know I can."

"I have had it up to here with your nescience, Antonio. We want her to submit to the Church, once and for all. Can you help us do that?" A white froth had gathered in the corners of the Archbishop's mouth.

"Calm yourself, Eminence," said the Bishop.

"But why excommunication, Ilustrísima? Do you really want her cast out into the world with nothing to guide her? No husband. No vows."

The Archbishop's cane hit him in the knees. "Tell me, Padre Antonio, you who were rebuffed by this daughter of a *criolla* whore, does she not spite the very patriarchs of our faith with every word she scribbles? Those plays! Those love poems directed not at Our Savior but at vicereines and viceroys. That scandalous *respuesta*! And now those books! Two volumes of her writings circulating in Spain! One of them comes with a warning, a *warning*, mind you, about the secret influence of the stars that motivated her affections for the Countess of Paredes. And another bears the signature of seven Spaniards who agree with her critique of Vieyra. Do you know how that makes me look to my friends in Spain and Portugal, that the Archbishop of Mexico is being told how to interpret the Bible by one of his own nuns? Are you so blind that you really believe this woman can recant?"

"I believe salvation is always possible, Eminence."

"Don't you understand, Padre Antonio? There is no room for women in God's community."

"But Juana is no heretic, Ilustrísima. I can vouch for that. She is completely misguided, and for that I must take a measure of responsibility for having abandoned her at a critical time. But to make her anathema, Eminence, is a grave mistake."

"Are you daring to correct me, Padre Antonio?"

"Forgive me, Eminence, that was not my intent. But we all know that Juana is not the equal of any nun. She is more than a woman. The very theologians that you refer to agree to that. Didn't one of them say that she was a man in every respect? Would we excommunicate a priest for doing what she has done, for writing, for publishing, for indulging in a life of the mind? She has committed no heresies."

"You're contradicting yourself, Antonio," interjected Don Manuel through a mouthful of sausage. "Earlier you said she was just a woman and a nun, and now you say she's more than a woman. You may be right. It isn't just the mind that she's been indulging. We've collected plenty of evidence to suggest that Juana and our former Vicereine were engaged in a, shall we say, particularly intimate friendship."

"Please, Manuel. Don't sour my appetite," said the Archbishop, grimacing again. "We can hear about it at the confession."

"I know nothing of a confession," said Padre Antonio, "save the one that she and I have been working on for the last seven weeks."

"We've decided—that is, the Bishop of Puebla and I have decided—that instead of the written chronicle that her Superior requested we permit her to write, there shall be a public confession, in the chambers of the Tribunal, to last as many days as it takes to divulge all of her sins and humiliate her before the world. That should take care of our *tenth muse*."

"But it is not a trial, Señores. Only a confession. And confessions are private."

"Not this one, Padre Antonio. Not if she wants to continue wearing the habit of Saint Jerome."

"Penitence and absolution are all she needs, Ilustrísima."

The Bishop burped behind his hand, then got to his feet and stood before Padre Antonio, thrusting his belly in the Jesuit's face. He reeked of garlic and cured meat, and there were oil stains on his sash.

"As her father confessor, *you* are in charge of administering the penitence, Antonio. We will let the Tribunal decide if she is worthy of absolution. All we need to know is that we can count on your influence with the inquisitors."

Padre Antonio scratched vigorously at his hair shirt and dared not look up lest the Bishop see the anger in his eyes. He had to accept that this was the penitence Juana's own sinfulness had sown. And no doubt it would be his last act of salvation before the merciful darkness closed over his eyes and returned him to his Maker.

"I am nothing but a soldier of Christ," he said, staring at the frayed hem of his cassock. "Who am I to question your command?"

Castling

1664–1670

Chapter 1

Uncle John glowered at them over his chicken leg, his icy gaze directed first at his wife, then at Juana Inés. His jaws popped as he crunched the cartilage at the tip of the bone. Aunt Mary's eyes blinked like butterflies. Juana Inés kept hers steady on her uncle's face.

"Where were you two today?" he asked. The bone cracked between his teeth.

"We went to Mass, Husband," Aunt Mary interjected before Juana Inés volunteered an answer. "And then we stopped at the apothecary's to pick up the herbals for your infusions."

He ground the bone to the marrow, spit the shards on the floor, then took a sip of wine. "Nowhere else?" He rubbed his tongue over his teeth, sucking bits of flesh and bone out of the gaps.

Aunt Mary lowered her eyes and shook her head.

"They're lying to you, Father," broke in Nico, the elder of their two boys. "I saw them at the hanging."

"I saw them, too," said the youngest, Fernando. "And Juanilla was using Mamá's funny spectacles, the ones she uses when she goes to the theater."

The color in Aunt Mary's cheeks matched the carmine of the roses on the table.

"María, look at me." He waited for her to meet his gaze before continuing. "Are these boys telling the truth? Did you two go to the execution?"

"Yes, Uncle, we were there," said Juana Inés, unable to tolerate her aunt's humiliation any longer. "The whole city was there. It was a public spectacle, not a clandestine ceremony."

"I don't care what it was, Doña Insolencia. I remember distinctly telling you last night that I didn't want either of you anywhere near the Plaza Mayor today. Hidalgos' wives and nieces don't attend hangings."

"It was difficult to avoid, Husband," said Aunt Mary, raising her voice to him. "We had marketing to do after Mass, and the apothecary's shop is right in the arcade."

Uncle John slapped Aunt Mary's face with the back of his hand. "Fine example you set!" Dark dregs of bone marrow flew from his mouth to the tablecloth. "That's why this *marisabia* has grown so insolent." He turned his frown on Juana Inés again, but she held his stare, challenging his authority with her eyes. It was the look that always provoked him to slap her. He got to his feet and reached across the table, arm in the air, but the kitchen maid's voice stopped him before he could strike.

"Excuse me, Señor."

"What do you want?"

"A message, Sir. He says it's from the palace."

"Who says? For Christ's sake, woman, show the man in."

Uncle John straightened his back and removed the dinner napkin from his collar, clearing his throat as the doors to the dining room opened. Juana Inés expected to see a liveried page standing there, but instead it was a small boy, a *mulato* from the streets, holding a scroll bearing the blue seal of the palace.

"Who are you?" asked Uncle John. The boy presented him the scroll and left his hand open for a tip. Uncle John waved the boy away, transfixed suddenly by the letter and the seal. "Give him something to eat," he said offhandedly, and Aunt Mary promptly got to her feet and escorted the boy out of the dining room.

"Open it, Uncle." Juana Inés couldn't keep herself from goading him.

"Open it, Uncle," her cousin, Gloria, mimicked her, kicking her ankle under the table. Juana Inés felt her eyes cloud over with the pain, but she didn't say anything or kick back, just sat there waiting for Uncle John to stop fussing with the letter.

"Look, it's addressed to me, Don Juan de Mata, *presente*," he read aloud, showing the handwriting to his sons. "My first summons from the palace. I knew this day would come."

"How do you know it's a summons, Uncle?"

"What else could it be, you imbecile? The palace doesn't send missives to inquire after one's health." Uncle John took his knife and tried to lift up the seal without breaking it, but it crumbled into waxy pieces over his plate. He threw the knife down and gingerly opened the letter, his eyes sliding back and forth across the page.

"I don't believe it!" he said.

"What does it say, Papá?" asked Gloria.

"María!" he bellowed, his voice echoing in the rafters. "María! Juana Inés has been summoned to the palace!"

Aunt Mary ran back into the room, her chest heaving. "What does it say?"

"*'Esteemed don Juan de Mata,'*" he read aloud, "*' . . . her Majesty, the Vicereine, la Marquesa de Mancera, requests the honor of making your niece's acquaintance. The court is anxious to meet the girl scholar who is stirring the talk of Mexico City. We look forward to an audience with her next Thursday after vespers.'* Signed, the Viceroy of Mexico."

"God help us!" said Aunt Mary, crossing herself quickly.

Juana Inés did not dare to breathe or look up from her lap. She kept hearing that phrase, *girl scholar who is stirring the talk of Mexico City*, and a sudden panic welled up that her uncle would refuse the Viceroy's summons. *Marisabia*, he was always calling her—*marí* for girl, *sabia* for scholar, as if the terms were mutually exclusive—in disdain of all her hard work with her studies. *Who ever heard of a girl scholar?* he would shout. *Are you trying to catch the eye of the Inquisition?*

It was true that Juana Inés had been reading since she was three, that she had taught herself the rudiments of rhetoric, geometry, and astronomy, and that she knew something of Greek philosophy and Roman law; it was also true that she had learned Latin in twenty lessons, but she did not consider herself a scholar, much less a prodigy as some chose to call her, to the utter horror of her guardians, who daily expected the Inquisition to accuse them of harboring a heretic in their midst. But the gossip flowed from the servants, and the city buzzed with the novelty of a girl who could read the constellations as easily as music.

"It's unnatural for a girl to know as much as you do, Juana Inés," her aunt had often admonished her. "You should learn how to embroider, how to crochet, like your cousin, Gloria. Those are safe things for girls to know. The Inquisition cannot fault you for good needlework."

Juana Inés did not argue with her aunt; in fact, she felt sorry for the poor woman who had the vocabulary and penmanship of a child, but she knew that her wits would not be threaded through the eye of a needle. She knew that her mind was the very pattern that the needle and thread tried to follow, the very fabric without which the pattern would be useless.

"May I go, Uncle? I would so like to see the palace."

"May I go, Uncle?" her cousin Gloria mimicked her again. "Weasel!"

"She deserves a good whack on the head for being such a show-off," said Nico.

Fernando threw a piece of bread at her. "Show-off!" he said.

"Stop it, boys," said Aunt Mary. "That's very unchivalrous."

"I don't know, Juanita," said her uncle, stroking the beard on his chin and gazing out at the twilit patio through the open dining room doors. "First I must find out what this is about. It could be beneficial to us, but then, again, you may have gotten this family into trouble. And then, of course, there's the issue of your punishment for disobeying me and going to the execution when I forbade you to be there."

"Told you she's becoming a nuisance," Nico said to his father, his black eyes glittering under the dark ledge of his eyebrows. "All the students are talking about her, saying she's really a boy in disguise."

"I knew it," said Aunt Mary, framing her face with her hands. "It's impossible to trust the servants. Who knows what stories they may be telling. This could be the end of you, Juanita."

Don't be a fool! she wanted to yell at her aunt, but the fear that her uncle would disallow the Vicereine's request checked her exasperation. She needed another approach, one that would appeal to the only logic her uncle understood.

"Not many hidalgos get an audience with the Vicereine, Uncle," she said quietly. Gloria kicked her ankle under the table again, smiling innocently so as not to draw her mother's rebuke. Juana Inés reached over and pinched her thigh as hard as she could, daring her with her eyes to make a sound.

"There is also the possibility that I may be offered a position at the palace," she added.

"Doing what?" snapped her aunt. "You're as useless as these boys around the house. What could you do for the lady Marquesa?"

"Read to her, I guess, that's all she knows how to do," said Fernando, and he buried his nose in the make-believe book of his two hands.

"The girl does have a point, Mary," said her uncle, taking a garlicky olive from his plate and popping it into his mouth. "If she were to be accused in any way, I doubt the Vicereine would want to make her acquaintance. Those matters are for the Inquisition to decide." His eyes gleamed like sapphires at the prospect of having a relative in the royal retinue. Juana Inés knew that she had baited him, but he had still to give his consent. She gave her cousins one of her haughtiest looks.

"She always gets her own way," moaned Gloria, rubbing her thigh under the table. "Even when she misbehaves and disobeys. Why doesn't the Vicereine want to see me? I'm the one who's the daughter of an hidalgo."

Juana Inés couldn't contain herself. "Because the court probably doesn't need another buffoon."

Gloria's dimples vanished into a scowl.

"Juanita!" said her aunt.

Fernando laughed. "Maybe they need a book rat!"

"Children, please, all of you are being totally insufferable. This is a grave situation," said Aunt Mary.

Uncle John sucked on the olive pit between his teeth. "This could be very good for us, María. Lend a little more weight to that coat of arms I'm still paying for."

Juana Inés jumped in. "I'd be happy to give you whatever they pay me, Uncle. If they pay,"

"I hope they pay," said Nico.

Uncle John drained his cup and stood up. "Well, I think I shall sleep on it, María. I have to decide if Juana Inés is even worthy of this honor. Tonight I fear she isn't."

"But, Uncle—"

"Juanita, I said I shall sleep on it. We have some time before next Thursday."

"Yes, but Uncle, you wouldn't want to offend the Vicereine."

"There she goes again," said Nico. "She's hopeless. She'd argue with the devil if she could."

"Quiet, Son," Uncle John snapped. "That kind of talk is precisely what the servants like to repeat. Now, Juanita, I will make some inquiries, and when I am satisfied that I know what the Vicereine's intentions are, I shall inform you of what we will do. *Buenas noches*."

For a week Juana Inés wandered aimlessly through the house, not able to concentrate on any of her studies, listless at Mass, so quiet at mealtimes she felt entirely absent from her body. Every day she lit a candle to Saint Jude, patron of impossible tasks, in the Cathedral and prayed fervently to all of the saints for their intercession. Then she would spend hours at Don Lázaro's bookshop perusing the shelves, but she was not really focusing on what she was doing, just biding her time and silently questioning her uncle's authority to determine what she could and could not do. By Thursday morning Uncle John had still not given his consent and Juana Inés was certain that he had decided against the visit. She was standing in front of a newly displayed shipment of diaries and writing boxes when the bookseller's wife approached her. "Congratulations, Doña Ramírez," she said. Juana Inés scowled.

"Don't tell me you haven't heard. We've recently been told that the Viceroy intends to offer you a position. How lucky you are, a young lady of your station at the palace."

"Señora! Are you quite sure?"

"Well, we could call it a rumor, I suppose. But we did hear it from a reliable source."

Impulsively, Juana Inés reached out and hugged the woman.

Don Lázaro was so impressed he offered to put a writing box on layaway for her, just in case the rumor proved to be true and she could afford the twelve pesos for the box and its hundred pages of parchment.

Juana Inés thanked them both, then hitched her dress up over her ankles and nearly ran the five blocks to her uncle's house, pausing only to buy a Catherine-wheel medal from a vendor in front of the Cathedral. As the patron saint of students and universities, Saint Catherine seemed a more logical saint to invoke than Saint Jude. Juana Inés was sixteen. She had survived the ridicule and stupidity of the Matas for eight years. The idea of living at court, even if just to scrub the floors of the palace, seemed like a miracle to her. Surely there would be a library of exceptional quality at the court. Surely the Viceroy would not fear the Inquisition.

"Where's Uncle's carriage? Has he left?" she gasped at the *mestiza* who was sweeping the vestibule.

"Your uncle's gone to the palace, Mistress. Your *tía* is waiting for you in the sewing room."

Juana Inés flew up the stairs.

Her aunt was altering one of her own silk dresses for her, and Gloria had hastily packed a trunk with all of her cousin's things just in case the Vicereine asked Juana Inés to remain at the palace.

"Why didn't you tell me, Aunt Mary! You know I've had my soul on a string for a week."

"Your uncle was very upset that you weren't here for breakfast. He wanted to announce it to you himself. It could have been your last meal with the family."

"I went to early Mass. I didn't know. Oh, Tía, do you really think they'll want to keep me?"

"According to your uncle's informants, that *is* the plan. If they decide they like you, of course. If you prove useful. Here, slip this on. I hope you don't end up wearing this dress to your *auto de fe*, Juanita." Her aunt mumbled through the pins she was holding between her lips. "What will I tell your mother if you're branded a heretic? She'll think it was my fault for being too lenient with you."

"Would they really do that, Mamá?" asked Gloria, eyes glittering. "Would they really drag Juana Inés through the city in a *sanbenito* and make her eat ashes in public?"

"Listen to me, both of you," said Juana Inés. "There's not going to be any *auto de fe*. There may be no position for me either, so don't think you can get rid of me so easily, Gloria. But don't worry. I'll do my best to impress the Vicereine."

That evening, after a tearful farewell from her aunt Mary, her uncle escorted Juana Inés to the court in his finest carriage. She had not gone anywhere alone with her uncle since the day he had brought her from her mother's house in Panoayán, eight years ago. The memory disturbed her, and she blinked hard to dispel it. He wouldn't try anything now, she told herself, but just the same she moved over as close to the window as she could.

"Your aunt's dress becomes you, Juanita," said her uncle.

"Thank you, Uncle," she said. She crossed her hands in her lap and stared out the window until they arrived at the main entrance to the palace. A footman in a green velvet coat and cap helped her out of the carriage. They were led past a large patio with a turreted gazebo in the center of a rose garden to a waiting room with long benches lining the walls. She and her uncle were the only ones waiting.

"I expect you to behave as befits the niece of an hidalgo," said her uncle, pacing the length of the hall.

"Yes, Uncle."

"I have made all the necessary arrangements. Now it is up to you, Juanita."

"I know that, Uncle."

"Don't be belligerent!"

Juana Inés checked her tongue and concentrated on the diamond pattern of the lace cuffs on the sleeves of her dress; trapezoids, they were called, a geometrical pattern that was easier to draw than to create with a crochet needle. Her uncle continued to pace, rehearsing in a loud mumble the introductions he was going to make. Just before they were admitted into the reception hall, Juana Inés took out her Catherine-wheel medal and wore it over her collar. In the huge salon the royal couple were seated on great gold armchairs, dwarfed against the backdrop of an enormous fireplace. On either side of them stood lords and ladies of the court, all dressed in dazzling velvets and silks, and behind them the last coral light of the sunset arched across the marble walls.

Juana Inés did not hear the initial presentations. She had glued her gaze to the Vicereine's eyes and pleaded silently to be taken in, to be saved from the ignorance of the Matas. The Viceroy, Don Antonio Sebastian de Toledo, Marqués de Mancera, twirled the end of his thin mustache, his eyebrows raised as he studied Juana Inés's face.

"You say she taught herself Latin?" the Viceroy asked her uncle.

"Well, she did have the help of a tutor for some time, Excellency, but in the main, she was the one who did most of the tutoring. She knows many other subjects as well; you see, Juanita is a most studious girl. She impresses all of our friends with her conversation. Of course, we don't really understand why . . ."

"Does she play any musical instruments?" the Viceroy interrupted.

"Oh, she's quite a musician, Your Eminence. She's an expert on the mandolin *and* the *vihuela*. She loves to cook, but she doesn't know much about sewing . . ."

Juana Inés's fingers had turned to wood. She knew what was coming next.

"We must have a demonstration," the Viceroy said, and snapped his fingers to a page.

"Bring a mandolin from the music room," the Viceroy ordered. "Quickly."

The page bowed and scurried from the hall. Her uncle continued to extol her virtues as a musician, but Juana Inés hardly heard him. She was trying to decide on the most appropriate thing to play. The piece had to be both modest and original, but it needed to live up to her uncle's praises, and so had to be . . . what was the best way to describe it? . . . haunting. She had to play the most haunting, most delicate piece she had ever written.

The Vicereine smiled at Juana Inés, leisurely fanning herself with a Chinese dragon.

"What will you play for us, Doña Ramírez de Asbaje?" the Viceroy asked Juana Inés.

"I would like to play one of my own compositions, if your majesties have no objection." The meekness in her own voice surprised her.

"No objections at all, my dear. That would be lovely," the Vicereine spoke at last. "Does your composition have a name?"

The page scurried back into the hall.

"Hand it to the young lady," the Viceroy instructed the page. Juana Inés took the mandolin and fit the mahogany- and spruce-striped belly of the instrument to her body. Inhaling the scent of the virgin wood, she tuned the strings, aware of the significance of this performance, aware of the Vicereine's eyes, of the jeweled buckles on the Viceroy's shoes, of her uncle's nervous breathing.

"Juanita, the Marquesa asked you the name of the composition," her uncle said.

Juana Inés raised her head and looked at the Vicereine. "I call it 'The Cell,' my lady. That's the name of the room where I was born in my grandfather's hacienda."

"How very bizarre," said the Vicereine.

Juana Inés filled her lungs with air. With her left hand she clasped the neck of the mandolin. With the plectrum in her right she started to play. She had written the piece in the dark morning of her fifteenth birthday, upon awakening from a dream. Her grandfather was standing on a riverbank in a circle of light, leaning against a bishop's crook. To reach him, Juana Inés had to float across the river on her back, arms over her head, but when she reached the light it was a woman—not her mother or either of her sisters—a strange woman waiting on the riverbank, holding a black shawl. "Where's my *abuelo*?" Juana Inés asked. The woman said, "Don't be afraid. You're safe now." When she awakened from the dream, she could hear this music in her head. The notes carried the delicacy of baptism and the mystery of death, and so she had called it "The Cell." Her mother had given birth to her in that room, and eight years later her grandfather had died there.

Juana Inés plucked the last few notes, then set the instrument down on her lap and kept her eyes on the Vicereine's face.

"Excelentisimo!" said the Viceroy, tapping the fingers of one hand against the palm of the other. Beside him, the Vicereine stared at Juana Inés in a way that she could not decipher, a way that made her heart beat with a question for which she had no words.

"We have heard that you are quite a conversationalist," the Viceroy spoke to her directly, "that you can talk about any subject put to you. Is that true, Doña Ramírez?"

Juana Inés said to the Viceroy, "I doubt I know as much as you, Señor Marqués. I am a girl, after all, and have not had the benefit of a formal education. I have read a number of books. I have a good memory."

"If this girl had her choice between eating and reading, she would be a skeleton by now," said her uncle. "Why, she even renounced cheese . . ."

"She will not have to make that choice here," the Viceroy replied, smiling at Juana Inés under the tails of his mustache. "Would you like to stay at the palace, Doña Ramírez, and be a lady-in-waiting to la Marquesa?"

"Sir, I would be a slave to la Marquesa," Juana Inés answered, the relief in her voice thick as powder.

"Well, Señora Marquesa," the Viceroy turned to his wife, "do you have an opinion to offer?"

"I believe, Husband, that you have made a wise decision," said the Vicereine, closing her fan and tilting her head to one side as if to study Juana Inés from a different angle. "I am sure Juana Inés will be quite an inspiration to me."

Juana Inés looked down and tried to keep her chin from shaking, but she could not control the tears of gratitude that streaked her face and slipped through the strings of the mandolin.

"And I believe the girl is baptizing the mandolin," said the Viceroy, chuckling. Juana Inés jumped up and tried to dry the instrument with her silk sleeve.

"Never mind," the Viceroy told her. "It's yours, to continue enchanting la Marquesa." To her uncle, he said, "Can she begin immediately?"

"This very evening, if you wish, Excellency."

"Excellent! I like a fellow who thinks ahead. Welcome to the palace, Doña Ramírez."

Juana Inés threw herself at the Vicereine's feet and kissed the brocaded hem of her dress over and over. "Thank you, Lady! Thank you!" was all she could say.

The Vicereine's hand came near her, and for an instant Juana Inés held her breath, but she was only reaching down to look at her medal. "What a fascinating image," said la Marquesa, holding the silver medal against her palm. "Tell us what it means, Juana Inés."

"It's Saint Catherine of Alexandria's wheel, Señora, on which the Roman emperor was going to torture her for refusing to marry him. It's the symbol of her resistance to his will."

"Very original," said la Marquesa, "but really, I insist you get up from the floor."

Juana Inés obeyed, smoothing the wrinkles at the back of her dress.

"Aren't you going to bid your uncle farewell, child?"

Out of the corner of her eye, Juana Inés saw that the Viceroy and her uncle were walking slowly toward the door of the great hall, going over the terms of her service, no doubt.

"Good-bye, Uncle," she called out, for the Vicereine's sake, though deep in her heart she wanted to wish him a good riddance.

"Tell me, Juana Inés," said la Marquesa, "do you play dominoes and cards? None of my ladies seems to have the same passion for the gaming tables that I do." Juana Inés heard the titter of ladies' laughter on the edge of her awareness. "I shall expect you to be my partner from time to time."

"For you, Lady," said Juana Inés, "I will learn to speak Latin in reverse."

"A language game! Excellent idea," said the Vicereine. She clapped her hands at her retinue. "Ladies! It shall be a contest of tongue-twisters tonight. But, first, take the new Lady Juana to your dormitory and get her settled. I shall wait for you in my salon, Juana Inés, for a private supper."

Suddenly Juana Inés was enveloped in a blur of skirts and fans. She felt herself being half-pushed, half-carried from the hall.

"We've been here all this time," she heard someone grumble, "and she's never asked us to a private supper."

Chapter 2

9 December 1664

Dearest Mother,

Aunt Mary says the post is very reliable between the city and the provinces and assures me that you are in receipt of my last letter, but I have been at the palace nearly a month and still no word from you, so I can only assume that the letter was lost in transit. If you don't already know, then the news that I am now a lady-in-waiting to our new Vicereine will come as a happy surprise, you who were always afraid I would never find a suitable position, given what you used to call my black inclination for learning. There is not much time for learning at the palace, at least not the learning I used to do in books. I am always surrounded by people, and there seems to be an unspoken agreement that everyone must be of excellent cheer and solicitous demeanor at all times. This, along with the lack of time to read, has been the most difficult adjustment to make. I am not of a sanguine nature, as you know, and prefer the ways of the hermit to those of the minstrel, and yet here I have become very much like a court bard, and somebody is always asking me to recite a poem or play a song or participate in some guessing game. There's such an aura of pronounced good humor and bustling activity that even the slightest frown or sigh provokes rebuke. I know I should not complain and, in truth, that is not the purpose of this letter, but you know me best and know how difficult it is for me to smile and laugh all the time, and not crack open a book, and not spend time alone wandering in the garden, testing my memory. Still, who would have thought I would end up here? Won't you come to the city and visit me? And bring Josefa and María, too? I think I've forgotten what all of you look like, and you certainly can't expect me to look the same after eight years. I must go now. The siesta is nearly over and I've got to paint on my beauty mark and curl my hair again (that same stubborn hair that could never keep a curl for longer than an hour) and go sit in the Vicereine's chamber with my mandolin. Please ask Josefa or María to write back.

Your other daughter,
Juana Inés Ramírez

After the first few weeks during which she had walked around in a trance of disbelief, exploring the many patios and halls and gardens and galleries of the palace, Juana Inés found life at court surprisingly superficial and yet excessively busy. La Marquesa gave her the title of personal secretary, which meant that in the mornings, after Mass in the palace chapel, she sat at the scriptorium in la Marquesa's salon and took care of most of her correspondence, after which she accompanied la Marquesa on her daily stroll through one of the gardens. Before lunch, she read aloud while la Marquesa embroidered with the other ladies; during the siesta, she played the mandolin in la Marquesa's chamber to help her sleep; in the afternoons, she posed for paintings in la Marquesa's patio dressed in silly costumes; and in the evenings, after vespers, if guests did not have to be entertained, if there was no *galanteo de palacio* scheduled, no special performance in the palace theater, she always served as la Marquesa's partner in dominoes or card games.

Month by month, the Vicereine's demands on Juana Inés increased, so that by the end of her first year of service she was known not just as the secretary but as the Vicereine's *favorita* and closest companion. The Viceroy, too, sought her company, and enjoyed debating with her and challenging her in chess. She allowed him to win part of the time, but they were both more engrossed in their conversation than in their game, and he took to calling her Athena-in-waiting when only the Vicereine was around.

Aside from all of her usual duties, she was required to attend every possible public event with the Viceroy and Vicereine, including plays and bullfights, to accompany them on carriage rides through the Alameda and picnics in Chapultepec, to amuse their guests with her musical skills, to sit beside the Vicereine at all affairs of state, to participate in intellectual banter with the courtiers, and to ride as part of the royal entourage, immediately behind the Señora Marquesa's palanquin, in the Octava processions of Corpus Christi. Thus her first two years at the palace were like a perpetual circus, and though she knew that somewhere the sand was slipping through the hourglass, she could not pull herself away from the spectacle of life at court. For the first time since her grandfather's death, Juana Inés was basking in attention.

In gratitude for the sonnet she had written to commemorate the death of King Philip, the Viceroy ordered a silver inkwell made in the shape of an owl with garnet eyes, the dedication engraved on the bottom in tiny letters. *For our Athena-in-waiting. Fondly, Leonor y Antonio, Virreyes de México, 1666.*

The Viceroy also established an account for her at the bookseller's, one book a month, anything she wanted as long as it wasn't banned. The first thing she put on the account was the balance she owed on her writing box—Pandora's Box, she called it.

She had no time to write or study, of course, except in the hours between curfew and matins. Leaving the other ladies to their nightly gossip about one or another of the courtiers, she would wander down to the Viceroy's library in the west wing of the palace and sit at the huge oak table by the window. She liked to open the shutters and listen to the sound of the fountain in the courtyard below while she worked, the noise of the night market in the distance. The Viceroy had cleared one of his cabinets for her to use, giving her the only key, and here she kept her small library, her journal and notebooks. Pandora's Box, too, she kept in the cabinet, under its own lock and key.

By the time the bells struck for matins, her eyes burned from straining under the smoky glare of the oil lamp, but, if she was fortunate, the cobwebs of anxiety that had gathered during the day would have burned away. She knew that the source of this anxiety was more than not having time to herself, was something as vague and diaphanous as a dream that she could not name, though at times she filled her entry in Pandora's Box with incoherent musings about this feeling that was both melancholy and apprehension.

On the nights when her studies soothed the agitation in her mind, she would walk back slowly to the ladies' dormitory, lingering on a bench in the main courtyard, listening to the nightingales in the magnolia trees and farther off, the voices of the Carmelite sisters from the nearby convent singing their matinal *alabanzas*. On those nights when anxiety would not be quelled, when even writing in her diary seemed an exercise in private torture, she went to the palace chapel where the court priests gathered to chant the midnight Office. She would sit at the back of the chapel, at the foot of the niche of Saint Peter, her grandfather's patron saint, and absorb the deep timbre of the plainsong echoing in the nave, which at times made her weep and at others lulled her into eerie dreams.

Once on her way out of the chapel she had run into the Vicereine sleep-walking through the courtyard in a gossamer nightdress. The dark aure-oles of her nipples stood erect, the dark patch of her pubis clearly outlined against the cloth, and she was looking for Juana Inés, calling to her in a loud voice that somehow melded with the priests' chanting. Suddenly some-one tapped her on the shoulder and she woke up. The head chaplain was bending over her, scowling and pointing to the door.

In the mornings she found it difficult to awaken in time for Mass, and usually she would be the last one to leave the dormitory. Still lacing up her bodice or pinning on her mantilla, she would run from the gallery of the east wing all the way across the four patios of the palace to enter the chapel by the side door and creep to her place behind la Marquesa's chair. She could hear the other ladies whispering to each other as she struggled to catch her breath. La Marquesa would give a quick look over her shoulder and shake her head very slightly.

"I don't know why you like to stay up so late," la Marquesa complained one morning at breakfast. "Look at those hollows under your eyes. You're ruining your complexion, Juanita."

"It's the only time I have to study, Señora. I try not to disturb."

"You always wake *me* up when you come back from wherever you go," said the lady Eugenia.

"And me," said the lady Cristina.

"We're all *desveladas*, thanks to her," said the lady Hilda.

"Perhaps I should ask my husband to give you a separate room, Juanita. I don't want any squabbling among my ladies."

"We're not squabbling, Marquesa," said the lady Hilda. "We just want her to understand that her nocturnal habits affect all of us."

"She's not the only one nodding off in Mass," added the lady Cristina.

"I do not nod off!" said Juana Inés.

"Ladies, please! You're disappointing me. I see that I shall have to move you immediately, Juanita. Get your things together after breakfast, and I'll have a page collect them and take them to your new room. I think I'll put you in my own wing."

"Forgive me, Marquesa," said the lady Eugenia, "but I don't think any of us would find it fair for the youngest and . . . and less privileged among us to have her own room."

"I agree with the lady Eugenia," said Juana Inés, terrified of the disfavor of her companions. "I want no special privileges. Perhaps if I had more time during the day—"

"And now she wants to shirk her duties," said the lady Cristina.

"Her duties are to please me," snapped the Vicereine. "And it pleases me for her to continue with her studies. She's the court scholar, don't forget. Tell me, Juana. Am I absorbing too much of your time? The truth."

"Not at all, Señora."

"Of course I am. I'm taking up all of your time, and that's why you have to resort to these midnight forays in the library. Let me see. You've grown so indispensable to me—"

Juana Inés noticed how the other ladies looked at each other and rolled their eyes.

"Please, Marquesa, you need not do me any special favors."

The Vicereine ignored her. "I suppose I could do without you on my walk in the mornings and in the salon in the evenings, as long as we don't have guests, of course. Would that be enough, do you think? Or would you prefer the siesta hour to the evening?"

She had grown accustomed to working at night and could not imagine trying to study in the noise and bustle of the day. And also, the truth was she had grown fond of the evening activities in the Vicereine's salon. Between hands of whatever game they were playing, the courtiers who had gathered around the table would always make some jest in Juana's favor, or pose some riddle that only she seemed capable of deciphering. This caused much laughter and good cheer and made her very popular with the gentlemen, even though it was the Vicereine's approval and gaiety that she most sought.

"Perhaps the siesta hour would be best," she told la Marquesa.

"Oh dear, I forgot how much I rely on your mandolin, Juana."

"Let her work in the morning," said the lady Eugenia. "One of us can always accompany you on your walk, Marquesa."

And so it was decided that Juana Inés would study after she had finished the correspondence. She had to move her books and journals out of the Viceroy's library because he was always engaged with his counselors in the morning, but la Marquesa gave her a small room off her own parlor with a bay window that overlooked the palace orchard and had it outfitted with a large desk, a locking book cabinet, and a cushioned armchair. Juana Inés asked for the key to the room, and kept her diary and notebooks locked in the cabinet when she herself was not locked in all morning and even at night, for her body could not rest until she had written out the day's events and feelings. At times she missed lunch, and la Marquesa would be cross with her, but the Viceroy praised her for her discipline and application, not knowing that she spent most of her time recording her feelings rather than reading the history and philosophy volumes she bought from Don Lázaro.

3 September 1666

I am haunted by a strange melancholy that is one part homesickness, another part loneliness, and in its third part a longing of some kind that I cannot or must not name. How absurd to be lonely at court when I am surrounded by ladies- and gentlemen-in-waiting, the latter of whom continually seek my company almost as much as la Marquesa or the Viceroy. The ladies humor me but like me not. When I first came to court none wanted to share her bed with me, and so I was given the trundle bed by the window, where—I heard them whispering—they hoped I would catch a chill and have to leave the palace. The Vicereine tolerates no illness in her retinue, they say. They little realize that the air I breathed on my grandfather's ranch in the foothills was much colder than the air in the city. And I am happy to have my own bed, no matter how lumpy.

I am the only *criolla* among the ladies, as well as the youngest, and they don't understand or appreciate how it is that I have become la Marquesa's *consentida*. They are all fine Spanish ladies, they say, though I have heard it from some of the courtiers that a few of my companions are just as *criolla* as I and that others made the voyage from Spain as infants and have lived in Mexico almost since the beginning of their lives.

Don Fabio de García y Godoy and I debated whether or not they could be considered *criollas* if they were not born in New Spain but have spent all of their lives here, bred on the air and water and light and customs and language and food of the New World. What distinguishes them from one like me when the only difference between us is that my birthplace lies at the foot of the volcanoes and theirs on the other side of the ocean? We look the same, speak the same, share the same heritage. Is birthplace, then, I asked, enough to determine status? Has the society in which you grew up, in which you learned your skills and values, nothing to do with who you are? Don Fabio, staunch *sevillano* that he is, does not think so. Birthplace, he says, is everything. The very soil of one's birthplace marks one's destiny. Notice, he says, the difference between the cultured people of Seville and the barbarians of Barcelona or the superstitious imbeciles of Galicia. What about all the *léperos* begging in the streets who hail from Spain, asked the swarthy Don Victor, a *criollo* like me. This country, says Don Fabio, is responsible. They became dissolute as soon as they set foot on this land of vice and dissipation.

What descriptor, I asked, would he give to the people of New Spain? By then we were surrounded by the rest of the court, including la Marquesa and the Viceroy, and I saw that Don Fabio was getting somewhat agitated at the attention. He thought about my question and shook his head. He had no descriptor for the people of New Spain, he said. As it was not his country he did not know the natives. And the other peninsular gentlemen threw their *reales* into the hat: savages, one said; magicians, said another; primitives; thieves; sloths; mules; drunks. Even the Viceroy offered his opinion: like the slaves, he said, the Indians were nothing but insurgents, always plotting some revenge against their masters.

I had just finished Bernal Díaz del Castillo's lengthy *True History of the Indies*, and I was seized by an allegiant fury that compelled me to give them all a lesson in the history of the conquest of the Aztec empire. I pointed out that it was on the foundations of that illustrious civilization that the Crown of Spain had built a colony. They were not thieves, sloths, mules, or drunks before the Spaniards came, I told them, dragging their diseases and their spirits with them and ripping anything they wanted out of the land, including the native women. And they were only considered savages and magicians because they placed their faith in augurs and idols rather than in the symbol of the Cross; and what difference was there, really, between human sacrifice and the countless deaths resulting from the religious wars of Europe? Did they not know, I asked, that the calendar of the Aztecs, their astronomical skills, their coda were so advanced they could predict their own downfall, which the arrogant mind of the Spaniards could only attribute to sorcery? Primitives do not build pyramids or roads or plazas or fortresses, or aviaries, I said. And Spanish greed, I added my final point, looking at the Viceroy, wreaked infinitely more damage on the country and its people than any abject insurgency by the castes.

28

I was so upset I could not sit at the *merienda* with them and begged la Marquesa to forgive me, that I had a headache and had lost my appetite. She came to my study after the curfew bells carrying a jug of chocolate and a sweet bun on a tray.

"I thought I'd find you here," she said. "The ladies say you haven't even been to the dormitory. I thought you had a headache, my dear."

"You shouldn't have troubled yourself, Lady. Truly, I am not hungry. I am still too angry to be hungry."

"Of course you're angry. These nationalistic debates always end this way. But why vex yourself over that foppish Fabio? He gives *sevillanos* a bad name. We're not all that obtuse. Come, Juanita, drink your chocolate."

I realized then that I had not moved from my chair and that la Marquesa was still standing. "Forgive me, Lady," I said, jumping up to give her my seat. "Please, sit. Can you stay a while?"

"When I gave you this little room," she said, trying to fit the swell of her skirts and petticoats between the arms of the narrow chair, "I didn't realize it would become your cell, Juanita. You've an entire palace in which to roam, and yet you cloister yourself in here."

For no reason I started to weep, and she made me sit at her feet and put my head in her lap and she stroked my hair over and over, her finger-nails grazing the skin of my cheek, my ear and temple. "Such little ears you have, Juanita. I think you need pearls to set them off."

I wept even harder, unaware until it was too late that I was ruining the black velvet of her dress with my tears. She is still in mourning for the King, and we all must wear black, a color that suits my strange despondency. When the tide of that emotion finally ebbed she told me it was time to go to bed and walked me to the ladies' dormitory with her arm around my waist. Ever since then, the melancholy has deepened, and I cannot look at la Marquesa without thinking of her fingers and her voice and her thighs beneath the crinolines of her dress.

25 November 1666 (Feast Day of Saint Catherine)

I feel like Saint Catherine today, pursued by someone intent on distract-ing me from my work. After our little debate, Don Fabio has not left me alone. For two months now he insists on sitting beside me at all meals, on being my partner at cards (unless, of course, la Marquesa is playing, and then it goes without saying that I will be her partner), on escorting me to the plaza or the Cathedral or the arcade or the bookshop. At first I felt flattered by his attentions, and somewhat vindicated as the ladies Cristina and Hilda both have their eye on Don Fabio, but his constant presence at my side has gotten tedious, and I am completely bored by both his courtliness and his deference, which are but thin disguises for seduction. When I try to pick an argument with him nowadays he graciously bows his head and praises me for my cleverness. *Marisabia*, he calls me, *his marisabia*. Yesterday he actually tried to kiss me as we returned from the bullfight, and pretended to be offended when I told him that I did not appreciate his truculent advances. I have had to seek a private audience with the Viceroy and request his help in removing the annoying Don Fabio. He laughed heartily at my descriptions of Don Fabio's behavior but agreed to employ him as an undersecretary to give him something to do other than chasing the ladies-in-waiting. What an odious life to have a man at one's side at all hours, especially one who won't even argue.

13 January 1667

The Christmas season is over at last (not even a moment in which to scribble here), and I have plunged myself into my studies. It's the only way in which to displace this anxiety that will not be excavated. I know that spending so much time with la Marquesa triggers that quivery feeling in my belly, especially now that Lady Eugenia is ill and cannot attend to her in the bath. I can't understand why my hands want to linger on the lovely architecture of her body. Her flesh in the soapy water feels like the softest, purest silk. She says I have the best fingers for washing hair, that she likes the way my nails scrub her scalp and make it tingle. I scrub harder and swallow the words that want to fly out of my mouth: your head is the sun and I a meager planet held in its orbit. Where do these words come from? These thoughts that press into my dreams and leave a trail of dampness on my thighs, a humor that is not urine or menses.

Dear God, dear Virgin of Sorrows, is there no remedy for this feeling that aches like an affliction and yet produces such illicit pleasure? Did Eve taste the apple of her own free will, or was it something in the nature of the rib that formed her which made it impossible to resist the snake?

"I have an outstanding idea, Señora," the Viceroy announced to the court one spring afternoon at the midday meal. "The palace is going to sponsor a tournament between our brilliant Juana Inés and the most erudite members of the university. I'll call together *catedráticos* from every field—theology, music, poetry, philosophy, physics, mathematics, astronomy—and we'll challenge them to find a gap in Juana Inés's education."

"But I'm only eighteen, Your Grace," Juana Inés tried to dissuade him, the fried cornmeal of the squash-blossom quesadilla sticking in her throat, "and nothing but a lady-in-waiting. Surely I have not learned enough to participate in such a contest. Not yet."

"Nonsense," the Viceroy said. "If you can answer their questions the way you play chess, I am certain that you will astonish and outwit them all. Don't be modest, Juana Inés. I can't abide modesty in intellects like yours."

Don Fabio turned his large brown eyes to her and pouted his lips. "Excellent idea, Your Excellency. I'm sure it will prove to be quite an entertainment. Don't you agree, Juana Inés?"

A few of the ladies at the end of the table exchanged whispers behind their fans.

"No, Don Fabio, I don't agree. I can't find anything entertaining about public humiliation."

"Bah! You've read Virgil, Ovid, Heraclitus, Pythagoras, Galileo, no doubt, and Aristotle. It is you who will humiliate them, Juanita," said the Viceroy. "You're a humanist. You can discourse about anything. I know this for a fact. The professors, on the other hand, specialize in the narrow confines of their fields. A specialist in mathematics would not be able to answer a question about physics if his life depended on it."

"Sigüenza might," offered one of the gentlemen-in-waiting.

"If he stopped chasing after all the ladies, he might," chuckled the Viceroy, and several of the ladies giggled.

"Most unbecoming for a Jesuit," said Don Fabio.

"And I think it unbecoming for a lady to compete with men," said the lady Cristina.

"Do you, now?" said the Vicereine, her lips pulled back in a false smile. "Would you prefer that she compete with me, perhaps?"

The lady Cristina turned red as a strawberry and looked down at her plate.

"It shall not be a competition, I tell you," insisted the Viceroy. "More of a recitation, a tournament of memory. I have complete faith in the mnemonic powers of our Juana Inés."

He's confusing memory with knowledge, Juana Inés said to herself, but allowed him to believe whatever he wanted.

"What do you say, Juanita? Are you amenable?"

"As you wish, my lord." She pinched herself under the table for all of the time she had wasted ruminating about her sinful desires when she should have been memorizing theology.

"Excellent!" The Viceroy pushed his chair back from the table, calling to his undersecretary to follow him. "We have letters to write, Fabio. A tournament to plan. Lady?" He turned to his wife. "Mark your calendar for, let me see, how much time would you need to prepare, Juanita?"

She blushed at the suddenness of this decision. "Three months?" she said.

"Very well. Mark your calendar for three months from today. That would be, that would be," he snapped his fingers at his undersecretary.

"Midsummer," said Don Fabio.

"Very good. Midsummer. Classes will be out and the professors will be idle. We'll be out of mourning then, too. Perfect timing. I tell you, Juana Inés, you're a genius."

The Vicereine smiled at her from across the table. "If you cannot go to the university, my dear, then the university must come to you."

Chapter 3

11 July 1667

Bless me, Padre, for I have sinned; my last confession was on Saint John's Day. Forgive me for not going to the confessional, but I couldn't speak this sin aloud, Padre, and I may not, may never, be able to speak it in writing. By now you may already know, perhaps you have guessed it from the wretched demeanor I display when I am in Her Ladyship's presence. A vernal fever, the ladies call it, laughing at the way it has affected some of the courtiers, and yet I know that what afflicts me is not connected to the season, nor is it natural to my sex. But there is naught that I can do about it, Padre, just as I cannot alter the color of my eyes or the shape of my bones. Punish me as you would punish the vilest sinner, but do not make me say this to you. Pull out my tongue, Padre, poke out my eyes, lock me up in a convent. Do what you will, just do not make me speak. I beseech the most pure, the most benevolent, our Lady of Guadalupe, to save me from this ugliness. Hide me under your robe, dear Lady, crush me under your feet like a serpent.

"Open this door, Juana Inés, or I shall have one of the masons take it down," said la Marquesa from the other side of the barricaded door. "What is the matter with you, girl? Do you have the pox that you quarantine yourself in this way?"

But Juana Inés could not answer. She dropped the quill on the parchment and felt the ugliness swell within her, spilling out of her eyes like innocent tears.

"I understand that you must be afraid, Juana," called la Marquesa. "But the Viceroy and the professors are all waiting for you in the salon. You don't want to embarrass the palace, do you?"

If only you knew about me, thought Juana Inés, about this sin I cann confess. But la Marquesa was right. If she refused to participate in the tournament, the palace would be put to shame, and she could not let her ugliness contaminate the Viceroy's plans.

Again la Marquesa ordered her page to pound on the dormitory door.

"Yes, my lady," she answered la Marquesa's entreaties at last, "I'm on my way."

"Thank God you have recovered your senses, girl. Do hurry. Everyone has already finished dinner. I'm afraid you won't have time to eat, dear."

"I'm not hungry, my lady," called Juana Inés, holding the confession she had just written over the flame of a candle. She stashed her writing box under the bed, opened the wardrobe, and gazed at her fine gowns, all gifts from la Marquesa, but she could not wear anything that would stimulate the ugliness and distract her. In this contest the only thing that mattered was her memory; her body and face were inconsequential, and so she would wear the plainest gown, the black one with the white lace collar and ivory buttons.

In the mirror, her eyes looked as though she had rubbed them with prickly pears, and her skin was the color of maguey pulp. She poured water into the basin and wet her hair. She would braid it simply, with a black ribbon, and would wear no jewelry, not even the cameo that her mother had sent her and certainly not the necklace that la Marquesa had given her for her eighteenth birthday or the pearls that set off her ears. She pushed the heavy bureau away from the door, expecting la Marquesa's page to be waiting for her, but the gallery was empty except for slave girls draping cloths over the birdcages.

Inhaling and exhaling slowly to loosen the muscles in her throat, Juana walked to the great hall where the contest was to be held, worrying about the questions that would be put to her. Deep in her mind she that the Viceroy's faith in her intellect was not unfounded—she hard enough at her studies to merit at least a licentiate from the of that she had no doubt. But here she was, on the day she most wits sharp and focused, preoccupied with this thing, this yearn- driven her at last to transgression.

to think about something else. What would they ask about the- eakest subject? The difference between Calvin and Luther . . . d not get out of her mind that scene which had finally cat- n she'd been trying to confess in Pandora's Box.

months, she had devoted herself entirely to her books. She

eschewed all company, particularly the Vicereine's, refrained from Carnival and Corpus Christi, took her meals in her little study, and requested that a pallet be brought in so she could sleep there and not be a nuisance to her roommates. Through willpower and her own natural inclination for study, she had managed to rout her melancholy and subdue her longings. But then last night, when she had come back to the dormitory to allow herself a good rest on her mattress the night before the tournament, she saw that scene which the devil had undoubtedly saved for her perdition.

It was late, as usual, and all the ladies were deep in sleep when she crept into the dormitory. Not wanting to rummage in the wardrobe for her night shift, she had removed everything but her undershift and slipped between the downy covers. She was about to lay her head on the pillow when she heard giggling down in the patio of the *doncellas*, the private courtyard of the ladies-in-waiting. She cracked the shutter. It was a full moon just after matins, and a silver light inundated the patio. She saw that it was the lady Eugenia down there with one of the courtiers—Don Victor!—and they were standing close together by the fountain. He stood behind her, tickling her neck with his tongue, his hands squeezing her breasts, his hips practically grinding into Eugenia's backside.

She clung to the windowsill, and knew that she shouldn't be watching but could not pull her eyes away until she heard one of the ladies moan about the light she was letting into the room through the open shutter.

Before she even knew what she was doing, she was under the covers and her fingers had found the source of all her longing. She did not stop touching, probing, rubbing, grinding her own hips into the pillow until Eugenia returned to the dormitory smelling of horse sweat. The bells struck prime. Only then could she sleep, as she had not slept since leaving Panoayán—the heavy, innocent sleep of a sated child. But she was not innocent. She was far from innocent.

"You made it, Juana."

A masculine voice pulled her out of her anamnesis, and she realized that she was standing outside the great doors of the east salon and that one of the porters had spoken to her.

"It looks that way, Silvio," she retorted, hoping that an angry facade would cover up any signs of the affliction. She did not wait for him to push open the door.

The chamberlain and his assistants were serving cups of hot chocolate to the forty examiners seated at the front of the hall. The Archbishop, Fray Payo de Ribera, the noblest hidalgos and their wives, students from the university, the families of the ladies- and gentlemen-in-waiting, all had been invited to witness the contest, and an entire section of the room was filled with Dominicans, Franciscans, and Jesuits; among these sat Padre Antonio Nuñez de Miranda, the court's father confessor and spiritual adviser, the kind of priest who, it was rumored, knelt to the whip as passionately as to the Cross and stained the walls of his quarters with his own blood. Juana Inés felt exposed. Surely the ugliness in her soul would be apparent to Padre Antonio if not to Fray Payo or to the abbot of San Francisco. For an instant, she felt her memory and everything she had learned and stored inside it evaporate in the heat of her fear.

"There you are, Juana Inés," said the Viceroy, getting to his feet as she entered the hall. "Gentlemen, it is my supreme pleasure to introduce you to the court's protégée, the Vicereine's friend and companion. Doña Juana Inés Ramírez de Asbaje."

Juana Inés stood beside the bench that had been placed in front of the audience and curtsied. "Forgive me for keeping you waiting. I have been indisposed," she said, her voice trembling.

"Should we postpone the tournament, Juana?" asked the Viceroy.

"I would not want the professors to think that I am surrendering without a struggle," she answered, sitting down. "I am quite ready to begin, thank you, Señor Virrey."

"Very well," said the Viceroy, turning to face the audience. "Fray Payo, good Fathers, esteemed ladies, noble gentlemen, as you know, we are here to test our protégée's education, which, as you also know, she has gained without the aid or direction of teachers. We shall see if our dignified professors from the University of México can find a gap in Juana Inés's education, or, indeed, if Juana Inés will find a gap in theirs."

One of the professors in the audience guffawed into the satin puff of his sleeve.

"Señor López," said the Viceroy, "since you are in such a sanguine humor today, I will give you the honor of asking the first question." The Viceroy resumed his place in the purple velvet chair beside la Marquesa.

Juana Inés avoided the gold-green light of the Vicereine's eyes but looked straight into Padre Antonio's to ascertain whether he knew about her secret. The priest nodded at her paternally, and Juana Inés felt her fear dissolve and her memory stir back to life. She knew that the pallor of her face and her red-rimmed eyes and quivering voice betrayed her, made her seem the vapid, frightened girl whom the professors had come to patronize or to embarrass. But she was determined to win this contest; if she could only keep her logic intact and not feel like a monkey performing in the Plaza Mayor, her victory was certain.

"Doña Ramírez," the professor named López commenced, "since we are to begin with Philosophy, as well we should, I would be most honored to hear from your learned lips the five conditions of the solitary bird, according to San Juan de la Cruz."

Juana Inés closed her eyes and concentrated on the image of her journal of quotations, saw her hand copying out the very text that Professor López was now asking her to repeat.

"He must fly to the highest peak; he must not be afraid of solitude; he must sing to the sky; his color must not be definitive; his song must be very soft. And I will add, Sir, though you didn't ask me to expound upon this symbol, that San Juan de la Cruz was talking about the human soul. I recorded the passage in my notebook because it was the first time I had ever come across an idea that made me weep, and weeping, Sir, is not my nature."

"What do you say, Señor López?" asked the Viceroy, turning to face his guest. "Has she satisfied your curiosity?"

The professor pressed his lips together and nodded reluctantly. "I acknowledge your astute assessment of the girl's memory, Excellency," he murmured.

"Next!" called the Viceroy.

An older professor with his wig slightly askew stood up.

"Ah, Don Jorge," said the Viceroy. "I trust your question will prove somewhat more of a challenge to our protégée than the last one."

"Once upon a time," the old man spoke, his voice croaking like a bullfrog's, "the art of poetry along with all the other arts was considered nothing more than imitation, an artifice that imitated the one true art. What did the Greeks have to say about poetry, young lady, and about the phenomenon of inspiration?"

Bless me, Father, for I cannot keep from sinning, deep and terrible sins that flourish like poisoned mushrooms in my dreams.

"Doña Ramírez, would you define mathematics according to Pythagoras, please, and explain Euclid's contribution to the field as well as the Archimedean principle?"

There is love in my heart, Father, but it is a vile love, an unnatural, unnameable love, and yet, so deep, so pure it feels almost holy.

"A question from the faculty of Music, perhaps," suggested the Viceroy, cutting a sardonic grin at the audience. A man in a brown velvet cap with a green tassel got to his feet.

I have violated the Vicereine's kindness, Father. She has trusted me, loved me, been overly generous, and I have sullied her with my ugliness. As Saint Augustine says: "I muddied the stream of friendship with the filth of lewdness and clouded its clear waters with hell's black river of lust."

"Would you explain the difference between Deliberative, Forensic, and Epideictic Rhetoric, please, Doña Ramírez, and then construct a syllogism based on a popular enthymeme that illustrates the latter?"

I help her bathe. I braid her hair. I pour her chocolate. I wait on her, as I am supposed to do, Father, as her other ladies do. But none of them, I know, are tainted as I am. They grumble among themselves about how willful she is, how bad-tempered she is, how she treats them no better than slaves.

"You were speaking earlier of the nature of light and spiritual illumination, Doña Ramírez. Let us now examine the subject of light in a less esoteric, more mundane manner. I am alluding, of course, to the sun and will ask you, specifically, albeit circumlocutiously, about Copernicus. What theory did Copernicus propose that caused such an uproar in the Holy Office? And who and what proved Copernicus to be right?"

I know they're right, Father, but I don't blame her. She's an artist trapped in a woman's body. I understand her. I, too, feel trapped in my body.

"Would you name the four texts of the Code of Justinian, Juanita, and explain their use in Roman law?" asked the rector of the university, the Viceroy's good friend.

I was not always aware of how I felt, Father. It came upon me last week, while we were . . . while I was . . . we were in the garden. La Marquesa was doing a sketch she wanted to call "Athena Among Calla Lilies," and she had me posing for her in a yellow sheet fashioned to resemble a Greek tunic. She had snapped a calla off its stem and tucked it behind my ear, and I suggested to her that, as the patroness of war, Athena would probably not wear flowers in her hair. I tried to convince her to change the title of the sketch to "Aphrodite Among Calla Lilies," but she laughed at my sug-

gestion. That would lack originality, Juana Inés, she said. Everyone expects the god-
dess of love to be surrounded by flowers, not the goddess of wisdom and patroness of
war. I want to depict Athena as she might have been without the armor, a lithe, care-
free, voluptuous Athena, unburdened by thoughts of war, innocent yet succulent, like
the callas.

"Have you any scholastic, or even scientific, evidence, Doña Ramírez, for this quaint conjecture of yours, this inconsistent premise, that women can aspire to the same mental and spiritual dimensions as men? That women are, in fact," the anemic-looking professor of Rhetoric looked around the room, chuckling, "*equal* to men?" Others joined the chuckling.

"It is not an inconsistent premise, Señor de la Cadena," she responded, her face flushed. "It is Holy Writ that God made Man in His own image and that Woman was created from Man. Thus it follows that Woman, too, was created in God's image. The enthymeme demonstrates rather than re-futes Woman's equality to Man, since one was created in imitation of God and the other was created in the imitation of the imitation of perfection. Since we know that God makes no mistakes, His reproduction of Himself was perfect, as was the reproduction of the perfect image. It is not pos-sible, then, for Man to be more perfect than Woman since both have been created in the perfect image of God."

"Well argued, Juana Inés," called the Vicereine.

Several of the professors turned to glare at la Marquesa. Beside her, the Viceroy was keeping score on a tablet. For every question she answered, Juana Inés received a point; for every question she could not answer, the professors scored. So far, she noticed, only her column had registered any points.

"Another question from the Faculty of Mathematics and Astrology," called the Viceroy. "Doctor Sigüenza, we haven't heard from you yet."

A young man with a balding pate and long stringy hair got to his feet from among the priests. He wore the cassock of a Jesuit and the thick spec-tacles of a scholar.

"Doña Ramírez, do you believe in the influence of the zodiac on a per-son's character and destiny? The Maya had a way of interpreting the heav-ens through letters of their alphabet—"

And then la Marquesa made a comment about the color yellow, about how it set
off the hazel flecks in my eyes and removed the melancholic pallor of my skin. I never
noticed what an expressive mouth you have, Juana Inés, la Marquesa said, and my

knees buckled. It may have been la Marquesa's unusual description of the lilies that disarmed me, that made me so susceptible to the sound of her voice, or perhaps the sun had been beating on my head too long (we had been out there all morning), but I started to feel very confused. I felt an attack of vertigo coming on, and my whole body itched as though I had just been enfolded by a swarm of bees.

I had to sit down. La Marquesa was alarmed; she blamed herself for causing me what she interpreted as sunstroke, and immediately called one of the maids to bring a fan and a pitcher of water. She had me move to the grape arbor where it was cool and shady, and she actually fanned me, herself, crooning to me as though I were her own daughter. But it was not a daughterly feeling that I was feeling. And it was not a daughterly instinct that made me lay my head on her breast and intoxicate myself with her closeness. Father, I'm so ashamed. So frightened. I love her so much.

"I didn't quite hear that, Doña Ramírez."

"Forgive me, Sir," said Juana Inés, realizing that she had wandered too far into that dangerous hemisphere of her mind where logic had no roots. "Would you repeat the question, please? I suppose I'm getting rather tired."

"Of course you are, my dear," said the Vicereine. Turning to the Viceroy, she added, "Perhaps, Husband, we have seen enough. I, myself, am convinced that what I have witnessed here today is the equivalent of a royal galleon fending off the bothersome arrows of a few canoes."

"Yes, Madam, an exquisite analogy," said the Viceroy, "but I should like to hear our galleon's response to that last question. Do proceed, Don Carlos."

"I was asking our girl scholar if she had any idea what the letter O symbolized to that very advanced, though admittedly pagan, civilization of the Mayan people," said the young Jesuit, Padre Antonio's colleague, Carlos de Sigüenza y Góngora. He stood with his arms crossed, his eyes huge under their thick lenses, and winked at her.

"As you know, Sir, there is not much written about the history and philosophy of ancient México beyond what your own illustrious pen has written," she answered, "but in my grandfather's hacienda where I grew up, there was a Mayan gardener who told me a story about three sacred letters; I believe they were the T, the G, and the O. He was a very old man and I a very young girl, starving for stories. Unfortunately, all I remember of that story is this: Once upon a time, there was a great and blessed tree known as the Tree of Life that grew as high as the grooves of the Milky Way, the spiral path through which the gods traveled, through which existence unfolded, and the fruit of this tree was the human mind, ripe and round as a pomegranate, its seeds filled with that he called "The Nothing and The Everything."

"Enough of this pagan chattering!" a voice called out. It was Padre Antonio, who was now also on his feet behind the Archbishop, his face white as bone. "The zodiac! The tree of life! The spiral path! The equality of women! I'm shocked, your Excellency, that you have permitted this girl to spice her studies with such arcane and profane reading!"

"Scandalous to be sure," said Don Carlos, winking at her again.

The Archbishop scowled at Padre Antonio.

"A royal galleon, indeed," the Viceroy said, standing up. "With a score of forty to zero, I declare the court's protégée the winner of the contest." He applauded and the rest of the audience followed suit, but Juana Inés could sense that the air between their palms had become as taut as her own vocal chords.

"We have refreshments and a string quartet waiting on the patio, everybody," announced the Vicereine.

Pretending to ignore their shifty glances and shaking heads, Juana Inés watched them—the murmuring Señoras, the indignant caballeros—follow la Marquesa through the arched doors of the salon. She had expected la Marquesa to felicitate her in some way: a kiss, an embrace, even a smile. But she had not so much as looked at Juana Inés, and she felt paralyzed on her bench, abandoned. Two meters away, the Viceroy, the Archbishop, and Padre Antonio were arguing about her education.

"How can she know if something is forbidden when she has no teachers?" the Archbishop asked Padre Antonio.

"As censor for the Holy Office, Ilustrísima, I must report the girl. Her soul is in danger of excommunication if she continues with these heretical studies."

"Let us be reasonable, Padre Antonio," said the Viceroy. "You have known for as long as the girl has lived at the palace that she is an omnivore of books and that she has mnemonic capacities of magnanimous proportions. Is it her fault that she remembers things she shouldn't? Will the Holy See excommunicate a young girl for having a good memory?"

"Joan of Arc was roasted at the stake for listening to angels," said Padre Antonio, "and she was a national heroine."

The Archbishop chuckled. "You are overzealous, Antonio," he said.

The black magnet of Padre Antonio's eyes pulled Juana Inés's gaze away from the lace collar of her dress.

"Look at her, Ilustrísima," said the priest. "She knows she has wronged God and our Mother Church, do you not, Juana Inés? Come here, child. We must speak of the future of your soul."

Juana Inés walked like a somnambulist toward Padre Antonio, her victory over the professors dragging behind her, heavy as a cross.

"Please forgive me, my dear," the Viceroy said. "I had no idea the tournament would result in this. I trust that Padre Antonio," and at this the Viceroy cast a sidelong sneer at the priest, "will not condemn my soul if I congratulate you for a performance that not only exceeded my wildest expectations but also increased my admiration for your talents, and, I'm sure, won you the respect of your colleagues. For, despite your sex and your age, you are, indeed, their colleague, my dear. Of that I am now convinced."

"I must agree with the Viceroy," said the Archbishop. "Congratulations, Juanita. If only some of my prelates had your good sense."

From the courtyard came the keening of the violins. The Viceroy lifted her hand to his lips and brushed his mustache over her fingers. "May I escort you to your victory reception?" he asked.

"I would like to speak to the girl in private, Sire," said Padre Antonio. The Viceroy nodded, and he and the Archbishop left the salon. Now Juana Inés truly felt abandoned. Padre Antonio raised his right hand over her face. She flinched, expecting the priest to strike her, but he only drew a cross in midair, her doom or her salvation.

"I know you are no heretic, child. And I understand the Viceroy's point about your memory and your voracious appetite for books. I have, therefore, a proposition to make, a way of directing your mind toward higher learning while saving your soul at the same time. How would you like to be a bride?"

"Marriage?" gasped Juana Inés, clasping her Catherine-wheel medal.

"The ultimate marriage," said the priest, his eyes glittering like obsidian.

She closed her eyes and imagined a man's hands on her body. A man's lips and beard on her face. Her belly swelling with children. Her mind shriveling like a prune. "Oh, no, Father!" she cried, clutching at his wide sleeves. "Please, don't make me get married. Please, Father."

"An earthly marriage is not what I mean, silly child. In that black dress,

I see a humble and obedient bride of Christ, of the Carmelite order, perhaps. *Yes*, the Carmelites will cleanse that vanity of yours that has led you into dangerous waters."

"Carmelites, Father?" Juana Inés felt her lungs contract.

Padre Antonio looked up at the candles in the chandelier and made the triple sign of the Cross. "I see, now, the infinite wisdom of your plan, O Lord," Padre Antonio seemed to chant.

"But I'm registered as a daughter of the Church, Padre," said Juana Inés. "I have no father, no dowry; I could never be a nun. I'm . . ."

What was she? . . . What else could she be?

"I'm a sinner, Padre."

"Of course you are, my daughter," said Padre Antonio, "of course you are."

Chapter 4

Juana Inés lasted less than three months with the Carmelites.

"Holy Mother of Christ!" la Marquesa cried out when she appeared suddenly in the rose garden of the palace. "Is that you, Juanita? You frightened me! You look like Lazarus returned from the dead! Nothing but a sack of bones! What have they done to you?"

Standing in the shade of the magnolia trees before her easel, her smock streaked with different colors, la Marquesa curved her arms open and enfolded Juana Inés. "What did they do to you? My angel. My poor angel. You look starved. Look what they've done to your beautiful hair!"

She inhaled the scent of the oil paints on la Marquesa's skin, and was awakened to the softness of la Marquesa's breasts against the bones of her chest, to the sudden hunger she felt, and to the sudden pain in all of her joints as the numbness of three months dissipated under la Marquesa's touch.

"I read the Order's *Spiritual Guide*," la Marquesa was saying, "that obscene pamphlet. How could I have placed your life in their hands? Hair shirts to sleep in and hemp sashes bound to your breasts! How insane of Padre Antonio to send you to that torture chamber of a convent! He could have taken you to the Hieronymites or the Augustinians. The man's a sadist! Those Carmelites are criminals. They promised me they would take care of you. Didn't they ever feed you, my poor dear Juana Inés?"

She did not tell la Marquesa that it was her choice to stop eating, that the pain she felt at having left the palace had closed her stomach. At first the Carmelites praised her for her strong will and devotion. They imagined that she fasted for some holy purpose. To them Juana Inés was a visionary, another Teresita. She lived on pain and air. Occasionally, someone gave her a sponge soaked in honey water. Later they tried to feed her broths, tried to awaken her appetite with the scent of freshly baked bread, but she had no appetite, no desire to live, no strength even to open her mouth.

She could not stand without collapsing. Padre Antonio came to hear her last confession, and all she could say was *Marquesa*. He told her that she was a weakling, that he knew she was using her fast as a ploy to return to the palace. He never figured out that *Marquesa* was her confession. *Marquesa* was the signifier of her sin. The Carmelites felt betrayed when she left. Their visionary was nothing more than a homesick girl.

"Why didn't you send word, Juana Inés? The Viceroy and I would have taken you from there if we'd known."

"They didn't allow us to write, Señora. They confiscated my pens and my notebooks, my mandolin, even the jade rosary you gave me. I did try to write once. I stole some parchment and a quill and a chunk of ink cake from the infirmary, and hid them in the folds of my cincture. But one of the sick nuns saw me and reported my infraction to the abbess."

"Did Padre Antonio know you were leaving today?"

"The abbess told him."

"And he let you come by yourself? Half-dead as you are?"

"Saint Joseph's is a block away from the palace, Lady."

"Still, he should have had the decency, if not the compassion, to escort you back here. He was very quick about taking you to that house of iniquity, wasn't he? When the Marqués returns from Santa Fe and finds out about this, when he reads that torture manual they call a spiritual guide, I am sure he'll rebuke Padre Antonio. Come, Juana Inés, there's our refreshment."

La Marquesa held her waist firmly as they walked over to the small marble table by the fountain at which Juana and the Viceroy had used to play chess in the afternoons. One of her ladies had brought a tray of hibiscus water and sugared lime shells stuffed with coconut.

"Juana Inés, this is Estér," la Marquesa introduced the girl who was pouring two glasses of the cool red *agua de jamaica*. "She was your replacement after Padre Antonio took you away from me."

Juana could not look at the girl without wondering if she, too, was afflicted by the same ugliness that had driven her away from the palace. But no, the girl was innocent. In her eyes she saw nothing but the azure tiles of the fountain.

"Thank you, Estér, you can leave us now. Sit down, Juana Inés. Here, let me hold the glass for you."

She took a sip and her jaws clenched from the tartness. She had had nothing but water and the raw whites of eggs for a week to give her the strength to leave Saint Joseph's.

"You read the diary I left for you in my writing box, my lady?" she asked after la Marquesa had taken a nibble of her confection.

La Marquesa dabbed at her lips with a lace napkin. "Of course I did. You know I read everything you write. It was kind of you to leave that for me."

"It's a good thing I didn't take it with me or else it, too, would have been confiscated."

La Marquesa shook her head, keeping her eyes on her glass. "That would have been a pity. It's such a beautiful box."

"Had I known I would be a coward and not be able to withstand the novitiate, I would never have offered you that obscene chronicle."

"I found nothing obscene in there, Juana Inés."

"Now you know why I left the palace?"

"I suspected some inner turmoil was afflicting you."

"And you didn't accuse me with Padre Antonio? You suffered my presence? Why, Señora?"

"Need you ask me to explain my love for you, Juana Inés? What was there to accuse? Your innocence? Your confusion? Your need for love? You spent only eight years of your life at your mother's side. You see in me a substitute for her. Where is the sin in that?"

"Forgive me for contradicting you, Señora, but I have never once—not with the Carmelites, not at the palace, not even with the Matas—never in the eleven years that I have lived away from my home have I longed for my mother as I longed to be back here with you these last three months. I couldn't live without you. What I feel for you *is* a sin, I know that. But I've been to purgatory, my lady. I was leeched and bled and cupped, I wore sashes of camel hair and whipped my back till it bled, and yet the sin is still there. Even my fevers couldn't burn it away."

"Love is never a sin, Juana Inés. Love is our very soul. Like the sacred Word, it has no gender," La Marquesa said softly.

"Have you asked Padre Antonio's opinion about that, Señora? Or your husband's? What do you think they would say if you told them what I have written in my diary? Do you think the Inquisition would consider my love for you daughterly love? Or would they cry 'blasphemy!' and 'heresy!' and light the torches in the Quemadero?"

"Really, Juana Inés, you do tend to exaggerate matters. Nobody has been burned in the Quemadero for decades. That isn't done anymore. It's terribly uncivilized. Besides, nobody is going to find out, *cariño*. I've burned the pages, for your own safety as well as mine. Men and priests don't understand that there are different forms of love, that a woman may love another woman perhaps more than any man could ever love his wife, or that a woman may love another woman in whose arms she feels the warmth of a mother's love. Because men don't understand these things, they can be cruel, and so it's best not to talk of this again. But please, Juana Inés, don't stigmatize your feelings. Don't hurt your spirit. One day the right man will make you forget all of this."

"I do not want a man, Marquesa."

"I see that in my selfishness to keep you close to me I neglected my own duty. Lady Eugenia and Don Victor were wed just weeks after you left. The lady Hilda found a good match with the son of the widow Calderón, and they shall wed in the spring. I must ask the Viceroy to make inquiries for you."

"Please, Marquesa, don't waste your breath. I will never marry."

"But you're still young, and very beautiful, Juanita. Of course you'll marry, and have bright, lovely children, too."

"If my survival were to depend upon a man, Señora, I would already be underground."

La Marquesa reached for her hand, stroking Juana's wrist with her paint-tinged thumb.

"You're fifteen years younger than I am, and just a few years older than my own daughter whom I haven't seen in all of the years we've been in New Spain, so you see, *cariñito*, it's difficult for me not to mother you. But when you speak as candidly as this, when I recall those verses in your diary, I close my eyes and try to divorce your words from your sex, and I feel . . . how shall I describe it . . . I feel flattered . . . more than that . . . I feel *moved* by the depth of your devotion."

She could contain herself no longer. "I don't know what desire is, Marquesa," she said, clasping la Marquesa's fingers, "except that it has your face, your body, your scent."

La Marquesa lowered her eyes and pulled her hand from Juana's grasp. The edges of her face were flushed. Her eyelids trembled.

"Forgive me for embarrassing you, my lady."

La Marquesa shook her head but kept her gaze on the plate of pastries.

"There's nothing to forgive, my dear. You are who you are and I shall always love you as the daughter I found in New Spain. All I ask is that we never discuss this again. That you not write any more verses that may compromise our safety. That you keep your dreams to yourself and not risk having them read by unsafe eyes."

"I swear it, my lady!"

La Marquesa looked up and Juana saw that the green-gold rays around her dark irises had been replaced by glints of gray ice. "If it will make it easier for you, my dear, I shall ask Estér to continue in your place. It's clear you need time to sort through your feelings."

She forced herself to maintain her equanimity. "Marquesa, when I'm strong again, I'll serve you as I did before, but only as long as it takes me to find another position. I can't live here and pretend that I don't feel the way I do."

"You must do as you wish, my dear. But for now why don't you go and lie down. You need much rest after what you've been through. I can move you to a private chamber if you would prefer not to sleep in the ladies' dormitory."

"If I can have my little study back I shall be happy to sleep there."

"Perhaps it is another cloister that you seek."

Juana felt a cauldron of shame bubbling inside her. "Perhaps."

For months afterward she did not see la Marquesa except at the afternoon meal, and even then they hardly spoke. When she came to la Marquesa's room in the evenings to help her bathe as had always been her duty, she was informed by Estér that la Marquesa wanted her to rest and recuperate her strength. When she asked to have a mandolin tuned so that she could play for la Marquesa during her siesta, Estér told her that one of the other ladies was already performing that task. When a bout of the fever returned, it was Estér who ministered to Juana, bringing her herbal infusions and wet cloths. When the Viceroy arrived from the northern province of Santa Fe, he consumed Juana's time with long stories of his journey and even longer games of chess, oblivious to his wife's silence and withdrawal from their company.

La Marquesa would absent herself for days at a time, taking Estér and three of the other ladies and her usual bevy of slaves and footmen to visit friends in Puebla or to the house in Chapultepec or to the mineral baths of Belén. Juana was left in charge of the Viceroy's social calendar. In her absence the Viceroy grew irascible and fought with everyone, particularly with Fray Payo, the Archbishop, who was suddenly not welcome at the palace. When la Marquesa returned, the Viceroy would sponsor a dance or a *galanteo de palacio* that Juana was expected to organize and supervise. And she was expected to sit between the Viceroy and the Vicereine on their Sunday carriage rides through the Alameda and amuse them with her observations, but always an hidalgo and his wife were invited to join them in the *paseo*, and mostly la Marquesa avoided Juana's gaze.

With the Viceroy's permission, Juana Inés started meeting her Aunt Mary in the Cathedral for Sunday vespers. Gloria was getting married. Nico had fathered twins. Uncle John was afflicted with gout, for which she was not sorry. And Fernando had joined the royal navy and was stationed in Vera Cruz awaiting his first passage to la Coruña.

"God, that I could change my life like that!" she told her aunt.

"Always wanting what you can't have, Juanita," her aunt said.

The best and worst news was that her sister Josefa had come to live in the city with her second common-law husband, Villena, but that, insanely jealous, he never let her out of his sight and withheld permission for her to visit any of her family. She sent a letter to Josefa through her aunt, begging her to come and visit her at court, but she never received a response and never found out where she lived. A rumor had it that their mother's husband, Don Diego, had a mistress in Mexico. She wrote her mother but could not bring herself to ask about Don Diego. Her mother's response, in the penmanship of a public scrivener, was full of stories of "the children," Don Diego's son and two daughters. "*Inesilla is smarter than Antonia,*" her mother wrote, "*and she reminds me so much of you, Juanita, with her insatiable curiosity and a mind much older than her years. One of these days I shall take the girls to visit their big sister at court.*" She did not expect them, and of course they never came.

She studied little during this time and forced herself not to write, as she had promised la Marquesa, though this vow she found difficult to keep. Late at night, as usual, she would write and rewrite stanzas of a long poem about the irrational effects of love and the need for discretion, changing the pronouns from feminine to masculine in case la Marquesa discovered it. A loving torment, she called it, a grave agony, a delirious, tyrannical longing and treacherous pain that caused her to become easily irritated and to offend the very one for whom she would give her life. Once la Marquesa had asked her a favor, to fetch her embroidery frame from the sewing room so that she could show the Viceroy the new pattern she wanted to use on the Christmas tablecloths, and Juana pretended to be so immersed in her next move on the chessboard that she did not hear la Marquesa's request.

On the cold, rainy morning of Juana's twentieth birthday, la Marquesa came to her room and gave her a copy of Plato's *Symposium*, a book so censored by the Inquisition that anyone caught with it would become the immediate prisoner of the Audiencia.

"You must not keep this," la Marquesa had whispered, "but you need to read it. Happy birthday, *cariño*."

"I miss you, my lady," said Juana before la Marquesa could leave the room.

La Marquesa paused at the door. "My husband wants to arrange a small gathering this evening in your honor, Juana Inés. We can speak then if you like."

Juana wept for an hour after she was gone, wanting to cast the book out into the courtyard for everyone to see. On the first leaf, the book was dated "*12 de noviembre de 1668*" and dedicated with a cryptic exhortation: "Beware. Incendiary material." Folded into the book was a page from Pandora's Box, the last entry she had written in the diary, which la Marquesa said she had burnt.

13 August 1667
Tomorrow I depart for the Convent of Saint Joseph's and I feel strangely removed from my body, as though I were watching myself make the motions of leaving the palace. Why am I always leaving somebody whom I love? First my family in Panoayán, then my aunt Mary, now la Marquesa and the Viceroy. And how does one prepare to leave the world in body without leaving it in soul as well? Do I pack anything? What do I take? Will I be allowed to keep my books, to write in my diary? Will I wear sackcloth and go barefoot as it is said the Carmelites do? Or do novices get a reprieve, and yet why should we if we are in the process of becoming daughters of the strict Saint Theresa?

In two days it will be the Feast of the Assumption, and outside the throngs of vendors have already gathered in the Plaza to prepare for the celebration. They have come from their villages in the hills and the outlying provinces with goods of every sort emblazoned with the image of the Virgin.

I have no heart for joining the other ladies today as they shop for the special sweets that la Marquesa likes to distribute to the hordes of children waiting beneath her balcony. A few have tried to convince me to go with them. "It'll be our last day together, Juana Inés. Don't you want to see that fellow who winked at you in the arcade one last time?" How little they really know.

Even la Marquesa reprimands me for brooding. "You'll be cloistered enough once you enter that convent, Juanita. You should go out, mingle with the crowds, join the festivities. You have one more day of freedom, my dear. Why spoil it by closing yourself off like this?" But they cannot move me out of this strange inertia. I watch the servants tie the bunting to the shutters of the palace, drape the Viceroy's colors from the balconies, line the balustrades in ribbons and streamers, and all I want to do is bury my head under my pillow. I feel so old and the thought of leaving weighs me down like a hump on my back.

But I must stop this self-pity and not waste my last day with la Marquesa closed up in this room. Enclosure awaits me for the rest of my life. La Marquesa is right. Today I am still free. I will go and take my place behind la Marquesa on her balcony and watch her watching the activity in the Plaza. The haggling of the vendors, the jugglers and the players rehearsing their skits, the members of the different guilds and fraternities setting up their stalls, the horde of pilgrims. I want to absorb every inch of her body with my eyes. That she could hear my heart with her eyes I would not even be able to look at her. But I shall not be the target of her gaze, and so I can revel in the feast of her presence. God forgive me. I cannot help this desire to confess how I feel. Perhaps I will leave her this diary as a testament to my sins. I'll leave her my Catherine-wheel medal, too. To remind her.

The convent is but a block away, and yet I feel as though I were embarking on a journey to the other side of the world, a journey from which I will never return.

The shame of it brought a fresh onslaught of weeping, and Juana Inés crumpled up the page and cast it into the flames of the brazier. She heard the Cathedral bells tolling for High Mass, but it was cold outside, and she could not bring herself to attend. Nor could she attend the afternoon meal with the others. She would stay in bed and see what insights la Marquesa offered through Plato's book.

She had read excerpts of the *Symposium* in other texts, but they were select and fragmented quotations that never revealed the true nature of that discourse, which was in actuality a philosophical debate on the meaning and character of Eros, of Love.

For Phaedrus, Love was the oldest, noblest, and mightiest of the Gods who provided virtue and happiness after death. Pausanius divided Love into two categories: heavenly love, which young intelligent men seeking spiritual illumination felt for each other, and common love, which was nothing more than physical desire for women and boys. The physician Eryximachus agreed with Pausanius's dichotomy but pointed out that both forms of love existed in the body and that knowledge of both was essential to his profession. For Agathon, Love was not the oldest but the youngest of the Gods, the very poet of life who gave order to the universe.

Socrates, of course, disagreed with all of his colleagues, stating that Love was neither a God nor a mortal, but a *daimon* or spirit that lived in the void between the Gods and mankind. Moreover, said Socrates, according to the wise woman Diotima who was his mentor in matters of Love, the only desire that attended Love was the desire for that which it could not possess, the desire not for good or for beauty or for carnal knowledge but for immortality. Because of this desire for immortality, Diotima had said, men begat children and gave free rein to their ambitions, seeking fame to carve their names in the scroll of eternity. Indeed, Love was linked to creation, Socrates said, but there were different ways of manifesting that desire. Creation could be a bodily impulse of the sort that engendered children; or it could be a spiritual impulse, a marriage of minds that involved the quest for wisdom and virtue; or—the best of all—creation could be a poetic impulse that gave birth to the immortal writings like Homer's or Hesiod's. Next to this passage, la Marquesa had written in minuscule letters in the margin:

This is your desire, Juana Inés. It is love of learning, not love of the body, that you feel.

But it was Aristophanes' definition that nearly choked Juana Inés, for, according to this ancient writer of comedies, once upon a time, when humankind had four hands, four legs, and one head with two faces, there had been three sexes: Man was composed of two male bodies, Woman of two female bodies, and Man-Woman, or the Androgynous One, was made of a male and a female. Because their strength and courage was doubled, humankind grew arrogant and actually launched an attack on heaven. To punish this great infraction and teach human beings the lesson of humility, Zeus decided to split them in half and, with the help of Apollo, refashioned humankind into its present state. Forevermore, Man, Woman, and Man-Woman have searched for their other half, and this, said Aristophanes, this pursuit and desire for wholeness was what constituted Love.

> Men who are a section of that double nature which was once called Androgynous are lovers of women. . . . The women who are a section of the woman do not care for men, but have female attachments; the female companions are of this sort. But they who are a section of the male follow the male, and while they are young, being slices of the original man, they hang about men and embrace them, and they are themselves the best of boys and youths because they have the most manly nature.

Juana read and reread the passage, alternating between joy and despair. Fantastic as Aristophanes' story seemed, at least it explained the origin of her feelings, at least it brought her desire out of the deep mire of shame in which she'd been wallowing for more than a year.

And yet she realized that la Marquesa was not her other half, for if Aristophanes was right, when the two halves met, they recognized each other and clung to each other and tried to become one again. La Marquesa clearly had descended from the Androgynous sex, which is why she clung to the Viceroy and expressed her desire for immortality through the begetting of children. Juana, on the other hand, had descended from the Female sex, which is why she felt this inborn attachment to la Marquesa and why she expressed her love and desire through a poetic impulse and an inclination for learning.

She copied the passage from Aristophanes into a notebook and then wrote la Marquesa a note in the margin of the book, beside Aristophanes:

> I see now, Señora, that you are right, and I can never thank you enough for the Promethean illumination this has brought to the dark labyrinth of my heart. I miss you so much that my side aches, and I imagine that Adam must have ached this way when he discovered that rib missing.

With the note, she had made the text even more incendiary. La Marquesa would burn it, she knew, but what did it matter? The book had served its purpose.

She marked the page with a piece of ribbon, wrapped the thin volume in an old scarf, and had one of the slaves deliver it to la Marquesa, more certain than ever that she needed to leave the palace. And where else could she go but to the one place where she could continue her studies and where they would not be expecting her to seek and find an other half, a half that did not belong to her. And who else would help her to return there but Padre Antonio?

At her birthday gathering she felt surprisingly sanguine and chatted with everyone, accepting compliments with an unusual aplomb and agreeing to any petition for a recitation or a song. The Viceroy gave her a chess set of her own, the pieces fashioned in an Egyptian style and carved of black onyx and white marble. La Marquesa returned Pandora's Box, filled with a ream of gilt-edged parchment, *to replace what was lost*, she said on the card. The courtiers and ladies had put their funds together and bought her a pendulum clock, to remind her, they said, not to stay up so late with her studies. She drank more wine than she was used to, and the instant she felt the twinge of melancholia brought on by the wine she kissed everyone, thanked them profusely for an unforgettable birthday, and retired to her little study, followed by two pages who carried her gifts.

For a month she attended rosary in the chapel, on her knees the entire time as the Glorious Mysteries, the Sorrowful Mysteries, the mysteries of her own heart slipped through her fingers. With each rosewood bead, each decade of Hail Marys, each Paternoster, each Credo, each Act of Contrition she begged Saint Jude and the Virgin of Guadalupe to give her the strength to make this choice. It would be, she knew, a permanent choice. No running back to the palace this time. And, of course, returning to her aunt's house was out of the question. At last, on the feast day of Saint John of the Cross—*de la Cruz*, she thought, *I will take his name*—she was ready to appeal to Padre Antonio.

"Bless me, Father, for I have sinned."

"Speak, child. God is listening."

"I have deafened my ears to the call of God, Father. For twelve months I have been hiding under the wings of the palace, avoiding the truth that nightly haunts me in my dreams."

"What have you dreamt, child?"

"It's an old dream, Father. The first time it came to me I was fifteen and I didn't remember the important symbols as I do now. I see a man holding a gold bishop's crook. Before him there is a river, and behind him there is a house, a great glass house. The man is calling to me, not with words but with his will, and he tells me that in order to reach that house made of glass, I have to float across the river on my back. But I'm afraid, Father. And I resist the man's call."

"What do you fear, my daughter?"

"I'm afraid of the strange woman who always appears after I cross the river. She hands me a black shawl and takes me up to the glass house. I can never return to the river."

"It is enclosure that you fear, Juana Inés. As well as obedience. Who is the man?"

"I used to think it was my grandfather."

"No, *hija mía*, the man is Christ. The river is the barrier between sin and salvation. The glass house is your soul. Don't you see? Christ is calling you to His house, for He lives in your soul. But the house is also the Church. The man is also a bishop. The river is also a place of baptism."

"God is calling me back to the convent, isn't he, Father?"

"My daughter, I am overjoyed at this news. I have been observing you all of these months since your return from the Carmelites. I have seen you praying in the chapel every afternoon, kneeling there before Our Lady with such a look of devotion in your face, though I also see sorrow and confusion. I know now that you returned here, not to hide from your calling as I once thought, but to strengthen it at your own pace and through your own efforts. The Carmelites, perhaps, asked too much of you. I should have sent you elsewhere."

"La Marquesa suggested the Hieronymites, Father, or the Augustinians."

"Yes, they are milder orders. Perhaps la Marquesa is right. The House of San Jerónimo is a good house. For a *criolla*."

"After what happened at Saint Joseph's, Father, I am ashamed to ask the Viceroy to sponsor me again."

"Indeed you should be, Juana Inés. Despite the difficulties, you dishonored us all. But leave your sponsorship to me. I believe I can persuade one of my good friends to put up the three thousand pesos they ask at San Jerónimo. I daresay our affluent Don Pedro Velásquez de la Cadena would enjoy nothing more than proclaiming his sponsorship to the Viceroy. He is still bitter about that spectacle of a tournament. It was, after all, a public disgrace for his brother—a very distinguished professor of Rhetoric, as you know—and the other professors to be upstaged by a girl."

"It was never my intention to disgrace, Father."

"Worry not, my daughter. De la Cadena blames the Viceroy, not you. I daresay, his sponsorship would help him feel vindicated. He has the opportunity to show the Viceroy how to redirect your studious mind toward higher illumination and remove you from public spectacles. I shall go to him forthwith and then write to the prioress of San Jerónimo."

"I am ready to go whenever you send me, Father. I know I cannot escape the fate that God has given me."

She closed her eyes and saw the image of Aristophanes' Woman, two heads on one neck. The face on both of them was her own, one framed by a nun's veil, the other wearing the pointed yellow hat of a penitent.

Chapter 5

The convent of Santa Paula of the Order of Saint Jerome lay four miles south of the palace, just past the Santa Rosa canal, on the same street as the city's meat market. Both cloister and church were surrounded by a red volcanic *tezontle* wall, along which grew immense agave cactus. Farther down along the southern causeway Juana Inés could make out the fields and smoky shacks of San Juan de Letrán where the Negroes and mulattoes lived, and, just to the west, the cupola of the church of Regina Coeli, the richest of the city's convents.

In the courtyard of the church she emerged from Padre Antonio's surrey like one in a dream, unsure, still, that she could live up to her vows and remain in the cloister forever. She already had failed once, last year, when she had run back to the palace after only three months in the Carmelite novitiate. She had not understood that joining a convent was like death in life; she had not been prepared for the sacrifices she had to make. Does the bullfighter enter the ring knowing it will be his last *faena*? Does the sailor embark upon a journey from which he knows he will never return? Looking up at the bearded image of Saint Jerome carved over the arched doors of the church, she made the sign of the Cross, fervently entreating him to give her resolve and resignation, then followed Padre Antonio around the corner to the convent's portal.

"Before I ring this bell, daughter," said the priest, "is there anything you wish to confess? I see a quavering in your chin."

"No, Father. I'm not quavering. It's just a solemn moment for me, that's all."

"Have you no doubts to confess? No second thoughts? I will not tolerate another humiliation from you, Juana Inés. Once you enter here, you will not leave, no matter how ill you make yourself. You will live and die in this convent."

She swallowed the tart liquid that had suddenly come up in her throat. "I understand, Father. I have no doubts, truly."

Padre Antonio pulled on the rope to the right of the portal, and almost immediately a pair of dark eyes appeared at the grated opening. "God give you grace, Sister. I have brought another sheep for your flock. Please announce us to the Mother Superior."

"We have been expecting you, Padre Miranda," said the gatekeeper in a voice that reminded Juana of the more coquettish ladies-in-waiting at the palace. "Please meet me at the gate to the second *locutorio*."

At the appointed *reja*, Juana Inés heard the jangle of keys, the squeak of the hinges, the rusty grate barely opening to let them through.

"*Adelante, por favor.*" The gatekeeper's face was veiled, but she had the gnarled hands of an old woman. They followed her past a tiny flagstone patio crammed with potted geraniums and a flowering acacia tree. "I've sent a *criada* to inform Mother Paula that you've arrived, Padre." She pushed open the long shutters that served as doors to the reception room. "Please take a seat."

Juana Inés nearly gasped at the elegance of the room, so unlike the dark locutory of Saint Joseph's with its austere benches and bare granite walls. Here, tapestries lined each wall depicting scenes of the Virgin of Guadalupe's appearance to the Indian, Juan Diego. Turkish rugs stretched beneath plush chairs and marble-topped tables. A large vase filled with poinsettias decorated the richly carved chest, and the afternoon light slanted through the floor-to-ceiling shutters. On one side of the sideboard in the corner stood a porcelain pitcher and basin, on the other side, a quill and inkstand and a leather-bound guestbook.

There was a grille, of course, and a less lavish room on the other side of it with no tapestries and no Turkish rugs and only a small, grated window higher than the door. But there were the same velvet cushions on the armchairs, a twin sideboard holding a vase of roses and carnations, and a large, gilt-framed painting of Madonna and Child.

"As you see, my dear, the Hieronymites are not driven by the same master as the Carmelites."

"It's not what I expected." She could not keep the delight out of her voice.

"You should be quite comfortable, here, Juana Inés, spoiled as you've been by the Viceroy. Ah, there's Mother Paula."

From a narrow door on the other side of the grille came two nuns in black veils and flowing white tunics with dragging sleeves, hands hidden under their long black scapulars. Above the escutcheons pinned to their chests, their faces seemed so alike they could have passed for sisters, the same sad eyes and rosy skin of the religious, though the eldest one limped like an arthritic.

"They don't cover their faces, Father?" she whispered.

"As I said, *hija mía*," he said aloud, "these are not the modest daughters of Santa Teresa."

In a gesture that was even more shocking, the gatekeeper nun came up behind them and unlocked the door to the grille so that the two nuns actually passed into the guests' side and stood in the same room, face-to-face with her and Padre Antonio. The priest took a step back to put more distance between them.

"Good afternoon," said the younger nun, who nonetheless looked older than la Marquesa by a decade. "On behalf of the Sisters of San Jerónimo, we bid you both welcome. Won't you please sit down, Padre Miranda, and make yourself comfortable."

Padre Antonio shook his head. "This is not a social call, Sor Catalina. I have come only to deliver another sheep for your flock." He turned to the older nun. "Mother Paula, this is Juana Inés Ramírez de Asbaje, the one with the notorious reputation as a girl scholar. You may have heard of her."

Juana Inés curtsied to them.

Sor Catalina's eyes lit up like green flames. "Indeed, we have, have we not, Mother?" she said. "The *consentida* of the palace. Welcome to our humble house, Doña Ramírez. I am the *vicaria*, Mother Superior's first assistant."

Mother Paula gazed at Juana with her sad gray eyes and nodded her welcome.

"She has served the Vicereine as lady-in-waiting for the last four years," said Padre Antonio. "She had an abbreviated novitiate with the Carmelites, so convent life will not be new to her, but I regret to say that she has been dreadfully pampered and indulged, and her spirit was not strong enough to withstand the regimen of the Carmelites. She does, however, demonstrate a sincere desire to serve God and to channel all of her intellectual abilities toward higher learning." He reached into the hemp sack he used as a pouch and brought forth a small scroll. "This is her letter of patronage from Don Pedro Velásquez de la Cadena. You may claim her dowry directly from him."

"Thank you, Padre Miranda," Mother Paula spoke at last, her voice as serene as her eyes, "for gracing our flock with such an exceptional sheep.

Are you certain we cannot offer you a repast for all your trouble? Not even a cup of chocolate?"

"The best refreshment for me, Mother, will be to see this child walk through those doors and bid farewell to the sins of the world."

"As you wish, Reverend Father," said Mother Paula. "Sor Catalina, please take Sister Juana to the headmistress of the novices."

Sister Juana, the title reverberated in her head. From now on I will be Sister Juana. She felt a chill crawl up her spine.

"Does she know, yet, what name she wants to take, Father?" asked Sor Catalina.

"De la Cruz," she said quickly, "Juana Inés de la Cruz, after Saint John."

"A good choice, child," said Mother Paula

"Pray hard, then, Juana Inés de la Cruz," said Padre Antonio, "that the Holy Spirit may soon drench your soul in humility and grace."

She curtsied again, to Padre Antonio this time, then remembered her trunk of books and clothes still strapped to the surrey. "And my books, Father? My things?"

"Everything you need will be provided here," he told her.

"But we have no library, Father," Sor Catalina objected, "nothing to accommodate the needs of a scholar."

"She is *not* a scholar, Sor Catalina. She is a wayward girl whose only needs are to steer her soul back in the direction of her heavenly Father. I am taking that trunk of yours, Juana Inés, and donating its contents to the Colegio de las Niñas."

"But, Father—"

"Perhaps, Padre Miranda," Mother Paula interceded in an almost indifferent equanimity, "you would consider donating the contents of Sister Juana's trunk to our own *colegio*. The boarders could certainly use some new books, and, of course, Juana, you won't be needing any of your regular clothes, save a few undergarments (forgive my indiscretion, Father). We can donate those to our *beatas*, bless their souls, who work as hard as the maids and are as devoted as any sister."

Juana Inés was going to protest. She didn't care about the clothes, but those were *her* books, given to her by the Viceroy, and nobody but *she* could keep them. She opened her mouth, but a glance from Sor Catalina told her to keep it shut and listen.

"I suppose it would save me a trip to the poor quarter," acceded Padre Antonio. "I shall need help dragging it in."

"Worry not, Father," said Sor Catalina. "I'll send my maids out to fetch the trunk forthwith. Come along, Mother, Doña Ramírez, I mean Sister Juana, we do not want to be late for nones. With your permission, Padre Miranda?"

"You may withdraw, Sister," said Padre Antonio. "Juana Inés, I expect to see you as a *monja flórida* by next Easter. I, myself, will light the candles in the church and bear the expense for your veiling ceremony."

She curtsied again. "Thank you, Father."

"Study hard, discipline yourself well, and consecrate all of your thoughts to the Almighty. That is the formula for godliness."

"Yes, Father."

"Good day, Padre Miranda," said Sor Catalina, taking Juana's hand and leading her to the other side of the grille, her eyes glowing triumphantly. "Don't despair, *hija*," she mumbled under her breath. "You shall have your books, and anything else you want, as long as I have any influence with the Mother Superior." Sor Catalina's hand felt warm as bread.

Mother Paula stayed behind a moment longer, signing a paper for Padre Antonio, and Sor Catalina told the gatekeeper to see to the unloading of Sister Juana's trunk. Then the three of them passed through the inner door that opened out to a narrow vestibule. Juana heard the gatekeeper nun locking the grille behind them, but she did not turn back.

Beyond the iron gate at the end of the vestibule, they passed a eucalyptus-shaded patio that ran the length of the south wall of the temple.

"What are those?" Juana Inés asked, pointing to three small structures built against the temple wall. They looked like privies.

"Confessionals, child," said the Mother Superior. "Lower your voice."

Sor Catalina stopped and pushed aside the dark serge curtain of one of the confessionals. Inside, it was tiled in yellow fleur-de-lis and smelled of church incense.

"After you have taken your permanent vows," Sor Catalina explained, "you will never again set foot in the nave of the church, where the common confessionals are. Only the *profesas* use these. And we take Communion from a grate between the lower choir and the nave."

"Novices, too?"

"Novices, too, child," said Mother Paula. "Enclosure during Mass applies to all of us."

"Let's hurry," said Sor Catalina. "The headmistress is most eager to meet you. She's never had such an illustrious pupil before."

In the huge central patio of the cloister, a four-tiered terra-cotta fountain, round and deep as one of the pools at the palace, graced the middle of the courtyard, rimmed by rows of potted flowers: geraniums, orchids, irises, lilies of all colors. Across from the fountain was the well. Roses in every hue climbed the columns and the arches around the courtyard and twined through the balustrades of the upstairs galleries. Bright pink bougainvillea spilled from the railings. Bordering the lower gallery, red and blue hibiscus trees grew between orange azaleas, their flowers larger than the span of her two hands. All along the perimeter of the convent grew an inner fence of blue agaves and prickly pear cactus, heavy with fruit. Birdcages hung off the lemon trees. Wild rosemary grew between the flagstones. The air smelled of citrus and afternoon rain.

Then she noticed the girls. Nothing but women and girls all around her, save for an occasional toddler in short pants chasing after a maid. Young girls in short white veils, older ones who looked like novices in long white ones, nuns of all ages in black veils and scapulars—all engaged in myriad activities in the verdant shade of magnolia trees and weeping willows. Maids from all of the castes—from *negras* to *mulatas* to *mestizas* to *zambaigas*—scurried to and fro in their green aprons and bandannas. Maids were not allowed to show themselves in the courtyards of the palace, but here they were everywhere. Sweeping the galleries, carrying linen and wood, hauling buckets of water and baskets of fruit, their constant movement reminded her of Panoayán. So did the sound of a rooster crowing not too far away.

" . . . at *recreo* time," Sor Catalina was saying. "Some of us like to spend our free time out here with the girls, but most of our Sisters prefer silent contemplation in their cells."

"There are more of you?" asked Juana.

"There are over three hundred living souls in this convent, child," said Mother Paula. "Between the sisters and the novices and the boarders and the *beatas*."

"What's a *beata*, Mother?"

Mother Paula pointed to a woman in a short brown veil and black apron over a brown dress trimming dead buds off the rosebushes. "Lay sisters," she said. "They pledge their lives to the convent but don't have the money to profess."

"They look like shadows," said Juana Inés, noticing another one harvesting prickly pears.

"They're invisible," said Sor Catalina. "That's what they want."

"Never talk to a *beata*," said Mother Paula. "And try to keep your tongue silent, child. We know that you have an inquisitive nature, but bear in mind that a quiet novice makes a better first impression."

Just as a handful of Sisters closed around them in a cloud of black and white, she took a deep breath, holding the scent of the magnolias and the rosemary and the approaching rain, the familiar scent of the hacienda that signified home.

1 February 1669

What a strange world I've come to, a world of women and prayers and constant bells. It's beautiful here but there's such an aura of sadness to everything, completely different from the palace where even the slightest hint of sadness would draw attention. Maybe I'm confusing the silence that prevails in the Sisters with a melancholia that really isn't there. I guess that is something I will have to learn, this inner silence, but how can I be silent when there is so much to think about, so much to see and discern and explain. I don't miss la Marquesa, yet. Difficult to miss her after only a few days, especially as Sor Catalina gives me so much attention. Sor Mariana, our headmistress, tells me to be careful, that it isn't good for a novice to be favored this way by the Sister Vicaria. She doesn't believe me when I tell her this always happens to me; I'm always someone's favorite. La Marquesa's, the Viceroy's, the courtiers'. I'm not trying to be. Vanity, she calls it, and says that this is the sin that will haunt my novitiate. I explain the meaning of vanity to her, that it is pride in oneself and not the preference of others, but she tells me to open my Manual for Novices and read the section on Modesty.

"It's your eyes," she says. "You have no modesty of the eyes, Juana. You hold your head up too high; you carry yourself with pride, you call too much attention to yourself when you move, and when someone speaks to you, you look at them directly in the eyes. You're doing it now."

"Am I supposed to hang my head like a cow? Or be invisible, like a *beata*?"

"Oh, Juana. Life in the convent is going to be so difficult for you."

"I don't understand, Sister. How do my eyes make Sor Catalina favor me?"

"The eyes are the windows of the soul, Juana. If we keep the windows open, one and all can look in and in looking can get caught in the beauty of the soul and not want to leave. That, I think, is what has happened to Sor Catalina."

"Are you saying that I've charmed her with my eyes?"

"I am saying, Juana, that you must close your windows, let nothing and no one distract your soul, for in distracting yourself you distract others."

Modesty of the eyes, of the head, of the body, of the arms, even of the feet—and that is only one of the virtues we novices must learn. There are so many others: obedience, humility, patience, gratitude, diligence, perseverance, penance, chastity. And each one has its interior and exterior acts that we must practice, its motives and explanation that we must learn by rote.

For the rest of the day, I will practice modesty of the eyes, whatever that means.

3 February 1669

I've made a friend. Her name, or rather the name she wants to take, is Andrea de la Encarnación. She's of the Diocese of the Incarnate Heart of Jesus and seems to be genuinely devoted to this vocation. Sor Mariana considers her the most pious of the novices and says she wouldn't be surprised if Andrea weren't elected Mother Superior of the Order one day. She counsels me against developing a particular friendship with her. Friendship, she says, especially of one particular person, greatly compromises the virtue of silence and leads to the temptation of speaking, which interferes with the practice of perfection.

For as pious as she is, though, Andrea seeks my company. She's an orphan, she told me, placed in San Jerónimo by an older cousin, her only living relative. I told her about my mother sending me away after Abuelo died. I'm an orphan, too, in a way, I said. She wanted me to talk about the Carmelites, but I told her nothing. Just that I'd become ill and had to leave. That's nobody's business but mine. She loves my stories about living at the palace, though.

"Why did you join the convent, Juana? Surely you could have stayed at court. It sounds like you had many friends there, people who loved you, perhaps even a young man who would have asked for your hand."

How can I tell her the truth of what brought me here?

"A young man would have asked for more than my hand, Andrea, and *that* I wasn't prepared to give him."

"Stop it, Juana," she said, blushing. "You shouldn't think unchaste thoughts."

"That's why I'm here, Andrea. To protect the chastity of my thoughts."

I'm helping her memorize the virtues. She's amazed by how much I can remember (even though she is infinitely better at practicing what they preach) and I've shown her a few of my favorite mnemonic devices to help improve her memory.

6 February 1669

The food here is much better than it was at the palace, and yet when I lived there I found it to be the most delicious food I had ever eaten, though often too rich for my finicky stomach. They serve no delicacies here, but every-thing is cooked in delicious sauces and scented with a variety of herbs and spices that I find difficult not to savor (it's one of our virtues to abstain from the pleasures of the tongue). The head cook in the refectory is from the coast of Yucatán and her cooking reminds me so much of Francisca's kitchen in Panoayán, the same rich smells of roasting chiles and garlic and fresh cilantro and the dark spice of chocolate. Today's meal is my favorite so far, a pork stew with garbanzos and potatoes in a saffron sauce. The nuns eat in their own kitchens; only the novices eat at the refectory tables, along with Sor Mariana, of course, and her assistants, Sor Beatriz and Sor Rosario.

I sit on Sor Mariana's left and Andrea on her right. I can tell, already, that all of the others see us as the favorites of the headmistress. So odd to live amongst so many women, all of us dressed in the same white veils and tunics, studying the same books, weaning ourselves away from our indi-vidual natures.

10 February 1669

My mother sent a letter, congratulating me for having entered the con-vent. "I knew all your education would do you good, someday," she writes, "and I'm just grateful that you found a place in which to make good use of all your learning." She wants to send me Francisca's daughter, little Jane (I'm sure she's not little anymore; she was four when I left Panoayán, she must be sixteen or seventeen by now), to attend me in the convent, but Sor Mariana won't allow it. I think I'll write to la Marquesa about this. Why shouldn't I have my own maid? The other sisters have lots of maids. I'm not always going to be a novice. And it would be nice to have Jane here, a piece of home after so many years.

Chapter 6

Sor Catalina struck the triangle to bring the Friday chapter meeting to order. Juana was sitting in the back rows of the chapter room with the other novices, the white rows, they were called. Only the full-fledged nuns could sit in the front, the pews arranged so that the congregation sat in two half circles, facing each other across a wide aisle. At the head of the room, beneath a huge black crucifix suspended from the rafters on thick ropes, sat the executive table: the Mother Superior, the *vicaria*, the archivist, the treasurer, and the chief *vigilanta*.

In the two weeks that she had been at San Jerónimo, Juana had already discovered the factions that vied for control of the convent, thanks to Sor Rosario, the headmistress's assistant who took pride in keeping the novices informed of the political currents that ruled their Order. According to Sor Rosario, the Chief Vigilanta, Sor Clotilde, had been nursing an old resentment against Sor Catalina for fifteen years. Ever since Mother Paula de San Bartolomo had chosen to favor Sor Catalina with the title of Vicaria, Sor Clotilde had made it her mission to undermine Sor Catalina's authority any way she could. Outlandish bribery and bizarre threats pronounced during mystical trances were Sor Clotilde's methods, and through them she had won control of the disciplinarians—*vigilantas*, they were called—and all the minor positions on the executive board, including the gatekeeper, the mistress of the larder, the sacristan, and the infirmarian. Now she was after the archivist and the headmistress of the novices.

"Sor Mariana, of course, cannot be swayed," Sor Rosario had said, "so none of you needs to worry about that, but keep your eyes peeled, girls, and your ears, too. And always," she raised her index finger in front of her face, "*always* keep your voice low so that nobody can hear what you're saying." She bobbed her head slowly, for emphasis. "The *vigilantas* have very long ears."

Although Sor Catalina was not the Mother Superior, Mother Paula allowed her assistant to run Friday chapter any way she pleased, stepping in only when Sor Catalina got caught up in personal arguments with Sor Clotilde or when an administrative decision needed to be made. Otherwise she would sit beside her assistant at the executive table praying her rosary while Sor Catalina listened to grievances and meted out the penitence she deemed appropriate for each infraction.

"The archivist will now read this week's list of grievances," said Sor Catalina.

Clearing her throat, Sor Luisa de San Simón—*cara de caballo*, some of the novices called her because of her elongated chin—glanced sideways at the Chief Vigilanta, and waited to be told to speak. Sor Clotilde nodded to her. She cleared her throat again and opened the Book of Grievances.

"The *vigilantas* received a notice from Sor Mariana accusing the Mother Superior of favoritism in the affairs of the novices," Sor Luisa read rapidly, not daring to glance up from the page.

Juana noticed that Sor Catalina's gaze swung like a pendulum between Sor Clotilde and Mother Paula. The other two *vigilantas*, the very thin and pale Sor Melchora de Jesús and the very tall Sor Bernarda de San José, sitting together in the first row, stared down at their scapulars. Sor Mariana, the headmistress of the novices, stood up. ·

"Forgive me for interrupting, Mother, but I swear by the holy rosary that those words never came from my lips."

"Lips are not the only things that speak, Sister," said Melchora across the aisle. "Surely you remember the note you sent Sor Clotilde about the new novice? Or will you not admit to that either?"

"I do not deny having written a complaint, Mother," said Sor Mariana, her voice trembling, "but I did not accuse the Mother Superior of anything, and I certainly never used the word *favoritism*."

"What was the nature of your complaint, Sister?" asked Sor Catalina, fixing her green gaze on the headmistress.

"The new novice, Sister Juana Inés de la Cruz, remarked to me that her mother was going to send her a slave as a gift for joining the Order, and I told Sister Juana that she could not keep a slave until she had taken her permanent vows and was given her own cell. Apparently, Sister Juana wrote to the Vicereine about this, and now Mother Paula has granted her permission to receive the slave. *That* was the nature of my complaint, Sor Melchora."

Juana felt betrayed. She could not confide in anybody here. Even those who pretended to help her, like Sor Mariana, were in truth simply judging her every action. She had been here only a fortnight and already she could see Moors on the coast, as her grandfather used to say.

"I see," said Sor Catalina. "The rest was interpretation, I gather. Please sit down, Sor Mariana." She turned to the Mother Superior and said, "It appears we have a debate on our hands, Mother. Shall I proceed?"

"With all due respect, Mother," said Sor Clotilde, "but I disagree. The issue is clearly not debatable. It *is*, after all, one of the convent rules that novices do not own slaves."

"Sor Elena, *por favor*," Sor Catalina called on one of the elder nuns, "you who were so long our archivist, and who are so well versed in the rules of the convent, is what Sor Melchora says an accurate statement?"

"Perhaps it is an understood rule," said Sor Clotilde. "Novices do not have the same privileges as we do, Mother."

"Moreover," added Sor Melchora, "allowing the novice to own a slave would contradict the final vows that she is preparing herself to take."

"I was speaking to Sor Elena if you don't mind, Sisters," said Sor Catalina. "Elena? Do you recall anything to this effect in the Order's regulations?"

"I can answer that, Sister Vicaria!" said another nun, getting to her feet. She was taller than a man and had a voice that matched her masculine build.

"I defer to my pupil," wheezed old Sor Elena. "Her memory is probably better than mine. She was my apprentice for many years."

"Proceed, then, Sor Rafaela," prompted Sor Catalina. "Tell us what you know."

"It is certainly true, Mother Paula," said Rafaela, her gaze nailed to Sor Clotilde's, "that novices do not get the same privileges as we do, but owning a slave is not contradictory to our vows since we all own slaves. Sister Clotilde should know this."

"What you are saying, then, Sor Rafaela," said Sor Catalina, "is that ownership of slaves by a novice is denied on the basis of rank and privilege, but there is no such rule per se?"

"Not that I remember," she turned to Sor Clotilde and added, with a sneer, "in the ten years that I served as apprentice to the archivist."

"Of course I know this, Sor Rafaela," said Sor Clotilde, sneering back. "The problem is not really the slave. The Order of San Jerónimo does not require us to renounce our servants, but it does require that novices keep to the regimen of the novitiate, and this includes living en masse rather than separately as we do. If Sister Juana were permitted to keep a slave, she would need a cell of her own. A novice with her own cell has never existed in the history of the convent of San Jerónimo."

"Do we even have a history, Sister?" Sor Catalina interrupted. "I mean, is it written down so that we can refer to it?"

"Perhaps, Mother, we can take a survey and see how many of us can recall a situation like this," suggested Sor Melchora. "Think back, Sisters," she addressed the congregation. "Try to remember your own novitiate. Who of you in your tenure here has ever heard of a novice living in her own cell?"

Everyone turned to look around the room. No hands were raised.

"You see, Sister Vicaria," said Sor Melchora, standing directly in front of Sor Catalina. "Regardless of whether we have a written history, it seems obvious to me that if no one has ever heard of a novice living in her own cell in the House of Saint Jerome, we must assume that such a situation is an anomaly, maybe even an aberration, which could, if seen in a particular shade of light, be perceived as a subversive act, worthy of inquest and punishment from our superiors. Frankly, Mother Paula, I am surprised that either you or the Sister Vicaria has troubled yourself over the issue at all."

"Is it permitted for a novice to speak?" asked Juana. She had not planned to say anything, but the errors in logic being displayed at this meeting were more than she could bear.

"You will sit down at once!" ordered Sor Mariana. "Novices *never* speak unless they are called upon by the Sister Vicaria."

Sor Catalina stood again. "I call upon our little Sister Juana to speak," she said, striking the triangle for emphasis. "Stand, Juana Inés, let us hear what you have to say in your defense."

Juana got to her feet and assessed the faces looking back at her. Accustomed to being the center of attention, she felt perfectly at ease at this opportunity to demonstrate her powers of logic. "It is not in my defense that I speak. With all due respect to Sor Melchora, Mother, I find it necessary to point out that it is a sweeping generalization to assume that because something has never been done in the history of the convent it is an aberration. The argument is, in fact, a non sequitur. That conclusion may hold true in particular circumstances, but to generalize and apply it to all situations would simply refute the most basic laws of reason."

As Chief Vigilanta, Sor Clotilde had the right to administer any means necessary to correct an errant sister. Striding to the middle of the chapter room, she ordered Sor Mariana to bring her insolent charge to the front. Sor Catalina glanced at Mother Paula again, then kept her eyes averted as the *vigilanta's* scourge bit into Juana's palms in angry lashes. Juana tried not to flinch. Not even her uncle had beaten her thus, and of course no one at the palace had ever laid an angry hand on her.

"You must learn to discipline your tongue if you want to be true to your vows," Sor Clotilde said, her eyes like shards of brown glass.

Juana stared at the welts and knew she would not be able to write for several days.

"Thank you, Sister," she said, quoting from the novice's manual, "for helping me quell my rebellious spirit."

"You may return to your seat," said Sor Clotilde.

"May we proceed, please?" asked Sor Catalina, clearly irritated by the display of discipline.

Sor Mariana rushed in from the adjoining laundry room with a wet towel for Juana's hands.

"I believe, Mother," said Sor Melchora, "that this matter requires your attention."

Mother Paula made the sign of the cross over herself with the crucifix of her rosary, pinned the rosary back on her shoulder, and placed her elbows on the table. She looked first in Juana's direction, then at each of the *vigilantas*, narrowing her eyes at Sor Clotilde, and finally spoke.

"Sor Luisa, please record carefully what I am about to say. What has emerged most clearly from this so-called debate is, in fact, an issue that has been troubling me for the fifteen years that I have been the abbess of this house. I say that the House of San Jerónimo needs a written chronicle of its history. We have been negligent about that task for too many years. It is my decision, and it will be supported, you may be sure, by the Archbishop's permission, that Sister Juana Inés de la Cruz, because of her reputation as a scholar, be assigned that task. To that end, she will write her last will and sign her testament of faith as soon as we can get a royal scribe and a witness to make the note official. Thus, she will live in her own cell, attended by her own slave, and, apart from the obligatory Offices, Friday chapter, and classes with her sister novices, she will be exempted from all other duties that pertain to the novitiate."

"What will the Tribunal say, Mother," Sor Clotilde interrupted, "if it finds out about this breach in etiquette? Will we not all suffer the consequences? Will the House of San Jerónimo—"

"Neither the Tribunal nor the Audiencia will concern itself over this matter, Sister. A convent is subject to its superiors, that is true, but we are also allowed to govern our own house and assign any tasks that we deem necessary for the survival of the Order. It is my belief that an Order without a history does not survive, and I have no intention of leading us toward that destiny of oblivion; our own father, Saint Jerome, was a chronicler and a scholar. Do you think it just that an Order dedicated to his memory should have no chronicle of itself in New Spain? Sister Juana?"

Sor Catalina smiled openly at the congregation.

Juana rose, her beaten hands cupped in front of her short scapular.

"Do you feel that you can take on this task and produce a piece of scholarship worthy of our patron saint?"

Sor Mariana shook her head at her, but Juana pretended not to see. "I would be honored, Mother, if I could be given the opportunity to follow in the footsteps of San Jerónimo and devote my life to this task, though I find myself unworthy of such distinction."

"We are all unworthy, Sister, and yet your accomplishments do not go unnoticed. The task is yours. May you complete it while I am still of this world. Furthermore, let it be written that none of us shall ever take a scourge to Sister Juana again. It would not bode well for the convent if the palace or the Archbishop were to find out that their protégée is being mistreated. Now, I have ruled, and Friday chapter is closed. Sister Juana, please follow us to the priory."

Sor Catalina struck the triangle three times, and the congregation filed out to the cloister in absolute silence.

In the priory, Mother Paula dictated two letters to Sor Luisa—one addressed to the Vicereine to apprise her of the outcome of the meeting and the other to the royal scrivenery, requesting that a scribe be sent forthwith to witness the signing of Juana's testament of faith.

Juana was not taking permanent vows. That would come only after she had completed the requirements of the novitiate, and from there, she could never turn back. She had a full year in which to change her mind, but why would she do that when it was clear that the convent was her only haven from a life dictated by her gender rather than her mind? At least here she could forget her gender and follow the path of illumination instead. *Piety is not the same as illumination*, Juana, a voice said inside her, but she ignored it, telling herself that it was possible to enrich the spirit at the same time that one cultivated the intellect.

15 February 1669
I, Juana Inés de la Cruz, novice of this convent of Our Father Saint Jerome, hereby declare: that I am within the year of approbation during which, according to the decree of the Holy Office, I can sign my testament and renounce whatever goods that may belong to me; in order to do so, I beg Your Grace to grant me license to sign my testament and renunciation before any Royal Scribe, that I may receive grace, with justice; in service, etc.

The following evening, Mother Paula received a response from the palace, which Sor Catalina promptly took to the novice's dormitory to share with Juana.

DEAR, ILLUSTRIOUS MOTHER PAULA,

It has been brought to our attention that you have granted our beloved Juana Inés the honor of recording the convent's history. As a symbol of the court's gratitude for your warm reception of the talents that our dear Juanita brings to your Holy House, my husband, the Marqués de Mancera and Viceroy of New Spain, has decided to purchase a cell in her name. Cost is, of course, of little consequence, and we encourage you to find the cell you deem most appropriate for her to fulfill her duty. She will, of necessity, require enough space to accommodate her growing library, without which she cannot accomplish this distinguished scholarship. Please remit the bill to the palace as soon as Juana Inés is installed in her new cell.

Your sincere admirer,

Leonor Carreto, Marquesa de Mancera

P.S. Should it be necessary to dislodge another Sister from the appropriate cell for Juana Inés, please offer her, in compensation for her trouble, an allowance equal to one year of room and board, and attach this amount to the bill.

Isabel Ramírez arrived two days after Juana had signed her name to the convent's Book of Profession. Except for the woman's voice and her tight embrace of fragrant vanilla, Juana did not recognize her own mother. More than twelve years had passed since they had last seen each other. A young boy accompanied her, and behind them stood Francisca's daughter, Jane— with whom, Juana remembered, she had played school in Panoayán. Also in tow were a notary public and three witnesses. Jane was four years younger than Juana, and yet called her by Francisca's epithet, "la niña Juana."

"Because she has immediate need of someone to attend and serve her—" her mother dictated to the notary in Sor Catalina's office, "I make this complete and irrevocable donation for life to my daughter, Juana Ramírez de Asbaje, of this *mulata*, who is sixteen years of age, a little more or less, born and raised in my house, daughter of Francisca de Jesús, also my own slave."

The notary asked her mother to slow down.

"By this letter I cede, renounce and transfer all of my right, action, property, and ownership of said *mulata*; so that, from this day forward, my daughter may make use of her in any way she will, selling her, donating her, or transferring her without the convent or its management impeding it in any way, and, even less, assuming any right over her. I accept that this donation cannot exceed the fifteen *sueldos* permitted by Law—"

The witnesses, she could tell, were getting bored. Sor Catalina fanned herself impassively.

"—will never revoke this either by testament or codicil or any other expressionable way—"

Juana watched Jane, amazed at how exactly she resembled Francisca: the same stocky figure, tawny skin, and black eyes pulled into a perpetual squint because of the tightness of her braids.

"—for this is my express will, and may any faults or defects of this document be amended."

After she had finished dictating the letter, the scribe and the witnesses were surprised to learn that, despite her acumen, Doña Isabel could not write and so could not sign her own name to the note. One of the witnesses signed his name over her mark. Juana was allowed to skip her lessons and obligations for the rest of the day so that she could visit with her mother and half-brother in the *locutorio* until vespers. Mostly, they listened to the boy, Diegito, little Diego, for whom she felt an irrational antipathy. Once in a while Juana caught her mother's tear-filled gaze on her and looked away lest her own eyes betray her. When the bells struck for vespers, Juana did not allow her mother to touch her, certain that she would break down if she felt her mother's arms around her again. She watched them leave through the bars of the grille and then hurried to the lower choir for vespers. At prayers, her voice wheezed through her taut vocal chords, but at least she managed to keep the tears in check. It was not she but the abandoned eight-year-old child in her who wanted to weep.

To reach Mother Paula's cell at the southeastern corner of the convent, it was necessary to climb a series of narrow stairwells that looked out onto the flowery rooftops and terraces of cells that had been added on to the main body of the building. From the gallery that ran in front of Mother Paula's cell she had a clear view of the main patio and of the belfry on the other side of the convent.

The cell consisted of two rooms connected by a kitchen and, up a short flight of stairs, a large parlor with a black-and-white-checkered floor, a pair of arched windows that looked out on the volcanoes, and a small cubicle containing a tiled bathtub. She had no idea that the Hieronymites lived in such splendor. She had been expecting a single room, no larger than the size of her study at the palace, and here Mother Paula was ceding an entire apartment.

"I'm moving in with Catalina," Mother Paula had told her. "The stairs are getting too difficult for me to manage. Go up and take a look at my old cell to see if it suits you, my dear. You can keep all the furnishings if you like, except for my rocking chair."

"Don't add avarice to vanity, Juana," Sor Mariana counseled. "In doing so, you lead even the Mother Superior to temptation."

"I didn't ask her to give up her cell," Juana tried to defend herself, but Sor Mariana gestured for her to be silent.

"Understand, Juana, that your actions will breed the vices of jealousy, envy, and resentment among your sisters, and that you will reap what you sow."

Juana could not be bothered with platitudes right now.

With Jane and the help of Sor Catalina's servants, Juana cleared out what she didn't want from Mother Paula's cell. She kept the bed and the small bureau at its side, the double wardrobe with its beveled oval mirror, the dining table, the benches in the parlor, which she had moved down to the front room, and the three trestle tables and stools at which Mother Paula had tutored her students and which Juana would use in her study. The rest of it—rickety chairs, spindly side tables, chipped, sooty lamps, moth-eaten draperies, and a dilapidated old chest wormed through with termites—was taken to be auctioned to the poor.

Under Juana's relentless supervision, Jane and Sor Catalina's maids scrubbed and waxed the floors to a sheen, redaubed the walls, refit the stove and bathtub with new tiles, and repaired the broken shutters at all of the windows. With the Viceroy's permission, Juana ordered a new feather-erbed and pillows, lace curtains for the parlor, leather-backed chairs for the dining table, talavera dishes from Puebla and silver cutlery from Taxco. She gave Jane the small room off the kitchen and outfitted it with a nar-row bed from the infirmary, a trunk, and a table. For her study she had a special desk made, twice the size of the one she had used at the palace, with shelves on each side and a secret compartment under the main drawer; she also ordered enough book cabinets, in a fine dark walnut, to line three walls from floor to ceiling.

It took half a year for Juana's cell to be exactly as she wanted it, dur-ing which time she completed her novitiate studies and lived in the dor-mitory with the rest of the novices. While the novices were engaged in the labors of the convent—some in the flower fields harvesting lilies for Easter and *amapolas* for Corpus Christi, some in the orchard picking fruit for the summer preserves, some in the laundry room starching and dying mantillas—Juana sat in the archivist's modest library doing research for the history of the Order of Saint Jerome in New Spain. She found the books dusty, worm-eaten, and damp. Many had broken spines and ruined bind-ings, and she requested permission to send out the most damaged ones for repair. Her old friend, Don Lázaro, would give her a good price.

By the day of their veiling ceremony, she and Andrea had passed all of their examinations with honors and won the two top prizes in their class. Standing together before the altar to receive their black veils and scapulars, their linen tunics and coifs, their immense rosaries and escutcheons inlaid with the image of the Annunciation, their heavy gold rings—everything blessed by Padre Antonio and anointed with a smoking censor—they were graced with the audience of not only the Viceroy and Vicereine, the Arch-bishop, and several representatives of the Church and city councils but also of half the nobility of Mexico City.

Later at the festivities in the largest of the *locutorios*, fully arrayed in their habits and wearing garlands of lilies, roses, and violets over their veils, they each received a special blessing from Fray Payo, while outdoors the cloister blazed in the light of *luminarias*, and fireworks were sent up from the gatekeeper's patio. Padre Antonio wandered around as if his own granddaughter were being celebrated.

It was the first time the Vicereine had met the rest of Juana's family, the first time Juana had met her own half-sisters and seen her older sisters, María and Josefa, since she had left Panoayán. Aunt Mary was there, too. It was odd having them all there, especially those three who formed a triangle in the abstruse geometry of her affections: her mother, who had turned her out; her aunt, who had taken her in; and la Marquesa, who had motivated her to leave the world. She had forgiven her mother years ago, when she understood that having been sent away from Panoayán had saved her from a fate like Josefa's, locked up in her husband's house, breeding children like rodents. Her aunt she could not blame for anything other than being too typical a member of her gender, tenderhearted but misguided, and hopelessly her husband's slave. It was la Marquesa whom she could not forgive, standing here fawning over her as though she did not know how Juana felt, as though she had not read with her own eyes those verses and confessions Juana had written.

"This cannot be the same Juana Inés I knew at court," la Marquesa said to Doña Isabel, adjusting the rosary pinned to Juana's shoulder. "She was so young and timorous the last time I saw her."

"She was even younger when I saw her last," interjected Josefa, standing on the other side of Juana, smoothing the back of the veil. "I always knew she would be something grand."

"She never settled for being just a girl," added her mother.

Andrea smiled. "Or just a novice."

"Remember, Josefa, when Juanita used to follow us to school?" said María. "Can you believe it, Marquesa, she told our teacher that Mamá had specifically requested that she teach her how to read, but that it had to be kept secret so that she could surprise our grandfather on his birthday!" Everyone laughed.

"And she was just three years old!" added Josefa.

More laughter.

"Always had to have her own way," said her mother. "Why, she even wanted me to dress her as a boy so that she could attend the university!"

"When she lived with us all she wanted to do was see bullfights," said

Aunt Mary. "We lived close to the ring, and she absolutely loved watching the bullfights from the rooftop of our house. She was alway so—"

"Different?" said la Marquesa.

"Macabre," said her aunt.

"Unique," said her mother. "Like none of her sisters."

"She had more in common with my sons than with her cousin, Gloria," said her aunt. "Except that she loved cooking. I remember all those quarrels we used to have about needlepoint." She omitted mentioning the sharp slaps she administered each time Juana dropped a stitch. "How she hated the sight of the sewing basket."

"She still does," added Andrea. "You should see how often Sor Mariana has to scold her for lagging behind in the sewing room!"

"Oh, but Señoras," la Marquesa began, clasping her hands dramatically. "What I witnessed and you, unfortunately, missed. The way our Juana Inés handled those," she lowered her voice, "pompous professors. It was absolutely *impresionante*. This girl's mind is the finest treasure of New Spain."

Juana was beginning to feel ridiculous as well as hungry, but she knew it would be impolite to leave the ladies talking and head for the sideboard. Besides, her uncle John was standing with the rest of the men, drinking wine and eating olives, feigning interest in the Viceroy's conversation, and yet unable to keep his glance from roaming across the room and settling on his niece and her young friend. Andrea, of course, was oblivious to his attentions, but Juana felt her neck grow warm each time she noticed him, and all the cloth around her head made her feel dizzy and out of breath.

At one point la Marquesa intercepted his gaze, saw Juana's discomfort, and glared at him with open animosity, clearly reading his intentions.

"I know this will be the best life for you, my dear," said la Marquesa loud enough for the men to hear. "There are so many lechers out there, no young woman is safe anymore. Don't you agree, Señora Mata. Your daughter is married, I hope?"

Shortly afterward, her aunt and uncle left the reception, and Juana was able, at last, to breathe normally. "Thank you," she whispered to la Marquesa, and la Marquesa squeezed her hand.

"Juana, let's have some cake," said Andrea.

"You go on, Andrea. My mother and sister will go with you, won't you, Josefa?"

"Another piece of cake?" asked her mother. "Oh, why not?" Josefa and her mother each linked an arm in Andrea's and wandered over to the sideboard. La Marquesa stayed beside Juana.

"Did he always look at you that way, Juana Inés? No wonder you were so confused at court."

Juana could not bring herself to look at the Vicereine. She shook her head. "He was not the one who confused me, Marquesa."

"I can't imagine what would have become of you had I not brought you to the palace. And now look at you! You make me so proud, Juana Inés, and the Viceroy, he's beyond words."

The ladies had joined the men at the sideboard. La Marquesa pulled her to a bench in the corner and made her sit down. "Tell me, Juanita," she said, her voice barely above a whisper, "you have everything you want now: a noble profession, your own cell, a family who loves and admires you, and the support of the most important people in the city. Tell me, *cariño*, are you happy? Have you found your place at last?"

Boldly, Juana took la Marquesa's hand in hers, brought it to her lips, and kissed the fine bone at her wrist. "Having you near me makes me happy, Señora. In your absence I am simply content, but profoundly grateful, yes, that I have found the path to my salvation."

"Come, Laura," called the Viceroy from the doorway, using the nickname he had given his wife, "we won't let you monopolize our girl today! You must see these *fuegos*, Juanita!"

"Excuse me, Señora," she said, releasing la Marquesa's hand and getting to her feet.

Andrea joined her, and together, crossing their arms under their new scapulars as Sor Mariana had taught them, they strolled out to the gatekeeper's patio to watch the fireworks and mingle with the guests. Padre Antonio stationed himself beside her, beaming with self-satisfaction.

"You did it, Juanita," he said. "Now you belong fully to God."

I belong to no man, she thought. She smiled and looked up at the gold sparks setting fire to the black silk sky of Anáhuac, the weight of the veil on her shoulders.

When the festivities were over and she and Andrea filed to compline with the other nuns, Juana knew she had made the right choice, the only choice. In her cell, she spent a long time studying herself in the mirror that hung between the two long cabinets of the wardrobe. Her face, framed by the white coif and black wool of the veil, seemed quite small, almost girlish, though she was nearly twenty-one years old and already starting to wrinkle around the eyes. She had the Ramírez hazel eyes and black brows and that small, heart-shaped mouth that she and her sisters had inherited from their mother; but that nose, thin at the bridge and slightly wider around the nostrils, the inward slant of her teeth, that tiny cleft in her chin—these characteristics, she was told, betrayed her Basque blood and could only have been handed down from her unknown father.

To allow her entry into the convent, which accepted no illegitimate daughters, Padre Antonio had lied about her parentage, using family name as an argument against illegitimacy. "That you never knew your father doesn't mean you didn't have one," he told her. "A bastard is a nameless child. You have your father's name, you just don't have your father."

On the one hand, she knew it was a lie. On the other hand, it seemed a logical explanation.

The Middlegame
1672–1680

Chapter 7

Through the wooden slats of the grille that divided the *locutorio*, Juana watched her friend, Don Carlos de Sigüenza y Góngora, work the bellows over the brazier on his side of the room. They had known each other since the famous tournament at the palace, but almost immediately afterward he had been expulsed from his Order for misconduct and had spent the better part of three years attempting to be reinstated. Finally, he had been appointed chaplain of the Amor de Dios Hospital and had secured a teaching post at the university. Now he was the newly elected Chair of Mathematics and Astrology.

When Don Carlos had first started joining the Viceroy and la Marquesa on their regular visits to the *locutorio* of San Jerónimo, he had impressed Juana as a rather frail and phlegmatic man whose constant complaints about the cold air seeping through the open windows seemed to Juana an indication of a weak mind. How mistaken she had been about that mind, and about the spirit nesting in that meager body. Of all her visitors, Don Carlos was not only the most consistent, coming as he did every Thursday afternoon, but also singular in that, as he often said, he sought her company to sharpen his rhetorical and poetical skills. Every Thursday for two years now, if she had no other guests, they listened to and commented on whatever manuscript each was writing, and they discussed Cicero and Longinus and Kircher and Cervantes and his own distant relation, Góngora, in intricate detail. Generous to a fault, Don Carlos was constantly lending Juana his books and forgetting to collect them.

"If you were a man, Sor Juana, what name would you like to have?"

"You ask such strange questions, Don Carlos."

"In that you and my students have the same opinion, Madre. But there is a good reason for my question. What name, tell me?"

"The only time I wanted to be a man, and not truly to *be* a man but rather to be allowed a man's privilege of a formal education, was when I was five years old. What is the purpose of your question?"

"Last week you told me about how you yearn to take a voyage and see the world. That gave me an idea for a *relación* I'd like to write some day, about a Caribbean youth, a slave probably, who becomes a sailor and sails around the world. Since you germinated the idea, I thought the youth should have your family name, Ramírez, but I need a first name, too, and I can't think of one that would fit this youth who is meant to represent you."

"I like the idea of making him a slave, if what you want is to represent me, but why Caribbean and not of our own soil?"

Don Carlos stroked the dark parentheses of his mustache with both index fingers, his red lips pursed as he thought about the question. Their ages were but three years apart, his sun in Aquarius, hers in Scorpio, he a creature of the air, she of water (how he would hate it if he knew she was constructing him in astrological terms), and yet the hunch of his spine, his thick spectacles, the bony knees crossed under his cassock, the expanding forehead, the wise intensity of his gaze cast the image of someone much older.

"I've only traveled as far east as Yucatán and as far south as Oaxaca," he said, now stroking the stubble under his chin, "so it's not as though I know anything about the Caribbean. But when the idea for this *relación* first flashed in my mind, I saw this youth as Caribbean who somehow, due to his outstanding cleverness, his way with words, his way with nautical instruments, ended up on the coast of Yucatán, from there to journey to Mexico City, where he would become something important."

"Like a teacher at the university, for example?" asked Juana, seeing in the imaginary character a sketch of Don Carlos's own personality. "A professor of mathematics, perhaps?"

"No, no, not a teacher. There is nothing less stimulating than giving lectures to a herd of dull-witted boys with pulque on their breath. Oh, don't remind me of the university, please, Sister. I still owe them sixty-five pesos."

"Perhaps if you showed up to lecture more often you wouldn't be fined so excessively," said Juana. There was little that irritated her about Don Carlos anymore except his lack of seriousness about his classes. He had competed brilliantly for his post, Fray Payo had told her, putting his opponents to shame with both the quality of his discourse and his passion for mathematics, and yet he loathed teaching. He wanted to experiment, he said, research, question, write; he had no time to prepare superficial lectures and examinations, to counsel students, to meet endlessly with colleagues. There was too much to learn, too much changing in the world of science to waste his time educating fools interested only in the charlatan science of astrology rather than in the quest for truth through mathematics. Let the adjuncts cut their teeth teaching them to play with the zodiac, he said, or let them teach themselves. He had Descartes to read, and Kepler, and Kircher, and Galen and Abelard—the forbidden fruits on the tree of knowledge that kept the blood pumping through his bones, the light faceted in his eyes. Juana understood his quandary, and yet she found it unfair and selfish of him to ignore his students altogether, to deprive them of the wisdom he could impart.

"Very well, not a teacher," she said. "What about a scientist? A Nostradamus of science."

"Or a poet," he said, pursing his lips in that delicate way of his, "who can compose sonnets in Spanish and Latin and Nahuatl and even in the difficult dialect of the Negroes, Caribbean that he is."

"I don't think they speak Nahuatl in the Caribbean, Don Carlos."

"But this Ramírez character is more than clever. He is a genius and can learn languages as easily as a parrot learns to mimic. And you're right, he should be a scientist as well, but *not* a Nostradamus. Sor Juana, you surprise me!"

"The character shares your disdain for astrology, then?"

"It is the intelligent thing, Sister."

"And yet sailors must rely on the stars when there is no sun or moon to guide them, Don Carlos. Perhaps as a scientist he would abhor astrology but as a sailor he would steer by the stars."

"Indeed, Sister, you are a poet and a rhetorician at one and the same time."

"And so this character of yours is both poet and scientist. I'm beginning to think, Don Carlos, that what you're creating with this Ramírez is the phantasmal offspring of our two minds."

Two red stains crept into the hollows of his cheeks. He removed his spectacles and held them up to the light of the window, then wiped them vigorously with the hem of his cloak.

"Did I embarrass you?" she asked. "You seem embarrassed, my friend."

He adjusted the spectacles over his face but did not meet her gaze. "Perhaps we should begin our workshop," he said through taut lips. "I have a thesis on Saint Thomas and Quetzalcoatl I'd like to share with you."

"Another monograph on the Aztecs?" she asked.

"More of a religious treatise than a historical one this time," he said. "Do you have anything?"

"Just another commission from the Cabildo, I'm afraid."

"Would that *I* received commissions," he said. "The canon pays well, I'm told."

"Not especially," she said, wondering if it had been her immodest comment about offspring that had made him uncomfortable. "And you certainly wouldn't have time to write the adventures of this multitalented Ramírez."

As she expected, he blushed again. "Really, Don Carlos, I don't understand what it is I'm saying that keeps flustering you."

He crossed his arms over his chest and looked her, finally, in the eyes. "It's not something we can discuss across this grille, Sor Juana."

"Then we shall never be able to discuss it because we shall always have this grille between us, Don Carlos. Only with female visitors of the highest rank am I allowed to dispense with the grille. Not even my mother is allowed that privilege."

"The grille is symbolic of what I'm alluding to, Sister!"

"Very well, if it's so difficult for you to talk about that you must speak in riddles, then don't tell me. I don't have a mind for riddles today. Perhaps your treatise on Saint Thomas and Quetzalcoatl is clearer."

He moved so quickly out of his chair that at first it seemed as though the light had changed in the *locutorio*. She blinked, but there he was, standing right against the grille, his thin face filling the space between two slats. There was something nervous and breathless about him that alarmed her, made her spine stiffen against the back of her chair. He wet his lips with the tip of his tongue before speaking.

"You were right about Ramírez," he said.

"About him being the offspring of our two minds?" she asked, her voice strained.

"When I was dismissed from the seminary I swore never again to let my heart dominate my reason," he said. "I was a simpleton then, a victim of the lust that used to boil in my loins. Please, Sister, don't look at me with that horrified expression, I'm not saying I feel that for you at all. It's unfortunate the Jesuits won't take me back, celibacy is second nature to me now. But I do feel very attracted to you, Sor Juana. Your mind is a magnet to my mind, a negative charge to my positive. I see us bound by something greater than human love; lust for knowledge, perhaps, devotion to learning, to reason. And then I wonder if I'm fooling myself with these lofty ideas. I wonder if my desire to consummate our minds is not really a mask for my desire to love you as a man would love a woman."

Anxiety had gnarled in her stomach as she listened to his declaration. What if Melchora had suddenly entered the *locutorio*? Or one of the novices she used as her spies, or even just Jane bringing them their hot chocolate? She realized she had a crick in her neck; her palms had grown slippery. What could she possibly say to this confession? That she felt betrayed, insulted, harangued, repulsed? This was her friend, her companion in letters and learning. What was he doing talking about desire and consummation? She had not taken her eyes off him, and she saw that the red stains in his face had spread to his forehead and his ears, down to the inverted exclamation mark of his goatee. His fingers were curled around the slats of the grille, knuckles sharp and white.

"I see that I have displeased you," he broke the silence. "I suppose you never want to see me again. I'll go now, if you like."

She started to shake her head, but the pain in her neck stopped her. "I'm not accustomed to dealing with declarations of that nature, you have to understand. Forgive me for asking so many questions."

He pulled himself away from the grille. "It is I who should apologize, Sor Juana. If you wish, I will never disturb you again."

"You don't disturb me, Don Carlos. I count on your visits, on the work we do together. And I understand how you feel. I, too, have known that kind of perplexity. I, too, have been the victim of sinful passion. It's a stubborn vice."

"Indeed it is, Sister. And stronger, I've found, in minds consecrated to reason."

"It's a constant duel," she said.

"Yes, exactly!" he said.

"Please have a seat, Don Carlos. Let's forget all this nonsense and continue with our workshop."

"Thank you, Sor Juana, thank you for being so noble about this."

"Nobility is not a quality ascribed to women, is it, Don Carlos?"

"And yet you possess so much of it, Sister."

"According to a gentleman from Peru (who shall remain nameless) I possess too many masculine qualities."

"That is preposterous. A Peruvian said that?"

"Oh yes, it's an interesting letter. I should show it to you. It came accompanied by some clay pots. Rather poetic, don't you think?"

"An insult accompanied by a gift? I hope you returned them to the sender."

"The pots are essential to the insult, Don Carlos. Reminders of my gender, the vessel of life, the weaker sex. As it is I did a bit of husbandry and sowed some geranium seeds inside them." She laughed at her own pun. Don Carlos stared at her.

"I wish you would tell me the name of this Peruvian. I would give him a piece of my mind—"

"If a man were to defend me, that would only feed his argument. Believe me, Don Carlos, he's getting a good chunk of my mind as it is. I'll be finished with my reply for our meeting next week. I'll read it to you then."

"What is *your* argument, Sor Juana? If you've already started to draft your response, you must have a guiding logic."

"My approach, I think, is to overwhelm our Peruvian friend with allusions to Greek mythology, but my main line of reasoning is based on the etymology of the word *woman*, which is *uxor*, the name given in Latin only to married women. As I am not married I am not a woman, for what defines a woman is her wedded relationship to a man. Because she has not had intercourse, a virgin is not a woman; and a nun who has forsworn all worldly relationships, but especially those with men, is a virgin, and therefore, not a woman. '*Con que a mi no es bien mirado,*' I tell him, '*que como a mujer me miren, pues no soy mujer que a alguno de mujer pueda servirle.* To see me as a woman is unseemly, for I am not a woman who as woman can serve a man. I know only that my body, not to either state inclined, is neuter, abstract, guardian of only what my Soul consigns.'"

"Truly, Sor Juana, I believe I'm going to begin using your writing in my classes."

"And risk increasing your fines, Don Carlos? I wouldn't hear of it."

"Your discourse is the epitome of reason. Your words have such precision, such mathematical exactness."

She heard a knock behind her. To her relief, it was Jane bringing their chocolate and nougat. She set the tray on the sideboard, curtsied, and was about to leave the room, but Juana asked her to stay and listen to Don Carlos's story about an adventurous youth named Ramírez. Even with the grille between them, she felt safer with Jane there.

That night she slept badly. Images she had buried in the most recondite corner of her mind stirred back to life, and the dream she had not had in years emerged from the dark lake of memory.

"You're going to live with Uncle John and Aunt Mary, Juana Inés," her older sister, Josefa, had said. "Stop squirming and let me braid your hair. We have to hurry. Our uncle is an hidalgo now; he has much business to attend to; he's not used to waiting for little girls."

Uncle John had gone to Puebla to purchase a coat of arms from an old hidalgo whose entire family had fallen prey to the pox. On his way home to Mexico City, he had stopped over at Panoayán to pay his respects to his father-in-law, only to find him laid out in black.

"But I don't want to leave Panoayán, Josefa."

"Aren't you happy? You get to live close to the palace with all those students and fine ladies. You're the one who wanted to go to Mexico City, remember? Constantly nagging Mamá to send you to the university."

"That was a long time ago, Josefa. I don't want to go away now."

"Well it's all been arranged, Juana Inés. Abuelo wanted you to live in the city when he died."

"It was Abuelo's idea? He knew Uncle was coming here?"

"That's what Mamá says. It was in his testament. Now hurry up. Oh no! The groom is bringing the mules up from the stable! He's leaving, Juana Inés. Put your dress on. *¡Apúrate!*"

She walked out of her grandfather's house feeling that she would never return. The small trunk her mother had packed was strapped to the back of the skittish mule she was going to ride. While her uncle said his farewells, the groom lifted Juana Inés onto the animal, its coarse hair prickling at her calves. She did not turn around, knowing that her mother held baby Diego in her arms and that her stepfather, Don Diego, stood beside her, neither of them waving good-bye, just standing there, watching her leave.

Her sisters, Josefa and María, waved their lace handkerchiefs from the balcony of her grandfather's library. "Adios, Juanita. Take care of yourself. Don't give Aunt Mary too much trouble."

The animals' hooves clattered on the cobbled drive that led to the gate of her grandfather's hacienda. She nearly cried when she saw Francisca and her little girl standing by the gate. "Adios, *niña*," Francisca called out as they passed, her dark face shiny with tears. She could hear the girl,

Francisca's youngest, named Jane after her, bawling, "Qué pasó? Qué pasó? Porqué se va la niña Juana?"

"Juanita, are those tears I see dripping down your little face?" asked Uncle John, turning around on his mule.

She shook her head and looked down at her gloved hands, wishing she could strip off the gloves and the stockings and this stuffy starched dress and this silly bonnet and jump into the creek and float away.

They rode past the crowded plaza of the village, chased by the children of the Indian women squatting by their pottery and baskets, their bundles of wild herbs, their piles of firewood and yams.

"We'll ride down to Chalco and spend the night," her uncle said. "From there we'll take a canoe into the city. Have you ever been in a canoe, Juanita?"

Again she shook her head. The bouncing of the mule was making her head hurt, bringing her breakfast up in her throat. And she couldn't stop thinking about the last conversation she'd had with her mother.

Why are you sending me away, Mamá?

This is your only chance to leave here, my love. Don't you see? God sent your uncle to us just for this, so he could take you home with him. Your aunt tells me they have a wonderful home not too far from the plaza. You'll have a cousin who's your age and friends of quality! It'll be so exciting! Don't worry, *chaparrita*, we're not that far away, you'll see. You can still see Popocatepetl and Ixtaccihuatl from the city. We'll be much closer than you think.

Abuelo didn't want me to leave, did he?

Your abuelo was very ill, sweet one, he didn't know what was going on anymore.

I don't want to go, Mamá.

There's nothing more for you here, Juana Inés. Both your sisters will soon be wed, and I have little Diego to look after now, and your stepfather. I won't be able to spend as much time with you as before, and with your *abuelo* gone, who are you going to play chess with? We won't even have his library anymore; we've had to sell Abuelo's collection.

You sold his books? All of them?

Would you like to take a book with you? I'm sure it won't be missed. Go on, Juanita. Take any book you want.

I want his almanac. And his book about flowers, too.

Josefa, go get what she wants and pack it in her trunk. You're being so brave, Juana Inés. Abuelo would be very proud of you. And don't worry. Every time you look up at Popo and Ixta you'll feel me next to you. And you can write me as many letters as you want.

Will you write back, Mamá?

You know I don't write, *mi amorcito*. But I'll be thinking of you, every day. Now come here. Hug your Mamá real tight.

Juana Inés would always remember the scent of vanilla on her mother's skin.

She and her uncle passed the smell of burning copal and marigold emanating from the cemetery of the Sacred Hill where her grandfather had been buried the week before. The road to the schoolhouse in Amecameca where she had learned to read. The canal that bordered the house where she'd been born in Nepantla. The parish of Chimahualcán where she was baptized. The market of Yecapixtla where her grandfather used to bring his wool and wheat to sell. At each place that marked a moment in her memory, she would turn around to look at the volcanoes, Popocateptl and Ixtaccihuatal, making sure they stayed at her back.

They stopped in the shade of a huge ahuehuete tree just beyond Tlalmanalco to eat their midday meal of bread and olives and dried meat. Afterward, her uncle spread a *sarape* and leaned back against the trunk of the tree. He placed another *sarape* on his lap, and called Juana Inés to sit there with him so that he could tell her a story.

"What kind of story?" she asked, not leaving the rock on which she was sitting, scribbling letters in the sand with a twig.

"The story of a princess."

"I don't like princesses."

"How about an adventure story?"

She ate the last of her olives, staring at the bright stripes of the *sarape*, and wished he would leave her alone.

"I know," he said, yawning. "I bet you like stories about magic. Do you know the one about the magic lamp?"

"No."

"No, *Uncle*. You're eight years old, Juanita. You should know how to address your elders properly. Just because you grew up on a ranch doesn't mean you shouldn't have any manners."

"No, Uncle, I don't know the story about the magic lamp," she said.

She spotted a tarantula ambling in the direction of the mules. Far away she heard the church bells from the monastery of Tlalmanalco announce the afternoon service. Her grandfather had died in the afternoon.

" . . . the boy's name was Aladdin," her uncle was recounting, "and he was very sad because the dungeon was cold and dark and he could hear his brothers feasting and laughing upstairs."

"Why was he in the dungeon, Uncle?"

"You're not listening to me, Juanita. Aladdin is in the dungeon because his brothers are jealous of him. When their father died, you see, Aladdin received all of his wealth, the castle and the lands and the livestock and the title of hidalgo. So the brothers decided to put Aladdin in the dungeon and starve him to death so that they could take his inheritance and divide it among themselves. Many days passed and Aladdin was very thirsty and very hungry and very cold, but every night he dreamt—"

"I don't think you can survive many days without water, Uncle."

"Juanita, stop interrupting. Listen to the story. Every night he dreamt of a beautiful girl who told him to seek the magic lamp. 'The lamp will save you, Aladdin,' the girl said to him. 'Find the lamp. It is close to you. Find the lamp and rub it three times.'

"At first, Aladdin didn't pay attention to his dream, but one day, weak with hunger and cold, he decided to do as the beautiful girl said and he got on his hands and knees and started looking for the magic lamp. The dungeon was darker than a moonless night, and it was very large and full of bones, but at last Aladdin's search led him to the magic lamp tucked into the farthest corner of the dungeon. Although it was too dark for him to see the lamp, Aladdin knew that it was made of the finest gold; the oil smelled of the sweetest almonds. Aladdin held the lamp gently, his fingers exploring the long, curved spout—"

Juana Inés had been watching the hawks circling above the fields of sugarcane and cacao that colored the foothills while her uncle told the silly story, but the change in his voice drew her attention back to him. Uncle John had his eyes closed. His knees were bent, and his hands were buried under the *sarape*.

"'Rub it three times, Aladdin,' the beautiful girl had said, 'rub it three times and a genie will appear.'"

She noticed that her uncle's hands were moving under the *sarape*. His knees twitched.

"Again Aladdin rubbed and again, nothing happened. 'I wish the beautiful girl were here to show me how to do it,' Aladdin said aloud, and suddenly, there she was, the beautiful girl sitting beside him."

Uncle John opened his blue eyes and fixed them on Juana Inés. "Come here, Juanita. Sit here, on my lap."

She felt something pulsing in the pit of her belly. Of a sudden she felt afraid. She saw herself leaping like a deer and running back to Francisca and Josefa and Mamá.

"Juanita? Weren't you brought up to obey your betters? Come here, I said."

She could not see the volcanoes through the dense branches of the tree. The road was entirely deserted save for the mules and the tarantula and the hawks flying in the distance. She was completely alone.

"You will do as I say, Juana Inés Ramírez, or I shall turn you out into the street as your own mother has done. Now come here."

She did as she was ordered. He wanted her to sit astride his legs.

"That's a good girl, right there. Now, take off your gloves."

She unbuttoned her gloves and yanked them off, tearing at the seams. He folded down the *sarape* and showed it to her, the most horrifying thing she had ever seen. She clenched her eyes tight to keep from seeing it.

"This is the best part of the story," he said, his voice grown husky. "Open your eyes."

She obeyed.

"Now, spit in my hand and I'll show you how to bring the genie out." She spit in his hand and saw him shudder as he rubbed her spit all over the stiff thing sticking up against her apron.

"Watch me." He was rubbing faster now, his other hand gripping himself between the legs. She could feel his thighs flexing and the motion reminded her of sitting on the mule. The pulsing in her belly had spread down past her navel and up into her throat. She saw the image of the man who was her father, one of the few times she had ever seen him, bending over her mother in the bed. Her mother's back was turned toward him, and the man was shaking her shoulder, mumbling threats and a bad name. Finally her mother sat up in the bed weeping and the man slapped her. Leaving the room, he nearly tripped over Juana Inés in the doorway. He took her hand and tucked her back into bed with Josefa and María.

"'Your wish is my command,' said the beautiful girl to Aladdin. 'What do you desire, Master?'" Her uncle's voice had changed again; he sounded hoarse and as though he were running out of breath. "'Your wish is my command. What do you desire, Master?' Repeat that, Juanita."

"Your wish is my command what do you desire master," she said. Somehow a woodpecker had flown into her chest and gotten trapped in her rib cage.

"Let's pretend you're the genie and I'm Aladdin," said her uncle."

Juana Inés stared at him. If she ran as fast as she could she could get to the monastery and the monks would send for her mother.

"Play along, Juanita, or you're going to make me angry. You don't want me to leave you here in the middle of nowhere, do you? Not with all those cannibals and *cimarrones* running loose through these hills. Now put your hand on it, Juanita."

"Uncle, please, I don't want to hear the rest of the story. I feel dizzy. Can we go now?"

He took her hand and crushed her fingers in his grasp. "I desire that my genie rub the lamp."

A breath shuddered through her. She bit her bottom lip to keep from crying.

"'Rub it three times, Master. Let me show you how!' Say that!" He thrust his hips up and the thing caught on her apron.

"Rubitthreetimesletmeshowyouhow," she mumbled, yanking her apron back, terrified.

"There's a genie waiting for you inside, Juanita, who will grant all your wishes if you're very good. Rub the lamp." He guided her hand, keeping his own fingers clenched between hers.

The lamp was hot, the spout oily.

"'Up and down, Master, up and down, Master!' Say it, *hija de puta!*"

"Upanddownmasterupanddown." She was going to cry. Her teeth cut into her lip. Every time he jerked her hand down, thick hair grazed the inside of her wrist. It was beginning to smell of wet wool.

"'It's coming, Master! The genie's coming!'" Her uncle panted.

His legs trembled under hers. Sweat streamed down his neck and dripped into his ruffled collar. Suddenly, his fingers curled tightly. She tried to pull her hand away, but it was pinned in his grasp, and she felt the thing throbbing under her palm. Suddenly her uncle sat very still, and the olives she had eaten gurgled up into her throat. She vomited on the *sarape* just as the hot oil of Aladdin's lamp spurted through her fingers.

"Get off!" her uncle said, casting her off his legs and dashing the soiled wool to the ground. "Look at what a mess you've made."

She scrambled to the other side of the trunk and cried with abandon, calling for her mother, her sister, her grandfather, Francisca, the Virgin, anyone, please, take her home.

"For God's sake! You'd think I'd hurt you!" She heard him urinating against the tree. "Let's go! You've spoiled my siesta. And pick up that *sarape*! You're going to wash it as soon as we come to a stream. You better pray you haven't ruined it or your aunt Mary will skin your hide."

He did not come near her or speak to her the rest of the journey. At the inn in Chalco they slept on pallets in a room with other travelers. By sunrise they had taken their breakfast of atole and cold mutton, and were on their way to the embarcadero. Under the dark canopy of the flat-bottomed canoe, Juana Inés could no longer see the volcanoes. Surrounded in morning fog, with nothing but the sound of the oars breaking the water and roosters crowing in the distance, she understood that she had left her childhood in Panoayán. She had no alternative now but to grow up in Mexico.

For weeks after she arrived at her uncle's house, she could not look her aunt Mary in the eye, feeling wicked and dirty for the incident at the ahuehuete tree. She slept with her cousin, Gloria, and her uncle never bothered her again, but still she dreamt that she had slaughtered the genie that emerged from Aladdin's lamp. Dressed in a *sarape* and wearing her uncle's face, the genie hovered over her bed, and she stabbed him over and over with her quill until even the outline of his form was mired in a pool of bloody ink.

Chapter 8

The disease penetrated the intestines and caused a putrescent black substance, thicker than both water and blood but looser than the softest of stools to emanate from the raw anuses of the patients. They were novices, mostly, and Sor Rosario, and a couple of lay Sisters who worked in the novices' wing—all of them burning with the fever, their eyes glazed and shiny as tiles. Their faces clammy and mottled, lips parched, teeth chattering, they shivered and thrashed under the bedclothes, excreting the black substance at all hours so that their bedding had constantly to be changed and their bodies washed. Undergarments and nightgowns had to be dispensed with, for it was difficult to keep up with the laundry and to scrub the stains and the stench out of the cloth. Even the bedding came back streaked with gray and yellow.

This much she remembered. But how had she come to be here in the first place? Why had she been helping Sor Elvira in the infirmary? She tried to raise her arm, look at the bite wound on her hand, but she found that she was strapped down to the cot, arms and legs, strapped down. The effort of trying to move woke the cramps in her belly, and she felt the substance coming out of her in a hot gush. She opened her mouth to call out for Sor Elvira but could not find the strength to use her voice. Her vision, she realized, was all blurry, and her eyes kept rolling back in her head.

She slept again and this time dreamt that she had placed her tongue between the legs of one of the novices, tasting the bitter flavor of her infected sex.

She had never done this kind of work before, not even with the Carmelites where she had done her share of floor scrubbing and laundry, and a kind of admiration for Sor Elvira dawned on her, motivated her. This, she mused, must be what being a true nun was all about. This perpetual giving of the self, thanking God for misfortune, learning the rhetoric of compassion.

"We lit a candle to Saint Joseph for you, Juana," she heard, and a panic seized her that she had never left the Carmelites. She was still there at the convent of Saint Joseph's, and Sor Elvira was the infirmarian trying to get her to drink water and eat bread.

"Juana, are you confirmed?"

No! she wanted to yell. *I left Saint Joseph's. I left the palace. This is San Jerónimo. I am in the convent of Santa Paula of the Order of Saint Jerome. I have taken the name Juana Inés de la Cruz.* Her body convulsed of its own accord.

"Elvira! Look! She's having a seizure!"

"Calm yourself, Mother. It's just the fever. We're doing everything we can."

"I knew it would be too dangerous. I should have listened to my instinct. Why did I let her convince me?"

"Juana can be very persuasive, Mother."

"She said it was a vision. The Lady of the Apocalypse. There was talk of an epidemic. Should I not have believed her?"

"She has never been a visionary before."

"That's what I told her. 'Since when are you visited by the Holy Ghost, Juana?' I asked her. Maybe it's just indigestion. But she didn't think so."

I don't want them here, Mother. Tell her not to send them. It isn't fair, doesn't she see that? Why should I have to do this for her? I don't owe her anything.

She had received a letter from her mother, informing her that after much deliberation, she and her husband had come to the decision that their daughters, Juana's half-sisters, fourteen-year-old Antonia and twelve-year-old Inés, were to be enrolled as boarders at San Jerónimo. It was the only way to protect their purity, her mother wrote, and, if it wasn't too much trouble, could they prevail upon Juana to accept the girls in her cell? The Mother Superior had informed them that there would be no more room in the boarders' dormitory for at least a year but that Juana's quarters were large enough to accommodate another bed, if, of course, Juana gave her consent. Don Diego would deliver the girls in time for the feast day of Saint Jerome at the end of September, and Juana should write and let her know if there was anything she needed for the girls to bring with them, anything at all. She was aware that she would have to provide sheets, blankets, pillows, and funds for the girls' room and board (the Mother Superior had already reduced the tuition by half, bless her soul). And she would be sending sacks of cacao and sugarcane for the convent's kitchen.

The postscript said that Madre Catalina had advised that the girls be known as Juana's cousins.

Juana had crumpled the letter in her fist and paced her study. This is beyond belief! she thought. My mother casts me out into the world at the age of eight and doesn't see me for nearly thirteen years and now expects me to assume responsibility for her two brats! Cousins, indeed! Everyone at the convent knew that her mother had a second husband and a second family. She had only seen the girls twice when her mother had brought them to Mexico City, first to attend her veiling ceremony and then last year on her birthday. Both times they had struck Juana as incorrigibly spoiled, particularly the young one, Inés, who kept interrupting the adults' conversation with annoying statements. Inesilla, her mother called her.

And the other one, dense as a watermelon, letting her sister do all the talking while she sat there twirling the ringlets in her hair.

And now they're coming here! To live with me! With what right? she called out. Why doesn't my mother care for her own children? She wanted to scream. There had to be something she could do to prevent this. Who did her mother think she was, anyway? She was assuming a kind of trust and familiarity that Juana did not share. She had no obligation to take those girls. Absolutely none. And yet, how could she tell her mother that she did not want to do this? That she resented the years those girls had spent at their mother's side while Juana passed from the Matas to the palace to the convent like a dog without an owner?

She couldn't breathe. The air had grown hot and heavy in her throat and she couldn't inhale. She felt her head shaking and a liquid moving back and forth in her ears. The colic squeezed and squeezed at her entrails.

"Breathe, Juana!" She felt a cold palm slap her face.

"Juana, breathe!" Another slap.

"The water, Mother, please, get me the water."

A shock of cold water on her face, in her throat. Choking her. She coughed, then willed herself to draw a deep breath.

"Good, Juana. Yes, breathe. Slowly, slowly."

"I think the fever's passing, Mother."

"Sometimes it gets worse after the fever."

"What do you mean, worse?"

"I can't bleed her anymore. We have to wait and see. We have to pray."

"Shall we get Padre Antonio?"

"Dear God, why did I listen to her?"

Think, Juana, think! she told herself. *Forget the pain. Try to remember how you got here, what brought you here.* Someone dribbled water into her mouth, and she sucked the moisture off her lips.

Her students were outside preparing for the play they were putting on in honor of the Feast of the Assumption. The Viceroy and la Marquesa and the patrons of the convent had been invited, and the boarders were busy making little lace baskets and filling them with rose petals and orange blossoms to distribute among the guests. Juana had sent her music class out to the cloister to rehearse the *villancico* that she still had not finished, even though she had been working on it for weeks. But her mother's letter had rattled her, angered her, and she had wasted much good time fretting about how to keep her mother from getting her way.

She could hear them so clearly, the girls' voices ringing out in the cloister. *Quiet, attention, for Mary is singing! Listen, attend to her voice, Divine!* They were rehearsing the refrain, and she noticed that their pacing was off, but couldn't bring herself to go outside and correct them. Then she heard a lay Sister come out of the infirmary and tell the girls to quiet down, that they were disturbing the sick Sisters. She went to the window to call the girls back into the schoolroom when the idea struck her. The lay Sister had just crossed the courtyard with a pile of chamber pots to be slopped, and she remembered that Sor Elvira, the infirmarian, had dozens of patients afflicted with typhoid.

If I volunteer to help out in the infirmary, maybe I can catch the disease. My mother wouldn't think of sending me her brats if she knew I had typhoid.

Think about the consequences of this, Juana, a voice said inside her. *Typhoid is a serious illness, and Sor Elvira's methods haven't proven very effective against it. Wouldn't it be easier to write your mother and tell her you refuse to foster the girls, or at least make up some reasonable excuse for why you can't comply with her request.*

But the voice knew nothing of Juana's heart. It was the voice of logic, the voice that belonged to her rational self, and it was not her rational self that felt deserted by her mother and insulted by these girls. It was not her rational self that would have to deal with the tide of emotions that would ebb and flow through her veins and that would prevent her from studying, from writing, from thinking. When her emotional self took control, all she ever felt was pain and anger and ennui, and the only thing she got out of it was wasted time. Her entire way of life was at risk, she reasoned with herself, and so she had to take an extreme measure to safeguard it. Surely her rational self could see the logic in that.

She would wait until after the performance before taking her decision to the Mother Superior, she decided, but by sunset, as the *beatas* arranged the chairs in the patio and hung the stage curtain between two balustrades in the courtyard, the actresses and the choir rehearsing one last time before the doors opened to their guests, Juana had worked herself into a numbing headache so that she was not able to supervise the performance from behind the curtain as she usually did, or come out afterward for her bow, or attend the small reception that followed in the patio. The headache, she figured, worked to her advantage and would only lend more weight to the story she was concocting for the Mother Superior.

At first Madre Catalina would not hear of Juana's assistance in the infirmary, but Juana convinced her by inventing a vision—brought on by the neuralgia, on the Feast of the Assumption, no less—in which the Lady of the Apocalypse had spoken to her about a great sacrifice she had to make for the sake of the Order.

"And you're willing to do this, Juana?"

"Mother, what else would you recommend? You could send a proxy for me, I suppose, but then that could bring down even more wrath."

"It *is* odd that none of the other convents have reported an outbreak. Maybe this is God's wrath. But what have we done to deserve it, Juana?"

"That's what I mean, Mother. There's no way of telling. Perhaps our faith is being tested."

"I wouldn't be surprised. It seems we get more and more girls placed here out of convenience than out of faith."

"Believe me, Mother, if it hadn't been the Lady of the Apocalypse that appeared to me, I wouldn't have bothered you with this—whatever it is—this message."

"And perhaps what it means is that, if you take this on, if you heed Her command, you will have passed your test, Juana, and the illness will not afflict you. Is that possible, or entirely foolish?"

"It's definitely possible, Mother."

"Well, then, what else can we do?"

"I'm at your disposal, Mother."

"You shall be commended for this, my dear. I shall bring up the subject of this vision at Friday chapter and make absolutely certain that the rest of the Sisters appreciate the sacrifice you've decided to take on for our sake. I shall tell Sor Rafaela to record it in the archive."

"Not necessary, Mother."

"You know why the vision came to you, don't you? Because you're the only brave one around here. None of the others would have told me about this. Had I been the one visited, I probably wouldn't have said anything either. Who in her right mind would want to expose herself to typhoid? Not, of course, that you're not in your right mind, Juana, but visions—"

"I know what you mean, Mother. Don't worry. I'll take all the necessary precautions."

Juana left the Mother Superior's office feeling perversely elated. She went straight to the infirmary, exchanged her long veil for the short one worn by the infirmary staff, pinned up her sleeves, and got to work slopping chamber pots. Sor Elvira was so relieved at getting help that she knelt where she stood and prayed a decade of Credos.

At some point in the middle of the first week Juana regretted her decision. She could not stomach food, and when she slept her dreams took her back to the infirmary where she continued to wash and wipe and smell the effects of the disease. By the end of the week it was too late to turn back. One of the novices she had been sponging down bit her hand in her delirium and drew blood. She knew it would just be a matter of time before the infection spread into her body. Even Sor Elvira, known to have withstood every pestilence that had passed over the convent in two decades, teetered on the edge of infection. Sor Elvira's assistants both fell ill at the beginning of Juana's second week, and three days later Juana dropped the load of soiled linens she was taking to the laundry as a pain stronger than ten colics twisted through her bowels.

"Daughter, can you hear me?"

She saw her grandfather bending over her, but then the face came into focus and she realized that it was just Padre Antonio and he was rubbing a rancid oil on her forehead.

"In the name of the Father, and the Son, and the Holy Ghost."

What did that oil mean, anyway? She knew it meant something, not baptism, not initiation into the family of Christ, something else, something terminal, like death. And then she understood what it was he was doing, and she kicked her feet and tried to writhe out of the bindings that fastened her to the bed.

I'm not dying! she tried to tell Padre Antonio. Get away from me! I don't want your last rites! Get that oil off me! But the monotonous sound of his praying wouldn't stop, and the oil dripped down her temples.

Another time she was sure she saw la Marquesa bending over her, felt la Marquesa's cool hands on her cheeks, her cool lips on her lips, la Marquesa's breath on her face as she whispered Juana's name. Wake up, Juana. I want to talk to you. Won't you wake up for me?

Finally, she opened her eyes and the fever was gone, the infection reduced to a headache and an unquenchable thirst. Her tongue felt like a slab of dry meat in her mouth. The flesh of her stomach had grown concave between her hip bones. Madre Catalina and Andrea were sitting on stools on opposite sides of the bed, and she realized she was in her own bed rather than in the infirmary. She wore nothing but her undertunic, and her skin smelled of rose water and Castile soap. She saw a basin of gray water and a pile of wet towels at the foot of Andrea's chair.

"My friend," she managed to say, "thank you."

"Don't tax yourself," said Andrea. "Here, take some tea."

She could taste nothing, but the warm liquid soaked into her tongue, moistened her vocal chords, seeped into the parched walls of her stomach.

"Enough, enough," said Andrea. "It's got honeycomb and a little laudanum. It'll make you vomit if you take too much."

"The danger's passed, Juana," said the Mother Superior, patting her hand. "Saint Jerome has interceded for you."

"But Saint Jerome isn't the patron saint of contagious diseases, Mother, that's Saint Roque."

She could speak barely above a whisper.

Madre Catalina stroked her face. "Don't you remember, *hija mía*? It was you, you kept calling to him, begging for his intercession. 'Not Saint Joseph,' you said, 'Saint Jerome!'"

"You kept shouting, 'Get me out of here! I'm dying in here!'" said Andrea, "so we brought you back to your cell, and still you wouldn't respond to any treatment."

"I thought I was somewhere else," Juana said, and swallowed more of the tea. Madre Catalina kissed her hand.

"We were so worried," she said. "Padre Miranda came. La Marquesa, too. She almost wept when she saw you."

"La Marquesa came . . . here? To my cell?"

"Brought her own doctor," said Madre Catalina. "I've had the novices praying for you in the parlor."

"And now you're well again," said Andrea, smiling and straightening the bedclothes. "The Lady has given you back."

She finished the tea. "What Lady?"

"She doesn't remember," Madre Catalina said to Andrea. "The Lady of the vision, Juana. It was a severe test she posed for you."

She remembered the reason for her self-inflicted illness. "Did you inform my mother? My sisters—"

"Your *cousins*, my dear, will arrive in December. We did not want to alarm your mother until we were sure that you would not pull out of this, so we simply requested that she wait another month or so to dispatch them to us. As soon as the doctor told us you were out of danger, I sent a letter."

Of course! How utterly idiotic could she be? Her illness had not prevented anything, and she had risked losing her life for nothing! She wasn't even confirmed! She could have ended up in purgatory for all eternity. She cast her head back on the pillow and let the tears come. She could hear the voice of her rational self gloating. *Another way out, a more effective way out,* the voice said, *would have been to confide in Madre Catalina and let her prevent the girls from coming.* Why hadn't she thought of that? Tears slid down into her hair.

"She needs to rest, Mother," said Andrea, picking up the basin and towels.

"You'll be fine, dear. Don't be afraid. You're safe now."

Don't be afraid. You're safe now. The very words of that old dream she had used to get herself into the convent. The tears felt like water pouring down the sides of her face. She heard them open the door, and the sound of the novices praying the rosary drifted over her like a dream. She slept and did not want to wake up, but there Andrea would be with a bowl of chicken broth or an infusion of chamomile. There Jane would be rubbing her feet and hands with camphor oil to stir the circulation back into her limbs. There Madre Catalina would be in the middle of the night nodding off over her prayer book. And finally her body healed and there was nothing she could do but sit up and dress herself for prayers.

Sor Rosario, she learned, had died of the disease, as had four of the novices and one of the *beatas*, and every door in the convent was draped with black ribbons. Out of respect for the dead, the Sisters exchanged their white veils for black ones and wore the gossamer fabric over their faces for an entire month, eschewing all visitors for the duration of their mourning.

Andrea was never far from Juana's side, in case the illness recurred or she was visited by any more apocalyptic visions—neither of which happened.

"Did the Lady really appear to you, Juana?" she asked on their return from compline one evening. They had lingered in the lower choir so that Andrea could say a special decade of Paternosters to the Sacred Heart. "What did she look like, the Lady?"

"I really couldn't see her that well," said Juana, not daring to confide the truth of her ploy even to Andrea. "The fever made everything so blurry."

"So you saw nothing at all? No angels hovering at her sides or devils writhing under her heels or souls raising their hands to be pulled out of purgatory? That's what all the mystics report seeing."

"Actually," said Juana, drawing on her own knowledge of mystic texts to provide a persuasive description of the vision, "the blurriness gave way to clouds fringed by rays of light, and her voice seemed to come from the clouds, though I was able to distinguish her outline very faintly. At first I thought it was my grandmother speaking to me. She said she was the mother of my mother and spoke of a sacrifice I had to make to prove my love for her."

"I thought it had something to do with the Order. That's what Madre Catalina told us."

"She chose me, she said, as the representative for the Order, so that my sacrifice would really be proof of the Order's devotion."

"I guess it makes sense that it would be you, Juana. I mean, you're not the most devoted daughter of Saint Jerome. And yet you were chosen. How fortunate you are!"

"I suppose," said Juana, "but I had no idea it would be so dangerous."

"Faith hurts, Juana."

They were standing at the fountain now, each one going her own way toward her cell—Andrea to the one-room hovel she had selected and Juana up the stairs to her apartment—and it was just past twilight and the lanterns had been lit throughout the courtyard and Juana felt a sudden impulse to embrace her friend, just because they were alone and she loved her for her innocence.

"My goodness, Juana. What was that about?"

"Have you noticed," said Juana, "the difference between faith and hope?"

"Don't change the subject. You know we're not allowed to touch."

"I have found—no, wait, listen, don't go—I have found that faith is about belief in something certain, while hope is wedded to expectation and desire. I think that when we confuse hope for faith, and when our expectations and desires are thwarted, then we feel that faith hurts. But if we believe only in that which is certain, faith can never hurt, because it is based on truth. Does that make sense?"

"What am I going to do with you, Juana? You disobey our vows so easily, without intending to do any harm, and yet you compromise my faith continually and all I can do is *hope* that one day you will truly be visited by the Holy Spirit."

"Hope hurts, Andrea," she said, but her friend had walked away and there was no one to listen to her except the cats hunkered between the orchid pots on the edge of the fountain.

Instead of returning to her cell, she went to the garden to pick a tomato for her evening snack. Fireflies hovered over the beds of oregano and sage that grew on either side of the gravel path. The sound of crickets in the orchard, the toads singing in the canal just on the other side of the convent wall reminded her of quiet evenings at the palace when all of the court had withdrawn early and Juana had the grounds to herself.

But there, at least, you could walk out of the gate if you wanted to, she reminded herself.

Escorted by a page, she liked to take walks around the Plaza Mayor, winding through the rows of shacks in the marketplace, stopping here and there to admire a Chinese silk or an Indian weaving. Across the canal in the arcades of the municipal building, she would watch the young lovers kissing surreptitiously in the corners, or the students who congregated at the outdoor tables of the *pulquerías* discussing the different subjects of their studies. Occasionally she would eavesdrop at the scribes' tables, listening to the pathetic stream of lovesick verses being dictated by their heartbroken clients. How she missed those long walks, which always ended at Don Lázaro's bookshop.

Here, you're locked in, Juana. Your whole world is bound by these walls.

I came here of my own choice, though. Of my own free will.

What free will? You had no other choice, Juana. Not with your inclinations.

Chapter 9

Antonia and Inés arrived in the second week of December. Juana did not meet her stepfather in the locutory, nor had he requested to meet with her. His only transactions were with Madre Catalina. Led by Sor Clara, the new gatekeeper, the girls and their luggage trampled into Juana's cell. She would not, naturally, share a room with them, and so she had moved her bedchamber upstairs, partitioning the west end of the library to accommodate her bed and wardrobe and bureau, leaving the room downstairs to her sisters. Inés complained about the size of the room, about the thin mattress on the creaky old bed they had to share, about the distance of the privy from the cell, about the lack of maids to attend them, about the fact that Jane was permitted to eat with them at table.

"Mamá would never allow this!" she said. "Would she, Antonia?"

Antonia picked at her chicken and rice.

"You're not in Mamá's house now, are you?" said Juana, realizing that she was now in charge and that they would have to do whatever she said. This, then, would be her revenge on these two who had grown up at their mother's, *her* mother's, side.

"I shall take my meals in my room then!" snapped Inés.

"You shall eat at the table, señorita, or not at all. You are not here on holiday or on retreat. You are here to study and to learn, humility above all. You will attend all of your classes, every single day, and return here only for the midday meal. At recreation time you will make yourselves useful in the kitchen or the laundry. That is my working time and I do not want you anywhere near my cell. After vespers, you are to retire to your room to read and study. You will not attend compline or matins. And you will limit conversation while you're here; endless chattering disturbs my peace of mind and my studies. On Sundays after Mass, and only if you behave, you will be allowed to help Jane with the marketing. If marketing is beneath either of you, of course, you will remain in your room the rest of the day. The trick is to stay out of my way and be almost invisible to me. Antonia, will you please repeat what I said?"

The girls wrote endless letters to their mother, begging to be removed from Juana's cell, to be taken from San Jerónimo and Mexico City altogether. Juana intercepted the letters and burned them in the brazier. Her mother had not heeded her own letters when she had pleaded to be allowed to leave the Matas, why would she heed the petitions of these two?

On the third Sunday in March her aunt Mary came to visit her in the locutory, dressed in black. Her uncle John had died, she said, of a venereal disease. Since her children had all married, there was nothing left for her in the city and she was preparing to return to Nepantla.

"Now that she's alone again, your poor mother—"

"Why is she alone? Has Don Diego died?"

"She didn't tell you? Did you think he was coming all the way to Mexico just to drop off his daughters at the convent? He has a family here. He's left your mother."

"My God, Tía. That's scandalous!"

"All I can say is that John may have had his faults, all men are the same that way, but at least he never abandoned his family."

Juana swallowed hard. "My poor mother."

"I wouldn't pity your mother. Isabel was always the strongest of all of us. Still, poor woman, I think she loved Don Diego. Unlike your father or that other man who just used her. I, myself, was never in love with your uncle (may he rest in peace), but we respected each other and he provided well for us. I couldn't ask for much more. But your mother, Juanita, has always been the provider, hasn't she? She's a soldier, that Isabel. And look at the daughter she bred."

"You bred me as long as she did, Tía. And la Marquesa did the rest."

"La Marquesa, yes, we're all grateful to her. You truly did blossom at palace. How are you taking the news of their departure, dear?"

"Whose departure?"

"By the Virgin's veil, Juanita, are you still so ill that you don't read the gazette? Or is your nose always buried in your books? The Viceroy and la Marquesa are returning to Spain. They're awaiting orders from the King, but they're expecting to leave on the next Flota."

The chocolate turned to acid in Juana's stomach. "That's two months away!"

"No, not this year's Flota. The next one."

"I can't believe she hasn't told me. Tía, are you quite sure? You can't always trust rumors."

"The courtiers are all talking about it. Your cousin, Nico, is the one who told me. He's got friends at the palace, you know."

She could waste no more time chattering with her aunt. "Tía, would you mind very much waiting for me to write a note to la Marquesa? I would so much appreciate it if you would deliver it for me."

"I suppose that would be alright. Are you allowed——"

"Thank you, Tía. I shall return shortly. Help yourself to more chocolate."

She swished out of the locutory and nearly ran to the archivist's library. She had no time to go all the way to her cell to write the note. Sor Rafaela glowered at her over her books but did not ask her what she was doing. She pulled a fresh sheet of parchment from under the writing surface and wrote the note without sitting down.

19 FEBRUARY 1673

MY DEAR MARQUESA,

I have just heard rumors of your imminent departure from New Spain and though I do not wish to burden you with reproach, I would very much like to express my regret at having lost your confidence. I have not seen you since I recovered from the illness, but knowing how busy the palace is before Easter, I attributed your absence to that occasion. Now I can only assume that you no longer count me as one of your friends. If I am wrong in that assumption, I beg you to visit me and reassure me that the rumors of your leaving are false.

Yours always,

Juana Inés

La Marquesa did not come but sent a note in response apologizing for not having told Juana the news, reassuring her profusely that she could never lose the Vicereine's confidence or friendship. Juana read the note so much she memorized the content:

I love you as much as you love me, my dear. If I have not told you of our plans it is because the thought of never seeing you again pains me more than leaving this land that I have grown to love with such allegiance. I will come to visit you after Easter.

   Your friend forever,
   Leonor Carreto de Mancera

When Saint John's Day came and still she had received no visit from la Marquesa, Juana sent Jane to the palace to investigate if they had already left, her heart hanging by a thread.

"They're still here, Madre, but the maids say her ladyship got sick again and hasn't left her room in weeks."

"Got sick *again?* She didn't tell me she was ill. What's the matter with her?"

"Water in the lungs, they said. Or fire. One of the two."

"Jane, for God's sake, you're my only link to the outside world. I wish you'd pay attention."

"Whatever it is, they say she's dying, Madre!"

Juana went to Madre Catalina to ask for permission to leave the convent and stay with la Marquesa until she healed. Now that she had experience with the sick—

"Absolutely not," said Madre Catalina. "You're just healing yourself. I have no intention of exposing you to another infection."

"But Madre, la Marquesa is like a mother to me—"

"I'm sorry, Juana. You know I accede to anything you want, but I thought I'd lost you to that fever. I will not risk losing you again."

"But I'm healthy, Madre—"

"Don't beg me, Juana. I cannot allow this. Please, understand."

"But, Madre—"

"You heard the Mother Superior, Sister," said Sor Bernarda, the new *vicaria* elect, coming in from the outer office. "Don't you have classes to attend to? Your students are complaining that they never see you."

At night Juana wrote in Pandora's Box and composed verse after verse of vapid poetry that only reflected her frustration at being caged. Antonia and Inés bore the brunt of it. If they slurped their soup or made noise on the stairwell or spoke above a whisper in their room, she scolded them. She forbade them to write any more letters to their mother, and once, when the gatekeeper announced that their father was waiting for them in the locutory *she* went to see him and in less than two minutes explained that the girls were not at leisure to receive visitors, that that was a privilege earned after a year in the convent.

"But they're only boarders," he protested.

"Precisely," she said. "Good afternoon, Don Diego. I shall let them know you inquired about them." She did no such thing.

Jane made regular rounds to the palace and befriended several of the Vicereine's slaves, so she was able to bring Juana detailed reports on the progress of la Marquesa's health. The summer heat, it seemed, had been particularly vexing for her weak lungs, but now that the weather was turning cool, la Marquesa was able to sit out in her garden and breathe more normally. Juana sent her a menthol ointment that Sor Elvira recommended and a sonnet that, after months of working on it, she finally considered fit for la Marquesa's eyes.

> In the life that always yours has been,
> divine Laura, and always shall be,
> Fierce Fate with mortal foot pursued me,
> triumphantly asserting my ruin.
>
> Amazed was I at her audacity:
> for if under her domain we kneel,
> she has no power here to wield,
> since you control my destiny.
>
> To cut the thread that she did fail to spin
> I saw the mortal scissors yawn.
> But, Fierce Fate, I said therein;
> know you not that only Laura reigns under this sun?
> Thus, she ran away and let me win
> death only for your person.

It was her way of telling la Marquesa what la Marquesa already knew. Using the conceit of her own illness, Juana tried to exhort la Marquesa to health by reminding her that Juana's life lay in her hands, that not even Fate herself owned her like la Marquesa did.

The last time she saw her friend was on her twenty-fifth birthday. Juana had been unable to keep from quarreling with her for she had brought her retinue rather than come alone, and Juana found it impossible to speak her heart, even in the convoluted syntax of allegory.

"My darling Juana, need you tax my mind so? I tire so easily after the illness."

"Sisyphus tired daily, Señora, and yet he wasn't allowed to quit his punishment."

"I know you're angry at me, *cariño*, for leaving, for not telling you we were leaving, but the affairs of state are complicated to arrange, Juana Inés, and nothing is ever certain until the last moment."

"Persephone was the goddess of spring as well as the queen of the dead."

"Really, Juanita, you're most exasperating today! I wanted to celebrate a last birthday with you. Don't you like your gift? I had the mandolin made just for you. Come over here, Juana Inés. Kiss me. Play for me. Let us be friends again."

Juana did not move. Madre Catalina had conceded to the Vicereine's request that Juana be allowed to sit on the same side of the locutory with her, but Juana had refused the privilege. She took her usual seat on her own side of the grille and watched la Marquesa through the bars, her heart shredding in silence.

When la Marquesa and her ladies ended their visit, Juana went to Madre Catalina's office to inform her that she was taking a vow of silence and solitude until the Viceroy and the Vicereine left Mexico in April.

"That's five months away, Juana. Why do you insist on these bizarre punishments for yourself? Besides, don't you want to greet the new Viceroy when he pays his visit to San Jerónimo?"

"I have lost all interest in the palace," said Juana. "As far as I'm concerned, there will never be a Viceroy like the Marqués de Mancera."

It was said that the new Viceroy, the Duke de Veragua, had won his post by outbidding his competitors, but the rumor was that he was old and sickly and not expected to survive the long journey to New Spain.

"I understand the pain of your loss, Juana," said Madre Catalina. "When I lost my fourth son I brought myself here to the convent to escape that pain. But you're so young, my daughter, to be hurt like this."

"I have not felt young since I left Panoayán, Mother."

Madre Catalina sighed and called to the *vicaria*, ordering her to find a substitute for Juana's classes.

For the first time in the five years of her profession, Juana resorted to genuine prayer and discipline, and would not permit Jane to go near the palace lest she hear something impossible for her heart to resist. Four days after the Duke's official entrance into Mexico, on the day of the Virgin of Guadalupe, the death bells started to toll and Juana was certain that la Marquesa had died, but it turned out to be the Duke of Veragua, whose reign had not lasted a week. La Marquesa did not even know until it was too late that she would never see Juana again.

1 MARCH 1674

JUANA INÉS,

The Marquis and I have been so regretfully busy these last weeks packing for our trip that we have not had the time to pay you a visit. Today I came to see you on my own, but was informed that you have taken a vow of silence and total solitude. I must say, *cariño*, that I was disappointed by the news. We have such few days left in Mexico. I find it rather selfish of you to have withdrawn from us in this way. Perhaps you will reconsider. It will take us a full month to reach Vera Cruz. Word has reached us that the Flota will be ready to sail by the beginning of May, so we depart Mexico City on the 2nd of April. I would very much like to see you once again before we leave.

Leonor Carreto de Mancera

12 MARCH 1674

Still no word from you, Juana Inés. I cannot believe that you will deny me the pleasure of your company after all that we have meant to each other for the past ten years. At least send me word of how you fare. I have instructed the page to remain outside the convent for your response. I am filled with anxiety over the journey, Juana Inés. Please do not add to my distress. I await your response,

Leonor (the Vicereine)

ESTEEMED MARQUESA DE MANCERA,

Your note has been delivered to Sor Juana Inés de la Cruz. Since Sor Juana cannot comply with your request, I have taken the liberty of responding to you myself. I assure you that our Juana is faring well, deep in prayer and meditation. She has taken it upon herself to write fifteen new offerings for our rosary to the Virgin Mary. To aid her in her task, she has chosen to fast as well as remain silent, but her maid tells me that she is maintaining her strength with *caldos* and rice water. Thank you very much for your concern. Let me reassure you that Sor Juana is as dear to all of us in the house of San Jerónimo as she is to you, and that we shall always look out for her welfare. I am certain that I speak for Sor Juana in saying that she will miss your company tremendously and that she wishes you a serene journey.

On the seventeenth day of March in the year of our Lord, 1674,
In service,
Mother Catalina de San Esteban, Prioress
Convent of Santa Paula of the Order of San Jerónimo

Madre Catalina had decided it would be best not to disturb Juana's pledge of solitude and silence and had never delivered any notes to her, keeping them in her own cell until the royal couple had left the city and Juana emerged from her meditations. It was her duty, after all, she told Juana later, to guard the hearts as well as the souls of her daughters in religion. And Juana's heart, as that old *dicho* said, was like a clay jug that had gone to the well too many times.

1 APRIL 1674

MY DEAREST JUANA INÉS,

It is the eve of our departure and I cannot sleep. I paced the balcony long after the curfew bells, thinking of you in your cell. Remembering our good talks in the *locutorio*, your maid's delicious confections, your lovely music, that grace with which you wear the veil. You have quite an imposing presence in that habit, *cariño*, and it makes you seem much older than your twenty-five years. Indeed, you seem more of a priestess than a nun.

I realized tonight as I was pacing that you are wiser than I, who am fifteen years your senior and still petulant, kicking at the door of your solitude like some spoiled child unaccustomed to not getting her way. I understand now that your solitude is a shell you have drawn around yourself. And I also understand, Juana Inés, that your love was the most precious gift Mexico offered me. I shall always carry that gift in my breast and perhaps it will heal the cleft in my heart that grows wider as the hour to depart draws closer. I shall never forget you,

Juana Inés Ramírez de Asbaje. Please write to me as soon as you can. I know I shall have to wait a terribly long time to receive your letters, but I shall force myself to be patient. Meanwhile, I will gaze at "Athena Among Calla Lilies" and remember all that you ever said to me. May God and the Virgin bless you as you deserve. Your friend who loves you,

Laura

P.S. I ordered a special chair to be made for you, with broad arm-rests and good support for your back. The palace carpenters will deliver it when it's finished. Please accept it as my farewell gift to you. Each time you sit in it, remember how much you mean to me. Adios, Juana Inés. Don't forget me.

One morning three weeks after la Marquesa's last note, returning from confession with Padre Antonio, Juana met Andrea and Madre Catalina heading toward her cell. The Mother Superior's eyes were rimmed with tears. Andrea carried a note and something dangling from a gold chain. Juana recognized the Catherine-wheel medal immediately.

My dear Juana Inés,

I regret to inform you that our beloved Laura fell ill on the journey and is gone. She was taken from us by a pestilence that claimed her life within two days. Her ravaged remains needed to be buried immediately. Her heart was very weak and sad at leaving Mexico. None could save her. She lies in the sacred ground of the convent of San Francisco in Tepeaca. Her soul is now in the garden of her Maker, may she rest in peace. Now I, too, shall leave my heart in New Spain. Yours in sorrow,

Antonio Sebastian de Toledo, Marqués de Mancera
21 de abril de 1674, A.D.

Juana could not weep. She kept a vigil in the choir every night for a week, forcing herself to remember every detail of her four years at the palace—recalling la Marquesa's face and voice, the scent of the pomade she liked to use in her hair, the way her eyes glowed whenever Juana recited poetry to her or played a brilliant hand of dominoes, her habit of rubbing a front tooth with her pinkie when she concentrated on her cards—and yet none of it helped bring Juana's sorrow to the surface. Though she felt spikes in her throat and belly as she lay prostrate on the cold flags of the choir, she could not weep. This she had feared more than anything, this hardening of her heart. She had been preparing for la Marquesa's departure for years, telling herself over and over that one day she would lose her entirely to that void across the sea. And now she had gone to an even deeper void, taking the knowledge of Juana's secret love with her. She slipped the chain with the Catherine-wheel medal over her head and vowed never to remove it again.

Chapter 10

May they die with you, Laura, for you died,
these affections that long for you in vain,
these eyes that you deprive
of the lovely light you once ordained.
Death to my unhappy lyre in which you graced
in which you graced . . . death to my unhappy—

"Sor Juana! Are you out here?"

The Mother Superior's voice startled her. She had come to the small stone chapel in the cemetery to compose her second requiem for la Marquesa. The chapel was used only for the funeral services of the *beatas* and so remained empty most of the time. On days when her spine ached from hunching over her desk so long, when the book-lined walls of her study felt like they were closing in, Juana claimed the abandoned chapel as her own. Afternoons, she liked to sit out here and watch the rain, inhale the scent of rosemary growing wild between the graves. It had been eight months since la Marquesa's death, and she was just beginning to emerge from a melancholia that had numbed all of her senses.

At the sound of Madre Catalina's voice, she opened her eyes and tried to hide the displeasure she always felt at interruptions. She peered out the cross-shaped slit that served as a window and saw Madre Catalina approaching. A young girl in China Poblana dress walked beside her. She sighed and went to meet the Mother Superior on the flagstone path that led down to the graveyard from the garden.

"Yes, Mother, were you looking for me? I was praying the rosary, as you know." She tried to keep her gaze away from the girl's bright raiment. The girl's eyes were downcast.

"Forgive me for interrupting you, Sister," said Madre Catalina, dimpling as she smiled, "but I don't think you'll mind. I've come to offer you a gift."

Ever since her most recent reelection as Mother Superior, Madre Catalina had not stopped giving her gifts of one sort or another. Juana linked her hands under the black cloth of her scapular and tried to appear interested. "Another one, Mother? Surely you are too indulgent with me."

"Girl," Madre Catalina said to the Chinita Poblana, "you forgot to curtsy to our illustrious Sor Juana Inés de la Cruz."

The girl could not have been more than ten or eleven years old. She curtsied, still not looking up, and Juana let her eyes sweep momentarily over her red skirt, green sash, yellow blouse, and lavender shawl embroidered in pink orchids. She wore several strands of blue glass beads, gold filigree earrings, and red ribbons in her braids. She even had a beauty mark on her left cheek. A weathered leather *morral* hung off her shoulder. "And who is this, Mother, who is so resplendent in our somber house?"

"My name is Concepción." Raising her head quickly, the girl spoke before Madre Catalina could do it for her. Not unusual for her *castiza* blood, she had eyes of different colors. "I am the daughter of María Clara Benavídez." Juana heard a discernible *criolla* lisp in her words.

"Quiet!" Madre Catalina chastised her. "This is not a *pulquería* where you can blabber whenever you wish. Sor Juana was speaking to me, didn't you hear?" Madre Catalina held her gaze on the girl, but the girl did not look down. "Don't look at me with those crossed eyes!"

"My eyes are not crossed, Madre. One is brown like my mother's. The other is green like my father's mother."

"*¡Insolente!*" said Madre Catalina, slapping the girl across the mouth.

Juana flinched as the heavy gold band on the Mother Superior's finger struck the girl's lip. "You were saying something about a gift, Mother?" she said quickly.

"Well, now you see what sort of gift it is. She's an insolent ingrate to be sure, Sor Juana, but my son's bastard nonetheless, daughter of that *castiza* who runs his pulque tavern. It seems she has some skill with the needle and apparently with the quill, and it is my son's wish that she be fostered here until her twenty-fifth birthday, under my protection. He could have turned her out like a common Indian, but good man that he is, he even gave a dowry for her, and has also paid for her education at the girls' orphanage."

Juana felt a contraction in her chest, a surge of grief and recognition, as though she were listening to the details of her own childhood.

"Did you board at the orphanage?" Juana asked.

"No, Madre," said Concepción, curtsying again. "We have a *vivienda* above the *pulquería*. My mother and I have always lived there. She made Don Federico bring me here because she says she didn't want me spoiled in the *pulquería*."

Madre Catalina rolled her eyes and shook her head. "You can't ask an elm tree to produce pears," she said to Juana. To the girl, she added, "We don't discuss such things in the House of San Jerónimo. Remember, this is a holy house."

"Would you like to see my sampler, Madre?" the girl asked. She had already unbuckled her satchel and pulled a furled linen cloth out before anyone could answer. Holding it like an offering in both hands, the girl presented the sampler to Juana.

Juana unrolled the linen and held it up against the early afternoon light. In the first row was a progression of roses, from a slim, tight bud rendered in Castile pink to a fully opened carmine bloom. In the second row, leaves of eight distinct types were etched to perfection in several hues of green. The third row contained the heads and beaks of a variety of birds, not quite as perfect as the roses and leaves, but well detailed: gray-blue dove, green parakeet, crimson-crested rooster, golden canary, a black *cenzontle* with a red bead for an eye. In the last row, the letters of the girl's name were written in a calligraphy of silk thread, each letter artfully sketched and decorated with its appropriate flourish.

"This is lovely, Concepción," said Juana. "You're quite the artisan."

"Thank you, Madre." The girl took the sampler back and slipped it into her bag.

"I thought she might be useful to you in your work," said Madre Catalina. "With all of these new commissions you're getting, you could use an assistant of some kind, couldn't you? I thought she might make a good secretary, or a page at least, to run errands for you between here and the Cabildo."

"Tell me, Concepción," Juana looked directly into the girl's eyes, "did you etch these letters in ink before you embroidered them, or did you stylize them with your needle as you embroidered?"

"I used the stencil at school," said Concepción, "then I filled in the letters with thread."

"So this is not your calligraphy we're seeing."

"But it *is* my needlework, Madre."

"And how does your penmanship compare to your needlework, would you say?"

The girl narrowed her eyes and thought about her answer. "I don't work on my penmanship like I do on my embroidery, so I guess my handwriting isn't so pretty."

"Good answer, Concepción. Honest, above all. From what you tell me, I conclude that you would rather embroider than write."

"I like coloring with thread, Madre. I didn't do much writing in the *pulquería*."

"Let me guess: you're ten years old or thereabouts, right? You must have learned your letters, your numbers, a bit of music?"

"I learned everything I need, Madre, and I turned twelve on the feast day of the Immaculate Conception."

"Quite an irony, don't you agree, Sor Juana," interjected Madre Catalina, "that this most mixed of all half-breeds, and bastard to boot, should come to light on such a feast day? There's nothing immaculate about this one."

"Yes, quite an irony, Mother," said Juana, turning her attention back to Concepción, who was clearly biting her bottom lip to keep from responding to the Mother Superior's comment. "But you do know your letters?" Juana insisted.

The girl nodded, gazing obliquely at Madre Catalina.

She has been taught to hold her tongue, thought Juana, already charmed by the girl's stoic impudence. "If you qualify to become my secretary, Concepción, you'll spend most of your time writing, and there'll be very little time for needlework."

The girl held her gaze. "Your secretary?"

"Does that suit you?"

"Or would you rather be peddling spirits to drunks and lechers?" asked Madre Catalina.

"How do I get to qualify, Madre?"

"A bit of dictation, I think. But, Mother, what about logistical considerations? Will she be staying in my cell or yours?"

"It would be best if she stayed with you, Sor Juana. We all know the late hours that you keep with your commissions."

"She will require her own cot, of course."

"This one has no need of a cot," said Madre Catalina. "She's used to sleeping on a *petate* like all of her caste."

"I have always slept in my mother's bed," said Concepción, "except when my father came to visit. You don't think your son ever lay on a *petate* like a common Indian, do you, Grandmother?"

It took the Mother Superior a few seconds to close her mouth. When she recovered from her shock, she slapped the girl again, drawing blood this time from her already bruised upper lip. The girl covered her mouth and blinked before the tears could slip out of her eyes.

"This insolence is incredible, an embarrassment beyond words," said Madre Catalina. "Forgive me for wasting your time, Sor Juana. As much as I would like to do this favor for my son's sake, nothing could compel me now to keep this demon's tongue among us. Her skills be damned! She returns this very day to that pigsty she came from."

Juana grazed Madre Catalina's shoulder to divert her attention and keep her from striking the girl again. "I am sure, Mother, that her spirit can be quelled with hard work. Leave her to me."

The girl looked down at the cobbles.

"But are you sure, Sister? You have seen that she has no respect, no sense of propriety at all, not even for an elder such as I. She could give you infinitely more trouble than she's worth."

"Yes, that's possible, Mother. But you won't, will you, Concepción?" She wanted to put her arm around the girl's shoulder but instead simply cupped the girl's chin in her hand and lifted her face. Her eyes were tiny pools of green and brown liquid.

"You'll cooperate and obey, isn't that true, Concepción?" The girl's tears spilled onto Juana's fingers. Juana pulled her hand away from the small face and stared at the teardrops still clinging to her fingertips. Concepción looked at the ground again, wiping impatiently at her eyes.

"Stop that hypocritical crying!" commanded Madre Catalina. "Well, Sister, you know best. But the minute she gives you any trouble, don't feel obligated to keep her. I'll get her to slopping chamber pots and scrubbing floors as befits her status."

"I'll keep that in mind, Mother. For now, though, perhaps you would be so kind (I would do it myself but you see I haven't been able to finish my rosary) as to ask Sor Lucía to find her a cot. If she's to be trained as a secretary, she'll have few hours in which to sleep, but she will require a mattress, a pillow, and bed linen to achieve the quality of rest that is necessary for a clear and alert mind. I don't want her sleeping on the floor. My cell is cluttered enough as it is."

"Do you see, Doña Insolencia, what kind of mistress you're going to have?"

"Thank you, Madre." Concepción curtsied to Sor Juana a third time.

"Stop that ridiculous bending. You're not in church. Come along now," Madre Catalina shoved the girl to one side, "we've intruded on Sor Juana enough as it is. We've got to find you some decent clothing, too. Can't have you running around like a peacock in the midst of all these pigeons."

"My maid's name is Jane, Concepción. When you get to my cell, tell her I said to put your cot in the girls' room. I'll see you after nones."

"Oh no, Juana, I wouldn't hear of such a thing," said Madre Catalina, shaking her head curtly. "It's enough that you've even accepted this up-start's presence. To have her sleep in the same room with your cousins, a lowly china among *niñas de razón* . . ."

"Antonia and Inés won't mind sharing their room, Mother. They're hardly there as it is. Besides, Inés will be leaving us next Easter, and hopefully Antonia will follow soon after. Concepción can use their bed when they're gone. In the meantime, a cot will suffice."

Madre Catalina sighed deeply and shrugged. "Whatever you say, Sor Juana. It *is* your cell, after all. *¡Vamos, muchacha!*"

"Yes, Grandmother."

Madre Catalina stopped in her tracks. "In here," she muttered through clenched teeth, "I am not your father's mother. I am the Mother Superior of this house, and you shall address me only when and if I ever speak to you again. Understood?"

Juana heard the girl mutter something in response, but she was already drifting back to her requiem, her shoes crunching on the rocky soil that led back to the stone chapel. The girl's tears on her ink-stained fingers had stirred an image, and the image brought the rest of the poem with it:

> Death to my unhappy lyre in which you graced
> echoes, which now, lamenting, call your name,
> even these awkward strokes are nothing
> but black tears from a pen in pain.
>
> May precise Death feel pity
> and remorse for not excusing you,
> and may Love mourn her bitter luck,
> for once, anxious to behold you,
> she wished for eyes,
> which now do naught but weep for you.

Her throat felt as though she had swallowed eggshells.

The bells announcing the midafternoon Office saved her from another bout of grief-induced neuralgia, and Juana realized she would have to hurry to reach the church before the newly elected, fanatic head of the *vigilantas*, Sor Melchora, locked the door of the antechoir to discourage tardiness. She rushed out of the cemetery and headed for the shortcut that wound through the orchard and led to the side gate of the cloister. The mandarins still hung from their branches, deep orange globes that glowed like Chinese lanterns, but the peach, apricot, and plum trees had surrendered their fruit over the summer. At the eucalyptus-shaded walk that led to the temple of Saint Jerome, Melchora waited, hands on her hips.

"Really, Sor Juana," she said, checking off a name in her ledger, "after six years of profession one would expect you to remember the holy hours."

Nones, the Office that marked the presentation of Jesus in the Temple, was the one canonical hour that Juana permitted herself to enjoy. She needed that space of music and solace that preceded the afternoon rain. She could write best during the rain as long as nobody paid her a visit in the *locutorio*. But she had few visitors now that la Marquesa was gone. Even Fray Payo's visits had become scarce now that he served as both Archbishop and Viceroy. Only Don Carlos continued to see her on a weekly basis.

Rippling like the sweetest water over a bed of quartz, the voice of the new novice, Sister Felipa, flowed into Juana's head, washing over the knots of grief that had piled up at the back of her neck, at the base of her spine, in the dark well of her throat where la Marquesa's name lay buried.

"In the mornings when she's back from Mass, she likes her chocolate very hot and frothy," Jane was saying as Juana walked through the front door of her cell. "After the siesta, *if* she takes a siesta, which she usually doesn't, she wants an *agua fresca* of some kind. If she doesn't take a nap—"

Juana shut the door quietly behind her, inhaling the scent of fried plantains coming from the kitchen. She wondered to whom Jane could be talking, surely not Antonia and Inés who were still at classes, and who only set foot in the kitchen to pass to or from their room. She unfastened her leather cincture as she climbed the stairs to her quarters.

" . . . I do the errands and the cooking," Jane continued. "A woodcutter delivers wood to the convent every morning, but you still have to chop it to fit into the stove and the braziers. You have to ask Artemisa, she's the head cook in the refectory, to lend you the ax. I do the cooking, the marketing, the ironing, and I sweep the upstairs and clean her rooms. She don't like anyone else to clean her rooms."

"Jane!" Juana called down from the entrance to her study. "Bring me a glass of *tamarindo* water and stop all that chattering. I have work to do." She walked in to the familiar smell of ink and tallow and leather bindings, unpinning the long rosary from her shoulder. The Turkish carpet that Madre Catalina had given her to celebrate her fifth anniversary as a *profesa* hung from the rafters to separate the dormitory from her workroom.

She hung the rosary and the belt from their hooks inside the wardrobe, unpinned the escutcheon from her scapular, and removed the heavy cloth of the veil, feeling, as always, like a player in a drama stepping out of her costume. She poured water into the basin on the bureau to refresh her face, rinsed her mouth, then fastened the shorter, lighter veil into place over the head binding. *Recreo* time had begun and she would have at least three hours to work before vespers. But first she needed to read those notes, a flagellation of the spirit that did not correspond to the paltry lashes she was forced to give herself every evening before retiring. She reached down for her writing box, took the small key out of her tunic pocket, and brought the box to her bed, aware that she was holding her breath. Tucked into the laminated pages of the pearl-encrusted Book of Hours that had been la Marquesa's gift to her when she took her permanent vows were the three envelopes with their royal seals. She read them again, very slowly, trying to imagine la Marquesa's fingers holding the quill, her hand moving over the parchment. She could not bring herself to reread the Viceroy's note informing her of Laura's death.

"Here's your *tamarindo* water, Madre," Jane called from the other side of the Turkish carpet. Juana wiped her eyes with the trailing tip of her sleeve and thanked Jane, frowning at the intrusion.

"Set the glass on my desk, will you?" she said, folding the letter back into its envelope. "And open the shutters, please. You know I like to watch the rain in the afternoon." She replaced the notes and the prayer book under the pile of diary sheets in the box and returned the box to the wardrobe.

"You're having *platanitos fritos* with your tea today, Madre," Jane told her as soon as she emerged from her dormitory. "Do you want them with cream or plain?"

Rubbing at her temples, Juana sat on the red leather seat of the chair la Marquesa had given her, which she used at her main desk.

"Madre? Cream or no cream on your plantains?"

"I don't care, Jane. Just bring me whatever you're going to bring me and stop all this chattering. How many times do I have to tell you not to talk so much?"

Jane pursed her lips. "I'll send the new girl with your tray," she said. "Sorry I bothered you."

"Since when do we have a new girl?"

"Don't you know?" Jane said, unlatching the shutters. "The Mother Prioress brought me a *castiza* today and told me to take charge of her."

Juana had forgotten all about her transaction with Madre Catalina. "That's Concepción!" she said, stirring her *tamarindo* water with an index finger. "She's not a maid, Jane." She lowered her voice, "She's Madre Catalina's granddaughter."

"That China Poblana?" Jane narrowed her eyes. "More like the granddaughter of a tramp!"

"Well she's not; she's well educated, unlike you, and she's going to be my assistant. I want you to call her by her name. How would you like it if I referred to you as that *mulata*?"

Jane tossed her head back like an angry bull. "All the other Madres have two or three maids. The Mother Superior has one for the washing, one for the cooking, one for the cleaning, and one to care for the old nun who lives with her. Why do I have to be the only maid around here?"

"The old nun is Sor Paula. Don't be so disrespectful. I know that you're overworked, but you know I can't stand useless prattle. I can barely tolerate Antonia and Inés, and they're students, they're gone all day." She drew a deep breath to dissolve the tension that suddenly gripped her solar plexus.

"It's not fair, Madre. Look at these calluses on my hands! Look at my back! I'm turning into a *jorobada* from all the work I have to do around here! My mother said you would be good to me and you're not!" Jane turned around and stalked out of the study, wiping at her eyes with angry strokes. Juana followed her to the top of the stairs.

"Did Sor Lucía have a cot delivered for Concepción?"

Jane descended the staircase without answering.

"I want Concepción to sleep in Antonia and Inés's room. Get her to help you move the cot in there. I want you to tell her what time we get up, what time we eat, what time we pray. Tell her where the privy is, and don't forget to set another place at the table for her. You will treat her civilly or I'll send you packing back to Panoayán!"

Juana returned to her study and slammed the door. She knew she was responsible for Jane's impudence, but she couldn't treat Jane the way the other Sisters treated their slaves. She was Francisca's daughter and once her childhood friend, obediently sitting in her chair while Juana—*la niña* Juana, as she was called—taught her the alphabet.

"You don't want to be an imbecile, do you?" she used to ask, and the little girl, not knowing the meaning of the word, would shake her head vehemently, later running to tell her mother that *la niña* Juana was teaching her not to be an imbecile. But Jane had no mind for letters. It was the language of the kitchen that she had to learn, for, unlike *la niña* Juana, her mother beat her if she didn't remember to grind the corn or the chocolate or the pods of peppers drying in ristras over the stove. Concepción knocked at the door.

"Jane told me to bring your tray, Madre," the girl called out.

"Come in, come in, Concepción. What are you waiting for?"

Concepción walked into the room, balancing the tray on her head with one hand. She was dressed, now, in the drab green uniform of the convent maids.

"Where do you want this, Madre?"

"Bring it over here to my desk," Juana said, watching the girl gracefully manipulate the heavy tray. "What dexterity you have, Concepción."

"What does dexterity mean, Madre?"

"It means that despite the awkwardness of that tray, you carry yourself with confidence."

"My mother taught me. I used to carry trays heavier than this in the *pulquería*."

"What else did your mother teach you?"

"How to use a machete to get rid of drunks."

"Good skill," said Juana. She placed some plantain slices on the saucer of her teacup and a dollop of cream on top. "Here, try these. Jane's the best cook in all of Mexico, even if she is a big grouch."

Concepción took the plate, looking around the room for a place to sit. All of the chairs were piled with books. Juana watched her out of the corner of her eye as she poured her tea. Still holding her plate, the girl ex-

amined the rows of bookshelves, the mismatched tables strewn with papers and opened volumes. She dipped a plantain slice into the cream, popped
it in her mouth, and licked her fingers.

"Are all of these books yours, Madre?"

"Not all of them. Some are borrowed, some are still being paid off."

"How many are they? Hundreds?"

"A thousand, maybe two."

"You've read all these?"

"That's what books are for, Concepción. Don't you like to read?"

The girl shrugged, but did not turn to face her, transfixed now by the
view of the snowy crests of the volcanoes rising out of the fog on the southeastern horizon of the valley.

"What happened to your pretty clothes? That's a maid's uniform you're
wearing. If you pass your dictation test you won't have to be a maid and
you can go back to wearing your own colorful clothes. Would you like that?"

"I think the Mother Superior was going to burn them," said the girl,
eating another piece of plantain as she bent over the chessboard laid out
on the small table under the windows. "She's afraid I brought lice from the
pulquería."

Juana shook her head. "Poor Madre Catalina," she said, "she's so ignorant. There's nothing worse, Concepción, than ignorance."

The girl turned to face her. "My mother says the worse thing is humiliation."

Juana raised her eyebrows but kept her response to herself: that's one
of our vows, obedience is another word for humiliation. She sipped the
black tea, enjoying the girl's presence.

"Does your mother know how to read?"

Now the girl was squatting in front of the bookcases, perusing the ti-
tles on the bottom shelves, her empty saucer placed carelessly on a book.
"Of course she does, Madre. But she's bad at numbers. That's why she made
Don Federico pay for my schooling, so I could keep the accounts for her."

Juana glanced at the clock. "Take that plate off that book, Concepción.
I hope you haven't ruined the cover."

"Sorry, Madre." The girl wiped the book with the hem of her apron,
then brought the saucer back to the tray. Outside, the rain had started.

"We have a chessboard in the pulquería. The students like to play sometimes. Can you teach me how to play, Madre?"

"Depends on how well you do on this dictation test. Are you ready to get to work? Time is literally slipping through the glass." She tapped the hourglass on her desk.

Concepción shrugged, casting her gaze down to the tiles of the floor. "I'm not really that good at writing, Madre," she mumbled. "I'm better at numbers."

"We'll see. You may just end up being Jane's assistant instead of mine."

"I wouldn't mind helping Jane. I know how to work in the kitchen."

"Yes, well, let's see if we can't put your schooling to use first. I hate to see an education go to waste." She turned the hourglass then got up from her desk and went to clear a space on one of the tables. She had placed quills and inkwells all over the room so that she would not have to interrupt any sudden trains of thought searching for a pen. She took a sheet of used parchment from its stack and placed it on the table. "Drag that stool over here, Concepción."

The girl did as she was told, knocking into the table as she sat down.

"First thing to remember is that we always use both sides of the paper before we throw it out. It's too expensive to only use one side. This stack in the middle is the high-quality parchment. We only use that on final copies of special documents. For all other documents—I hope you're paying attention, Concepción, I don't like to repeat myself—for all other documents we use the paper in this third stack for final copies. I keep the bottles of ink on the top shelf of my desk. The knife for sharpening the pens is over there in my penholder. I never use that knife for trimming the wicks on the lamps, otherwise the pens get greasy and ruin the parchment. Let Jane take care of the wicks. Are you ready to begin? Why aren't you holding the pen?"

The girl took the pen from its slim holder and dipped it into the inkwell. A drop of ink soaked into the top of the paper as she brought her hand down.

"Don't wipe it, it'll just get worse," said Juana, annoyed already. "You'll have to learn to gauge how much ink to take. Now, here goes the first line. I'm going to dictate a verse, Concepción. Write it down exactly as I say it, including the punctuation. 'May they die with you,' comma, 'Laura,' comma, 'for you died,' comma." She spoke slowly, enunciating each word. "New line, Concepción, 'these affections that long for you in vain,' comma, again new line, 'these eyes that you deprive,' comma, last line of the stanza, 'of the lovely light you once ordained,' period."

"You once what, Madre?"

"Ordained, Concepción. 'lovely light you once ordained.' Let me see."

Though not illegible, the handwriting was very awkward and inconsistent.

May they dye with you Lara for you dyed,
these afecshons that long for you in vane,
these eyes that you depribe
of the lobly light you onece orrdaned.

"Of the twenty-nine words I dictated, Concepción, you misspelled eight of them. Eight of twenty-nine is what percentage, since you're so good at numbers?"

"About one-third, Madre."

"That's right. Thirty percent of this document is incorrect, not to mention the fact that it took me ten minutes to dictate one stanza and that the handwriting is horrible."

The girl hung her head. "I told you, Madre."

She had left the pen inside the inkwell and Juana could see the ink soaking up into the stem of the quill. Juana pressed her fingertips to her temples and told herself to be patient, to remember the girl's age and background. She could not treat Concepción the way she treated her students. Of course! That was the solution! She picked up the bell on her desk and rang for Jane.

"I don't have time to give you penmanship and orthography classes, Concepción, but I *can* ask Sor Beatriz if she'll allow one of her novices to teach you. It should take no more than a couple of months to get your writing into shape. Take the pen out of the inkwell, please."

"Yes, Madre."

Juana rang the bell again. "Where is that Jane? Maybe you'll have to ask Sor Beatriz yourself. It'll do you good to go out and explore the rest of the convent. Just ask anybody you see how to get to the novice's wing. What's the matter?"

The girl looked like she was about to cry. "I miss my mother," she said, chin trembling.

"Yes, well, that happens, Concepción. We all carry around somebody that we miss. Now go on, go look for Sor Beatriz. Tell her to come talk to me. And try to forget about your mother for now. I don't know what the arrangement is, but I doubt Madre Catalina will let her visit you very often."

"Can't I visit her? How am I supposed to keep her accounts?"

"I really don't know, Concepción. You'll have to ask Madre Catalina, but don't do it today if you know what's good for you. Go on. You'll be fine. Come back here after vespers."

Juana refilled her teacup and went over by the window to gaze at Popocateptl and Ixtaccihuatl in the rain. As a girl she had thought of those volcanoes as her guardian angels, watching over her grandfather's hacienda. On the days when her sisters refused to take her to school with them, she would sneak a book from her grandfather's library, go to her favorite hammock, and read aloud to the volcanoes, who always listened. When she had had to leave Panoayán the volcanoes reminded her of her grandfather, buried in their shadow in the cemetery of the Sacred Hill. Now the volcanoes made her think only of the way to Vera Cruz where la Marquesa had met her death.

She turned to the altar she had made on top of one of her bookcases.

"Concepción. Before you leave—"

She stopped the girl just as she was slipping out the door. "Si, Madre."

"I have a piece of velvet I want you to embroider for me, for my altar, here. And the novices make a beautiful silk thread. You seem to be good at flowers. Can you do calla lilies, do you think?"

"She won't listen to us, Father. And Mother Superior is hopelessly indulgent with her as well. All of the Sisters are incensed."

"All of them, Sor Melchora?"

"All of the ones who confide in me, yes, Father. She's become the bane of our existence."

"She is also the convent's boon, don't you think. Look at all the patronage your Order has received since she's been here, thanks to their Majesties."

"Well, her protectors have left, Father, and we see no reason for Juana's privileges to continue."

"Have you discussed this with the Archbishop?"

"How can we? Fray Payo protects her."

"Precisely. And am I supposed to oppose the Archbishop?"

"You are her father confessor, Padre Miranda. Can you not make her see what enemies she is making of all of us?"

"I thought you were beyond such passions, Sor Melchora."

"I confess, Father, that I have not yet achieved perfection, that my stomach roils with anger when I see how crowded Mother Catalina and Mother Paula live while Her Highness lives in one of the largest cells of the convent."

"That was Mother Paula's prerogative, Sister, to give up her cell. And from what I have heard, you don't exactly live in a shanty."

"At least I didn't displace anybody, Father, and I earned that cell through my own diligence."

"I am not interested in the living arrangements of San Jerónimo, Sister."

"And what of that diary that she keeps, then? Surely that must concern you. She isn't working on the history of Saint Jerome, nor on any of the tasks commissioned by the Cabildo. She's writing in a diary. Surely *that* deserves your remonstrance, Father."

"How do you know what she's writing, Sor Melchora? Has she shown it to you?"

"Her own relatives, those so-called cousins of hers, showed me samples of what she writes. I tell you, Father, we're harboring a demon in the House of Saint Jerome."

"Sor Melchora. You will never utter those words again. As penance for your evil-mongering tongue, you will be silent for a week."

"But, Father . . ."

"Starting now."

Padre Antonio heard her muttering under her breath as she left the confessional on the other side of the wall. That Juana, he thought, shaking his head. She draws enemies like a lodestone. He closed his eyes and waited for the next sinner to enter the confessional, massaging the pain in his knuckles. First the right hand, then the left, he rubbed each gnarled bone, silently thanking God for this affliction that kept him from forgetting that Christ had died for his sins.

Someone cleared her throat on the other side of the screen. He waited for the usual preamble.

"Father Miranda?" The voice sounded young.

"Yes, have you come to make a confession?"

"Not exactly, Father."

"Then what do you want, and who are you?"

"I am not a *profesa*, Father, only a boarder."

He felt his jaws grinding. "Father Nazario speaks to boarders. I do not. You're not even supposed to be in there."

"Yes, Father, I know, but what I have to say is for Your Reverence's ears only."

He squinted to see if he could make anything out of the speaker's face through the lattice of the screen, but his eyesight was getting cloudier by the day and he could distinguish nothing.

"Proceed, then, and be quick about it. There are others waiting to take their turn."

"It's about Sor Juana, Father."

He shook his head. Two complaints about Juana in one day. Surely Melchora was behind this.

"Which one? De la Cruz or de San Antonio? They are both my daughters in religion."

"De la Cruz, Father."

"Well?"

"She does not observe the rules of society, Father. She treats her slaves and servants as though they were equal to people of quality—"

He rolled his eyes in the dark. Now he knew who it was.

"—and also she writes verses to someone who is dead, Father."

His eyes blinked rapidly. "What manner of verses?"

"Love verses, Father."

"Have you read them?"

"With my own eyes, Father."

"To whom are these verses dedicated? To a man?"

"No, Father, to a woman. La Marquesa de Mancera, I believe."

"La Marquesa was like a mother to Juana. She is still in mourning, you know."

"I do not think one would write such verses about one's mother, Father."

"If she is writing verses about la Marquesa, they are requiems, no doubt commissioned by the Viceroy. Requiems are adulatory in nature. I see nothing wrong with Sor Juana's actions, nor do I see it as any of my concern how she treats her slaves and servants. Now if you will please do me the favor—"

"Would you like to hear one, Father? I copied it before she mailed it to the Viceroy."

He heard the crackling of parchment. The child was persistent.

He let out an audible sigh. "Proceed, then."

> "'In love with her beauty the Heavens
>   stole Laura to their heights,
>   for it was indecent that the purity of her light

should illumine these miserable valleys;
'or because mortal beings, fooled
by the lovely architecture of her body,
in awe of such beauty, failed
to judge themselves fortunate.
　　'She was born where the red veil
of the East moves toward the birth of the ruddy star,
and she died where with ardent passion,
　　'the sea gives sepulcher to her light:
in divine flight she rotated
like the sun around the earth.'"

God have mercy, thought Padre Antonio, feeling himself blush in the dark.

"Father? Did you hear it?"

"I heard it, I heard it. It's a requiem, I told you."

"Perhaps it is, Father, but not to a mother. 'Lovely architecture of her body'? 'Ardent passion'?"

"Yes, yes, no need to repeat it."

He heard the parchment crackling again.

"Let me have it," he said. "Fold it up and slip it through the lattice."

She did as he ordered. He took the folded parchment and stuffed it into his satchel. "Are you finished?" he asked.

"I just thought you should know, Father."

"You did the right thing. Now go, and may God forgive you."

"Forgive me? For what, Father?"

"For bearing false witness against your own sister. Out of my sight. Never come to me again. And tell those who are waiting to come back next week. I've no mind to hear more confessions today."

He sat in the confessional until the blood ceased to pound in his temples. He had no idea what to do about Juana, how to correct that strange passion of hers for verses and dramas. And it would do no good to take this requiem to the Archbishop. While he protected her, Padre Antonio's hands were tied. He left the church by the door that led to the street, not waiting for the meal that Mother Superior always served him in the antechoir after confession. He was in no mood to indulge in the pastry-covered hypocrisies of a nunnery.

Chapter 11

5 February 1675

(Feast Day of Saint Agatha)

I wonder what I've gotten myself into. Concepción is more of a problem than I thought. The girl herself is no trouble, and is very helpful to have around when I need errands run to the Cabildo or the bookshop. She's already alphabetized and categorized my library, but she's still working on her penmanship with Sister Felipa, so she's not much good as an amanuensis yet.

19 March

Feast of Saint Joseph. We were at Mass when the earthquake hit. This is the worst we have experienced in several years. The more exaggerated of my sisters vouch that the earth trembled for as long as it took to pray three Credos, but in truth, it was only a moment, though the violent shake sent immediate cracks down the walls of the choir and snapped off the hands of some of our statues. A cry went up among the followers of the Sacred Heart and Saint Rita as they watched the plaster hands of their saints crash into the flagstones. And now Father Nazario has declared this a day of fasting and atonement, which means nothing but bread and water for the rest of the day. Too bad I didn't eat my breakfast before Mass. Have been so hungry lately. Must be all of this increased tension since Concepción arrived. Inés has not stopped complaining that she and her sister have to share their room with my servant. They've even written their father, as if Don Diego could force his will on me. Enough that he had me dispatched from Panoayán, that he's burdened me with fostering his two spoiled whelps, that he abandoned my mother. If he has anything to say about this arrangement with Concepción I'm going to suggest that he take his daughters out of my cell as soon as possible. I don't care what my mother thinks or says. The last time she visited all she could talk about was "little Diego," who is now twenty years old and a militia man in Puebla. "Little Diego" who clung to her bosom while my beloved uncle Mata "escorted" me away from Panoayán and brought me to Mexico. "Little Diego," the only male of my mother's six children and for that her redemption and only reason for living. I have the taste of quince in my mouth, and nothing but tepid water with which to wash it down.

3 April

Sister Felipa is working wonders with Concepción's instruction. Not only is she helping perfect her penmanship and honing the girl's reading skills, but she's even been teaching her Latin. Would that I at Concepción's age had had more of a companion than an inkwell, more of a teacher than a mute book. How generous of Sister Felipa to have offered her time to work with Concepción, although I believe she has an ulterior motive. I suspect she's extremely lonely. The poor woman's been here over a year already and still hasn't made a single friend among the novices, nor has she been allowed to take her vows. The convent can be such a cruel place at times. I hear rumors buzzing about that Sister Felipa's swarthy features and the wealth she donated to the convent are attributed to a Jewish ancestry. Daniela, the treasurer, confided to me that Sister Felipa's dowry exceeded the required three thousand pesos twelvefold times. They say she studied music at the convent of Coeli Regina as a girl, but was subsequently removed when her family suffered a terrible tragedy.

21 April

First anniversary of la Marquesa's death. I can't believe that an entire year has passed already, that Laura's body is turning to bones in the salty earth of Tepeaca. Finished the third requiem and sent it off to the Marquis. I don't think I'll show it to Don Carlos. Mustn't make my feelings so public, and I couldn't bare any criticism anyway. He wouldn't enjoy my reference to Ptolemy, nemesis of Copernicus.

2 August

It's been more than three months since I've written. Writing the last requiem plunged me back into that gloomy numbness where everything ceases to interest me, where all I want to do is look out the window and remember her face, her voice, the way she used to wink at me when we were winning at dominoes. Mother Catalina allows me to indulge in my despair, but the other sisters, Melchora, especially, complain at Friday chapter that I do nothing for the convent. I don't work in the sewing room or the gardens or the kitchen, she says. I spend all day in my cell, reading and writing who knows what, and still I haven't produced a finished version of my history of the Order of Saint Jerome in New Spain. After six years, she asks the congregation, shouldn't I have something to show for the extra privileges I've enjoyed?

17 September

Sister Felipa tells me that my "cousins" have been talking about me behind my back. They were overheard yesterday in the schoolroom discussing my illegitimacy. Indeed, I am registered as a daughter of the Church since the honorable Don Pedro de Asbaje who claimed both my mother's heart and her innocence failed to own up to his promise and never returned from the other side of the ocean.

But what could anyone have expected, anyway, of a wandering gambler such as Don Pedro Manuel de Asbaje whose only reason for marrying my mother, so my aunt Mary used to say, was to absolve my grandfather's debt? Seems the only time my grandfather lost a chess game was to Don Pedro, years before Josefa, María, and I were born. Our family's fate sealed by a chess game.

As soon as she is more advanced in her studies, I will begin teaching Concepción how to play chess. Andrea is not very good at it, and Mariana and Beatriz just want to gossip over the board about the new novices. Madre Catalina calls it a "gentleman's game," and never bothered to learn it. And so I am reduced to playing with my grandfather's ghost if I want a good challenge. I remember how every afternoon gentlemen would ride in from the neighboring haciendas to play a game with him, and I would sit on a little stool at Abuelo's knees, absorbed by the strategy of the jumping knights and the all-powerful queens who could move in any direction they pleased. Feast of Saint Hildegard of Bingen today. One of my favorite holy rebels.

12 November

My twenty-seventh birthday. My mother and Josefa and María's eldest girl, Isabelilla, whom Josefa is fostering, came to visit, joined later by Fray Payo and Don Carlos. Fray Payo brought me a kilo of that thick Turkish coffee that helps me stay awake long past curfew. Don Carlos gave me his old telescope; he wants to train me, he says, in astronomical mathematics.

My mother and sister just shook their heads. "No wonder she's so happy here," commented my mother. "Look at how she's indulged."

Madre Catalina permitted all of us to sit in the same room together, without the grille between us, and Jane prepared a delicious flan to accompany our hot chocolate, and I asked Concepción to read some verses for us out of *The Aeneid*. The best gift was when my mother announced that the son of a friend of Don Diego's who is finishing his licentiate at the university has asked for Inés's hand. They will marry as soon as he completes his degree. My faith in the miracles of Saint Jude has been restored.

When the bell rang for vespers, my mother, Josefa, and Fray Payo took turns at hugging me. How odd to feel a man's arms about me. I was so tense my spine started to ache. Even my ears felt flushed under the veil. Then Josefa held me so tightly I couldn't breathe for a moment. I had to push her away. The last person to have held me that close was la Marquesa. Thank God that Don Carlos simply shook my hand. Belilla wanted to hold my hand all the way to the gate, and I noticed that Concepción looked jealous. They're only two years apart, but Concepción seems so much older while Belilla has an innocence about her that reminds me of myself before I was taken from Panoayán.

Just before they left, Belilla kissed my cheek and whispered through my veil: "I want to be just like you, Tía." Strange child. If only she knew what she was saying.

Navidad

Fell asleep during Misa de Gallo last night. Luckily it was too dark in the choir for Agustina or the twins, María and Marcela de San Onofre—all sycophants of Melchora's—to notice; Andrea sitting beside me is much too prudent to report such an infraction. It was midnight and exhaustion hung off me like a cobweb. For three weeks I've been preparing the boarders for the skit they perform on Nochebuena for their relatives and other guests of the convent: three weeks of supervising rehearsals during *recreo*, mending costumes with Lucía, quibbling with Daniela about the cost of candles for lighting up the stage, listening to the girls' perpetual chatter.

During the performance I kept remembering that just two years ago la Marquesa sat among the guests in the patio, wearing a lavender dress with black velvet sleeves slashed from shoulder to elbow, a black lace mantilla draped over her flaxen locks. I remembered the *amapola* scent of her perfume, the alabaster coolness of her hands, the frescoes of her eyes. Needless to say I couldn't concentrate on the play; I barely managed not to weep. I begged Madre Catalina to excuse me from our communal dinner in the refectory, came to my cell, tried to read, but the melancholia took over. I could not, of course, expect to be excused from Midnight Mass, but during the homily, the darkness, the exhaustion and melancholia, the smell of wax and frankincense, the drone of Father Nazario's voice lulled me to sleep.

When I awoke everyone in the choir and down in the church was on their feet, chanting the Paternoster, and one of the twins was standing beside me, watching me with those unsettling colorless eyes of hers and writing my name down in her *vigilanta*'s notebook. I'm expecting Melchora's visit any minute, but I'm sure she'll do more than reproach me or add another mark to my name. Madre Catalina pays no attention to her, but I know well how ruthless Melchora's long tongue can be.

20 February 1676
(Feast Day of Saint Sebastian)

Just two months into the new year, and already I am tired of all the intrigues. So tired I don't feel like writing any of it down. Waste of good ink and paper. Suffice it to say that there are more rumors and *cábulas* invented about me than arrows piercing Saint Sebastian's flesh. Padre Antonio came to confess me today. I told him of my feelings toward my half-sisters and of my anger toward my mother for having burdened me with their care (seems she is always giving others the responsibility of looking after her children). I confessed that the girl I was training as my assistant (better not to name her in his presence) was now sleeping in my quarters, though I assured him that a thick Turkish carpet separates my dormitory from my workroom, where she sleeps now that the girls have banished her from their room. Padre Antonio asked me if I continued to mourn for la Marquesa and I told him that I had thought about her during Nochebuena but that I did not grieve for her as I did. I did not tell him about the three requiems I sent the Marquis, delivered secretly to the palace mails by Concepción. As penitence for falling asleep during Midnight Mass (Melchora told him, of course) he wants me to mortify myself every night for a week. He knows how I abhor the use of the whip, the sound of it most of all. How will I ever keep Concepción from hearing what I'm doing? What a ridiculous life this can be.

Ash Wednesday

Why do I let things like this happen to me? All I wanted was to investigate the progress Concepción is making in her Latin; she's still confusing her cases, and I wanted to see if maybe Felipa were making some fundamental error in teaching the girl. So I went down to the parlor during their lessons earlier and pretended to be inspecting Jane's work in the kitchen, when I was really eavesdropping on the lesson taking place at the dining table. Occasionally I would glance over to see what Concepción was doing, if she was paying attention to Felipa or daydreaming as usual, and one of those times I noticed the casual familiarity with which Felipa placed her arm around Concepción's shoulder, in a gesture of praise or encouragement.

I tried to talk myself out of approaching the table, knowing that I would interfere with the lesson, but I went to the table, nonetheless, and stood behind them. Of course, both of them were distracted. Felipa removed her arm from Concepción's shoulder, and Concepción kept looking over at me as if expecting me to make a comment.

"Ignore me," I said. "Pay attention to your work."

Felipa smiled nervously. "She's doing very well, actually, aren't you, Concepción? It's the grammar that she's still having some difficulty with, but she's got an excellent ear for dictation, and see—" Felipa held up a sheet of words, a spelling lesson, in both hands. "Her penmanship is quite refined and there are only three mistakes in her orthography."

Standing behind her chair, I noticed that the deep olive of Felipa's skin seemed darker against the cream-colored parchment. I took note of the pink, well-scrubbed ovals of her nails, the long, curled fingers, the pronounced curve of her thumbs, the knuckles well defined and sharp bones at the wrist brushed with dark hairs. I imagined the garnet ring that Don Fabio gave me so long ago on one of those fingers, the stone cut large and faceted in squares, the gold setting picking up the olive tones in her skin, and then I noticed that the ashes on Felipa's forehead, which we had all gotten at morning Mass, had gathered in the crease between her brows, and before I could stop myself I brushed the ashes off with the tips of my fingers. I felt such a contraction between my legs. I don't know what she felt, but I'm afraid now that I've exposed myself somehow.

"Yes, it's very good," I said, regaining my composure.

"We're making progress," she repeated.

"But not in grammar."

"No, but then you can probably teach her that as you go along."

"Are you surrendering, Sister?" Because I was standing and she sitting, I had her at a disadvantage. She could do nothing but look up at me.

"Not as long as you continue to need me, Sor Juana."

There was something in the way she said it that made me look away. "Your penmanship is nearly as fine as your needlework," I said to Concepción.

"Thank you, Madre."

"I'm pleased that you're satisfied, Sor Juana," said Felipa, and I felt another contraction at the thought of what would satisfy me.

"Perhaps you would like to stay for dinner with us. I know Concepción would enjoy that, and I believe Jane's stew is going to be delicious. She found some excellent chorizos at the market."

"Oh, yes, please stay," said Concepción, latching on to Felipa's arm.

"I doubt Sor Beatriz will give her permission," Felipa responded, rather stiffly.

"Of course not," I said, feeling flustered by my silly invitation. "I forget that you haven't taken your permanent vows yet. Excuse me, then, I need to return to my books."

You have elegant hands, I wanted to say, but Concepción was listening and Jane was in the kitchen. Now I sit here transcribing this confession and feel (it embarrasses me even to write it down), I feel as though I've been *intimate* with Felipa just because I grazed her skin, admired her hands, stood close enough to smell the starch in her veil. May God and la Marquesa forgive me for this weakness.

"Really, Antonio, I don't see what the problem is. Juana is unique among women. You can't expect her to be one of the flock."

"I am well aware of her uniqueness, Fray Payo. But her sisters in religion dislike this quality, and cannot understand why Your Ilustrísima continues to award her the privileges of one not consecrated to Christ. They bring me eternal complaints—"

"Bah." Fray Payo scowled, waving his hand as if to dismiss him. "Those women are a pack of envious bitches. If they're as religious as they pretend they should be flagellating themselves rather than complaining."

"It's those passionate verses she writes, Ilustrísima. Her own sisters copy them and take them to her enemies."

"Those girls should be removed immediately. Does Juana know that she is being betrayed?"

"They'll be leaving soon, Ilustrísima. One of them is getting married, I hear, the dangerous one."

"Have you told Juana?"

"I thought it best not to, Your Eminence. She would create such a scandal."

"So what do you suggest, Antonio. How do we quell these bitches?"

"Give Juana something to do, Your Grace, a commission from the Church Council, something religious to work on to take her mind off of poetry."

"That will take care of one problem, but I'm very concerned about those snakes in the grass. You must crush them, Antonio. I want them gone."

"I will write to the mother, myself, Ilustrísima, and ask her to take her daughters back."

"Absolutely not. Find out who she's marrying and tell him to get on with it. What that girl needs is a firm hand."

"That is often what I think of our Juana, Your Grace. I wonder if I should have married her to a man rather than to Christ. I think she needs more direct supervision."

"Antonio, don't play the simpleton. You know perfectly well Juana is not the marrying kind. Her kind is beyond the laws that men make for women. She's another Catalina de Erauso, I daresay."

Padre Antonio balked at the Archbishop's allusion to the infamous Basque nun who escaped her convent and deceived the world in her lieutenant's disguise: *monja alferez*, they called her.

25 March

As if to honor the Feast of the Annunciation of Mary today, I received a commission from the Church Council this morning. I am to prepare the *villancicos* for both the Feast of the Assumption and the Feast of the Immaculate Conception this year to be sung in the Cathedral. Fray Payo has convinced the Council that I deserve at least a modest honorarium for my trouble, and they've agreed to offer me 130 pesos for both pieces. I do need the money. My account at the bookseller's is shamefully past due.

30 March

I have just received a note from my mother in which she informs me that she and "little Diego" are coming to Mexico on Palm Sunday to pick up *both* girls and take them home. Inés's future husband wants to get married in the summer and she must get home to prepare her trousseau. Antonia, of course, must go everywhere with her sister, and so both of them will be out of my life at the end of Lent. Diegito, my mother writes, is most anxious to see his famous sister again. What a bother. But still, I have to be grateful. They're leaving. I've been awaiting this day for four years. Must light a candle to Saint Jude in gratitude for granting this difficult favor.

Palm Sunday

Antonia and Inés are waiting for me down in the parlor. Our mother has arrived, finally. They've been pacing downstairs ever since lunch. I can hear the swish of their petticoats, their shoes clicking impatiently against the tiles. Jane and Concepción were ordered to carry their trunks to the *portería*. As much as I want to see them gone, I relish making them wait. I told them it would not look well if they preceded me to the *locutorio*.

later

They're gone, at last, and I feel oddly empty. I always feel empty after one of my mother's visits. "Little" Diego stands over two meters tall now, and looks, I must admit, very impressive in his military uniform. He's a candid young fellow with kind eyes and a delicate grace about him, despite his size. He hugged me as though he had known me all his life, called me Juanilla, told funny stories of life in the militia, and ate the entire plate of coconut tarts that Jane made for the occasion. Josefa and Isabelilla came along, too. Poor Josefa, she looks even older than Mamá. She's had two miscarriages in the last year, and even though she's got four children already, her husband wants her to produce more. Belilla is a great help to her, she says, but now she's worried that Belilla wants to profess at San Jerónimo when she's older. Belilla sat beside me the entire time and played with the rosary beads of my habit and traced the image on the escutcheon with her finger and asked if my head itched under the veil.

After they had gone, I stopped by the priory to ask Madre Catalina not to send me any more boarders for the time being since I found them to be too intrusive, which had a pernicious effect on my state of mind, but she was vexed by something having to do with Melchora and Rafaela, and in a rank humor, so I dared not overstay my visit.

"It would be prudent for Felipa not to come to your cell so much until this is all over, Juana," she said as I was leaving. I have no idea what she meant, but I have noticed that Felipa has been unusually morose. No time to dwell on this, now. Must get back to the *tocotín* I'm writing in Nahuatl (with the help of Don Carlos, naturally) to balance out the Latin section in the First Nocturne of the *villancico*. What a difficult language Nahuatl is; Don Carlos says I remind him of Doña Marina, whom the Indians called Malintzin at the time of the Conquest, who spoke two native tongues as well as Castellano.

"She was a slave and a diplomat at the same time, Juana, like you."

Sometimes, he knows me too well.

Good Friday

Couldn't work. Spent the whole day either chanting at choir or walking in circles around the cloister, repeating the Sorrowful Mysteries until my throat parched. Old Sor Paula and those of our sisters who are overly devout lashed themselves as we circled. Others walked on their knees. Andrea carried the black crucifix from the chapter room, not as heavy as the bronze one in the choir, but heavy enough to bend her back. Those are the kinds of promises that Andrea makes to the incarnate Heart of Jesus. What a sight we must be for someone like Concepción, going round and round the gallery in our blood-streaked habits while the outside world prepares its bright costumes and gay floats for Sunday's *mascarada*.

22 April

Yesterday was the second anniversary of la Marquesa's death!

In all of this scandal around Sister Felipa, I have not paid much attention to the calendar. Please forgive me, Señora, for my negligence. Madre Catalina has had all of us looking for Sister Felipa for three days. The rumor is she's escaped from the convent. No one can find her. Beatriz says that all of her things are gone. Sor Clara, the gatekeeper, swears by the foreskin of Christ that Felipa did not leave by the convent's gate. Even the gendarmes who patrol the streets at night have been questioned, to no avail. It's possible, says Madre Catalina, that Felipa bribed them to keep their mouths shut. Melchora and Agustina are disappointed; they were so looking forward to tearing the girl's reputation to shreds at the next chapter meeting. They say they've collected some information that corroborates all of their suspicions.

"But why would she leave us? The girl has no family, nowhere to go."

"It's because she's a *judaizante*, Mother, and she knew we were onto her."

"That must be why she left Regina Coeli, no doubt."

"We have no proof of that, Sor Melchora."

"Why would anybody want to condemn the voicebox of the Holy Spirit? When she sang I could hear the very filaments of our Lord's breath woven into the fiber of ecstasy caressing my spirit."

"With your permission, Mother Paula, but the only thing more blasphemous than allowing a Jew to sing *alabanzas* to God is to defecate on the Eucharist."

"Sor Agustina! I expect you to scrub your tongue with a floor brush for that."

"As the saying goes, Mother, something good always comes of something bad. We may have housed an infidel, but at least her dowry has stayed with us."

These are the voices of my good sisters in religion!

I suppose there will be no more special tutoring for Concepción. Alas, I will now inherit the girl's bad Latin, but at least I can get her to start copying the verses I've completed for the Assumption.

29 APRIL 1676, A.D.

MOST ESTEEMED MADRE CATALINA,

I write you a sealed letter in the hope that my seal will deter certain persons in the House of San Jerónimo from intercepting this missive. The situation with Sister Felipa is of some concern to me, as you know. She was found last week, hiding in one of the *taquesquales* in the market, starved and terrified as a wild cat, and now the Tribunal has gotten involved. It would surprise me little if the unfortunate novice were to be dragged out to the Alameda and made the protagonist of an *auto de fe*. You know how the Tribunal enjoys setting examples. If, indeed, she is found to be a *conversa*, the Tribunal would have to be more tolerant. But if, in fact, Melchora's charge is proven and her family is declared to have been practicing *judaizantes*, I'm afraid there will be little I can do to change her fate. At the very least, she will get a "limpieza de sangre," which could prove fatal for one in her condition.

The documentation in the girl's favor is impressive, but we also have irrefutable evidence to support the claim that Felipa's family was implicated in moneylending. Some of the family's servants attest that candlelight rituals were held in a storage room every Friday after sunset. At these rituals, we are told, the grandfather read out of the Holy Bible, and the family alternated between very loud prayers to the Holy Trinity and very quiet prayers in a language that nobody could understand. Indeed, we are in possession of the family's Bible and it is quite clear that the latter part, the New Testament, was never touched; only the Old Testament seems to have been read and even studied. Sections have been underlined and the word "Adunai" appears throughout the margins. A person of quality has testified that every Pentecost, the family served bilious herbs and a flat bread baked without yeast which the family called "pan de galleta." Quite fortunately, the abbot of Saint Francis has written an excellent letter in favor of Sister Felipa. It was he, in fact, who suggested that she join the Hieronymites after the tragedy, as well as the one who encouraged her to call the family's death the result of an epidemic, when in truth the father and brothers were crucified in their own olive grove, their foreheads branded with a Hebrew symbol. The mother took her own life as a result. Poor woman. The abbot's letter and your own eloquent petition are our two strongest documents. We shall see what the Tribunal decides when it meets next week. Until then, I remain your friend and admirer,

> Fray Payo Enríquez de Ribera,
> Archbishop and Viceroy of México

1 June

Have just returned from Friday chapter and am so shocked by the news that I can barely form these letters on the page. Madre Catalina reported that Felipa was found dead in the Tribunal's dungeon this morning. There was a white crust on her tongue and human feces all over her face. The other prisoners said she was licking the floor of the jail cell as a penitence. The others voted not to observe any mourning for her as she was most probably a *judaizante*. What evil and cruelty lurk in this place.

16 June

Still can't shake the melancholy caused by Felipa's tragedy. How I regret not having paid more attention to her. Concepción went home to her mother for a week, and I was afraid she wouldn't come back. She's the only one who keeps me sane. Odd how I've grown to depend on her company. Perhaps it is that she grew up in that tavern and learned to deal fearlessly with the likes of men—and drunks, at that—which makes her seem so much older than her years.

8 August
Finally finished the *villancicos*, just a week before the Feast of the Assumption, and Concepción has taken them to the Cabildo. There's barely enough time to get the verses printed, but at least Fray Payo's faith in me has been restored. He was worried, he said, that I would let down the Council.

25 August
I am haunted by a vision of myself in a remote place, surrounded on the inside by all the books I have ever wanted, and on the outside encircled by fog. The best place of all would be a castle someplace far and very foreign to me, alone with my studies and my writing. Instead I find myself cloistered in this convent, connected to every political web spun by my good sisters, embroiled in little arguments that I must mediate or risk losing the support of Madre Catalina, and getting more resentful by the day that everything, literally, everything gets in the way of my writing.

5 September
It's a new election year and Andrea has nominated me for treasurer. I declined. I do not have the time or the desire or the inclination and especially not the wiles necessary to become part of the executive body of this convent. Elections aren't until October, but the campaigns, the afternoon visits, the Good Samaritan offers and sudden interest in one's health have already begun. As if I didn't have enough interruptions.

30 September
Day of Saint Jerome. The cloister is ablaze with candles and music. At times I forget where I am.

12 October
We're doomed. Melchora has beaten Madre Catalina by eight votes. Andrea is the only one of our side who got elected, and all she gets to do is keep the accounts. I suppose that's better than letting Melchora's side run the money. Who knows what dire straits they'd plunge us into in their false

piety. If my life here were a position I could leave, I would start looking for a new post immediately.

14 *October*

The ceremonies are over, the new administration is installed, and the first ruling has been made against me. Mother Melchora has ordered that all of my private writing privileges be suspended immediately, "for the good of my soul." Rafaela and the twins came to my cell to confiscate all of my writing instruments, not just the quills, but the inkwells and sandcasters as well, and all of the paper that I just finished paying for. I will not even be allowed to write letters. Thank God I had the foresight to build this hidden compartment into my desk, else they would have taken Pandora's Box. Madre Catalina tells me to write Fray Payo about this. "Establish your alliances immediately, Juana. The jackals will not wait to sink their teeth into your jugular. You must be equally ruthless, my dear, but do it with a white glove."

"I'm afraid I don't have your talent for subtlety, Mother," I said.

"As long as the Archbishop protects you, Juana, you've no need of subtleties," she said.

For the first time in the two years it has been that she gave her to me, Madre Catalina asked about Concepción. "How is that *castiza* working out for you, Juana? I hear she's quite smart."

"From such wood such a thorn, Mother," I said.

She laughed. "Juana, you are the epitome of subtlety. Come, walk me to my cell."

17 OCTOBER 1676

MY DEAR FRAY PAYO,

It is with extreme regret that I must inform you of my inability to complete the *villancicos* for the Feast of the Immaculate Conception which the Church Council commissioned from me in March. This is in accord with the wishes of our new Superior-elect—Mother Melchora de Jesús, under whose supervision I dictate this letter— who has ruled that for the good of my soul I must cease all activities that require the use of the pen. As I am sworn to obedience, it will not be possible for me to see this commission to its conclusion. I enclose herein the completed first suite of carols and rough drafts for the second and third suites which, alas, I did not have time to finish before the recent election, and trust you will find somebody else to complete the task. Please convey my deepest regrets to the Church Council. In service,

Sor Juana Inés de la Cruz
Monja de San Jerónimo

21 OCTOBER 1676

ESTEEMED MOTHER MELCHORA,

The resounding success of the *villancicos* in honor of the Assumption prepared by Sor Juana Inés de la Cruz has motivated the Cabildo to convey its deepest gratitude, both to Sor Juana, directly, with the enclosed honorarium, and to your humble Order, with this deed to the farmland in Chalco which a previous Superior of your house had petitioned some years back. The Council is greatly looking forward to receiving the *villancicos* in honor of the Immaculate Conception, and has authorized me to commission Sor Juana's incomparable services for the following feast days of next year: Saint Peter Nolasco, 31 January; Saint Peter the Apostle, 29 June; Christmas.

In addition, the Church Council would like to place Sor Juana in charge of the villancicos for the Feasts of Assumption and the Immaculate Conception for the next two years. She will receive a yearly sum of 360 pesos (in installments of 30 per month) in exchange for the time these commissions detract from her other conventual obligations. A royal scrivener accompanies this letter to witness the signing of the deed that will entitle your Order to the real estate in Chalco.

I remain humbly yours,
Fray Payo de Ribera,
Archbishop and Viceroy of México

23 NOVEMBER 1676

YOUR REVERENCE,

Thank you for granting the House of Saint Jerome control of that small farm in Chalco. Because we could find no one to run it for us, however, we have since sold it and the profits will be used to buy a plot of timber adjacent to the convent, where our own tenant farmers will be able to work it.

I am writing, however, for a different reason. Your protégée, Sor Juana Inés de la Cruz, whose writing privileges, as you know, were restored immediately as per Your Ilustrísima's request, is proving to be an incorrigible sinner. At our recent chapter meeting, she called me a *fool* to my face. The Sisters of Saint Jerome have asked me to write and beg for your intercession; you seem to be the only Superior to whom she will deign to show respect, as she will not even listen to her father confessor. We await Your Reverence's justice. In humility,

Madre Melchora de Jesús
Priora de San Jerónimo

27 NOVEMBER 1676

MOTHER MELCHORA,

I congratulate you on the wise use of the profits from your real estate and am looking forward, as is the Church Council, and, indeed, the entire constituency of the Metropolitan Cathedral, to Sor Juana's *villancicos* in honor of the Feast of the Immaculate Conception.

As to your complaint about Sor Juana, that she called you a fool: Prove the contrary and I will effect justice.

Sincerely,
Fray Payo de Ribera
Archbishop and Viceroy of México

Chapter 12

"Get me the syrup, Jane."

"You can't fry eggs in syrup, Madre."

"Why not?

"It don't work."

"Do you know what happens when you put a raw egg into hot syrup, Jane?"

Jane shrugged. "How should I know?"

"Well, that's what I want to find out. So get me the syrup."

Jane took the pan of melted *piloncillo* off its trivet in the brazier and brought it over to the stove, already crowded with platters and skillets and bowls.

"Stand back, Jane. This might be explosive." She chuckled, remembering the way another egg had splattered grease all over the kitchen after she had added water to the hot pan.

Juana cracked the egg in half and let it slip into the heavy sweetness of the syrup, fully prepared to jump back at the first sign of combustion. The egg separated, the yolk sinking to the bottom of the pan in a viscous halo, the white turning to lacy strips of grizzle.

"Come and look, Jane, it's safe."

Jane surveyed the kitchen in despair. It had been laboratory day, and Juana had asked Jane to gather a dozen extra eggs from the chicken coop for her experiments. The week before Juana had found a group of children spinning tops in the courtyard and had invited them all to her cell to continue playing with the toy while she studied its motion and gravity. A thought had occurred to her about how best to trace the design of the movement, and she had had Jane sprinkle flour all over the kitchen floor. When the girls set the tops to spinning on the flour, Juana noted that the faster they moved, the tighter the spirals they described in the white powder; when the tops slowed down, the spiral shape lengthened into an ellipse, and she imagined this must be the way the planets spun around the sun.

"What do you see?"

"Nothing but a waste of good eggs," said Jane, "and the last of our *piloncillo* gone to muck."

"What do you expect? We're learning about the universe here. Science is expensive, Jane."

"Are we finished, then, Madre?"

"For now." She wiped her hands on the kitchen apron that Jane had loaned her and went to the dining table to resume her notes, the bottom of her shoes sticking with each step.

"Will you be wanting your pineapple water today? I got some fresh *piñas* at the market."

"Clean up, will you? The floor's all sticky."

Jane brought the blue glass pitcher and a matching glass to the table.

"You know I can't lift the pitcher, Jane. It strains my back." Lumbago, the infirmarian had diagnosed, from sitting down all day. Would do you good to work in the fields, Juana, once in a while.

As if Juana ever had any time to waste on harvesting fruits and flowers for the convent.

Jane sloshed the pineapple-and-parsley concoction into the glass.

"Thank you, Jane." She took a deep swallow. "Delicious. Experimenting is thirsty work."

"You should try cleaning up after one of your experiments, Madre."

"And you should try minding your manners. Now leave me alone and let me concentrate."

She turned to a fresh page in her notebook and picked up her pen. From the parlor window that looked out over the courtyard came the sound of squealing girls, which she tried to ignore.

The nature of the yolk is completely different from that of the white. While a beaten yolk produces custard, the beaten whites produce meringue, and yet together they produce neither, though the omelet that is created by their mixture has the golden color and dense substance of custard and yet the fluffy texture of meringue. I must conclude that the kitchen is, indeed, a scientific laboratory and daresay that Aristotle would have benefited much from learning to cook.

Outside, the squealing continued. She got up from her chair and went to look out the window, hands rubbing her lower back down to the coccyx. Several groups of boarders were gathered around the fountain, jumping up and down in their excitement.

"What's going on out there, anyway? Why aren't those girls in school? They're noisier than Sor Clara's canaries!"

"It's lunchtime, Madre," said Jane, scrubbing at a burnt skillet with a wire brush.

"They're too loud! People are trying to work. Go out there and find out what they're so stirred up about. And tell them I said to be quiet. I can't concentrate on my bookkeeping with all that noise."

Jane wiped her hands on her apron and sauntered out of the cell. She was pouting about something again, and Juana could not be bothered with finding out what it was. She suspected it had something to do with her new rule that Concepción always accompany Jane when she went to the market. It had been reported to her by two of the refectory maids that Jane had developed a romantic attachment to some *zambaigo* blacksmith's apprentice, and it was in Juana's best interest to quell the romance before matters got out of hand. She could not have a lovesick maid running around the city or mooning and moping about the cell.

"Here comes Sor Rafaela, Madre," Jane called up from the landing on the gallery. "Looks like she's coming this way and she don't look happy."

Oh no, thought Juana, here we go again. Melchora probably sent her to see if I'm still prostrate. Juana placed her glass on the cupboard in the kitchen, removed the apron, and went to hide her notebook under a pile of books on the settee. Then she walked slowly to the entry to greet the *vicaria*. *You have to be diplomatic, Juana,* she reminded herself before opening the door.

"Buenas tardes, Sor Rafaela. Come in. May I offer you a glass of pineapple water?"

Rafaela shook her head curtly. "Mother Superior asked me to deliver this letter," she said, pulling a scroll with a cracked seal out of the wide bell of her sleeve. "It's from the Cabildo. Fray Payo has convinced the Church Council to commission *you* to design the Cathedral's triumphal arch for the new Viceroy's entrance." Rafaela's mouth wrinkled like a dry apricot. "Mother Superior said that, were it not that Fray Payo is the Archbishop, she would have declined on your behalf, knowing how behind you are with the accounts and how strained your health has been of late."

Juana read the letter for herself. "By November?" she said aloud. "But it's already Saint John's Day. I can't possibly design something of this magnitude in less than five months!"

"Shall I tell Mother Superior you have refused?"

"I can't refuse the Church Council, Rafaela. That would insult Fray Payo as well as the new Viceroy."

"Oh, you wouldn't want to insult the new Viceroy," Rafaela smirked. "Who would protect you if you did?"

Juana stared calmly at the *vicaria*, but her stomach had gone cold with anger. "Thank you for bringing the letter, Sor Rafaela," she said. "I'll have Concepción deliver my response to Fray Payo directly."

"Mother Superior hopes you will invest the 200 pesos offered as payment for the arch in the convent's real estate."

"I will use the money in the best way that I see fit, but do thank Mother Melchora for her suggestion. Is there anything else?"

"I am also supposed to inquire about the status of the accounts. Mother Superior sincerely hopes that you will not neglect them again in your enthusiasm for this new commission."

"Please thank Mother Melchora for her concern, Sister, and tell her that the accounts are now up to date, and she may examine them whenever she wishes."

"She will be relieved to hear that, I'm sure," said Rafaela.

And I'll be relieved when you get out of my sight, thought Juana, but she only bowed her head like a good nun and kept her eye on the door.

"You are so punctual with your worldly assignments, Sor Juana. Perhaps you could apply the same formality to your convent duties."

Juana did not respond. She would never give them the satisfaction of a reaction to their prodding. The *vicaria* swept out of the entry. Juana shut the door gently behind her. Pious as they appeared, her convent sisters had a streak of envy in them that not even weekly scourging could remove. Could she help it if the Church commissioned her work? If nobles and dignitaries and their ladies came to visit her in the *locutorio*? They enjoyed intelligent conversation and a good sense of humor. They liked her music and her verses and her plays. Her confections, they said, were the best of all the convents. In return for her hospitality, they brought her books, paintings, instruments—both musical and scientific—souvenirs from other lands, and other tokens of their gratitude and admiration. She did not ask for any of these things. Nor could she refuse them.

"Concepción!" she called out. "We have a new commission. Let's get to work!"

But Concepción did not answer, and for a moment she realized that she was alone in her cell: Jane and Concepción were off running their respective errands (though she could not remember having assigned a task to the girl) and there was no one requiring her attention. What a luxury, this solitude. She knew it would not last, but for now she had a new commission, the silence of an empty cell, and all her books and papers waiting for her upstairs.

She tucked the letter into her sleeve and returned to the kitchen. She had already eaten her midday meal, but all that experimenting over the stove and the excitement of this new commission made her hungry again. She took a lukewarm tortilla from the stack piled up by the stove, layered it with scrambled egg and avocado slices left over from lunch, and ate standing up. She supposed it *was* sinful to waste all those eggs when there were so many children in the city begging for alms.

Rereading the letter as she climbed the stairs to her study, she tried not to dwell on the pain in her lower back. Gabriela's massages had worked out the knots and most of the pain, but there was still a lingering throb at her coccyx that did not improve no matter what ointments Gabriela concocted.

What did it mean to design a triumphal arch for a Viceroy's solemn entrance into his new realm? What images should the arch portray? What entreaties would be necessary? The answers were elusive right now, but this she knew: she would have to work like one possessed by the nine muses to complete that commission on time. Even with Concepción's assistance, she would still be bent over her desk for five months. She would have to do something about the lumbago, get a professional *sobadora* to rub the pain from her back, or maybe just let Concepción do it. Her hands were stronger than Gabriela's.

At least now Melchora has no recourse but to remove her punishment, she thought smugly, remembering how the Mother Superior had found Juana cramped in her chair, unable to move more than her arm and her vocal chords, for she had spent all night at her desk balancing the ledgers and rereading *Antigone* to keep herself awake. As penalty for having missed Mass and the first Office, Melchora had, yet again, withdrawn Juana's writing privileges.

Midsummer was one the busiest seasons for the convent of San Jerónimo. Its flower fields supplied many of the churches in the city as well as

the palace and the parishes in the outlying districts. As if this weren't
enough, requisitions for the famous Hieronymite mantillas arrived daily,
sometimes from as far as Peru. To her chagrin, Juana had been voted treasurer in the last election, thanks to Andrea's nomination. How she dreaded
the monthly balancing of credits and debits, a job that always tempted her
into procrastination. The only good thing about it was that as an administrator she only had to teach one class rather than her usual three, and this
meant she could hoard some time for her own work. Still, it was never
enough, as she also had to attend meetings with the rest of the administrative body and sit there listening to the most vapid conversations. At the
next election, she was going to nominate Andrea for *vicaria*, or even prioress. Let her have to deal with the likes of that boring Melchora and that
self-righteous Rafaela. Maybe then she would understand why Juana was
always in a bad mood.

"Where is that Concepción, anyway?" she muttered aloud, pacing slowly
in front of her bookshelves. She had attended the Marqués de Mancera's
royal entrance in 1664 (she crossed herself at the memory of la Marquesa)
and knew that a triumphal arch had to be more than a symbolic doorway
into the realm. It had to pay homage, yes, but also serve as a kind of exhortation to the new ruler to improve the city in some specific way. She
couldn't remember, now, what the Cathedral's triumphal arch for the Marqués and Marquesa had looked like, or the city's arch, for that matter, except that it had been a florid affair with several panels and columns. Fray
Payo wrote that Don Carlos had been selected to design the city's arch,
and she knew that he would select some innovative conceit for his design.
She, too, would have to find a good allegory for the text and drawings of
the Cathedral's arch, something that could be rendered impressively in both
pictures and prose, convoluted enough to compete with Don Carlos's arch,
and regal enough to pay homage to this Don Tomás Antonio de la Cerda,
Marqués de la Laguna y Conde de Paredes. She laid the Archbishop's letter on top of a pile of open books and went to the mythology section of
her library.

The names Laguna and Paredes gave her an idea, evoked images of water
and ramparts. Wasn't Neptune the god responsible for the indestructible
walls of Troy? Fray Payo suggested that Juana find a way of weaving into
the fabric of the arch the Church's petition for the new Viceroy to finish
draining the city, repairing the roads and bridges, and completing the tower

of the Metropolitan Cathedral, as these were quite appropriate entreaties for the Church Council to make of the incoming potentate of New Spain. Luckily, the mythology section was at waist level and she did not need to bend down to pull out the books she needed: Homer, Ovid, Virgil, Apuleius, Horace, Herodotus.

"With your permission, Madre."

Jane's voice startled Juana out of her research and a bolt of pain twisted up her spine. "For the love of God, Jane! How many times must I tell you not to disturb me when I'm working?"

Jane kept her gaze on the checkerboard floor of the study. "Yes, Madre, I know, but you wanted to know what the girls was screaming about."

"Oh, the girls, I'd forgotten. Well, what is it? I'm busy."

"They're bringing a prisoner to the convent, Madre."

"A prisoner? What kind of prisoner?"

"They say she's the daughter of the *cimarrón* who got hung in the Plaza Mayor yesterday, Timón de Antillas. She was his spy, they say, and she was giving some kind of signal to the slaves of San Francisco. Timón de Antillas was going to burn down the whole monastery after the slaves escaped."

"I didn't know there was a hanging in the Plaza yesterday, Jane. Why didn't you tell me? I would have sent Concepción to see it for me."

"Concepción was there, and me, too. The whole city, it looked like. The bells tolled for hours."

"I don't remember hearing any bells other than the prayer bells."

"You never hear anything when you're working, Madre," said Jane.

"Funny that Concepción didn't tell me anything about it," said Juana. "And who told her she could go? She can't do as she pleases."

"We went to the market, Madre. You wanted squash blossom quesadillas yesterday, remember?"

"Concepción had to go with you to buy squash blossoms?"

"You said she had to go everywhere with me."

"It doesn't take two to buy squash blossoms, for heaven's sake! She should have gone alone."

"She don't know the difference between a squash blossom and a mushroom. Anyway, Madre, I can't be carrying everything by myself."

"What does this have to do with screaming girls, Jane?"

"The girls are squalling like cats in heat, Madre, because they thought the soldiers were coming inside the convent."

"I see. Very descriptive. I imagine Concepción must be part of the pack out there. No wonder she's not around. Go call her for me, please. We have so much work to do preparing for this new commission."

"Oh no, Madre, she ain't wasting time. She's out picking mangoes for your fruit salad."

Juana put down her quill and narrowed her eyes at Jane. "What?"

Jane fidgeted with her apron strings. "Since Madre Melchora said you won't be needing Concepción for a while, I thought she could help me instead. You know how much work I have."

Juana shook her head. "Why do you do this, Jane? Why do you insist on meddling with Concepción's time? I have told you a thousand times that Concepción is not at your disposal. Between her work in the fields, in the sewing room, and in my study, she has no time to be picking fruit for you or washing dishes or doing anything else that is your work. Don't think I haven't noticed that you make her go to the well twice a day and draw water for you, or that you make her wash the menstrual linen. Are you laughing at me, Jane?"

"But Madre Melchora said—"

"That was before I got this new commission from the Archbishop, and I've only got five months in which to finish a job that should take a year and a half. Now go find me Concepción, immediately!"

"I don't know what's so special about that girl, anyway. She ain't nothing but a *castiza*."

"It's taken me six years to train that *castiza*, and I don't intend to let you turn her into a scullery maid. Now, enough. Go do as I say. And, Jane, I don't want any fruit salad. Just bring me some more pineapple water, and bring our food up in a tray. For the rest of the year, Concepción and I won't have time to eat downstairs. You'll have to eat by yourself. And don't make anything with cheese. You know I don't eat cheese when I'm working on an important commission."

Jane stalked out of the study. Juana drew a deep breath to dissolve the uneasiness gathered in her solar plexus, then returned to her reading, submerging herself once again in the divine conspiracies of the Trojan War. She had nearly finished the story when she heard Concepción bounding up the staircase, taking two at a time in her typical zeal. From the kitchen, Jane shouted, "You idiot! I told you to bring mangoes, not peaches!"

Jane had disobeyed her again. She had not gone to fetch Concepción as Juana had instructed.

"She's a *princess*, Madre!" exclaimed Concepción as soon as she burst into the study. "And they've locked her up in the toolshed!"

"What are you talking about, girl, and where have you been?"

Concepción was good at pretending that Juana was not angry with her or annoyed at her absences. "The *cimarrón's* daughter, Madre. Her father was the king of the refugee slaves in San Lorenzo de los Negros. . ."

It still amazed Juana to see how much Concepción had changed now that she was a young woman of seventeen years. Her figure had grown stylized and graceful as a dancer's, with a narrow waist and the hips of a grown woman; there was an almost promiscuous arch to her nostrils, a catlike shape to her eyes, a well-etched fullness to her lips that at times made Juana uncomfortable and distracted her from her work. Were it not for her two-colored eyes, the girl would be quite a beauty.

" . . . Isn't that a pretty name? Aléndula. Sounds like a song, doesn't it?"

"Why are they bringing her here, Concepción? Why didn't they hang her? I've never known the Audiencia to be lenient or merciful with *cimarrones*."

"They say San Jerónimo interceded for her, Madre. When the Audiencia asked her what Timón de Antillas's band was doing in the city, she said they had just come to free her uncle who's a slave in the monastery of San Francisco, but somehow she and her aunt got separated and she got caught in the procession for Saint John and then when she asked for directions to San Francisco, someone told her how to get to Saint Jerome. When she looked inside all she saw was the image of the saint taking a thorn out of a lion's paw. At first she thought she was in San Francisco because she was told Saint Francis was always surrounded by animals, so she went inside and hid in a confessional until her father showed up, but she fell asleep and dreamt that the old man in the picture was pulling a nail out of her hand. Since San Jerónimo's the patron saint of orphans, they thought she was having a vision or that the saint was arbitrating for her, so the Audiencia sentenced her to life in prison here in the House of San Jerónimo."

"They've confused their Saint Jeromes," said Juana. "The one with the lion is the father of our house. The other one, the patron of orphans, is the Italian Saint Jerome, a minor saint."

"She told me—"

"She told you? You've befriended her already?"

"It's just that I thought I heard someone crying in the toolshed on my way back from the orchard, and there she was, all chained up. She told me what happened, Madre. How it wasn't true that they were going to set San

Francisco on fire and steal the gold from the church and start a big insurrection. They were just coming for her uncle, to liberate him from slavery, that's what *cimarrones* do, she said. But they got caught on the causeway before they even reached the city, only Aléndula was already here, you see, she had been sent ahead with her aunt. It was so horrible, Madre, watching them all get hanged and quartered! The dogs in the Plaza ate their entrails!"

Juana remembered the last execution she had seen from la Marquesa's balcony at the palace, how the crowd jeered as the thieves fell from the platform, how people took turns pulling at the chains from which the bodies dangled while the buzzards swirled over the Plaza Mayor.

"Do you suppose the soul issues out with the body's vapors and humors, Concepción?" she asked, startling the girl with her question. "Or does the soul really exist in the heart, as the Egyptians believe, and so remains trapped in the body until the body itself begins to decompose?" It was the same question she had asked la Marquesa that afternoon and la Marquesa had said that Juana must have snow in her veins the way she could make scientific observations of a corpse.

"I don't know. That's a horrible thought, Madre," said Concepción, stepping away from her. "Aléndula says her father took her heart with him. Now she doesn't have a heart. She says she would've preferred being hung at his side. She says a *cimarrona* must live free or die."

Juana held up both hands. "*Basta*, Concepción! We've wasted enough time! I want you to take a deep breath and turn all of this exuberance of yours into concentration."

"But, Madre!" The girl's eyes filled with tears. "She's a princess and now she's a prisoner here and they've locked her up in a toolshed. Don't you think that's unfair, Madre?"

"Whatever that girl's destiny is, Concepción, has nothing to do with you. I know it's all very exciting and very unfair, and I understand how tempted you are to participate in the pandemonium out there. But we have so much work to do between now and November, and I really can't have you wandering off without permission like you've been doing. And don't even think that you're going to have any time to visit this *cimarrón*'s daughter. She's a prisoner, so leave her alone."

"But, Madre, you should see what they've done to her. They've got her locked up and chained. Ankles and wrists. They say she'll have to work in the fields with those chains on. It's so cruel, Madre!"

"I'm sure it is, Concepción, but that's the way life is for most of us. Just remember you have your work to do and she has hers, and right now, for the next five months, I'm going to need all of your concentration. Now come along. I need you to rub my back. I can't sit here any longer."

"What about prayers? It's almost time for tierce. Have you forgotten?"

"I have a medical excuse, don't you remember. As well as a commission from Fray Payo."

"And your punishment, Madre?"

"What punishment?"

Concepción followed her past the Turkish carpet and into her dormitory. Leaning on Concepción, she knelt by the side of her bed, unpinned her rosary and her veil, and very slowly let herself down on the cool tile of the floor. Knowing exactly what to do, Concepción began kneading the knots in her aching spine. To keep herself from groaning with pleasure at the girl's strong touch, she thought about the work at hand.

Neptuno alegórico, she thought, that's what I'll title the arch. *Neptuno alegórico, Oceáno de colores, simulacro político*. In that flash of an instant in which she always conceived of her best work, from beginning to end, she saw the panels and the columns of the arch inscribed with an intricate labyrinth of arguments and poetry and illuminated with images from Greek and Egyptian mythology.

"I want you to copy those passages I've underlined in the books on my desk," she said, and then dropped into a lucid doze, wondering about the new Vicereine and how to incorporate her family names into the body of the text.

La Excelentísima Señora Doña María Luisa Manrique de Lara y Gonzaga. María, of course: *mar*, ocean, wife of the god of the sea.

She dreamt of an ocean holiday she had taken with la Marquesa in Oaxaca, sand glittering like gold in the pristine water, only in the dream they were naked, and la Marquesa was leading her by the hand, like Isis leading Nefertiti, to a bamboo-covered cove in the distance. When she turned to look at her, though, it was not la Marquesa at all, but a woman with dark eyes glittering from her alabaster face and black hair dressed in pearl combs, and lips that looked like tiny slices of watermelon, red and wet.

Chapter 13

She was awakened by a summons from the gatekeeper. She had a guest, Concepción said, bending over her. Don Carlos was waiting for her in the locutory. With difficulty, Concepción helped her to her feet, replaced her short veil with the long one, pinned her escutcheon back on the scapular, brought her a wet towel for her face. Her spine was in agony, but she said nothing. She had no repast prepared to offer her unexpected guest, and told Jane to bring him a glass of pineapple water and a plate of the shredded beef she had made for lunch.

She walked as fast as she could to the locutory, so anxious to see her friend that she forgot to curtsy in front of the crucifix in the cloister. She wondered briefly if any of the *vigilantas* were around, lurking by a tree or a doorway, taking notes on her actions, but it was still the hour of the siesta and the courtyard seemed deserted except for the cats sunning themselves on the flagstones.

"Here on a Wednesday, my friend?" she said upon entering her side of the locutory.

"Juana!" Don Carlos bowed. "Always a pleasure to see you."

They took their seats and didn't say anything for a moment. She could not fathom the purpose for his visit and waited for him to begin the conversation. He looked gaunt, as usual, though his eyes were alight with a kind of mischief.

"What good news, don't you think," he said at last, "that we'll be working on the same commission."

"The city council and the Church Council are different bodies, my friend," she said.

"I know, but at least we'll be working at the same kind of thing."

"And now you've come to tease me with all of the progress you've made, I suppose."

He pursed his lips and turned toward the bowl of plums on the table beside his chair. "Actually, I haven't even started. I'm having a bit of diffi-culty with the term *triumphal*," he said. He selected a plum and polished it lightly on the front of his cassock. "How are *you* interpreting the term, Juana?"

"I haven't really thought about it. It's just a symbol, isn't it?"

"Precisely! A symbol of Roman conquest, bloody battles, brutal deaths by the thousands. Don't you find the allusion inappropriate for New Spain, Juana, which was conquered more by religion than bloodshed?"

"According to Díaz del Castillo, who enumerates the countless deaths that resulted in the conquest, religion may have saved souls, but it did not save lives, Don Carlos."

He finished his plum in two bites and wiped the juice from the corners of his mouth with his sleeve. "Nor do these triumphal arches represent anything other than conquest, when they should, to my mind, describe a more humble entrance into a civilization that certainly rivaled Rome in accomplishment."

"I don't believe I follow your line of reasoning, my friend. I perceive a contradiction."

"The Viceroy's entrance ceremony denotes America's wholehearted welcome of its new ruler, does it not?" he asked. "And yet since 1586 we have been using a symbol of conquest to represent that welcome, when it is with humility and lack of choice that we accept our new Viceroy. And listen—"He took a notebook from his satchel. "—I've been doing research on the titles of some earlier arches. Mythological Political Aster, erected in honor of the Conde de Alva in 1650, Catholic Mars, the Cathedral's arch, and True Ulysses, the city's arch, to welcome the Duke of Alburquerque in 1653. And Panegyric of the Illustrious Aneas for our beloved Marqués de Mancera in 1664. It is all Greek mythology."

"That is the traditional approach, Don Carlos. I myself am going to use the Greek story of the Trojan War and Neptune's intervention for my arch, and thus exhort him to repair the damage of floods in the city."

"Why not exhort him to be an exemplary prince, instead? I believe that is going to be my approach. Rather than dwell on fabulous stories of the Old World, I want to remind our new ruler of the reality of history, of the Mexican empire that existed before Europeans set foot in this valley. I want to evoke the names of Chimalpopoca, Huitzilipochtli, Cuautémoc, and pro-duce a theater of virtues for the new ruler of our New World."

"A triumphal arch in reverse, perhaps?"

"Indeed, Sister! Let Mexico's mythology conquer the European. Let the prince be made aware that he treads in the shadow of the Plumed Serpent." He removed a piece of parchment from his satchel and handed it to her through the bars. "I thought you might like a copy of the Count's coat of arms."

She took the parchment. "Generous, as always. Thank you, my friend."

"What think you of my idea, then?"

"It's quite a conceit, Don Carlos, and you certainly have the command of Mexican history necessary to pull it off with some subtlety. I, however, given my position, will not be straying from the approved method."

"Not at all? That isn't like you, Sister. Not even the slightest subversion of form?"

"Well, there is a small detail."

Don Carlos grinned. "Yes?"

"You remember the contest between Poseidon and Athena," she began, but Don Carlos interrupted.

"Oh, good, a quiz." He closed his eyes for a moment, drumming his fingers against the arm of the chair. "Weren't they vying to see which of the two would be the protector of Athens?"

"Very good."

Jane came in to bring him his repast. He balanced the tray on his knees and ate with his fingers, taking first a piece of the boiled beef and following it with a slice of avocado and a bite of green onion.

"Given the name of the city, we know who won," he said, with his mouth full.

"There's a little more to it than that," she said. "According to one version of the story, they've been convened by the King of Attica, who is to be the judge in the matter, and he asks them to demonstrate what gift each would bestow on the city. Poseidon immediately plunges his trident into the earth and out springs a fierce horse in a wild gush of seawater. But Athena takes a stick from the earth and it becomes an olive tree, and this the King of Attica decides is a better gift than the horse and the goddess wins the contest."

He swished the *agua fresca* from side to side in his mouth. Juana half-expected him to gargle with it, too. "Didn't Neptune flood the city after that, Juana? Isn't that the pagan equivalent of our own Great Deluge?"

"I don't have to put that in. How many people know the myth, anyway? In fact, I could revise the myth a little and say that Neptune, in a demonstration of supreme reason, ceded graciously to the goddess when he recognized that a peaceful and bountiful olive tree was probably a better gift for mankind than a warlike and unruly horse."

Don Carlos started to chuckle. "What you're really saying, Juana, is that New Spain should be governed by the owl rather than the trident."

"Well, there is that other version of the myth that says that all the women voted for Athena and all the men for Poseidon, and since there were more women than men, the goddess was elected. Poseidon's revenge, then, was not limited to flooding the city. He took away the women's vote, and hence"—she raised her arms in mock surrender—"our current condition."

Now Don Carlos was laughing aloud. "You *are* bad, Juana."

"The worst, I assure you," she said. "But the detail I was referring to earlier," she continued, "is that while Neptune brought forth the horse, it was Athena who invented the bridle that tamed the horse. It seems that Uncle Neptune was always being outdone by his niece."

Don Carlos wept with mirth. "Indeed, Juana you've outdone me again. And no doubt you will do it so discreetly in your text that none will know the subtlety of your subversion."

"I hope you're right, my friend. I would not want the new Viceroy to think I'm suggesting that he needs a bridle." They laughed again, but Juana's merriment was tempered by the fact that the arrival of a new Viceroy meant the loss of a good friend. Fray Payo was returning to Spain to cloister himself in a monastery. He'd had enough, he'd told her at their last visit, of the public, political life and wanted to retreat back to his own land where he could spend his time praying and cultivating olives. "Nor do I want to offend Fray Payo. This will be the last commission of his I'll ever work on, you know."

"He's been charitable with you, has he not, Juana?"

"I wouldn't have survived convent politics without his help."

"No, I suppose not." He ate another plum. "And he's helped you stay afloat, economically, I mean, he's—he's taken care of you."

"I've worked hard for every cent I've been paid, Don Carlos."

"Yes, yes, of course, Juana. Forgive me. I guess I'm just envious that the Archbishop was never as charitable with me, never gave me any commissions that could have helped me take better care of my brothers. Even this assignment for the arch comes from the Corregidor rather than the Cabildo."

"Fray Payo did, after all, appoint you Royal Cosmographer," she pointed out. "That should help your income. It's a lifetime post." She wanted to change the subject. Discussing money with Don Carlos always irritated her; well she knew how often he brought himself to the brink of asking to borrow from her. "Do we know anything about Fray Payo's replacement?" she asked.

Don Carlos picked at his teeth with his thumbnail. "By right of seniority it should go to the Bishop of Puebla, Don Manuel Fernández de Santa Cruz. This would be a good thing for New Spain as the Bishop is moderate like Fray Payo but younger and in much better health."

"But we've heard that there's a Dominican coming a year after the new Viceroy arrives, a canon from Santiago de Compostela. Could it be the Jesuits are losing favor in Madrid?"

"I'd hate to think so, Juana. Do you know what a Dominican in the Archbishopric would do to us? We would have to sacrifice our intellectual achievements for spiritual fervor, no doubt. Not to mention what it's going to mean to you, my friend. The Dominicans are notorious misogynists."

Their visit was cut short by the nones bells, and Juana knew that she could not absent herself from another Office, especially not after having received a visitor in the locutory. She walked to the choir in a foul mood, not even bothering to return the greeting of the novices who preceded her into the church. Her mind was heavy with the preoccupation of Fray Payo's replacement. Whomever the Crown had chosen to take his place, she knew she would not have his kind of patronage again. As both Archbishop and Viceroy, he had had an authority that none could challenge, and, as his protégée, Juana's own authority in the convent had superseded that of Melchora for the last four years. Now that he was returning to his homeland, she was going to find herself in desperate need of another sponsor, and the only one who could even remotely match Fray Payo's influence was the new Viceroy. Thus this triumphal arch would have to serve an even deeper purpose.

The summer Feasts of Saint Thomas and Saint James passed and, having petitioned Fray Payo's permission to exempt herself from all manner of ceremony that would take time away from the arch, Juana stayed in her cell, finding more and more passages for Concepción to copy and drawing three-dimensional pictures of the arch on huge sheets of paper that Don Lázaro, the bookseller, added to her already exorbitant account.

By the end of July she had decided on the mythological scenes she wanted painted on the eight panels of the structure. The central image above the title would be of Neptune and his wife, Amphitrite, riding on a clamshell chariot pulled by two ferocious horses over the waves of a turbulent sea. This would denote the royal couple's entrance into New Spain across the turbulent Atlantic. To the right would be a city half-covered in water to denote Mexico's flooding problem, with Neptune riding in Juno's lion-drawn chariot overhead, casting his trident down to pull the waters back from the shore. Its corresponding image to the left of the central one would be the Greek island Delos, etched with exotic cities and copious trees and intricate cliffs to denote the ancient civilizations and raw beauty of Mexico, discovered by the grace of Neptune's trident that quelled the seas to permit passage. On the panels just below the second and third, respectively, would be a scene from the Trojan War with Neptune presiding over the victors and, on the other side, a scene in Neptune's palace depicting the god being paid homage by centaurs, ancient masters of science and metaphors for the Spanish *conquistadores*. The panel immediately above the flooded city would show Neptune placing the Dolphin constellation— symbol of prudent judgment—into the night sky. Its opposite immediately above the island panel would render the Neptune and Athena scene, showing Neptune's steed shrinking back into the sea under the great shadow of Athena's olive tree. And in the eighth panel above the first, a miniature reproduction of the Metropolitan Cathedral with its unfinished tower and Neptune standing on the Trojan wall surrounded by architectural instruments.

Satisfied with her allegories, she spent an entire week copying each scene onto a fresh sheet, making meticulous notes in the margins about the colors that should be used for every figure and section. At the end of the week, she sent Concepción with the bundle of blueprints to Fray Payo so that he could get the architects and artists to work building and painting the structure, and proceeded to work on the text.

By the Feast of the Assumption the allegory's abstract rationale was ready. This she had written specifically for the Cabildo, knowing that the interpretations for the different panels that were to be declaimed at the door of the arch needed to be in a less exalted style and more descriptive for the benefit of the masses in attendance at the spectacle. And, wanting to add a personal signature to the work, she was also going to write a special dedication for the Viceroy and Vicereine in which she would translate all the foregoing arguments and exegeses into a poetic explication of the arch. She would use the rest of August and all of September explaining the premises of each of the pictures and write the poem in October, at the end of which everything had to be submitted to the printer.

Two days before the Feast of Saint Jerome at the end of September, the gatekeeper announced that her aunt Mary was in the locutory and desired an urgent audience with her niece. She had not seen her aunt since she had returned to Nepantla and was surprised to learn that she was back in the city. Leaving Concepción a pile of pages to copy, she hurried down to the *locutorio*, asking Jane to prepare a pot of chocolate and bring it in to them as soon as it was ready.

She bit her tongue to keep from gasping when she saw her aunt. Looking drawn and starved, she sat on the edge of her chair, still in her widow's clothes, coughing gently into her handkerchief.

"Tía! My God, what's the matter with you?"

"Juanita," her aunt said, rising to grasp her niece's hands through the bars of the grille. She tried to smile, and Juana noticed how the creases on her face seemed almost like lacerations in the dry skin, how her eyes gleamed as though she were holding back tears.

"Tía! You don't look well."

"I'm ill, dear one. Some strange disease of the stomach. There's no hope, the medics tell me."

"How long have you been ill? What medics?"

"I should have come to see you long before it got this bad, but I kept hoping to get better. I didn't want you to see me like this."

"But, Tía, you looked hale when I saw you last. You were so happy about going back to Nepantla."

"I was happy, Juanita, very happy. Lonely, at times, with all my children here in the city, but at least I got to see your mother more often, and Antonia's family and Diego's family. They're all doing very well. Your mother's the same as usual, looking for new businesses to start. She's planted coffee now, you know——"

"Sit down, Tía, please," she said. She did not want to let go of her aunt's hands, but the pain had started again in her coccyx from all the hours she had spent in the last three months bent over her work and she needed to pace. Her aunt resumed her seat. Juana rang the bell for one of the maids to tell Jane to bring their chocolate.

"Don't trouble yourself, Juanita. I can't eat or drink anything. I'm on a strict diet and can only take some herb concoction that the medic has prescribed. Everything else comes right back up. I just wanted to see you before it became impossible for me to move around. Your cousin, Nico, brought me, but I asked him to leave me and come back later. I wanted to have you all to myself."

"Oh, Tía! I can't believe it! And I can't believe Mamá didn't say you were ill in her last letters."

"Your mamá doesn't know, *cariño*. I left Nepantla last month, as soon as the—" She coughed into her hand. "—the discharge started. I knew I had to get back here, be with my family again, before—"

Someone knocked on the door behind her. Jane came in with the tray of chocolate and slices of hard-boiled egg on pieces of bread.

"It looks so good," crooned her aunt. "Sometimes I really crave a *huevito*."

"Take it back, Jane," said Juana. "We're not going to need anything after all."

Jane mumbled something that she couldn't make out and left the room, letting the door slam.

"She's moody just like Francisca," her aunt observed, "except Francisca has grown very fat and very gray. Your mother's still a taskmaster, though."

"Tía, you're so resigned about this. How can you give up hope? How do you know that medic was telling you the truth. Some of our so-called medics don't even have an education."

"Believe me, Juanita, Nico and Gloria have not given up. They've brought every medic in the city, I think, and they all have the same opinion. I have a growth of some kind in my stomach. There's nothing they can do."

"Can it be removed, Tía? There are good surgeons at the Hospital del Amor de Dios."

"Glorified barbers is all they are. I don't think so, Juanita. Besides, the medics all think I'd die in the middle of the surgery. Who can survive having their belly cut open?"

Juana felt tears running down her face. She wiped at them with the tip of her sleeve.

"Juanita, my dearest. Don't cry. I didn't come here to upset you. I just wanted to tell you what a joy you always were to me, even when I most feared for you, I was inwardly so proud of your strong will and your intelligence."

Juana wiped at her eyes again.

"Also, I wanted to ask your forgiveness, if it's not too late."

"For what, Tía? For taking me in? For being a mother to me?"

"For never having told you—" She paused and looked over her shoulder, then lowered her voice. "—that I knew of your uncle's weakness for young girls, never having asked you if he'd done anything, well, anything inappropriate?"

Juana's stomach contracted. She could not look into her aunt's eyes.

"He took to the maids, mostly, but you were always so afraid of him, and wouldn't be in the same room with him by yourself. Did he . . . was he . . . offensive to you in any way, cariño? At any time? I'll never forget that strange comment la Marquesa made at your veiling ceremony, and she was looking directly at your uncle when she said it. Did you tell her something that you could not tell me?"

Juana stared at the gauntness of her aunt's face, the violet hollows around her eyes, the shame shimmering in her pupils, and she knew that it would do no good to confess the truth now. It would only add another cross for her aunt to bear to her deathbed.

"Of course not, Tía," she whispered, but the words felt like dust in her mouth. "You've done nothing that I have to forgive you for."

Outside the afternoon rain had started. Juana could hear the rumbling of thunder on the horizon. Her aunt narrowed her eyes, and Juana knew that she was trying to assess the truth of her words.

"You know the quality that I always admired, even more than your intelligence, Juanita?"

"Please stop, Tía. I don't want to talk about myself."

"Your compassion," said her aunt. "You inherited that from your grandmother, you know."

"Perhaps I learned it from you, Tía. Just as I learned what a real mother was in your care. For that I shall always be grateful to you."

Her aunt got to her feet. "Nico will be back any minute," she said. "I want to kiss you and hug you one last time. Would it be possible to open the grille?"

Juana rang the bell and asked Sor Clara to open the lock.

"But, Sister," argued the gatekeeper, "you know the rules. Only ladies of the highest rank. We need the Mother Superior's permission."

"Unlock the door, Sor Clara. Can't you see that my aunt is ill? She's come to say good-bye to me. Would you deny a dying woman's wish and carry that to your grave, Sister?"

"Oh dear! God have mercy! Nothing contagious, I hope," said Sor Clara, making the triple sign of the Cross over her forehead, face, and chest, all the while sorting through her key ring with her other hand. "Here it is! Señora," she curtsied clumsily, "please forgive me. I had no idea you were dying." She unlatched the grille, curtsied again, and rushed out to the rainy patio.

The gatekeeper's performance made Aunt Mary chuckle, but almost immediately she started to cough and the cough brought up a dark spume that she gathered into her kerchief and hurriedly stuffed in her pocket.

"Excuse me, Juanita," said her aunt.

Juana felt a stab in her chest. She reached for her aunt, and they held each other until Nico returned, Juana sobbing into the warm skin of her aunt's neck, remembering those first nights in Mexico when all she could do was cry for her mother and Aunt Mary would hold her and sing the ballad of the weeping Indian woman who had lost her children to the *conquistadores*. Much later, after she had stopped missing her mother, Juana would follow Aunt Mary all over the house, spending hours with her in the kitchen concocting recipes for the abundant variety of vegetables that grew in her aunt's garden.

For a week after her aunt's visit, Juana couldn't work, couldn't read, couldn't think of anything but her aunt's stoicism and the fact that she was losing yet another person she loved. In her dreams, her aunt bore the face of la Marquesa and la Marquesa grew thin and small and became her aunt, and once both of them were sitting in her study watching her work until Concepción awakened her and she realized she had just fallen asleep at her desk.

"I saw the printer at the market today," said Concepción. "He wants to know when we're getting the text for the arch to him. He said to tell you that the Widow Calderón has already begun printing Don Carlos's arch and he doesn't want ours to be late."

Juana had four more panels to explicate and could waste no more time indulging in melancholy.

Only after Concepción had delivered the full text of the arch to the printer did Juana allow herself to think about Aunt Mary again, and at night her heart swelled with guilt, remembering how unkind she had been to her poor aunt, how the more she read and learned, the more arrogant she grew and the more she judged her aunt a simpleton and a weakling. She always sneered at any of her aunt's attempts to make her happy. Even the graduate student whom Aunt Mary had hired to teach her Latin turned out badly, for Juana Inés had insisted that the man was more interested in decorum than declensions and had had him dismissed after only twenty lessons. In truth, he had wanted to teach her something that Juana had already learned from her uncle.

"Juana, you've kept us waiting," scolded the Archbishop as soon as she stepped into the *locutorio,* still breathless from having rushed across the orchard and the cloister. She had withdrawn to the chapel in the cemetery just after nones to pray for Aunt Mary and had fallen asleep over her rosary.

"I apologize, Your Grace." She noted that they had already been served a *merienda* of *buñuelos* and syrup.

"Come, let me introduce you to the artist who has won the commission to paint the panels of your *Neptuno alegórico.*"

Seated next to Fray Payo with his arms stretched across the back of the bench as though he were in a park rather than a convent locutory, the man was dressed completely in black, with a black cape and even a black ribbon wound in his blonde hair. His eyes were pale blue, and he looked German or Dutch except that he wore his hair tied back into a braid, like an Indian, and a gold hooped earring in each lobe.

"Despite his penchant for this . . . this buccaneer fashion," said Fray Payo, lifting an eyebrow at her, "he's a good artist. Sor Juana, may I present you Don Jorge de Alba, a distant relative of the Duke."

"Enchanted," she said, and stuck her hand through the bars of the grille.

"I am honored to meet you, Sor Juana," he said, with a pronounced accent to his Castilian. He shook her fingers lightly. "I hope I may do justice to that intricate arch of yours."

"They call him 'El Tapado,'" said the Archbishop.

"And why do they call you this, Señor de Alba? Are you in hiding?"

The Archbishop chuckled.

"But of course, Sor Juana. Like all good artists, I have many faces, and each one covers the other like this—" He lifted the black hood from his cape and let it drop over his face, covering all but his mouth. "—you see? A part always remains exposed. Your veil functions in the same way, does it not?" She saw only the white flash of his teeth and felt a strange shiver run down her spine. Laughing, he threw his head back and the hood slipped down his shoulders again. His eyes gleamed like aquamarines.

"He's a rare bird, there's no doubt about that," said Fray Payo, chuckling again, "but he can paint better than that foppish court artist that the Corregidor has hired to paint the city's arch."

"His Ilustrísima is too kind," said Don Jorge. "That foppish court artist is a well-known maestro in Madrid. His work is very fine, but, alas—" he dropped his wrist and affected a more pronounced lisp "—he is foppish, and His Excellency does not like foppish, therefore he does not like the man's work." He settled his wrist on his knee and looked at her. "But it is true that I can draw better than the maestro. Drawing is a plebeian skill, compared to painting. See for yourself, Sor Juana." He took a scroll of wrinkled pages from a large black satchel on the floor next to him and passed it to her through the grille. The paper smelled of paint and sweet tobacco. She unrolled the pages and examined the work.

"Since you can't be present, Juana," said Fray Payo, "I wanted you to see how it would look on the day of the triumphal ceremony of the twenty-ninth Viceroy of New Spain, so I asked Don Jorge here to draw the entire trajectory of the Viceroy's entrance, from the Plaza of Santo Domingo, where the city's arch will be installed, to the Plaza Mayor and the Cathedral."

Every detail had been rendered, down to the plumed hats and jeweled parasols of the lords and ladies gathered in the squares. Red and yellow bunting—the colors of the Spanish flag—adorned the balconies of the palace and great arches of carmine roses and golden sunflowers decorated the arcade. In the middle of Santo Domingo Plaza, opposite the flower-festooned portal of the Inquisition, the artist had drawn the arch that Don Carlos had designed for the city council in the shape of a three-dimensional pyramid, an oversized key to the city sticking out of its turquoise door.

"Is the city's arch finished, then?" she asked.

"Odd shape for a triumphal arch, don't you think, Juana?" asked Fray Payo.

"You know Don Carlos, Excellency. He likes to be different."

"Indeed, I do. I also know something of our new Viceroy. I daresay he is not going to be much pleased by Don Carlos's conceits."

"Surely Don Carlos means no offense, Excellency."

"I believe he is suggesting that the Crown take its cue from the pagan emperors who once ruled this land. You may be sure, Sister, that the Count of Paredes is neither dense nor incompetent. He is the brother of the Duke of Medinaceli, after all. At least your own arch does credit to the welcome of the Church Council."

In front of the east entrance to the Cathedral, dwarfing the portal of the great church, Don Jorge had drawn a monumental structure with a high arched doorway in the middle flanked by two lower doorways, also arched, and divided by four Roman columns. Above the arcature, sprawled across three rows, were the eight panels she had designed. A side view of the structure showed a depth of at least three human lengths.

"Will it be this deep, Excellency?" she asked. "More than an archway, it looks like a street the Viceroy will have to cross to reach the Cathedral."

Fray Payo spread his arms as wide as he could. "We're the Cabildo of the Metropolitan Cathedral of New Spain, Juana. We represent God's Kingdom in the New World. Of course, the entrance is deep."

"May I ask your permission to smoke my pipe, Sister?" asked Don Jorge, digging in his pocket.

"This is your house, Sir," she said. "Make yourself comfortable. And please, Fray Payo, help yourself to another *buñuelo*."

Juana studied the miniature paintings of the eight panels. They had little to do with her sketches, though they conveyed exactly the symbolism she had intended.

"I have taken the liberty of painting the second drafts as they will appear on the arch," said Don Jorge, "if they are to your liking, of course, Sor Juana. I hope you do not find my style too incompatible with your own."

El Tapado had rendered the images in hues of green and blue, punctuated here and there with gold leaf and other metals. The mother-of-pearl clamshell that Neptune and Amphitrite were riding in the central panel stood out from the frescoes around it like bas-relief. The houses of the flooded city on the right panel had been painted an ocher red to emulate the volcanic tezontle stone that predominated in the *traza*. The winged lions that pulled Neptune's chariot above the city had been rendered in bronze and gold leaf. In the panel that showed Neptune surrounded by the centaurs, he had painted a scarlet carpet under the god's golden chair and the man half of the centaurs was dressed in silver armor, complete with helmet and lance.

"It's amazing, Sir," she said, looking up from the pages at last, "how you have captured my meaning, in this panel especially, where I sought to weave Greek myth into the imperial history of the Spanish Crown."

"All I did was follow your directions, Sister," he said, grinning at her like a schoolboy.

"So you're pleased, then, Juana," asked the Archbishop.

"More than pleased, Ilustrísima." She bowed her head. "Grateful that you place such confidence in my abilities."

"None other in New Spain compares to you, Juana. It is a true *lástima* that you were born a woman. That mind of yours. You could have been something, Juana."

Juana's face twitched as if the Archbishop had struck her. She swallowed before speaking. He had meant to compliment her and had succeeded only in making her feel the shame that her gender connoted to him. "I try not to brood about God's will," she said. Don Jorge was gazing at her with the kindest eyes.

"Yes, God does work in mysterious ways. Had you been a man I probably would have had to surrender my post to you."

"I doubt it, Excellency."

"Or she could have been another Pope Joan, Excellency," Don Jorge interjected, "dressed in the robes of the highest patriarch. Or a lieutenant nun claiming the hearts of maidens across two oceans."

Juana could not believe she had heard him correctly. Why was he mentioning the notorious case of *la monja alferez*?

"Look what you've done!" Fray Payo scolded him. "Your libertine's tongue has offended my friend. She may be a nun, but she's still a lady. Now apologize at once."

The artist jumped to his feet and bowed so low his chin touched his knees, his cape falling like black wings to either side of him. "I meant no offense, Lady."

"None taken, Señor."

"Well, it's getting late!" said Fray Payo, rubbing his hands together. "We must take our leave, Don Jorge. Now that she's approved, you can get your crews started in the morning."

She handed the drawings back to the artist. "Thank you," she said, "for understanding me."

Don Jorge squeezed her hand like a friend. "*Fuerza*," he said, smiling, and then, under his breath, "I think in another life you would be an admiral, not a lieutenant."

A fortnight before the triumphal entrance of the Viceroy, in the dark morning hours of the 15th of November, the convent was awakened by the mad howling of the dogs. Through her telescope, Juana had been monitoring the skies all night and knew immediately that the strange luminescence hovering above the valley with its iridescent tail stretching back as far as the volcanoes was a comet, nothing to be superstitious about. Still, Melchora ordered everyone out to the courtyard, and all the nuns and novices, the *beatas* and the maids, even the boarders—all had to kneel on the flagstones and pray for salvation.

"It's a natural phenomenon, Mother," Juana tried to explain to her, but Melchora was too terrified to listen to a rational explanation.

"Kneel down, Sister!" she commanded. "Whatever this mystery means, we shall pray for deliverance and forgiveness. You may lead the rosary, Sor Juana. Since it's now Friday, we will pray the Sorrowful Mysteries, in Spanish, please, so that everybody can pray along."

"I didn't bring my rosary with me, Mother," Juana said, humiliated by Melchora's ignorance.

"Surely you know how to say a rosary without holding the beads in your hand, Sister," she said, and Juana had no choice but to lower herself to her knees and obey. They prayed until sunrise, and then all of the girls were allowed to return to their beds while Juana and her sisters trudged off to the choir for the first Office. Later that day, she received word that her aunt Mary had died in the night. She sent Concepción to the Cathedral to pay for a special Mass in her aunt's memory and kept silent for a week.

The day of the Viceroy's triumphal entrance, every belfry in the city tolled the Te Deum from sunrise to sunset. All the maids and boarders who had solicited permission were allowed to attend the spectacle. Juana baptized Concepción the official chronicler of the event. She was to take mental note of every detail and report back immediately after the ceremony at the Cathedral. Meanwhile, Juana and the rest of her sisters gathered on the rooftops of their cells—across the city, the roofs of all the nunneries were full—and heard clearly when the buglers' clarion announced the arrival of their new sovereign.

On the horizon, like a translucent moon in daylight, the comet hovered over the volcanoes. There were whispers among her sisters about the comet being a bad augur for the Viceroy's reign, but Juana, of course, knew better. She had sketched the view of the comet from her study window and saw that if she connected the palace to the convent and the convent to the point on the horizon where the comet had first emerged, it formed an isosceles triangle over the valley of Anáhuac. If Juana were to believe in signs, she would interpret that as a presage of good relations with the palace.

2 December 1680

The curfew bells are ringing, but I shall not be able to sleep tonight under the clamor of my beating heart. I should have known that the comet meant something, portended something, the minute I learned of Aunt Mary's death, I should have guessed it, but my rational self would not listen to any preternatural interpretation. Why don't I accept once and for all that there are such things as metaphysical signs, and that to acknowledge their existence does not always signify a superstitious mind? Even Don Carlos would agree with that. But not I, not the enlightened Juana Inés de la Cruz. Dear God, what shall I do? I know what this incessant turbulence in my chest means, this quavery feeling in my belly.

She looks like a queen. The entire locutory was ablaze with her presence. Beside her the Viceroy looked like a page. Perhaps it's that she's taller than he is, or that he was wearing no wig over the frizzled mane of his brown hair, only a broad-rimmed hat adorned with a single quetzal plume. Indeed, the only thing distinguishing his rank was his Viceroy's ring and the huge medallion on his chest. "Madam," he said to me, daring to take my hand through the grille and kiss it before all of the congregation, "your reputation precedes you. Our friend, the Marqués de Mancera, spoke very highly of you, and now that I have seen the product of your mind in that amazing structure you designed for our welcome, I can only opine that the Marqués was too humble in his praise."

Charmed as I was by his attentions, it was his lady I wanted to engage. She was dressed in a white brocade gown trimmed with golden chains, her dark locks covered in a gold filigree mantilla, a string of rubies trailing down her neck. A rosary of black pearls was wrapped around one wrist, an ivory fan dangled from the other. And her eyes, the color of smoky quartz, were like lodestones to my own. Even Madre Catalina noticed.

"You seem to have delighted our new Vicereine, Juana," she said as we returned from the locutory. "No doubt all your years at the palace taught you how to behave in front of royalty."

"The Viceroy, too, seemed quite impressed, don't you agree, Mother?" asked Andrea. "He couldn't stop kissing your hand, Juana!"

Would that I had been able to kiss her hand, I thought, and felt suddenly warm under my coif and veil. I shall wear a hair shirt and scourge myself in remonstrance of this pernicious inclination. May I burn in purgatory for my disloyalty to la Marquesa. To make matters worse, I'm supposed to be in mourning for Aunt Mary! *No tengo perdón de Dios.*

The Onyx Queen
1681 — 1688

Chapter 14

31 January 1681

My Dearest Marquesa,

Again, I turn my quill toward Heaven, where you dwell, and address my thoughts to you, though this time it is in apology that I speak, not despair. As you know, we do not celebrate birthdays in the convent, but one does not forget to count the years that pass, especially when a burning comet falls from the Milky Way only three days after one's thirty-second birthday. Although I scorned Melchora's fanatical interpretation of that beautiful and disturbing celestial light, a small voice within me said that the comet portended another cataclysmic change in my life. And, indeed, it did.

All the months that Concepción and I slaved over the triumphal arch, I convinced myself over and over that the feelings gnarling in my chest were but a consequence of fatigue, the excitement blooming in my belly nothing but a natural reaction to finishing that long and intricate commission.

But when I saw the comet, three days after my birthday and two weeks before the triumphal ceremony of the *virreyes*, I knew, somehow, that the portent was announcing a new liaison with the palace. And I knew, also, that temptation was blazing a trail into my life again. Like that dazzling orb which spilled its unearthly glow all over the valley of Anáhuac for fifteen nights, the bright orb and tail of temptation fades with daylight and flourishes again in the evening, especially in the hours between compline and matins.

I have prayed, my lady. I have kept vigils in the chapel. I have scourged myself as never before, hardly aware of the leather's bite, indifferent to the stripes of blood soaking through my tunic. From the day of the Immaculate Conception to Epiphany, I wore a hair shirt such as the Baptist wore to purify himself. Nothing has helped. The comet's burning light remains. The truth is again an alchemy of contradictions. You know what that truth is, my lady, my first love, and you know, also, how long I have mourned you. Seven years since your death I have stood by my window and gazed out on the volcanoes. I have seen myself as Popocateptl, smoldering, silent, capped with ice and snow, speaking to you, Ixtaccihuatl, the Sleeping Lady, in that language of dark smoke.

When I received your husband's letter explaining how you had died, so suddenly, the strange pestilence consuming your body so quickly, he said, as if your heart had just stopped pumping out of sadness at leaving this country that you had come to love so much, I felt responsible for your death, my lady, in a terrible way, a proud way, believing that you were heartbroken at leaving me. And I swore always to love you; I *married* you in my mourning, Laura. *That* has been the vow I have lived by these seven years, not obedience, not poverty, not enclosure, certainly not chastity (forgive my boldness; as one grows older, one is less ashamed to speak of the passions of one's body).

But now even that vow I have broken. I must confess, Lady: there is a new sovereign in my heart. *Never* will I love her as I loved you, but then *never* will you stand before me again; *never* will I smell your scent again; *never* will I hear your voice again; *never* again will we sit together in the chiaroscuro of our unspoken love.

Laura, I did not seek to fall in love again. Please believe that. Heavy as the cross of my mourning has been, I was resigned to carry it for the rest of my days, and it is still there in the silver crucifix that hangs from the rosary pinned to my shoulder. But there is light in my heart again after seven years of darkness, though it is only a comet's glow and could never rival the rays of Helios that once burned there.

She is of noble blood, a countess, our new Vicereine, a year younger than I. Her name is María Luisa de Manrique y Gonzaga, Condesa de Paredes (la Condesa to me, as you were once and ever shall be, la Marquesa). Although she and her husband have already paid their official visit to our community, and afterward stayed to dinner in the refectory, served a sumptuous feast of native fruits and cheeses and the Rioja wine they brought as a gift to the convent, la

Condesa has visited me several times on her own, on Saturday afternoons, when she arrives just after the siesta without her retinue of ladies-in-waiting.

We share a passion for poetry and philosophy, and, I daresay, the same loneliness and need of compatible friendship. As she says, her ladies are like a flock of elegant birds with no conversation. She does not call me *Sor* Juana when we are alone, just Juana or *amiga*. She has no compunctions about embracing a nun, and she teases me for my stiffness. Her appetite is even more voracious than Concepción's; from the way she eats, I know that she is a woman of passion (and a choleric temper, too!), a woman who is not afraid or embarrassed to take what she wants. (How silly, to be jealous of a plate of dates, to long for the fate of an orange and be peeled by those strong white fingers.)

In just eight weeks, we have already come to know each other so well. There are times when I am afraid she will read my thoughts, as Concepción does at times, and I get flustered and tongue-tied, a regular lovesick maid, at the possibility she will guess my true feelings. But if she has guessed, she is not repelled, for she keeps visiting me and bringing me gifts. How she loves my desserts! In exchange for my recipe for *huevos reales* and *postre de nuez*, she brought me a small telescope last week, meant not for the stars but for scrutinizing the tiniest bits of earthly matter. A microscope, it's called. (What an amazing instrument to add to my collection!) She has brought me a harp, a silver quill and matching sandcaster, a double inkwell for two colors of ink, an illuminated edition of *Don Quixote*, and, her latest gift, a mahogany box full of fortune-telling cards that she bought from gypsies before sailing from Spain. These, of course, I could not accept. How would I ever explain them to Padre Antonio?

As you can see, the woman is fearless, and I suppose *that* is the trait I most admire in her. She dismisses the gossip of the convent with a flick of her Persian fan.

"The abbess knows that the convent needs to remain on good terms with the palace," she said last Saturday, "and if I choose *you* as the convent's representative, if I choose to honor the convent through you, you are not responsible for my choices. Let them talk until they grow scales on their tongue, Juana. Meanwhile, slice me another piece of your nut cake and let us discuss your ideas for this brave and wonderful philosophical satire of yours. *Hombres necios que acusáis a la mujer sin razón, sin ver que sois la ocasión de lo mismo que culpáis.* Oh please, Juana, I know you haven't finished it, but do recite that wonderful opening verse for me again."

> "Stubborn men who accuse
> women without reason,
> dismissing yourselves as the occasion
> for the very wrongs you design:
> > if with unequaled fervor
> you solicit their disdain
> why wish them to behave
> when you incite them to sin?"

"How true, how true, Juana. They create us in their own image and yet they want us to resemble the Virgin Mary."

Would that I had la Condesa's courage. But she does not have to live in this house of intrigue and gossip. She does not have to wake up each morning wondering what new restrictions her Superior has wrought overnight, what new chastisements her father confessor will impose on her for keeping her intellect alive. She does not have an abbess censoring her thoughts, a *vicaria* and a trio of *vigilantas* taking notes on every one of her actions.

But if I admire her courage, la Condesa admires what she calls my inspiration, *the tenth muse*, she has baptized me, and of all possible reactions, I can only blush—I, who blush even less than I repent for my sins. Because of la Condesa's admiration for my work, I have become braver, not only in my writing, but in my own feelings for myself. I am no longer afraid of the nature of my love, Laura, this pure and selfless love I once called ugliness. I compare it to that bizarre and bloodstained love that the holiest of my convent Sisters profess for Christ, and to the hypocritical love that forks the other Sisters' tongues, and I know that my love is far from ugly; it is a blessed thing in this place of so much falsehood and fanaticism. Padre Antonio would deem it worse than ugliness, worse, even, than any mortal sin, but he is a man and knows only the laws of men. If he understands love at all, it is a man's love that he knows (though men have designed to dictate the kind of love a woman may feel).

I remember what you said to me the afternoon that I returned from the Carmelites after only three months in that austere novitiate. I was but a prodigal daughter disguised as a sack of bones, certain that you would have me not at your side, knowing what you knew of my inclination. You said: "Love is never a sin, Juana Inés. Love is our very soul. Like the sacred Word, it has no gender." And so now, at the age of thirty-two, I am resolved to express my love for María Luisa. Any verse I want to write, any gift I want to bestow, any sign I want to give within the bounds of this habit, I shall do it. And it will be so well done, that even when I lie in the earth, outlived only by my scribblings, none shall know what muse drove my hand. None but you, Laura.

I have asked Concepción to bring me the brazier from the bath. She is stoking it now, glancing this way, wondering why I want to burn what I have written. She frowns when I tell her that I am writing to *you*, that I am speaking to you the way Popocateptl speaks to Ixtaccihuatl, in the language of smoke, but she doesn't question. She knows too much about my own heart to question.

Receive the dark smoke of my love, Laura, and remember: Your spirit sleeps at my side.

> *Your devoted*
> *Juana Inés*

5 *February*

Last night in my bath I realized I was calmer than I've been in a month. Is it the quiet that precedes a storm, or the peace that comes with knowing that our friendship is as deep and meaningful to her as it is to me? I think I may have found my other half. Aristophanes' Woman could be no more whole than I am when we sit in the *locutorio* together. Even with the grille between us, we are bound by something deeper than flesh and bone. In many ways she is my complete opposite, but I suppose this makes sense, this balance of opposites on the same tree. Is this the secret of the Tree of Knowledge for which Eve sacrificed perfection? This knowledge that Adam could never have given her?

9 February

La Condesa and the Viceroy both came to visit me today. I felt awkward with him in the room, at first, accustomed as I've become to having la Condesa all to myself and not diverting my eyes from hers until she leaves. But the Viceroy is leaving next week, taking a trip to the north, to the province of Nuevo Méjico, where the Indians continue their revolt against the missions.

"Do you know, Sor Juana," he said, clearly trying to find a topic of conversation that would engage all of us, "that my couriers actually saw our comet while on the Camino Real?"

"It stretched that far, Excellency?"

"It was even seen in Seville, I'm told," said la Condesa. "Our Jesuit friend, Father Eusebio Kino, is writing a treatise about it that refutes Don Carlos."

"What is there to refute, Condesa? Don Carlos is simply clarifying the origin of comets so that they cease to frighten people of quality, like yourself, Lady."

"The origin of comets, Juana, is the Devil himself," she said.

"Even the Greeks understood the malignant power of comets," said the Viceroy. "Or do you share Sigüenza's views, Sor Juana?"

"Don Carlos says that comets are natural rather than supernatural phenomena," I said, "that they are not portents at all but signs of God's existence." I was leery of saying any more for I could sense that this was a delicate topic for la Condesa.

"We know what he says. What do *you* believe, Juana?" she asked, narrowing her eyes at me.

"I tend to agree with the scientific view——" I started to say, but la Condesa interrupted.

"Science is the work of the Devil, Juana. Surely you know that."

I couldn't help but grimace at her comment. I'd never known her to be superstitious. Surely *she* knows that the only Devil exists in the minds of the priests!

"What scientists are you referring to, Sor Juana?" asked the Viceroy. "Not that imbecilic colleague of Don Carlos's who thinks the comet is a ball of fumes from dead bodies on the earth, I trust."

"Descartes and Copernicus both had theories concerning the movement of matter in the void, Excellency, which could be applicable to comets. Descartes argued that there were vortexes in the Milky Way that could generate intense heat, and the comet could be a great spark shooting through the sky. Copernicus believed that there were celestial bodies constantly traveling in straight lines from beyond the stars."

"If God is the author of this portent, Juana," countered la Condesa, "why do scientists waste their time looking for origins outside of God?"

"That is the work of scientists—" the Viceroy began, but la Condesa did not allow him to finish. She got to her feet and said she had no intention of being contradicted by that *criollo* Sigüenza.

I winced at the comment, as I, too, am a *criolla*, and she knows it. "I doubt that it was his intention to contradict, Señora," I pointed out. "He did dedicate his manifesto to you, after all."

"What better way to mock me!"

"Don Carlos *is* Chief Cosmographer of the Realm, María Luisa. He's entitled to his ideas, even if they contradict prevailing dogma."

"This is a fine display of loyalty," la Condesa said, her face gone red with anger. "The two people I love most are both siding with that pagan-loving dolt, Sigüenza, and letting him dictate to us how we should respond to that ungodly presage. I'm leaving! If you want to sit here chattering behind my back, Tomás, so be it!"

The Viceroy raised his eyebrows at me, and all I could do was shrug in stupefaction. He reached for my hand to kiss it good-bye, and I wished him a safe journey. His hand felt so warm. All I could think as I returned to my cell was of that hand touching la Condesa, stroking away her anger in the carriage. Concepción was just preparing to bring our tray. I was going to serve Chinese tea today, and Jane's delicious pastries, stuffed with meat and olives and raisins. Now I shall have to send some to Madre Catalina and interrupt my work to write an apology, though I don't know what I did to merit such a reaction. Surely she cannot expect me to share her credulous interpretation of that silly comet!

19 March
Halfway through Lent and still no word from la Condesa. Now I know that she is both superstitious and rancorous. Could it be that she is jealous of Don Carlos? Or jealous, at least, of the fact that I am in agreement with his and not her views? I wonder if she's seen Don Carlos's new manifesto

yet. He has denounced the chicaneries of astrology and those who would rely on it to explain the comet. He is looking forward to the arrival of Father Kino for he hopes to find a broader mind and a mutual depth of astronomical discernment in a fellow Jesuit. He does not believe that Father Kino has been expressly commissioned to refute his own theories.

"Scientists do not refute each other with superstition," he told me.

We shall see. I had Concepción deliver another poem to la Condesa in which I pretended that I had just seen her, seen the effect of jealousy on her face, and resorted to a rhetoric of tears to beg her forgiveness.

> This afternoon, my dear, when we did speak,
> from your face and actions could I evince
> that with words I did not convince,
> my heart I wanted for you to seek;
>   and Love, which my intentions sought to aid,
> defeated what seemed impossible:
> for amid tears produced by pain,
> was my broken heart distilled.
>   Enough punishment, my love, enough;
> let no more tyrant jealousy torment you,
> nor vile misgivings conflict your calm
> with stubborn shadows, useless clues
> for already in liquid humor did you see and touch
> my heart unraveled between your hands.

Easter Sunday

A gift arrived from the palace this morning after High Mass, a crate of startled, gobbling turkeys, one for each nun, and pheasants for the novices. The gift has caused quite a commotion. It's been many months since we've enjoyed the luxury of turkey at our tables. There was a note stuck in the cavity of the one that came labeled with my name (at first I wondered if she was equating me with a turkey!). All the note said was, "If the humors of the heart must be distilled in order to persuade, then tears no less than hearts must be sacrificed to appease our inner tyrants." I am assuming that to mean she has forgiven me. Jane is cooking the turkey now in that rich and spicy chocolate sauce that Francisca used to make in Panoayán. The scent of it makes the roof of my mouth drip.

I allowed Concepción to help Jane in the kitchen. Every time she goes to visit that prisoner friend of hers in the toolshed she comes back in a choleric humor and spends the rest of the day being a surly bore. I can't tolerate her moods while I'm working. But also, the girl actually fancies the tedious work of grinding on the metate, my least favorite of cooking tasks. All afternoon Jane had her grinding peanuts and toasted sesame seeds and dried red chiles and bittersweet chocolate into a powdery paste. Now she sits across from me at her writing desk, and I can smell the spices emanating from her hands. How distracting!

Pentecost

Padre Antonio came to examine my conscience yesterday. He says he is "distressed" by my particular friendship with la Condesa. He has heard about her gifts and the verses I write in gratitude, and as penance he wants me to go into silence for a month to meditate upon my sins. He warns me that if I continue in my "rebelliousness" he will have to consider broaching my case with his superiors.

Last night, as a consequence of Padre Antonio's visit, I had that old dream of the bishop on the riverbank. In this dream, I can clearly see the bishop's face, and he wears the same round spectacles that Padre Antonio uses, but he has a goat's white beard hanging from his chin, so I know that the bishop is not Padre Antonio himself but perhaps has the same vision as my father confessor. The man is chanting the Paternoster. In one hand he holds a smoking censer, in the other a bottle of blue water, and I see that I am prostrate before him, my habit stripped to my waist, my back striped with lashes from his scourge. My hair, which is much longer in the dream, is a mat for the bishop's feet. He is purifying me.

14 July

La Condesa and I argued about human nature this evening, but what started out as a debate ended in a quarrel. How she hates to be contradicted! She says human nature is innately good, that original sin is but an invention of the priests (let the spies of the Inquisition hear her say that, and she will rot in a dungeon!), and I say that original sin is selfishness, that human nature is innately selfish, a defect that we can never hope to remove, only to control.

"I never knew you were so pessimistic, Juana," she said.

"On the contrary, my lady, my view of human nature is one of the few optimistic views I hold," I told her, "for it is not grounded in self-deceit."

"Do you imply that I deceive myself, Juana?"

"Lady, this is not a personal attack, and you should not feel defensive. We simply disagree about original sin. Surely our friendship is ample enough to allow some disagreements."

"And are you not being selfish, Juana, in expecting me to gainsay my principles and agree with you that disagreements in a friendship should be allowed?"

"I see that we have changed the subject, my lady, but yes, I *am* being selfish, I am expressing my human nature and expecting you to agree with me just as you expect me to be in accord with your views."

"You always twist my words around to your advantage, Juana."

"Now you attack me, Countess."

"I do not see how believing that we are innately selfish is an optimistic view. You contradict yourself, Sister."

"It is optimistic, Countess, because it allows me to do something about curtailing my greed, to be always on the alert for the shadow of greed in my life. I do not always succeed, but at least I am aware of my own short-coming and thus do not burden myself with the cross of guilt when my human nature gets the best of me."

"You do not convince, Sister."

"I did not think so, Señora."

26 September

Another quarrel with la Condesa today. I still disagree with her interpretation of the comet, and she has involved me in a silly scandal with Don Carlos and Father Kino. Now she has brought me a copy of Father Kino's absurd treatise on the comet, *Exposición astronómica de el cometa, que el año 1680, por los meses de Noviembre y Diciembre, y este año de 1681, por los meses de Enero y Febrero, se ha visto en todo el mundo y le he observado en la ciudad de Cádiz*. It is a refutation of Don Carlos's manifesto, and I must write a sonnet in favor of Father Kino's ideas if I expect to maintain my friendship with la Condesa. She is far too dignified to request it openly, but I believe my loyalty is being tested, and I know, although in reality I agree with Don Carlos that comets are not portents of disaster as the learned Jesuit suggests but natural phenomena of celestial origin, that I will eventually submit to María Luisa's will, at the cost of my friendship with Don Carlos. It is an unjust test, and she knows it. The choices that we are driven to make by our tyrannical hearts! She is twenty times more willful than la Marquesa, and I am twenty times more foolish for her love.

3 *October*

Sent la Condesa a birthday gift with Concepción, a tiny *retablo* of the Nativity etched out of ivory that Concepción found for me at one of the stands outside the Cathedral. I've had her looking in every silversmith's shop and *mercería* for a week trying to find some sort of Nativity scene, and this one— so small and beautifully carved, it can only be an import from Africa—is absolutely perfect. And Concepción is so good at haggling that she paid half its worth to the vendor. I've written a poem to accompany the gift in which I compare la Condesa's own birth to the Nativity (another sacrilegious glyph of mine). I hope she likes this gift best of all, though it be the most modest.

Don Carlos has said nothing about my sonnet in praise of Father Kino. He must know that I was coerced to write it, that I would never err on the side of the irrational and the ridiculous. And now I must return to my *loa* in honor of King Charles. I've already written two, at the behest of Fray Payo, but this one was commissioned by the Viceroy as soon as he returned from the north. Seems every new Viceroy must pay homage to his King with one of my *loas*. It must be dispatched in the next mail in order to reach Vera Cruz before the Flota sails back to Cádiz.

16 *October*

Argued with Concepción today when she returned from the market. She had ribbons wound in her disheveled hair and I could still see a trace of the beauty mark she'd painted near her mouth. Jane tells me she's been flirting with some gypsy juggler who's installed himself in the Plaza Mayor and that he seems very interested in Concepción. That's all I need, for my assistant to be trafficking with gypsies rather than making my deliveries and running my errands. She says she delivered the poems I sent to Don Carlos to enter in the university's poetry contest, but she wasn't focusing on what I was saying. I asked her why she looked so suspicious, but she denied it, her nostrils flaring the way they always do when she feigns innocence.

"I better not find out that you've been making a fool of yourself out there."

"Of course not, Madre!"

"And what happened to your *huipil*? The lace is ruined!"

"I tripped in the market, Madre, on some prickly pears. It wasn't my fault."

"Wasn't your fault? You know you're not supposed to wear that blouse unless we have guests. Take it off and wash it immediately."

Jane told me later that the girl *had* tripped, she hadn't lied about that, but that she'd left out the detail of the gypsy who appeared out of nowhere, turning somersaults like an acrobat, and helped her up. He disappeared with her into the crowd of the *baratillo* before Jane could stop them. I suppose Concepción is old enough to do what she wants with her body, but the thought of her dirtying herself with a man—and at the Thieves Market, of all places—is deeply disturbing!

25 *October*

Offended la Condesa today with my sarcastic tongue, and now I have promised to be silent. She was asking me if I'd never felt the urge to have children, and I told her I did have children, lots of children, every single one of my scribblings is a product of my urge to create, I said, which is all the begetting of children really means. She was horrified by my response and went so far as to call me a narcissist. On the contrary, I rebutted, Narcissus enjoyed staring at his own reflection in the water, which is what mothers and fathers do when they stare into the dumb faces of their progeny. When I stare at my own creations I see not myself reproduced in a childish likeness but a mind aspiring to exceed itself. Each line I write, I said, is a rung on the ladder of wisdom that I have been both building and climbing ever since I was a child. So forgive me for disagreeing with Your Highness, I said, but the only narcissist I know is the one who seeks nothing beyond his own reproduction. She was stunned, to say the least, by this dissertation, and even more so when I cut the visit short. I was shaking too much to continue.

12 *November*

My birthday again. Thirty-three was the year of Christ's crucifixion, and I feel as though I, too, were nailed to a cross. Three weeks have passed since my last quarrel with la Condesa, and still I have not spoken to her. It is my own pride and stubbornness that have crucified me.

later

I can barely write. My fingers tremble. My chest swirls with emotions that I must force myself to conceal. I have received a summons from la Condesa. She bids me to break my silence, to explain why I have cloistered myself in my dreadful pride. That woman could break Padre Antonio's will, despite his diligent misogyny. I must finish drafting that verse of apology, and pray that she will visit me today.

> And now your grave command
> shatters my mute silence;
> your wish, alone, is the key
> to my respect for you.
>   And, though loving your beauty
> is a crime without pardon
> I would rather be punished by guilt
> than by indifference.
>   Don't ask, then, my stern lady,
> that, having declared my intention,
> I make myself more wretched
> when I was graced with mockery.
>   If you blame my contempt,
> blame also your own license;
> for if you say I am not obedient,
> I say your mandate was not just.
>   And if my intention is guilty,
> my affection is also damned,
> for loving you is a transgression
> of which I will never repent.
>   This I find in my feelings,
> and more which I know not how to explain,
> but you, from what I keep silent
> will infer what I cannot say.

There are traces of my wounded pride in between the lines, but let her smell the bitter scent. Why should I hide that I am bitter about betraying my friend, Don Carlos, which is what my short temper with her is really about? I have missed her so much, though, and am thankful that she has come to pull me from the Cross. Now I must tell Jane to heat the water for my bath. Concepción will copy the verse in her graceful calligraphy on a gilt-edged sheet. If my muse does not deceive me, I will be receiving a guest this evening after vespers who will resurrect me from the tomb.

Chapter 15

Juana sprinkled sand on the copy Concepción had just completed and when the ink had dried, rolled up the parchment and secured it with a piece of silk ribbon. The *loa* was in honor of the Queen's birthday. La Condesa had commissioned it several months ago, before their most recent argument about the true intentions of la Celestina. To Juana, Salazar's character was an *alcahuete*, pandering her young charge's feelings to the highest bidder; to la Condesa, Celestina was a seducer and an instructor in the arts of love. Juana had grimaced at the interpretation, which was enough to send la Condesa into a fit of indignation. She had left the locutory without even giving Juana the opportunity to explain her reaction. Their arguments were becoming increasingly shallow and tiresome, and Juana had come to the conclusion that la Condesa thrived on the cycle of argument and reconciliation. I thrive on my own vicious cycle, she reminded herself; first I'm aggravated by her choler, then I worry that she never wants to see me again.

On her way out of the cell she ordered Jane to beat the chocolate into a good froth, and reminded Concepción to bring the refreshment tray as soon as she heard the bell. Her heart pounded as she crossed the courtyard, but by the time she reached the door of the *locutorio* she had calmed down, forcing herself to take deep breaths and slow steps.

Upon entering she noticed that the grille had been unlocked, and, instead of waiting for her on her own side, la Condesa was examining the picture of the Madonna on the nuns' side. It had always been the other way around, Juana crossing over to the guests' side on those privileged days when she was permitted to dispense with the grille. Today was no special occasion, and yet there stood María Luisa by the chair that Juana usually occupied during their visits. It did not surprise Juana at all that la Condesa intended to sit in her place.

Juana decided to play the game but to play it her way. She went to the guests' side, closed the grille, and took up la Condesa's usual seat. They had not looked at each other during the exchange of places. It proceeded automatically, each one understanding her own part in the script.

"Good afternoon, Sor Juana—" La Condesa thought it was her turn to begin.

Juana raised her hand. "I beg your pardon, Señora, but if we are going to do this correctly, we must follow the rules. The rule in this situation is that the person sitting on the guests' side must speak first. We nuns, remember, do not speak unless we are spoken to."

La Condesa slowly exaggerated her nod. She had to concede the point.

"I have the verses you requested," said Juana, omitting the usual formalities. But before she could continue, la Condesa took her turn.

"I, too, have something for you," she smiled, her eyes flicking to the table by Juana's hand.

Juana picked up the velvet box, noticing that on this side of the room the chair was slightly elevated and gave her an angled perspective above her guest. La Condesa told her to open her gift. Juana studied the little box; it was too rectangular for a bracelet and yet too narrow and small for a comb. She could feel la Condesa's gaze, but she kept herself from looking up, and lifted the lid. It was a cigarette case, with fretwork in silver and gold, an opal teardrop serving as the clasp. Inside were a dozen pale brown cigarillos, very slim and perfectly rolled.

"The tobacco is Cuban and very strong," said la Condesa, "from my husband's own supply."

"What's this?" asked Juana, lifting out the opal.

"That keeps the cigarillo in place as you smoke it," said la Condesa. "I thought it clever the way the clasp doubles as a clip."

"Quite clever," said Juana, genuinely delighted with the gift, but when she looked up, la Condesa was wiping the edge of her eye with a lace kerchief.

"Señora, is anything wrong?"

"Never mind, Juana. Aren't we having any refreshment? I was so looking forward to one of your confections."

For the first time they looked directly into each other's eyes. Juana held her gaze steady and la Condesa smiled, that coy, impish smile she used after every argument. Usually Juana resisted smiling back. Today she did not.

"It is so good to see you," she said.

"Aren't you going to smoke one?" said la Condesa.

"I don't think we're allowed to smoke in the *locutorio*, Señora. The gate-keeper is apt to report me to the *vicaria*."

"Since when are you so concerned about being reported? I have never known you to have difficulty doing what you're not supposed to do, Juana."

"I believe that was an indirect remark, Condesa."

"Not indirect at all. And you know exactly what I mean. If you pursue the issue, I guarantee you, Juana, that I will leave and not return."

Juana handed the scroll to la Condesa across the grille. "But you're on that side, now, Condesa. You can't go anywhere." She grinned.

"Very funny, Juana."

"Think about it," said Juana. "How would *you* be different if you knew that you could never leave a place, not even to step out onto the street, let alone go anywhere."

"How would *I* be different, or how would my life be different?"

"Well, both, naturally, but I mean specifically you, inside, the person you are. How would that situation affect the person inside and cause that person to change?"

"I don't know what you're getting at, Juana," said la Condesa. "Are you suggesting I have to change?"

"Condesa, you always turn my hypothetical situations into personal attacks. Can we please not speak about you, for once, and simply discuss the matter in a more abstract way?"

"If it's abstraction that you need, Juana, perhaps you should wait until Don Carlos's visit. I did not come to speak abstractions."

"What *did* you come to speak, Señora?"

"Really, this is getting tedious. Are we or are we not having anything to eat? I would have supped at the palace if I'd known we weren't to have a repast today."

"The bell is next to your own hand, Condesa. All you need do is ring the bell, and a servant will tell Concepción to bring us our *merienda*."

La Condesa rang the bell just as the Mother Superior strode into the *locutorio*. Startled to find the Vicereine sitting in the nun's chair, Melchora forgot to curtsy to the Vicereine and sought Juana's gaze through the grille. Juana hid the cigarette case in her sleeve.

"Sor Juana, what are you doing on that side? Why have you taken la Condesa's chair?"

"On the contrary, Madre," la Condesa said first. "It is I who dared to cross the line. Please forgive me. My husband says I am incorrigible sometimes. But you see, it has always been my desire to understand what it feels like to be in a cloister and removed from the world. In fact, we were just speaking of that before you entered."

"I see," said Melchora. "Very well, I shall not interrupt your—"

"Game," said la Condesa, filling in the word for the Mother Superior. "Another *galanteo de palacio*, the exchange of places."

"Yes, yes, I remember. Excuse me," she said, turning back toward the door just as Concepción pushed it open with the tray.

"Here's your chocolate, Madre," the girl said, quickly assessing the odd arrangement and proceeding calmly with her duties.

"What an exquisite *huipil* you're wearing, Concepción," commented the Vicereine. "What is that on the design? Birds?"

"Hummingbirds, Señora," said Concepción, setting the tray on the sideboard. "I embroidered it myself. I'll make you one, if you want."

"Don't be ridiculous, girl! Spanish ladies don't wear *huipiles*," said Melchora, scowling at Concepción.

"Oh, but it looks so comfortable, Mother. Don't you agree, Juana? Nothing cinching the waist or pressing down on the bosom." She pressed her palms on the soft mounds of flesh protruding from the top of her gown.

Juana coughed into her hand. Melchora bowed her head and averted her gaze.

La Condesa laughed. "Come, ladies! We're all women here, aren't we?" She turned back to Concepción. "I would like for you to make me one exactly like yours."

"I'd be happy to, Señora," said Concepción, "just get me the blouse you want and I'll embroider the design. The best booth for *huipiles* in the *mercado* is the one right next to the candle-maker—"

"I think I'll order one from Tehuantepec, of black Chinese silk," said la Condesa. "You do know how to embroider on silk, don't you?"

"With silk thread, naturally, Señora," said Concepción, pouring the chocolate, which, Juana noted, seemed rather flat. Either Jane had not beaten it into a froth as she had ordered or it had gotten cold during this vapid conversation about *huipiles*.

Concepción handed la Condesa her cup of chocolate and set the loaf of almond and *piñon* nougat next to the bell on the table.

"*Turrón de almendra!*" exclaimed la Condesa. "You haven't made this for me in a long time, Juana. Won't you join us, Madre?"

Melchora begged la Condesa's forgiveness and excused herself from the invitation, saying she had matters to discuss with the Sister in charge of the larder. Someone was helping herself to more than her share of eggs, she said, with a sidelong glance at Juana on her way out. La Condesa raised her fan to hide her face from Melchora and made a funny grimace at Juana. Juana sucked on her cheeks to keep from laughing. While Concepción cut generous slices of nougat for them, placing the slices carefully onto the blue and yellow Talavera plates that Jane used only for important visitors, Juana examined the cigarette case again, the cleverness of the clip, the tiny numbers on the stamp embossed on the back.

"It really is very kind of you to give me this," she told la Condesa.

La Condesa was chewing, and said behind her hand, "You did say you wanted to try them."

"How shall I explain them to Melchora?"

"All women of quality are smoking these days."

"I don't think nuns are included in that taxonomy."

"Of course you are. Haven't you noticed the difference between San Jerónimo and San Juan?"

"I've never been to San Juan."

"No good *criolla* has."

"Shall we smoke one together, then?"

"Go ahead, Juana. I want to enjoy your *turrón* and watch you smoke."

"May I leave now, Madre?" asked Concepción. "I have work to do in the garden."

"No," said Juana. "Go wait in the vestibule and make sure nobody comes in."

Juana waited until the girl had closed the door behind her. "Now," she said to la Condesa, "how do I do it?"

"Take the clip, clip it to one end of a cigarillo, that's right. Now light it. That's all. When you put it to your lips inhale very lightly. Don't take a deep breath, whatever you do."

Juana drew on the cigarette and exploded into a cough. Her throat had caught fire.

"You inhaled too much. Lightly, I said. Like a sip, not a big swallow."

"It burns," said Juana.

"That's because you're not used to it. I told you it was strong tobacco. Try it again."

Again Juana drew and fell into another coughing spasm. "Here," she managed to say, "I don't want any more." She tried to hand the clip to la Condesa.

"You haven't had any at all, Juana. Don't exasperate me. Do it again. I want you to know how to smoke. You have to be fashionable. Just because you're locked up in here doesn't mean you shouldn't know what's going on in the world. Even Queen María Luisa smokes, I'm told."

And just because you're so hardheaded doesn't mean I should damage my vocal chords, Juana responded silently, but she accepted the challenge and drew yet a third time on the smoking leaf. She absorbed the smoke very slowly, letting it trickle into her throat, feeling it fill the sacs of her lungs.

"Enough, Juana, enough! You've drawn too much again. You'll make yourself ill."

Juana released her breath and a stream of gray-blue smoke issued from her mouth, a small cough at the tail of it. There was a hint of camphor on her tongue. She drank some chocolate and lightly rinsed her mouth with the sweet warm liquid. Almost immediately she felt the effect. It started as a numbness in the roof of her mouth that spread out onto her lips and over her face, gathering in the middle of her scalp. She drank more chocolate and the feeling dissipated.

"Juana?"

"Forgive me, Condesa, I was focusing on the effect of the tobacco. For a moment there I felt almost lightheaded and very clear."

"I know what you mean. It can be quite addictive, you know. Some women smoke all day long. They start right after Mass and don't stop until vespers. It can rot your teeth if you do it too much."

Juana heard the bell ring in the gatekeeper's patio behind her and sensed that their visit was going to be interrupted. She tried to take another draft, but the thing had gone out. "They don't last long, do they?"

"Look, Juana, here comes Don Carlos with Padre Antonio."

Juana shot from her chair like a wind-up toy expulsed from its box. Before they entered she was sitting on the stool next to la Condesa, the cigarette case and half-smoked cigarillo hidden in the folds of her sleeve. La Condesa only blinked.

"Madam," said Don Carlos, bowing to the Vicereine. "We were returning from our Brotherhood meeting and saw your coach outside. Who could Her Highness be visiting, I said, but my dear friend and astronomical nemesis."

It was the first time Don Carlos had been in the same room with la Condesa since the comet fiasco of the previous year. Juana flinched at her friend's *indirecta*. Padre Antonio was assessing the seating arrangement with evident displeasure. He noted the cup of chocolate and plate of cake on the table beside the armchair, the empty velvet box.

"Is somebody sitting here?" he asked.

"That is my seat, Padre Miranda," said la Condesa. "You're welcome to it. I was just experimenting with sitting on this side of the grille."

"May I offer you some *turrón de almendra*, Padre? Don Carlos?" Juana asked.

"Nothing for me," said the priest, "I'm fasting today."

"Perhaps a thin slice for me, Sister. I can never resist any of your culinary delights."

She went to the sideboard and quickly slipped the remainder of the cigarillo into the case and hid the case behind the flower vase before serving her friend's refreshment.

"How have you been, Padre Miranda? I hear your eyesight is failing," la Condesa was saying.

"Perhaps, Madam, you wouldn't mind returning to your place," he said. "I find your presence on that side very disconcerting."

"But, of course, Padre. It was only an experiment." She rose from Juana's chair and went back to her usual seat.

"Rather like the French festival of fools in which paupers pretend to be royalty," said Don Carlos.

Juana handed the plate and cup to Don Carlos through the opening in the bars. La Condesa raised the cup that had been Juana's to her own lips and took a deep sip, keeping her gaze on Juana. Don Carlos dug into his dessert.

"I wouldn't call Juana either one, although it would please me to see her converted into the former," said Padre Antonio, sneering at the indulgence of the guests.

"And why should she be a pauper when the Mother Church is so rich?" asked la Condesa.

"Señora! You may be my superior, but I entreat you to watch your tongue. I am a *calificador* for the Inquisition and do not hear blasphemous remarks without impunity."

La Condesa rolled her eyes at Don Carlos.

Padre Antonio turned to Juana. "Mother Melchora tells me you've received a new commission, Juana. A *villancico*, I hope."

"No, Padre. The accountant, Don Fernando Deza, has asked me to prepare a *festejo* in honor of the palace that he wishes to present at his house."

The sound of forks scraping on porcelain punctuated the priest's stillness. "You do love to pay homage to the palace, don't you, Juana?" he said at length.

"It is a commission, Padre," she said.

"For which I imagine you are being handsomely paid," he said.

She ignored his remark. La Condesa narrowed her eyes at Padre Antonio.

"This *torta* is beyond excellent," exclaimed Don Carlos, trying to sway the conversation.

"I'll convey your compliments to Jane," said Juana.

"And what would be the argument of this homage, may I ask?" Padre Antonio was relentless.

"An homage has no argument, Father," Juana said, trying to keep her voice from going taut. "It pays tribute, as Don Fernando wishes to do, on the occasion of the Viceroy and Vicereine's third anniversary in México. It is a simple comedy of errors, nothing philosophical."

"I see. Does it have a title, then?"

"I'm calling it *Los empeños de una casa*," she said, "and it's about how mistaken identities converge on a noble house."

"And the protagonist?"

"Doña Leonor, isn't it?" said Don Carlos, wiping his mouth on the sleeve of his cassock. Juana shifted her eyes toward la Condesa and saw her immediate displeasure. Why couldn't he keep quiet? Just because he'd looked over her outline didn't give him the right to discuss her work so freely.

"Doña Leonor," Padre Antonio repeated. "How quaint. To use the name of our previous Vicereine to pay tribute to our current one."

La Condesa pulled a fan from her reticule and cast it open, not bothering to disguise her annoyance. "Really, Padre Miranda," she said, "to what do we owe this sudden interest in literature?"

"Correct me if my memory is at fault, Juana," he said, boring his black eyes into her own, "but have we not discussed this penchant of yours for secular scribblings, and did you not promise me to curb that temptation and dedicate yourself to reading Scripture, instead?"

"We did, Padre, discuss how to make the best use of this inclination of mine, and I did, as you know, compose those three *villancicos* that the Bishop of Puebla commissioned; and I've composed the carols in honor of the Immaculate Conception and of the Assumption every year for the last six years, not to mention those for the two Saint Peters." She pointed to the scroll in la Condesa's hand. "And now, as you can see, I've just completed a *loa* to the Queen, commissioned by la Señora Condesa, and am about to begin another *loa*, also commissioned by Her Majesty, to honor the King's birthday in November. I do not, however, remember promising you to forswear my other writings, Your Reverence."

"See here, Padre Antonio," said Don Carlos, looking vexed about their exchange, "this was supposed to be a friendly visit. Surely Sor Juana need not be reprimanded in the presence of our Vicereine."

"Coming from one with such a tarnished history in religion, Sir, that comment is uniquely appropriate." Padre Antonio got to his feet. "Still, I know that I am like a fly in milk in the present company. I'll leave you to your indulgences. I have matters to discuss with the Mother Superior."

They waited for him to leave and then la Condesa said, "More like a turd in milk."

Don Carlos burst out laughing.

"Juana, you've made me jealous. I didn't realize you were using the other Vicereine's name in *my* play!" She pouted her lips, and Juana had to close her eyes for a moment to keep from focusing on their soft, rouged texture.

"It isn't *your* play, Condesa," she said, eyes still closed. "And Doña Leonor actually represents me, not la Marquesa."

"Why couldn't you have called her something else, then?"

"If I may interject a literary analysis," said Don Carlos, placing his empty plate on the table.

"Please, my friend," Juana spoke up before la Condesa could object.

"What I hear in that name which is meant to represent our Juana is not Leonor per se but the French *le'honor*, meaning honor. Thus, it seems the most appropriate name for such an honorable character caught in the middle of all those convoluted *empeños*."

La Condesa cut her eyes at him and opened her fan again, fluttering it quickly over her face. "I hope you aren't going to tell me how it ends, too."

To Juana, she said, "I despise critics, don't you? They think they know everything."

"I was merely offering a humble analysis, Condesa," said Don Carlos, hand on his chest.

"Let me show you the gift la Condesa has brought me, Don Carlos," Juana said, seeing the need for a change of subject. She got up to retrieve her cigarette case.

"Look." She opened the case and offered it to him through the bars. Don Carlos took a cigarillo from the case and lit both his and Juana's with a twig from the brazier.

"It's so thin," he said, "I feel like I'm smoking air."

"They're meant for ladies," said la Condesa, still fanning herself.

"They're very light," he said, taking another puff. Juana noticed that he inhaled deeply and let the smoke issue from his nostrils in steady streams. He was obviously experienced at this smoking.

"What brings you today, anyway, Don Carlos?" asked la Condesa. "It isn't your regular visiting day, is it?"

"No, that's on Thursday," he said. "This wasn't meant to be a visit, actually, more of a warning than anything else, and then Padre Antonio saw me coming in this direction and attached himself, so forgive me, Juana, for bringing him and his bad mood into your salon."

"No need to apologize, my friend," said Juana, stifling a cough. "I know my father confessor."

Don Carlos turned to la Condesa. "Señora, what do you know of our new Archbishop? I hear very distressing news about him."

"We've not seen him at all since his arrival, except at Mass, of course," she said, holding her plate out to Juana for another slice of nougat. "He hasn't responded to a single summons to the palace. My husband is convinced he's avoiding us."

"That's precisely what I've heard. And do you know why? Sor Juana, you won't believe this. He doesn't want to be in your company, Madam, or in any lady's company."

Juana cut another helping for la Condesa and handed her back the plate. "He's come here to the convent," she said. "He's met with Melchora, I'm sure. She told us at chapter meeting, and these are her words, that Francisco de Aguiar y Seijas is the best thing that's happened to New Spain since the conquest."

"What a fool!" said Don Carlos.

"That's always been my opinion of her," said Juana.

"What does he have against ladies?" asked la Condesa. "He was born of one, or do you think he believes he was immaculately conceived from his father's thigh?"

"A Dionysian analogy, Madam," Don Carlos pointed out, stubbing the tail of his cigarillo out on his empty plate. "Spawned by a god and a mortal woman, and incubated in the god's thigh when the woman was struck dead by the god's brilliance. Very appropriate."

"You needn't condescend to la Condesa, my friend. She reads as avidly as we do," Juana said.

"Forgive me. I didn't realize our Vicereine shared our love of literature as well as astronomy."

"And several other subjects," added la Condesa, glancing briefly up at Juana. Juana felt her ears and neck grow warm.

"Well, I'm afraid the analogy stops there. The only thing the Archbishop indulges in more than misogyny is distributing alms to the poor and closing down *corrales de comedia*. Seems he abhors all manner of public spectacle, but especially plays and bullfights. He also rejects comfort, and wanders around in a torn cassock and tattered shoes."

"Good God," said la Condesa, "where does His Majesty find these specimens?"

"He was very revered in Compostela, actually. A devotee of Saint James who despises women with the same ferocity with which the saint persecuted Moors."

"Padre Antonio must worship the ground he walks on," said Juana, a feeling of dread taking root in the middle of her chest. "If he hates women and he hates plays, can you imagine how he feels about a woman playwright?"

"That's why I came to warn you, Juana. Is there any way you could postpone this commission of Don Fernando's?"

"How can I postpone it, my friend? He's already paid me half the honorarium, and the money has—" she felt embarrassed suddenly "—I've had to lend it to my sister, Josefa." Juana stubbed the last of the cigarillo into her dirty plate.

"Well, then, I suppose we shall have to entreat Padre Antonio to stand up for you," he said.

"And what are my husband and I, may I ask?" said la Condesa, her voice rising an octave. "Are we just painted on a wall? Do we have no influence?

Or do I need to remind you, Señor, that Juana has the full protection of the palace? There's nothing for her to fear, I assure you."

"Yes, Madam. But your husband's reign is not perpetual, and the Archbishop can remain here the rest of his life. She needs canonical protection as much as yours."

"Then I shall have my husband speak to Padre Antonio, as well as to the Bishop of Puebla. He's the one who should've been offered the Archbishopric in the first place, not this fanatic from Compostela."

"Yes, I know, Madam. Don Manuel is very bitter about it, but he's also way over there in Puebla and not here in our midst. As they say, Condesa: *amor de lejos es amor de conejos.*"

"I've heard it said another way," said la Condesa. "*Amor de lejos es amor de pendejos.* You needn't watch your tongue in my presence. Juana never does."

Juana felt herself blush again. Between the blushing and the dread, she could discern the onslaught of one of her headaches. She pressed her fingers to her temples and closed her eyes.

"There. Are you happy? You've upset her," la Condesa said to Don Carlos.

Juana opened her eyes and saw that la Condesa had gotten up from her chair and was standing right by the grille.

"It isn't good news," said Don Carlos, "but I wouldn't be a friend if I didn't warn you."

"Thank you, Don Carlos, truly. You know how I hate surprises," said Juana, sliding to the edge of her chair. "And now, you're both going to have to forgive me, but I must end our visit and see if the infirmarian can draw me up an infusion before I start seeing spots."

"Was it the cigarillos do you think, Juana?" asked la Condesa, reaching a hand through the grille. Juana tried to resist, but before she knew it her own hand was grasping la Condesa's, their fingers interlocked, her own sweaty palm pressed against her friend's cool one. Don Carlos sat stiff as a statue.

"It's me," she managed to say. "Too many emotions swirling around in me right now." For a flash of an instant, she contemplated bringing la Condesa's hand up to her mouth and kissing her palm.

"Does this belong to you, Sister?" Don Carlos was holding out the velvet box in which her gift had come.

"Thank you," she said, letting go of la Condesa's hand. She slipped the cigarette case back into the box and left without another word. There was still time before the next Office and she needed to feel the bite of the scourge on her back to quell this sudden desire to reach through the bars and plunge her hands into the milky cleavage of those breasts. What she would give to have the intimate knowledge of a corset, to live in the warm shadows of a petticoat! Dear God, she thought, I mustn't see her until this passes. All that talk earlier about *huipiles* and bosoms, the tight grip of those fingers on her own, the look of those glittering eyes piercing through her escutcheon and her scapular and tunic, straight through to her living heart. It was more than she could contain, much more than the scourge could alleviate.

12 *November 1682*

Have just received a note from la Condesa. She cannot come to celebrate my birthday, she says, because her doctors are sending her away for the benefit of her condition. She is with child, good God! She says they must go to the viceregal house in Chapultepec and not return to the city until the rains have quit, for the rains bring disease and a vile stench that poisons the streets and makes the air noxious to the life she's carrying inside her. The life she's carrying! That means I won't see her for six weeks. Why do I have to be punished for this? Her absence is the most severe penitence I can imagine. "I've had so many miscarriages in the past, Juana, that the doctors fear the very air I breathe could poison my child." It had never occurred to me that la Condesa wanted to give life, to bear children inside her body. Why did we never speak of it? Why did I assume she wanted to remain chaste of that experience as I do? And now her own health is at risk. Dear Mother of God, please keep her safe. Must light candles at the altar of the Lady of Mount Carmel. Keep her safe, Lady. I couldn't live if I lost her, too.

17 NOVEMBER 1682

MY DEAREST CONDESA,

For five days now I have had knots tied in my stomach. Hearing of your condition and knowing that so many weeks must pass before I see you has been such tortuous news. I tell myself to stop this nonsense. We each have our own destinies to fulfill and we both know that the choices we have made in the past have brought us to this moment of juncture and disjuncture.

I am waiting for Concepción to return from the market, and then I will dispatch her to the palace with this letter. I know you are leaving today. The convent is full of spies, outnumbered only by the spies that lurk at your own gates. And yet I cast caution to the wind. I ache to see you, to sit beside you, to watch you eat your favorite pastries and listen to your voice. You know I cannot write to you without the missive passing under the scrutiny of Sor Rafaela, and although the sealed letters that you send me are not opened, I am required to show them to the Mother Superior after I have read them, and I must read them in the Mother Superior's office. The silence is strangling me. The waiting. How will it be when your condition worsens and you cannot visit me at all, when you will be bedridden, waiting for the arrival of the one you carry inside you who will then occupy you with his constant care. Why do I assume you shall bear a masculine child? Perhaps because when he comes he will deliver you from your burden, and increase mine, or perhaps he will save us both from the very difficult particularities of our friendship. I send you this miniature portrait to remind you that I am mute and deaf and blind as this picture until we see each other again.

Always,

your Juana.

QUERIDA JUANA,

Today, after a fortnight of not seeing you, I feel utterly despondent. A cold rain has started and I watch it streaking the granite flags of the terrace. Chapultepec is absolutely dismal in the mist. I stand at the window looking southward, in the direction of the convent, and hope that you will not hold this distance against me, as it is by decree of the doctors that I am here. Happily, they have assured me that I can return to the palace by Epiphany. Tomás hears me sniffling and asks me if I've caught a grippe, and how do I answer him? The grippe I suffer from has no name, is nothing more than the despondency of missing you, and the desire to sit in your *locutorio*, listen to your voice, know what you're thinking. I have, you see, become accustomed to your odd ways and our conversations.

I imagine myself arriving at the convent drenched in rain, and you insisting that I must change my clothes in your quarters. I see your servant—the smart one who reads everything—bringing me a towel and one of your own shifts, and I swear by the Virgin's shawl that I can feel you watching me as I undress. You do not know that in the last few days I have been visited by you late at night; I know it is your image, an apparition that comes and goes softly, but I can hear your steady breathing, smell the scent of the incense that you like to burn while you write. In my dreams, your words flow across my body. I feel the pressure of your quill on my skin. In other dreams, I see you touching the beads on your rosary, your fingers moving on the dark cedar circles, one by one, and I become the small crucified body on the end of that rosary. I am as mute as the clouds and my only message to you, my only words to you, are like these drops of rain, siphoned away by gods and men. Perhaps it is my condition that is sowing such melancholy in me, but I think it of great importance suddenly, to tell you exactly how I feel, just in case anything happens. I quake at the thought that you may not know how reciprocal it is, this need to be with you. It occurred to me last night while we listened to the court poet reciting his sad verses in the large salon, the blue one, that you and I are like that image he was trying so desperately to weave into his sadly pedantic poetry: I am the sea and you the earth, and we are both bound and separated by, as you say, our distinctive choices. The sea bathes the shore in its liquid, briny humors; the sand contains the secrets the waves have pulled from the bottom of the sea.

I must go now. Tomás has ordered a posset for this grippe of mine. How do I tell him that you are the missing ingredient in the wine? I have taken your example and am having my portrait painted in miniature. You shall receive it when it's ready. I'm sending a page into the city to deliver this note directly into your hands; he has, I trust, enough *reales* to bribe your gatekeeper.

Please destroy this letter, and remember that I remain, always,
your melancholic María Luisa.
5th of December 1682

8 DECEMBER 1682

CONDESA,

The page, discreetly, will relate
how, the moment it was read,

I tore your secret into shreds
that shreds be not the secret's fate.
And something more, inviolate,
I swallowed what you had confessed,
the tiny fragments of your note,
to guard the secret that you wrote
and honor thus your confidence, lest
even one scrap escape my breast.

I await Epiphany like one awaiting the Queen of the Magi.
Jidl†

Chapter 16

"*Who* does the man think he is?" Juana exclaimed, her voice echoing in the priory.

"You must not raise your voice to the Mother Superior, Juana," said Rafaela, taking notes in her ledger with her tattered turkey quill.

"Why does Padre Antonio not come to me with his complaints, Mother? Why must he air his thoughts to everyone except the one concerned?"

"We all know how stubborn you can be, Juana," said Melchora. "His Reverence thought it best to come to me directly and solicit my help in saving you. Obviously Madre Catalina and Fray Payo were too indulgent with you."

"Saving me from what, Mother? From ignorance?"

"Don't act so innocent," said Rafaela. "You know perfectly well what Padre Miranda wants."

"Give up your worldly books," said Melchora. "And your scandalous verses. Forbear these secular commissions, these plays and comedies, that are leading you down the path of perdition. Devote yourself to the welfare of the convent, Juana, and to the salvation of your soul. You seem to forget that you renounced the world many years ago."

"Am I to refuse Don Fernando's commission for the festival, then? Should I disobey the wishes of a man who has been one of our most generous patrons? Or should I lie to him and tell him I cannot complete it? Is it Padre Antonio's desire that I insult the Viceroy and the Vicereine as well as Don Fernando?"

"His Reverence is beside himself, Juana," said Melchora. "He blames himself for his shortsightedness. He said he should have guessed that you would be as impudent in the convent as you were in the palace."

"He says, Juana," added Rafaela, "that he should have married you to a man instead of to Christ. Obviously you need a firmer hand, he says, more direct intervention and guidance since you are unable or unwilling to quell this stubborn perverseness of yours."

"Marry me to a *man?*" shouted Juana. She could feel the veins throbbing in her neck. "Since when did Padre Antonio have the authority to decide what became of my life? It was I who chose to profess. I who chose *him* as my confessor, just as I can choose another who is not so repulsed by my actions or so scandalized by my refusal to be coerced into submission. For fourteen years, he has done nothing but complain about my writings, about my studies, about my guests, *even* about my handwriting!"

"Masculine penmanship it is, Sister," said Rafaela. "Very unbecoming for a nun to have such illegible writing. I don't see how that secretary of yours can read anything you write."

"This is outrageous!" Juana fumed. "Masculine penmanship. Masculine studies. Masculine conversation. Masculine verses. Why is everything that edifies the mind ascribed to masculinity? Are men the only ones capable of writing, studying, or speaking? Or does Padre Antonio echo the Archbishop's notion that women have no minds or souls, and therefore need no spiritual or intellectual nourishment?"

"I doubt you're in a position to contradict our holy fathers, Juana!" said Rafaela.

"Are you implying, Juana," said the Mother Superior, "that Holy Scripture is not enough spiritual nourishment for you?"

Juana lowered her voice. "Perhaps you have not discovered this, Sisters, but without a well-developed mind, the soul is impoverished and susceptible to all manner of spiritual disease, greed and malice among them. There is much in Holy Scripture that cannot be understood without some knowledge of the sciences, unless one wants to continue repeating the same psalms and parables and say that one has studied Holy Scripture and has, therefore, become spiritually nourished."

"We're not here to engage in a debate with you, Juana. I convey only Padre Miranda's concerns for your salvation. He fears for you. The Archbishop is most displeased."

"The Archbishop's displeasure does not seem to prevent him from borrowing money from me," Juana pointed out. "Just last week he asked me to lend him another fifty pesos—"

"I told you, Mother," Rafaela interrupted. "She thinks she's *lending* the Archbishop money."

"I *am* lending it, and I am expecting him to pay it back, Sister. I have expenses of my own that I've not been able to meet because all my funds are currently tied up by His Ilustrísima. I've not been able to balance my accounts because he is using my money for repairing the casements in the archiepiscopal palace."

Melchora glanced at the hourglass on her desk. "It's almost time for compline," she said. "Check your notes, Sister Vicaria, and tell me if we've covered the important points of Padre Miranda's conference."

"About the gifts, Mother," said Rafaela.

"Of course, the gifts," said Melchora.

"That ridiculous Indian headdress," said Rafaela, reading from her notes, "that pagan diadem, that cigarette case!" She shut her notebook with a snap. "Really, Juana, have you no shame?"

"Padre Miranda has authorized me to put an end to this eternal gift exchange between yourself and the Vicereine," said Melchora. "I trust this will not require another debate, Juana."

"Of course it requires a debate, Mother," Juana responded. "Has His Reverence also the authority to dictate to the Vicereine what she can and cannot do? For it is her will and her wish to give me presents, and I am in no position to refuse them, nor can I accept these gifts without fitting reciprocation. If you want to put an end to the exchange, Mother, I suggest you or His Reverence ask the Vicereine to quit her generosity. I cannot compromise my virtues."

They looked at her as if they did not understand what she was saying.

"Gratitude is still one of our virtues, is it not?" She wanted to scream it in their bovine faces, but kept her voice measured and her eyes straight ahead.

"One needs to be a rhetorician to speak with you, Juana!" said Melchora, pushing her chair back and rising from behind her desk. "You have the most malevolent habit of making sense out of nonsense. I find it impossible to listen to you any longer."

"Padre Miranda's right. You *are* a mule in nun's clothing!" said Rafaela.

It was useless, now, to pretend politeness. She turned to leave.

"I shall pray for you tonight, Juana."

Juana looked over her shoulder. "And I for you, Mother. And I shall pray that the next time my father confessor has something to say about me, he shall have the charity to say it to my face."

Juana stormed out of the priory, tempted to slam the door behind her. Why wouldn't they leave her alone? Why did they insist on tormenting her with the same stupid questions about her soul. They knew she had work to do. This evening she had to finish Act One of *Empeños* so that Concepción could get to work copying the final draft. By the time Concepción was done with Act One, all of the scenes for Act Two had to be ready. But how could they be? With all of these interruptions she kept getting the plot confused, kept losing track of the subplots. The characters stepped all over each other, and now the male comic was upstaging the female comic; she could feel the audience getting lost amid the confusion. And now this. This, of all things. Padre Antonio talking about her behind her back, and to the likes of Melchora and Rafaela! Dear God, how she missed Fray Payo.

Just as she passed the chapter room the bells rang for compline. She knew it would be useless to return to her cell until after the final Office. She had lost another hour. She turned back toward the church and reached the lower choir before any of the others. For the first time since she had professed, she was early for an Office. She knelt before the image of the Guadalupana and said a quick prayer for patience. When the others filed into the choir Juana was already installed in her pew. Andrea took the seat next to her and made the sign of the Cross over her face and chest.

"How did it go?" she whispered as Melchora intoned the opening antiphon.

"They're wearing me out with their stupidity," Juana whispered back.

"There's talk in the refectory that you struck Jane again."

"And whose business is that? She's my slave, Andrea."

"Just as you are God's slave, Juana, and yet you fail to see the justice in it when the Mother Superior chastises *you*."

"*Et tu*, Andrea?" said Juana.

"You're becoming just like them, Juana."

"Sshh!" someone hissed behind them.

She tried to concentrate on the psalm, but Andrea was right. She had treated Jane in the same disparaging way that Melchora and Rafaela—and now even her own father confessor—were treating her, and yet she justified her actions by saying that Jane was her possession. When had she started believing that? This terrified her, the idea that she was somehow, despite her intelligence and all of her studies, becoming one of her sisters, adopting their illiterate views and cruel behavior, absorbing the vinegar that soured their own livers. She had to quit all this anger and come back to her senses. Analyze the situation without emotion.

She had been furious with Jane for six months, ever since she'd confessed that she was carrying a child and wanted to bring it to term. The thought of Jane intercoursing with men when she went to the market, of her returning here to the convent, to Juana's own apartment, reeking of filthy bodies and sweat, standing there cooking her food, touching the meat and the fruit and the bread she served to Juana—the repugnance roiled like nausea at the back of her throat.

Late one night, possessed by anger and disgust, Juana had gone downstairs to Jane's room and beaten her out of bed, kicking her out of the bedclothes and striking her face, both sides of it, several times, as hard as she could. The rage possessed her as nothing ever had—stabbing her like a cold blade in the spine—and she wanted to keep on beating and kicking, punishing that soiled body until she drew out its filth, but someone stilled her hand.

It was Concepción, standing there with a wet towel. The girl began sponging off her face, blowing cool air on Juana's skin. "Enough, Madre," she whispered. "Enough now. She's learned her lesson. Come, come back upstairs to your own bed. Just follow me."

The girl had thought Juana was asleep, that she was beating Jane in her sleep. It was the only thing that allowed her to even look at Jane, the farce that she acted without conscious intention. Poor, poor Jane. How unfair! And she had done it again, this evening, not with the same rage or desire to punish, but with a sense of eternal frustration at never having the cooperation she needed.

She had been pacing in the parlor, trying to think of a comical way to explain why the gendarmes had deposited Doña Leonor in Doña Ana's house while they pursued the murderer of Doña Leonor's cousin, Don Diego. He had been killed by Doña Leonor's lover, Don Carlos, when he had caught them trying to elope. Meanwhile Doña Ana was secretly in love with Don Carlos, although it was Don Juan who pursued her, just as Don Pedro, Doña Ana's brother, pursued Doña Leonor. She was just about to solve the riddle she had made of the plot, when Jane interrupted.

"Concepción says you're nervous, Madre. I can brew you a tea. Linden blossom is good for the nerves." Juana heard Jane's high-pitched voice ringing up the stairwell, shouting up at her like a common fishmonger, and she felt the blood rise to her head. Suddenly she was down the stairs in the parlor, spitting angry words in Jane's face.

"How dare you make all this noise when you know I'm working!" Juana had exploded. She could hear her heart pounding in her ears.

Jane's eyes narrowed. "I was just offering to make you a tea," she said.

"I am so sick of your shouting," said Juana.

"And I'm sick of you," Jane said. "Here I am trying to be nice to you." She turned her back on Juana and waddled off toward the kitchen, supporting the watermelon of her belly with both hands.

"Don't walk away from me!" Juana yelled, following her, and Concepción scuttled down the stairwell to see what was going on. Jane turned around, hands on her waist. She had grown so fat that her face and breasts looked as though they'd been inflated by a bellows.

"I should have put poison in your food a long time ago," she said.

"I don't want your stupid food. I want you to clean up. It stinks of old food in here!"

"I told you, Madre, I can't lift anything or bend down."

"You pregnant women are useless! La Condesa can't come to visit me because she's carrying low. You have us living in a pigsty because you can't bend over. You better wash these dishes!"

"I can't wash them without water. If you'd make that *castiza* earn her keep, she could help me, but no, she's too special, she's your sweetheart, I guess."

Suddenly, Juana reached out and slapped both sides of Jane's face, her hand stinging from the impact. She heard something crack in Jane's mouth.

Jane shook her head and walked away again, holding her jaw. Juana saw the humiliation pouring down her face, the pain inscribed in her grimace, but by then it was too late to stop herself. She grabbed Jane by the back of the hair and pulled her to a stop.

"Pack your junk!" she said through gritted teeth. "I want you out of my sight!"

Jane wrenched herself from Juana's grip and slammed the door of the room where she and Concepción slept, locking it from the inside.

"I know you beat me on purpose that night," Jane shouted from the other side of the door. "You're no better than a man, but at least a man gives me what I like."

"I'll go get the water, Madre," said Concepción behind her.

"No you won't!" Juana said. She rapped her knuckles on the door. "Jane. Did you hear me? Pack your things. You're leaving in the morning. I've had enough of you! I won't tolerate a whore for a maid, or a bawling brat in my cell. And if you don't obey me, I'll amend my plan and sell you to an *obraje*. God knows I need the money!"

She turned toward Concepción. "And you, *metiche!*" she yelled. "Have you finished your work?"

"No—no, Madre," the girl stuttered, her eyes wide as coins. "Almost."

"Almost!" Juana swooped past her and climbed the stairwell. "Let me see what you've done." She strode over to Concepción's desk. The stack of parchment on which she was supposed to have been copying Act One was blank except for eight lines from Doña Leonor's entrance soliloquy:

> Such was my eagerness to learn,
> from my earliest inclination,
> that studying far into the night,
> and with most eager application,
> I accomplished in a briefer span
> the weary toil of long endeavor,
> with diligence, commuting time
> through the fervor of my labor;

"This is all you've done?" she said through clenched teeth. "I told you that Don Fernando is coming to pick up Act One in the morning."

"You told me we'd be working late tonight. You know I'll be finished by daybreak. I'm not sleepy at all, Madre. Don't worry. It'll get it done. I promise. And I can go fetch the water for the dishes, too, if you want. It won't take long."

"You just want an excuse to visit with that prisoner. Don't think I haven't been informed that you steal out at night to visit her. Aren't you too old to be sneaking behind bushes?"

Concepción hung her head, and Juana felt a surge of tenderness for her. Juana's anger always dissipated around Concepción. "Where's the opening *loa?*" her voice softened. "You've finished that, I hope."

Concepción gestured to a pile of sheets on the corner of the desk. Juana picked up the pile and carried it over to her own desk to proofread, the choler she had unleashed still hammering through her temples. That was when she had gotten the summons from Melchora.

Damn this life and its perpetual interruptions! Juana thought while her sisters sang the closing antiphon of the evening Office.

"I don't know what to tell you, Juana," said Andrea, walking back from the church with her.

"But you're the archivist. You hear things, Andrea. What are they saying about me?"

"It's the Archbishop. He's filling them with *cizañas*."

"What did I do to him to merit such antipathy? I give him anything he wants."

"It's obedience that he wants. And he's put it into Melchora's head that you'll bring doom to this house if you don't mend your ways."

"Two-faced devil!"

"Juana! That's His Ilustrísima that you're cursing."

"He means to drain me of all my savings, and meanwhile he's spoiling my relationship with Padre Antonio and turning Melchora into an archenemy. Why do they do this to me, Andrea? Why do they hate me so?"

"It's your influence, don't you see? They know you don't fear them because you have the protection of the palace. You're more celebrated in New Spain than the Archbishop is. No prelate can tolerate that kind of notoriety, especially not when it pertains to a nun, Juana. You've been immodest. They think you're flaunting your power."

"Good evening, Sisters," said Sor Agustina, coming up behind them. "Watch where you're walking, there's a rat running around and the cats are frantic."

She walked past them, her *vigilanta*'s switch swinging from her cincture. In the light of the sconces, her figure cast a huge shadow on the flagstones.

"Do you think she heard us?" Juana whispered.

"Agustina specializes in eavesdropping. From the priory she can hear what the maids are saying in the laundry room. She can even hear when someone rings at the portal."

Juana shook her head. Of a sudden, she became fatigued and declined Andrea's invitation to supper.

"We were supposed to discuss the accounts, Juana."

"I'll send Concepción over with the ledgers," she said. "I need to work on that *festejo*."

"Will you take some advice, Juana?"

"You're the only one I trust to give me advice," she answered.

Andrea bent to whisper in her ear. "A demonstration of penitence, a vigil, perhaps, might help. Padre Antonio would hear about it, and so would the Archbishop. Buy yourself some time. Meditate, Juana. Look ahead. They're laying traps for you, believe me."

Juana nodded. Andrea was right. She did need that extra time to think. And both Jane and Concepción would benefit from being alone a few hours longer.

In a voice meant to be overheard, she said, "Forgive me, Andrea. I won't be able to join you for supper tonight. I'm holding a vigil to the Virgin."

"Next week then," said Andrea, her voice equally audible. "Pray for us, Juana."

"I'd promised to read to Madre Catalina this evening," she said in a lower voice.

"I'll do that for you, Juana. I should spend more time with her anyway."

Juana squeezed her friend's arm and turned back in the direction of the choir. She would even go so far as to prostrate herself at the foot of the Virgin's altar, but then decided against it in case her lumbago flared up. She had not held a vigil since her days as a novice, when she and Andrea liked to compete with each other to see who could last prostrate longer, and, of course, Andrea always won, for Juana, already in the habit of staying up late with her studies, fell asleep with her cheek to the marble and lost the contest.

Her oil lamp cast a sheen over the candlelit choir. The statues seemed to breathe, their inscrutable glass eyes following her as she wandered back and forth between the different altars on either side of the high-back pews where they gathered seven times a day. Saint Jerome had the place of honor at the front, and his devotees (some said they were his lovers, mother and daughter) Saint Paula and Saint Estochium guarded either side of the locked grate that separated the choir from the rest of the church, keeping the nuns forever caged in the convent. Tonight she identified with Saint Sebastian, dark arrows piercing his body while he stood tied to his stake. She unfastened the rosary from her shoulder and knelt at the saint's feet, but she didn't pray. Staring up at the wounds in Sebastian's neck, she began composing a letter to Padre Antonio, and realized she was going to dismiss him as her father confessor.

Both hands of the clock were on the III when Juana returned to her cell. The quicksand of exhaustion had been pulling at her eyelids for hours, and she hoped Jane had had the foresight to prepare a pot of chocolate mixed with coffee. It was the only thing that prevented her from falling asleep when she burned the midnight oil.

Downstairs, the parlor felt colder than usual. Jane must have forgotten to close the shutters; either that or she was airing the smell of fried food out of the cell. Upstairs, she found Concepción working her quill diligently over the page, an empty plate and cup at her elbow. The dark beverage in Juana's cup had grown a skin; her quesadillas sat in a pool of grease. Juana's stomach growled at the sight of food.

"You took a long time, Madre," said Concepción, inking her quill.

Juana sat down at her desk and took a bite of quesadilla. Squash blossom, her favorite. Poor Jane was trying to make it up to her when it should be the other way around.

"How much progress have you made, Concepción? I'm surprised you're still awake."

"I'm almost finished with this section, Madre. Is the last scene ready?"

Juana ate the last bite of quesadilla and wiped her mouth with the cloth napkin under her plate. The vigil had wearied her, but at least she knew exactly what she was going to say to Padre Antonio. And she knew, also, that she would have to send word to Don Fernando and beg his indulgence for the delay in delivering Act One of the *festejo*. This matter with Padre Antonio had to be resolved first. She barely had the energy to speak.

"Does your back hurt, Madre? Shall I rub it for you?"

Juana sighed deeply. "No, we have work to do. Put that aside for now. I've a letter to dictate."

"Right now? But I thought you said we had to finish this before morning."

"Don Fernando will just have to wait."

Concepción straightened the pages she had written and stacked them neatly on the corner of her desk, then she pulled a sheet of stationery from its cubbyhole and inked another goose quill.

"*Pax Xpti*," Juana began as she unpinned the escutcheon from her scapular. "*For some time now various persons have informed me that I am singled out—*"

"Slow down, Madre, please."

Juana took the pins from her veil while Concepción caught up. "*—that I am singled out for censure in the conversations of Your Reverence—*"

Concepción shook out her fingers, then pinched her cheeks to keep herself alert.

"*—in which you denounce my actions with such bitter exaggeration as to sug-*

gest a—underline the next two words, please—*public scandal, and other no less shocking epithets.*"

"—and other what, Madre?" Concepción blinked hard.

Juana repeated the phrase. She had already removed the veil and let it drop on the floor. Now she was untying the coif. "*Although my conscience might move me to my own defense*— Concepción! You're not falling asleep, I hope?"

Concepción snapped her head up. "No, Madre, no, just trying to keep up." She pinched herself again and kept writing, mumbling to herself the words that Juana was dictating.

"—*and that they listen to you as if to a divine oracle and appreciate your words as if they were dictated by the Holy Ghost, and that the greater your authority, the more is my good name injured*—"

A deep yawn made the girl pause.

"Get up, Concepción! Open the shutters! You need some fresh air."

Concepción did as she was told. "It's just that I've been sitting here since you went to compline, Madre," she said, holding her waist and turning her back sideways from the hip. Her movement reminded Juana of the belly dancers who used to perform for the Viceroy when she lived at the palace. The girl swung her shoulders from side to side again, her hips turning in the opposite direction.

"Why are you doing that, Concepción?"

"Doing what, Madre?"

"Distracting me like that. If you need to exercise why don't you run up and down the stairwell for five minutes?"

"I'm just so tired, Madre. I don't mean to disturb you."

There you go, again, Juana, she told herself, *getting impatient.*

"I understand you're tired, *cariño*. We're both tired."

The dark morning air felt like a swath of water on her face and neck. Juana wanted to take her clothes off and bathe in its coolness, but instead she just pulled the scapular over her head and let it fall on the rosary and cincture, which lay on the heap of black and white cloth at her feet. "Here," she said, "help me unfasten the stays of these sleeves."

Concepción untied the stays, and the heavy sleeves dropped to the floor. Juana's thin arms were nearly as pale as her tunic. A woolly smell rose from the dark hair in her armpits. She needed a bath.

"Shall I bring you something to drink, Madre? Something fresh?"

"I'll just drink this chocolate," said Juana, tousling her short hair with both hands. "The sugar will do me good." She drank from her cup in deep swallows. "Look, Concepción—" she pointed at Concepción's blouse— "you've got an ink stain on your *huipil*."

"I know, Madre. The pen slipped out of my hand earlier. I guess I was nodding off."

"We both need to freshen up," said Juana, getting to her feet. "Follow me. And bring all that stuff, will you?"

Concepción gathered up Juana's veil and scapular and sleeves, wound the rosary around her wrist, and followed her past the Turkish carpet into her dormitory. While Concepción hung everything up in the wardrobe, smoothing out the wrinkles in the cloth and coiling the rosary neatly into its box, Juana poured fresh water into the basin. From the top drawer of the bureau she pulled out two washcloths and dipped one into the water, wrung it out, and told Concepción to stand beside her. Juana realized that she stood a head higher than the girl, though the girl had a way of carrying herself that made her seem taller. Why had she never noticed this before?

Juana wiped Concepción's face with the wet cloth, her other hand supporting the nape of the girl's neck. She wiped the forehead first, then the cheekbones and the cheeks, then the chin, then down over her neck, and back up to her temples and her eyelids and behind her ears. There was something remarkably alluring about the texture of Concepción's skin, like soft, worn suede. Juana could feel her nipples hardening under the linen of her habit, as if the night breeze wafting into the room were making her cold, and yet her face felt hot, her armpits moist.

She wet the cloth again and wiped Concepción's forearms, pausing for a second at the back of each wrist and in the crook of each elbow, to cool the veins, she said, though her own veins were starting to throb at the feel of the girl's skin.

Stop this, Juana! You're wading in dangerous waters.

And yet there was a certain acquiescence to Concepción, the way she stood there and let Juana fuss over her, the way she held her breath when Juana touched her.

You're making things up, Juana. The girl is tired, that's all.

She took a deep breath and felt her vows sinking like stones into the pit of her stomach.

"Your turn now, Concepción," said Juana. Concepción opened her eyes to find Juana handing her the other washcloth.

The girl's hands trembled as she wrung out the cloth. She repeated what

Juana had done to her, held the back of Juana's head and wiped her face, her neck, each of her wrists and forearms.

"Why are you trembling?" asked Juana. "Are you cold?"

Concepción swallowed hard. "I thought we were in a hurry, Madre."

"Take your blouse off. Let's soak it and see if the stain comes out."

"Oh, no, Madre, it doesn't matter."

"You know I don't like to see beautiful clothes ruined, Concepción. Besides, you don't have that many nice things to wear. Go on."

Obediently, the girl raised her arms and Juana pulled the blouse over her head. She had no shift on underneath and stood there with her arms in the air, her small breasts exposed, the veins in her neck pulsing. Juana could not believe what she was doing as her fingertips grazed the girl's dark nipples.

"You have such beautiful skin, Concepción," she said, lowering the girl's arms to her side, "and hardly any hair on your body. That must be the Indian in you." She let her fingertips graze the girl's shoulders, the bones of her clavicle, down between her breasts and over the nipples again. The girl's skin grew goosebumps and she shuddered.

"I'm making you cold," said Juana. She tried to look at Concepción in the eye, but the girl had lowered her face.

Juana knew she should stop but couldn't keep her hands away from those breasts, firm and yet soft as ripe figs.

"Look at me, Concepción," she said, and the girl raised her face to Juana's. "How old are you?"

"I'm nineteen, Madre." Juana was exactly fifteen years older, the same age difference between herself and la Marquesa. She had been about the same age as Concepción when she'd declared the truth of her feelings and spoiled their friendship.

"Have you let anyone touch you before? Some man?"

Concepción swallowed but didn't answer.

"Who was it, Concepción?"

"Nobody, Madre. Just a gypsy I met at the Plaza."

Juana felt suddenly jealous. "You let that gypsy touch you?"

"Jane said I had to if I expected to learn about men. She said you'd never teach me anything. She said it would feel good, eventually."

Juana bent over and pressed her lips against the girl's mouth. Concepción tasted sweet, like chocolate. She smelled of civet. "Did that feel good?"

Concepción's eyelids fluttered, but she did not look away. "I don't know, Madre."

Juana kissed the girl again, parting her lips this time with her tongue and letting her teeth cut slightly into the girl's soft flesh. Concepción pulled her head back, the pink tip of her tongue rubbing at her lip.

"How about that?"

"It hurt, Madre."

"And the gypsy didn't hurt you?" She wanted to pinch the girl's nipples.

"Just the first time."

Juana felt her belly quivering with something that felt like anger but that caused a moistness to well up between her legs. "Get out of here," she said through clenched teeth. "You make me sick."

The girl swallowed, and Juana's eyes lingered on the movement of her throat. "But why, Madre? I'm old enough."

Juana wanted to slap her and kiss her at the same time. She pulled away and plunged her hands into the basin of cold water. "I would expect that behavior from Jane, but not from you, Concepción, not after everything I've taught you."

"But, Madre—"

"Get out!"

"What about the letter you were going to dictate?"

The letter to Padre Antonio. She had forgotten about everything. Juana felt the blood rise like hot steam into her face. "Get out," she yelled. "Or do I need to flog you to make you understand?"

Concepción's eyes bubbled with tears. "You've never raised your voice to me before," she said.

Juana's heart pounded in her throat. She bent over and plunged her face into the basin, feeling the water splash over the brim and onto her shoes. When she looked up, the girl was gone.

Chapter 17

20 December 1682

Dear God, what have I done? How could I have allowed myself to be so weak? I sit here stunned by my ability to complicate my own life. I tell myself it did not really happen, I did not really kiss Concepción, and yet I remember the precise smell and texture of her skin, a scent of civet and something sweet, like chocolate, and her skin—God and la Condesa forgive me, how I wanted to run my hands over the soft suede of her body, how I wanted to take the small figs of her breasts into my mouth. Even now, moisture gathers under my tongue as I think about it. If I had not become angry with her, I would have acted on the irrational possibilities.

I do not want this to mean anything. Not yet. Not ever. I want only the taste of it, the smell of it, on my fingers, and nothing more. Is that possible? She would never tell anybody, would she? She wouldn't expect me to explain it or apologize for it or ever mention it again, would she? Surely, she cannot continue in my service. This is going to haunt me, I know. Dear Mother of God, why did you allow me to surrender to this weakness?

Now I must stop thinking about this and get back to my letter to Padre Antonio. I really can't continue to trust him as my father confessor. I can stand no more of his fault finding. I am too sorely tried. What obligation is there that my salvation, if that's what it is, be effected through Padre Antonio? Can it not be through another? Is God's mercy restricted and limited to one man? I think I'll ask him those same questions in the letter.

Oh, God. Please remove the memory of her skin from my hands so that I can concentrate.

28 December

Worked all through Christmas, but at last the letter is finished. I have told Padre Antonio in no uncertain terms that if he cannot look upon me with the charity, discretion, and kindness of a father confessor, then he need not bother himself with me anymore, nor need our relationship be furthered. The letter is full of rhetorical questions concerning a woman's right to study and to write, and there is no small amount of recriminations against Padre Antonio's indiscretion. These are my favorite sections:

> Are letters an obstacle or do they, rather, lead to salvation? Was not St. Augustine saved, St. Ambrose, and all the other Holy Doctors? And Your Reverence, with such learning, do you not plan to be saved?

> What then is the cause of such anger? And of the injury to my reputation? Or holding me up as scandalous before everyone? Do I offend Y.R. in some manner? Have I asked you to assist me in my needs? Or have I disturbed you in any other spiritual or worldly matter? Did my correction fall to Y.R. by reason of obligation, of relationship, upbringing, plelature, or other such thing? If it is mere charity, let it be seen as mere charity and proceed as such, gently, for vexing me is not a good way to assure my submission, nor do I have so servile a nature that I do under threat what reason does not persuade me, nor out of respect for man what I do not do for God; and to deprive myself of all that can give me pleasure, though it be entirely licit, it is best that I do as self-mortification, when I wish to do penance, and not because Y.R. hopes to achieve it by means of censure, and then not given in secret with fatherly discretion . . . but publicly before everyone, where each can think as he chooses and speak as he thinks.

The letter is going to infuriate him, I know, but good riddance to him and his foul humor and his perpetual rancor against the inclinations God gave me. Now I must get Concepción to make a copy while I'm at prayers. Can't be in the same room with her without feeling a strange ringing in my ears. No doubt it is guilt for my disloyalty to la Condesa.

7 January 1683
Jane tells me that Concepción is still sleeping, that she has not been able to wake her all day, no matter how much noise she makes in the kitchen. There is a rumor among the maids who saw her coming from the garden at daybreak that she was returning from some nocturnal tryst.

"The gypsies were run out of town, Madre, but maybe her *gitano*'s come back. She's been preening like a—"

"Never mind, Jane, I don't want to hear the lurid details," I interrupted before she could further her description. "Let her sleep. I've been working her too hard, I think."

"Too bad you don't have the same consideration for me, Madre."

She's right, but how can I tell her that? Besides, it's her fault she's pregnant and gets tired more easily these days. I pray to the Virgin that Concepción doesn't end up the same way. I know I mustn't be so rigid with Concepción; she's a woman, after all, and her body has desires that must be quelled one way or another. But she doesn't need to soil herself with men to satisfy those needs. I should know.

1 February

Received a commission from the Church Council for *villancicos* in honor of Saint Peter, the Apostle. Another 100-peso honorarium, although the Archbishop has already claimed half of it, they tell me, for repairs to the orphanage, trusting that it is in my generous nature to contribute to the needy.

Still haven't sent my letter to Padre Antonio. Something tells me it is prudent to wait until I'm certain this is the right course to take. Must think of the consequences of my actions.

25 February

Sor Clara, the boarders, and the children of the maids are in an uproar. Melchora has just received a decree from the Archbishop that he is banning all dogs from the convent, and she has ordered the maids to let the animals out into the street. What a sight the courtyard is right now. Children of all ages and colors are clinging to the necks of the dogs, wailing in agony as though their own mothers were being taken away, while the novices chase after them, some wielding brooms, other clanging pot lids together. At least the clamor has roused Concepción out of the melancholy she's been dragging around for the past two months. Now she's out there with Sor Clara, advocating for the poor beasts.

What is the matter with that man? What harm do the dogs do to him or to us? How do they compromise our saintliness or pose temptations to our supposed austerity? At least the cats are considered necessary for the hygiene of the convent, but dogs have no function other than companionship and devotion to those who love and feed them. I suppose that, for Aguiar y Seijas, any corporeal attachment is sinful. Poor old Sor Clara. At least four of the dogs were her own personal favorites, four-legged escorts that followed her everywhere, including to church. Now back to that intermittent *sainete* between Act One and Act Two.

later

Concepción has returned and I can hear her telling Jane about the mystery of the dogs. It seems the Archbishop is incensed that our dogs eat better than the mendicants in the streets. From now on we are to gather all the scraps from our tables and have our maids distribute them to the beggars at the door. There is some suspicion that the dogs themselves will be turned into meat for the poor. The wailing of the children grows louder. Concepción tells me Sor Clara looks distraught and she's offered to stay with her for a few days. Why do I feel the girl is testing me?

3 March

Showed the letter to Don Carlos this afternoon. Did not want Concepción to deliver it to Padre Antonio before we had had a chance to discuss it, though I knew that my friend's naturally cautious nature would counsel me against sending it. He asks me to think carefully about the consequences, especially now that Aguiar y Seijas is on his saintly rampage.

"It isn't a time to lessen your friends, Juana," he said.

"But he has proved himself more of a foe than a friend," I argued.

"Perhaps that is how Melchora and her accomplices have made him out to seem. Have you ever thought, Juana, that they may want you to take this course of action precisely to leave you unprotected? Is it not hearsay, in the main, that he talks about you behind your back? Padre Antonio has no hair on his tongue. He says exactly what he feels to your face. Why should you believe these archangels of intrigue that he is faulty in his discretion?"

"I believe only what I feel, my friend," I said. "And for years now I have been feeling his growing antipathy toward me, and his anger at my refusal to submit to his will. It is not just my good sisters making up untruths. That is why, at the same time that I point out to him that I have a choice in the matter of who my father confessor is, he, too, has the choice to further our relationship or not. He can choose to be charitable and contrite for faulting rather than favoring me, as is his duty, or he can choose to forget about me and turn his zeal on someone more servile and less trouble to his spirit."

"I see that you have already convinced yourself, Juana. Nothing I could say could refute your own arguments."

"What would you do in my situation, Don Carlos?"

"I would probably keep my mouth shut, Juana, though my gender gives me a privilege that yours cannot afford. It is not a fair comparison. I could never know what it means to be in your situation."

More than anything else he said, it was this last that persuaded me to proceed with my decision to send the letter.

11 March

A new decree from the Archbishop. He is still on his crusade to weed the convents of New Spain of all particular attachments, he says, and will begin with San Jerónimo. Any maid who has been with her mistress for longer than a decade will be rotated to another nun. Legally, they cannot remove Jane since she is entirely my property, but it would be a difficult case to win against the Archbishop, as the Tribunal is wont to decide in favor of its prelate. The only solution, I've decided, is to send her back to Panoayán. It's my way of making it up to her after all those ugly rows we've had. Have to transfer her to Josefa first, and Josefa will take her back home. She can't leave until she's given birth, though.

It's Concepción I worry about. Received a cryptic note from her mother today. Seems she's marrying Concepción's father and leaving México altogether, going north, to Zacatecas where her husband and his brother own a mine of some kind. She doesn't want me to tell Concepción. What a shame. It would be the perfect way to get rid of her, but she is indentured to the convent, not to me, and I cannot dispose of her service as I can of Jane's. Why do mothers forsake their children for the men they marry? If I show her the letter she will probably go after her mother, and who knows what life she'll find in the north. I don't want to lose Concepción, but how can she stay after what we've done?

Maybe I can convince her to go with Jane to Panoayán. She would be able to use the skills I've taught her at the Amigas school in Amecameca, and surely she would prove helpful to my mother in running the hacienda. With her arthritis and that strange problem with her breathing, my mother isn't well, and her youngest daughters, my beloved Antonia and Inés, have both washed their hands of her now that they have their own families to think about. Only my eldest sister, María, is of any help to Mamá, but María has never been shrewd with the pen or with numbers. Concepción would be a godsend, to both of them. She will have to leave in secret, though. I must not be implicated in her leaving. I will arrange it so she is at the market on the day that Josefa comes to fetch Jane, and then they can pick her up on the way out of town. That will be simple enough. Concepción cannot continue here, especially not if she is to be transferred to another nun. Who knows what stories she could tell.

I mustn't allow myself to think about how lonely I'll be when she's gone. After that lapse in judgment, letting her go is the only reasonable thing to do. She sits at her desk and pretends nothing has changed, though at times I catch her looking at me while we work or eat and I swear I see tears in her eyes. Maybe it's just the smokiness of the lamp that makes her eyes water. I hope all she can read in my eyes is the dark refusal to discuss what happened.

Must write to Josefa about my plans for Jane and to my mother to see if she's interested in keeping Concepción. I suspect that *I* am the main target of the Archbishop's plan, and he means to weaken me by removing my servants.

The thought has just struck me: what will I do here all alone? No maid to attend me, no secretary to help me with my work. Or, will Melchora decide to fill my cell with boarders and thus prevent me from concentrating on my studies? Perhaps I should think about moving to a new cell. This one has no more room for all my books, though I could always turn the downstairs room now occupied by Jane and Concepción into an extension of my library. And the idea of utter solitude isn't repugnant to me, actually. It could be a scholar's paradise: solitude and room after room of books. If only I didn't have my good sisters and the Archbishop to contend with, I would feel like I had survived the purgatory of my daily existence. Still, I mustn't be alone or give Melchora cause to use my cell for an extension of the boarders' dormitory. I think I'll ask Josefa if Belilla is still interested in being a religious. She's already fourteen, I believe; old enough to enter the novitiate.

13 March

Still no word from Padre Antonio about my letter, but I have noticed (or perhaps this is a product of my imagination) that Melchora and Rafaela have a flare of triumph about their nostrils. They are suddenly quite smug whenever they speak to me. I suspect they know something that I don't.

"This is sheer obscenity," cried the Archbishop, glaring at the parchment as though it were bewitched by the Devil himself.

"Now you see why she dismissed me, Ilustrísima," said Padre Antonio. He bent his head back to rinse his eyes in the solution that Sor Gabriela had sent him with Juana's maid.

"And Payo did nothing about this? He let her continue with these repulsive verses?"

"Fray Payo indulged her, Your Reverence. I did my best to dissuade her from pursuing this path, to keep her true to her vows, but you see that I have failed, and now she dismisses me as though I were nothing but a servant." The saltiness of the solution burned like acid, and he thanked God for the sensation, praying that it would help restore some clarity to his vision.

"Padre Antonio, I don't think you comprehend the gravity of these words. Did you not read them? This is fodder for the Inquisition."

Padre Antonio resumed his seat opposite the Archbishop's, solution dripping down his face. "As you can see, Ilustrísima, my eyes don't do much reading these days, but I know what ungodly detritus issues from that pen of hers. I can only imagine it's gotten worse with practice."

"You cannot imagine such profanities. No true Christian could. Listen to this—"

Padre Antonio was going to protest, but there was no stopping Aguiar y Seijas.

> "'Semblance of my elusive love, hold still—
> image of a bewitchment fondly cherished,
> lovely fiction that robs my heart of joy,
> fair image that makes it joy to perish.
>
> 'Since already my breast, like willing iron,
> yields to the powerful magnet of your charms,
> why must you so flatteringly allure me,
> then slip away and cheat my eager arms?
>
> 'Even so, you shan't boast, self-satisfied,
> that your tyranny has triumphed over me,
> evade as you will arms opening wide,
> all but encircling your phantasmal form:
> in vain shall you elude my fruitless clasp,
> for fantasy holds you captive in my grasp.'"

Padre Antonio shook his head. He had lost the black lamb of his flock, and now she had no father confessor and no Fray Payo to protect her. Even Juana's own maid had betrayed her, bringing him the evidence that Melchora continued to accumulate against her. Someone had to get Juana to mend her ways, and if not himself or her Superior, then it must be the Inquisition.

17 March

It nearly happened again! Thank God my hands were chaste and my resolve—except for that brief straying of the lips—secure as a chastity belt. I was in bed trying to read, but my attention was focused elsewhere and I blew out the lamp to go to sleep. Sleep was elusive and I found myself tossing in one direction and then the other. I finally started to doze long past the curfew bells when of a sudden I felt her slip under the bedclothes beside me. At first I thought I was in that dream state between wake and sleep, but there was nothing phantasmal about her nakedness or about that musky scent of her skin. I could feel the warmth of her body through the cotton of my night shift.

"Get up, Concepción," I whispered to her. "You mustn't be here. Jane will hear you."

"Why don't you talk to me, Madre?" she whispered back, and the feel of her breath on my face made me shudder.

"There's nothing to discuss, cariño. We must forget it all happened."

"I can't forget. It's all I think about." Very gingerly, her hand traced the curve of my hip.

"Stop that, Concepción. This is wrong, and very dangerous. Jane could hear us."

"Kiss me, Madre. One more time. Please."

Her lips were almost on my own, and I tried to resist the magnet in them drawing me to kiss her. But then I let myself get drawn into the muskiness of that warm mouth, so moist and full of desire. It was everything I could do to keep my hands from wandering, though her body pressed against me and I could feel the hair of her pubis grazing my knee. Oh, Tantalus, the pain of unrequited longing when the fruit hangs so closely within reach!

Suddenly the girl started to weep against my neck, and I remembered her as a homesick child. I wanted to stroke her hair, soothe her pain, but knew that if I started touching that acquiescent skin of hers I would be lost. I let her have her cry and when she was quiet I asked her to return to her own bed.

"I'm sorry, Madre," she whispered. "I feel so ashamed now."

"You must forget about this," I advised, knowing I would never be able to keep my own counsel. "It isn't possible."

"But I feel so much for you, Madre. I didn't know how much until the other night."

My head started to pound. "You mustn't say that."

"But it's true."

"When you're young, it's possible to feel things very intensely for five minutes, Concepción." And then I found myself repeating the very words that la Marquesa had used with me: "It's possible that a woman may love another woman in whose arms she feels the warmth of a mother's love. It's your mother that you miss, don't you see?"

She sighed, and I heard her breath quiver as though she were about to start weeping again. I turned my back on her and prayed that she would leave soon, but she stayed on the edge of the bed, caressing my back. To think of all the times she's stroked my back, eased the tightness in my spine, the lumbago in my coccyx. I guess there's always been the intimacy of touch between us. It is absolutely essential that she go away to Panoayán. Must tell her about her mother in the morning.

19 March

Haven't seen Concepción for two days. When I told her that her mother had gone north and that I thought it was a good idea she went to Panoayán, she didn't believe me at first, even after I showed her the note her mother asked me to keep secret. She called me a liar and yelled out that I just wanted to get rid of her after what we had done. The only way to keep her still was to hold her against me with my hand over her mouth, and then I heard Jane's heavy footsteps on the stairwell. I am sure she saw me holding Concepción, and she's been behaving so strangely lately that I'm almost afraid to trust her. There is no doubt in my mind now that they both must leave. What a stupid thing I did with that girl. No doubt it will haunt me for years. Feast of Saint Joseph today. I have only three months left to complete the *villancicos* for Saint Peter. All of this foolishness with Concepción and that letter to Padre Antonio have kept me from concentrating on my commissions.

Concepción did not return until the Feast of the Annunciation, near the end of the month. Juana half-expected her to turn up pregnant. She looked tired and morose, with a gray tint to her skin and violet hollows under her eyes. Juana did not reprimand her, did not speak to her at all. When the girl sat down at her desk and asked Juana what she wanted her to do, Juana ignored her completely. Out of the corner of her eye she watched Concepción straightening out her bookshelves, organizing the notebooks in the trunk, scraping off the tallow that had caked onto the tables.

"I'm sorry I left, Madre. I just had to see for myself. She's really gone."

Juana took the ledger book out of the top drawer of her desk.

"I can't believe she would leave me like that."

Juana pretended to add one of the columns in the ledger, but she was listening.

"Her note says she'll send for me after my indenture's complete, but I know that's not true."

"I want you to get to work copying the first nocturne of the *villancicos*," Juana said.

The girl threw herself at Juana's knees. "Do you forgive me, Madre?"

She wanted to stroke the girl's hair off her forehead. "No," she said. "Now get to work."

The girl went to sit at her desk again, but it was clear she couldn't focus on the task and kept balling up the parchment each time she made a mistake.

"You're wasting good paper, Concepción. You know I can't afford that."

"Madre, remember when you told me once that I had more freedom than you, that, as a *castiza*, I could go wherever I wanted, once my indenture was over? And you said I could make my own destiny."

"No, I don't remember saying that. What's the point?"

"Aléndula says there's a difference between freedom and destiny."

"Is *that* what you're thinking about? No wonder you can't concentrate."

"It's important, Madre. Tell me. Is there a difference?"

"Look up, Concepción. Look around you. What do you see?"

The girl's eyes roamed over the bookshelves and the cluttered tables of the study. "Nothing different," she said, shrugging, "just your cell."

"It's a cage, don't you see? This cell is the cage of my destiny. Because I'm a *criolla*, I had two cages to choose from, this one or the one most *criollas* choose, which is marriage and childbearing, but that one would have gone against my nature, it wouldn't have allowed me to do any writing or studying. So, instead, I chose this habit, this life, as my destiny. Destiny is the cage each woman is born with, and we can't ever leave that cage. In that sense, I guess freedom is the opposite of destiny."

"Am I free, Madre? I'm not a slave like Jane or Aléndula, and I'm not a nun like you."

"What do you see when you look in the mirror, Concepción?"

The girl scowled. "I don't know, my face, I guess."

"A *woman's* face, Concepción. You're a woman with a good education and a keen mind, but no matter how intelligent you are or how much you learn, you'll never be thought of as a whole human being, and you'll never be allowed to be free."

"Because I'm a *castiza*?"

"Because you're a *woman*. That's the cage we were both born with, Concepción. It doesn't matter that you're a *castiza* or a *criolla* or a servant or a nun. If you're a woman, you have no freedom. All you have is the destiny of your body, and we're all slaves to that destiny."

Concepción went back to her copying, managing to fill an entire page without a mistake. Juana watched her from the corner of her eye; there would be more questions, she knew.

"Did I make you angry, Madre?"

"I'm angry at *them*. Just like my 'Philosophical Satire' says, those stubborn, bullheaded men who won't allow women to live according to our true nature when that differs from what they want us to be."

"I thought destiny came from God, Madre."

"God made man in his own image. Isn't that what we're taught, Concepción?"

"So you're saying that even if I leave the convent, I won't really be free."

"I'm not talking about physical freedom, Concepción. You can leave the convent, but you can't escape your destiny. All you can do is change it with the choices you make."

"Like you changed yours by taking vows."

"Exactly. And you could change yours, too. When Jane leaves—"

"You really *are* sending Jane away?"

"She's going back to Panoayán with my sister, Josefa, after her confinement is over."

"Does she know that?"

"Of course she knows that. And I want you to go with them, Concepción."

"But why, Madre? What did I do? Was it because of—"

Juana held up her hand. "It has nothing to do with that. The Archbishop is not my friend. He isn't any woman's friend, especially not a woman with learning, and he is particularly vexed with me because of my influence with the palace. He and Melchora would do anything at all to make my life miserable. As it is, they want to send Jane to another nun because she's been with me fourteen years. And no doubt they'll take you away, too. Don't you think it's better for you to go to Panoayán?"

"Even if I wanted to go, how can I if I'm still indentured here?"

"I'll find a way. If anything, I'll pay for your last six years."

"How much would that be, Madre? How much am I worth?"

"To me, you're priceless, which means that to them, you're not worth the air you breathe. But if I offer to buy out your time with the money I get for Jane, Melchora should have no quibble with that."

"Then why send me away, if I'm so valuable to you?"

"Because you are indentured to the convent, not to me, which means that Melchora can do whatever she wants with you. She can make you a refectory maid or sell you to an *obraje* if she pleases and there's nothing I can do about it under this new decree of the Archbishop's. That's why I'd rather you go to Panoayán. I know you'd be happy there, and you could use the skills I've taught you. You could keep the accounts for my mother, write her letters. Your education wouldn't go to waste."

She had not noticed until then that the girl was weeping. "Concepción, you have to understand—"

"I don't want to go to Panoayán and be somebody else's servant, Madre."

"We all have to serve, Concepción. That's what I mean. That's the destiny of this body we were born with. Do you want to get married and serve a man and his children? Would you prefer that?"

"Aléndula says there's a place near Vera Cruz called San Lorenzo de los Negros, a village of refugee slaves like her father where everyone is free, Madre, even the women."

"Aléndula is your prisoner friend?"

The girl nodded, wiping her face with her palms. "She's always talking about freedom, and about wanting to die because she says the child of a *cimarrón* should either live free or die. She says that if I set her free I could become a *cimarrona* and I could go live with her in her village of *cimarrones.*"

"I see. You want to abandon your learning and become a *cimarrona* now. And how are you and an escaped prisoner of the Audiencia going to get out of the city without being detected?"

"We'll be out of the city by the time they discover that she's gone, Madre. And Aléndula knows the way through the mountains. She's made that journey before when she came with her father."

"Have you located this San Lorenzo on the atlas? Do you have any idea where it is?"

"It's not on the atlas. Aléndula says it's a small village in the hills about five leagues south of Vera Cruz. Only Indians and *cimarrones* live there."

"Do you know what kind of life you can expect in a village of Indians and refugee slaves? At least in Panoayán there are schools and civilization and you can use your calligraphy skills to good advantage. Are you telling me that you would prefer a life of ignorance and filth to one of learning and compatibility with minds of your ilk? Is that an accurate summary of your deduction, Concepción?"

"My deduction, Madre, is that if you don't want me anymore, and you don't even want me to stay at the convent, then I should be able to choose for myself where I want to go. Aléndula says there are four choices to every decision: the safe choice, the wise choice, the foolish choice, and the choice that somebody else makes for you."

How old was that Aléndula, Juana wondered. She sounded so sensible.

"You want me to make the fourth choice," Concepción continued, "and I want to make the wise one. Aléndula says I'm nothing but another pair of hands for you and that, even if I'm not a slave, I'm still enslaved here, just like she is. Why not be a *cimarrona?*" The girl started to cry again. "I was happy here with you. I don't want to go anywhere, but if I have to go I might as well go where I can be free."

"Is that your conviction, then?" Juana went over to the chess table under the window, slid the drawer open, and took out the pieces. "I'll wager my conviction against yours," she said, arranging the pieces while she spoke. "If you win, you go to this San Lorenzo de los Negros, assuming you can even get your friend out of her chains. If I win, you go to Panoayán. Does that sound like a fair wager?"

"But I always lose, Madre," Concepción protested. "It's not a fair contest."

"I'll give you an advantage, then," said Juana, turning the board around so that the onyx pieces were on her side. "I'll be black tonight so you can take the initiative."

Concepción moved the ivory king's pawn two spaces. Juana followed with her queen's knight. They played for a time in silence, Juana's black army wreaking havoc on the white, and suddenly it occurred to her that sending Concepción to Panoayán would keep the danger alive, for there was always the possibility that she would tell somebody and that somehow word would reach Melchora or the Archbishop. It was stupid to hold on to the girl. Better if she followed her own mind and Juana never saw her again. She blundered her game on purpose, losing her knights and her bishops and one of her rooks, until at last the onyx queen was captured and Concepción mated her in three moves.

Concepción narrowed her eyes at her. "You let me win, didn't you?"

"Your argument won, *cariño*. The game gave me time to realize that your point is a reasonable one. You shouldn't make the choice somebody else wants you to make. If you want to choose the life of a *cimarrona*, it's your prerogative, and I have no right to stop you."

"What if I'm afraid to go, Madre? What if we get lost or if we're attacked by some wild animal?"

"If you trust this Aléndula, if her wits are about her and you trust she's telling the truth about knowing her way through the mountains, then I daresay you'll be safer in that wilderness than in the convent. In here, there are more beasts than you realize, Concepción. And at least you can say you own this decision. That's as close as we come to being the proprietors of our own lives."

"Aléndula says I've been a puppet so long I don't know how to listen to my own head."

"Fifteen years ago, Concepción, when I was deciding whether or not I could really be a nun, renounce the world and never set foot outside the cloister again, I wrote a sonnet. Listen to it, it might help you make up your mind:

"If the hazards of the sea were first considered
none would embark; if danger were well foreseen
there would be none to take a risk
nor would the fierce bull be goaded.

"If the prudent horseman were to ponder

the fury of his mettlesome brute
runaway in the race, none should
stay him with a discreet hand.

"But if there were one so bold
who, despite the peril, should want to govern
with an impudent hand the very Apollo's
rapid chariot bathed in light, everything for him
would be possible; he would not settle only
for a state that must last a lifetime."

"I don't understand what the poem has to do with me, Madre."

"It means that I gave in to my fear, *cariño*. That I chose this state of enclosure rather than risk seeing what the world had to offer me. Everything for you is possible if you aren't afraid of what you might lose. Every loss brings strength and courage. Don't be meek and settle for the safe path, as I did."

And then Juana got to her feet and stepped out from behind the chess table. Concepción stood up, too, and they faced each other like the queens on the same rank of the chessboard. Suddenly they were embracing, their bodies so close she could feel the beating of Concepción's heart, could smell the Castile soap in her braided hair. Juana gazed at her openly, and for an instant she felt the quivering of desire in her belly, and a small thing opening and closing inside her, but then she shook her head and stepped away.

"Are you sure you can get your friend out?"

"I can get the keys to the shed from Sor Clara. It's just that—"

"What? You need money?"

"Yes, and something else. Sor Clara has to bribe Sor Agustina. She's the one who has the keys to Aléndula's chains."

"What could be a better bribe than money?"

"Something of yours, Madre. A letter from la Condesa."

Juana felt her heart pounding in her throat. "Did you betray me, Concepción?"

The girl looked down at her hands.

"Did you?"

"I kept one of her letters, just in case."

"In case you needed to betray me?"

"In case there was no other way, Madre."

"Was that the letter I never received?"

The girl nodded.

"Where is it?"

"I gave it to Aléndula to keep for me until I decided."

"Are you sure you didn't give it to Sor Clara?"

The girl looked up. "I swear it by my mother's life, Madre—"

"You must destroy it, then, do you hear me? I don't even want to see it, just destroy it."

"But what will I give Sor Clara? She won't give me the keys otherwise."

Juana glanced around the room, her eyes pausing on the two desks and then on the crumpled papers that Concepción had scattered on the floor.

"Do you think you can fool Sor Clara?"

"Sor Clara can't read, Madre."

"Then copy 'Philosophical Satire' on a piece of stationery, only structure it like a letter with a greeting and a signature, and don't forget to date it at the end. La Condesa always dates her letters after the signature. You *can* copy her signature, can't you?" The girl nodded and went to dig the "Philosophical Satire" notebook out of the trunk that held Juana's writings. Meanwhile, Juana wrote a letter of introduction for Concepción and sealed the envelope. There was still a chance that the girl would remain in Panoayán. She took some coins out of the locked chest in her wardrobe and slipped them into a pouch.

"A peso buys a lot of food, a lot of pulque," said Juana, handing the girl the letter and the pouch, "so don't let anyone know you're carrying any money. Use the *reales* for lodging, if you can, or for bribes. Save the pesos for emergencies."

"What's in the envelope, Madre?"

"Don't trust the causeways. Buy a ride on a canoe to get you out of the city. You can go as far as Chalco and from there you can head for the hills. They'll be looking for you on the causeway. Panoayán is only a day's ride from Chalco, two days if you're on foot, I guess, but you can stop at my mother's house and she'll get one of our grooms to escort the two of you to Vera Cruz. I've written this letter for you to give her. When you reach Amecameca, ask for directions to the *finca* of Isabel Ramírez in Panoayán. Anybody can tell you where it is."

The girl stared at her blankly.

"Are you paying attention, Concepción?"

"It's all happening so fast all of a sudden, Madre."

"You must leave tomorrow morning, if you can, at first light, before prime. You don't want to risk getting caught by the night watchmen. In the morning, you can get lost in the crowd at the market."

Suddenly Concepción threw herself into Juana's arms, weeping. Juana held her close and kissed her lightly on the lips, tempted for a second to linger over that musky mouth. The girl clung to her, but Juana pushed her away.

"*Basta*, Concepción. You're wasting time. Now, go, and be a *cimarrona*. Write to me when you're safe, but sign your letters with the name *Jerónima*; that way Melchora won't know it's you, and won't incriminate me in your and the prisoner's disappearance."

"How can I thank you for everything you've taught me?"

Juana shook her head, unable to speak because of the stones that had suddenly formed in her throat. She reached over and removed the onyx queen from the chess table and handed it to Concepción. "Don't forget you have an education," she managed to say, then turned her back on the girl and left for compline.

When she returned from prayers, the cell was dark and felt almost desolate. She stood at the doorway of Jane and Concepción's room and was comforted by the sound of breathing, though she could see only one body in the bed. No doubt Concepción was out plotting her escape with the *cimarrona*. She hurried upstairs before the melancholia rooted, and found Concepción's old sampler on her pillow, the embroidered birds and flowers still bright against the musty linen. Her eyes went moist at the memory of the girl, how proud she had been when she'd shown Juana her needlework for the first time.

Dear Mother, she thought, keep them safe.

Chapter 18

She had heard something. The squeak of the front door. A floorboard creaking. Had Concepción overslept? Or maybe it was just Jane down in the kitchen. She got up and dressed for prime, knowing that today was going to be an interesting day if Concepción and her prisoner friend had managed to get out of the convent safely. In the kitchen, she found Jane groggy and lumbering under her heavy robe, bringing the milk to a boil for her morning chocolate.

"Concepción didn't come to bed again last night, Madre," said Jane, dropping a handful of freshly ground cocoa into the steaming milk. "I bet you she's gone back to that *gitano.*"

Juana cut a piece from the loaf in the bread basket and waited for Jane to fill her a cup with the chocolate. She did not want to speak of Concepción.

"Hurry up with that, will you?" she said, nudging the cup at Jane.

"Don't you want me to make a foam, Madre?"

The Te Deum bells started to ring.

"Just give it to me like that. Can't you see I'm going to be late again?"

Jane ladled the weak chocolate into the cup and Juana dipped her bread in it. They were not supposed to eat anything before morning Mass, but she needed something to settle the bile in her stomach or else risk vomiting in the choir. She wiped her mouth with the back of her hand and hurried to the church, praying that Concepción had gone and that she would never see the girl again.

"The star of light has risen," she chanted the morning hymn in Latin. "Let us pray to God, implore Him to keep our deeds free of sin during this day."

Every morning for fourteen years she had said that prayer. And every day she had sinned, venial sins, mortal sins, sins of the flesh, of the tongue, of the mind, of the eyes, of the heart. Now she had even abetted the escape of a prisoner. It would not be long now before her transgression was discovered.

"Listen, Juana," Andrea whispered against her veil on their way down from the upper choir. "I want to nominate you for prioress. Nominations are due in a week."

"You've lost control of your senses, my friend," said Juana, not bothering to lower her voice. She sped up her gait under the eucalyptus trees.

"Someone's got to wrest Melchora out of the priory," Andrea said, keeping up with her.

"How about you, Andrea? You're already the archivist."

"And you're the accountant. That's a more important post," hissed Andrea.

"I can't, Andrea. Nominate me to continue keeping the books. That's the most I can do."

"But Juana, *las santas* want you."

"Me or my influence with the palace?" She shook her head, tucking her arms under her scapular. "I'm sorry, Andrea. I can't. I've still got that *festejo* to complete, and who knows how long that'll take, now that—" She caught herself just in time. Even if Andrea was her friend, she would not be able to keep the truth about Concepción to herself. "—now that I've got another *villancico* due in June."

She left her friend standing by the fountain and hurried up the numerous stairwells to her cell. *Las santas*, as they had been facetiously christened by Rafaela, were that group of devout nuns that had followed old Sor Paula's example, and who tried in vain to return the convent to some modicum of saintliness. They were not Carmelites in the strict sense but shared the ascetic inclinations of the daughters of Santa Teresa. They strove for spiritual purity rather than political power, and in that were the diametrical opposites of Melchora's faction, called *las interesadas* by Andrea's group, which had descended from the now-deceased, politically interested Sor Clotilde.

Two refectory maids were hauling water and firewood into Juana's cell. At first she feared Jane's time had come, but Jane was just laying out her breakfast of papaya slices and a spinach omelet. The smell of warm corn flour filled the parlor. It was Concepción's favorite breakfast, and she felt another pang at the girl's absence.

"I needed water and wood, Madre. Who knows where that *castiza*—"

"Yes, Jane," she cut her off. "Thank you, *muchachas*, for your help." She gave them each a pair of *reales,* then locked the door behind them.

"That lazy Concepción was supposed to do that last night, Madre."

"She was busy. Now go on. Get me some sugar and lime for my papaya." She had not even gotten halfway through her meal when the loud clanging of the alarm bells brought everyone out of their cells and into the galleries and the patio.

"The prisoner has escaped!"

"Someone let the prisoner out!"

"Find the prisoner!"

"Send word to the Audiencia!"

Sor Agustina had stirred up a tumult among the maids, assembling them all in the courtyard to question them about the incident. Her fellow *vigilantas*, the albino twins María and Marcela, were already questioning the boarders and the novices.

"Let's go in, Jane. It's total chaos out here."

Jane followed her into the cell. "You don't think Concepción had anything to do with this, Madre, do you?" she asked.

"How could she?" said Juana, sitting back down to her breakfast.

"You know how she was always talking to that prisoner," said Jane, waddling past the kitchen into the room she shared with Concepción.

Juana held her breath, spooning the egg and spinach into a steaming wedge of tortilla.

"Madre!" yelled Jane. "She's gone, Madre!"

Juana heard Jane huffing back into the parlor. "She's gone, Madre! All her clothes and things are gone! Her trunk's empty!"

Juana dropped her food back on the plate and rubbed her forehead. It was not even midmorning and already a pulsing headache had gathered behind her eyes.

"What are we going to do, Madre? She must've been the one."

"I thought you said she was with that gypsy."

"She might be, Madre, but who knows? That Concepción was very attached to the prisoner, kept telling me how she wished she could save her."

"Oh, God," said Juana. Had Concepción told her plan to Jane?

Just then someone pounded on the front door. Jane nearly tripped over the brazier in her rush to answer it.

"Don't say anything, Jane," Juana hissed behind her.

It was Agustina, Melchora, and Rafaela—the Three Graces, as she called them. "Get out of the way!" said Agustina, shoving past Jane's belly.

Juana did not get up from her chair.

"Well?" said Melchora. "Where is she?"

"Who are you looking for, Mother?"

"That other *criada* of yours, who else?" said Agustina. "I said I wanted all the servants down in the courtyard."

Behind them, Jane was fretting at her fingernails.

"I don't know," said Juana. "Jane has just discovered that she didn't sleep here last night."

Agustina turned toward Jane. Jane lowered her arms and stood very still, eyes bulging with fear under her green scarf.

"And you? Why weren't you downstairs?"

"Don't be ridiculous, Agustina," said Juana. "Look at her! She can't even climb the stairs to my study, much less walk all the way down to the patio."

"You know something, don't you?" Agustina prodded Jane.

Jane started to shake her head but Juana nodded to her to speak. "Ye-yes, Madre. I mean, all—all I know is—is that her things are gone."

Agustina whirled back to glare at Juana.

"Please rise, Sister," said Melchora. Juana decided to obey.

"It would not behoove you, Sor Juana," said Rafaela, "to conceal anything."

"I know nothing about this," said Juana. "She was here last night, working until I went to compline. She wasn't in my study when I returned, so I thought she'd gone to bed. I haven't seen her since, but then that's not unusual."

"You! *Panzona!*" Agustina bellowed at Jane. "Come here and stand before us! And God help you if you don't tell the truth!"

Jane did as she was told, her hands clenched behind her back, and Juana saw that the poor woman's knees were shaking.

"Did that *castiza* say anything to you?"

Jane shook her head vehemently. Agustina narrowed her eyes at her.

"Where does she sleep?"

"With me," said Jane, pointing to the room beyond the kitchen.

"When was the last time you saw her?" asked Rafaela.

"I don't know, I—I—"

"You what?" yelled Agustina.

Jane swallowed. "I took an infusion to help me sleep." She rubbed at her belly. "I—I was having pains, Madre."

Agustina struck her with the short scourge she always carried. "Imbecile!" Jane started to cry into her hands.

"How dare you barge into my cell and strike my servant," said Juana through clenched teeth. "Go back to your work, Jane," she said softly, and Jane hurried back into the kitchen.

"With your permission, Mother!" called Marcela from the doorway. Beside her stood Sor Clara. "Come in, Sister. What have you discovered?" said Melchora.

"Tell her!" Marcela prodded the gatekeeper with her elbow.

Sor Clara would not look at Juana, and Juana noticed that she was holding a wrinkled scroll. She recognized the parchment.

"It was my fault, Mother," said Sor Clara, gaze pinned to the floor. "I gave the *castiza* the keys to the prisoner's shed."

"You what?" Agustina roared.

"She gave me this letter in exchange." Sor Clara handed the parchment to Melchora, then started to beat at her chest in manic mea culpas.

"'*Dear Juana, I hope this letter finds you well again. You really should take better care of your health,*'" Melchora read aloud. "'*Stubborn men who accuse women without reason, dismissing yourselves as the occasion for the very wrongs you design.*' What manner of letter is this, Juana?"

Juana opened her eyes and stared at Melchora. They were all in cahoots with each other, including the gatekeeper. "I have no idea, Mother."

"'. . . *who is more to blame,*'" Melchora read on, "'*though both be guilty of wrongdoing: she who sins for pay or he who pays to sin?*'"

"Excuse me, Mother," Juana tried to interrupt the reading, but the Mother Superior held up her hand and continued to read. Agustina, Rafaela, and Marcela were a rapt audience, each looking more scandalized than the other. Juana glued her gaze on Sor Clara, but the gatekeeper was still beating at her chest and would not raise her head.

"'*Thus, with much evidence I conclude that the duel is with your own arrogance, for in both deed and promise you conjoin flesh, world, and devil.*'" Melchora punctuated the last line with extra emphasis. "'*Always, your Condesa.*'"

Juana bit the inside of her cheeks to keep from grinning, and decided to play along with their charade. In their stupidity, they had given her the very weapon of her defense.

"Looks like your little secretary turned on you, Juana," said Agustina.

"I will submit this shameful evidence to the Archbishop, Juana," said Melchora. "We shall let him decide how best to punish you for this particular attachment to *your* Condesa, not to mention your participation in this scheme."

"And what will I be punished for, Mother? My secretary copying a private correspondence and using it to bribe our gatekeeper?" asked Juana. "The very fact that I was betrayed absolves me, don't you think?"

Rafaela and Agustina exchanged glances.

"We're talking about an indentured servant here, Juana, property of the convent," said Melchora. "Whether or not you authored this scheme, you were still her mistress."

"Does that make us the guardians of our servants, Mother? Do you, in fact, know what your servants are doing at every instant?"

"By decree, Juana, we are responsible for the actions of our *castas*," said Rafaela. "Which makes you responsible for this escape."

"That's preposterous logic," said Juana.

"I've got your logic mounted on my nose," said Agustina.

Rafaela joined in again. "You've meddled with a prisoner of the Audiencia and lost us a servant who was legally contracted to the convent for another six years. No logic is going to save you from the repercussions of this, Sor Juana!"

"Rafaela's right," said Melchora. "But I will not wait until the Audiencia decides to attend to this case. I'm sure the Archbishop will agree that your punishment should begin immediately." She turned to her assistant. "Sor Rafaela, have the *beatas* bring boards up here to nail shut Sor Juana's library—"

"You can't do that! That's my property!"

"Your property is communal property, Sor Juana," said Melchora, "and if I want to see that library nailed shut, so it shall be." She turned to the assistant *vigilanta*: "Sor Marcela, you go upstairs and take every one of Sor Juana's pens and inkwells. Make sure you look in all the drawers, too. There is to be no writing instrument left in her cell."

Juana's head pounded with fury. Her little bit of breakfast had become acid in her stomach. "What about my commission from the Cabildo? The Archbishop has already used half of what I was to be paid for them. I can't renege on the Church Council."

"You will write your *villancicos* in the priory, under the *vicaria's* supervision," said Melchora.

"This is outrageous," Juana said in a low voice, though in truth it did not surprise her.

Melchora shook the parchment in her face. "No, Sister, *this* document is outrageous. Your lack of modesty and respect is outrageous. That you don't appear contrite, or even surprised, by this escape makes it outrageously evident that you had something to do with it. Now listen well to the penalty you've incurred for the insubordination of your little *criada*: no writing, except that which Rafaela will supervise, no reading, and no visitors until the Audiencia has determined what fine you will have to pay for these transgressions."

"That could take years," said Juana.

"I'm counting on it," said Melchora. "And, furthermore, you will eat nothing but rice and beans for a month."

"You are forcing me to take a vow of silence to protest this action," said Juana.

"Take any vow you wish, Sister," said Melchora. "You've never been very good at keeping your vows, anyway." She turned to her chief *vigilanta*. "Agustina, go into the kitchen and remove all of Sor Juana's food, save the rice and beans. Distribute it to the beggars at the gate, if you will."

At the word *gate*, Sor Clara fell to her knees, mumbling something about the folly of Saint Peter and Christ's forgiveness.

"Give me the keys, Sister," said Melchora, holding out her hand. "The best punishment for you is to remove you from your post. I see that you've grown too careless for the responsibility of the keys."

Without a word of protest, Sor Clara untied the ring of keys from her cincture and handed them to Melchora, and then resumed her mea culpas. It was a theatrical performance, to be sure, and the gatekeeper was playing the part of the penitential conspirator. She could hear Marcela rummaging clumsily through her things upstairs and said a quick prayer of gratitude that she had not decided to take her writing box out of its secret compartment last night.

As soon as Melchora and her brigade left, Marcela carrying Juana's quills and inkwells in her greasy apron, Juana went upstairs to assess the condition of her study. Her hands shook with anger when she saw the results of their invasion. Books had been pulled boorishly from the shelves and were lying about on the floor with their leaves bent and their spines cracked. All of her drawers had been turned out, their contents heaped on the tables, and there was ink smeared all over her desk and on the leather seat of la Marquesa's chair. She had expected to pay a price for Concepción's escape, but she never imagined Melchora would go so far as to vandalize her cell. She said nothing to anybody the rest of the day, resolved to keep her tongue silent until Melchora returned her writing instruments.

At *recreo* time, while Agustina and her albino assistants hammered nails through the boards across her bookshelves, Juana escaped to the *beata's* chapel in the cemetery and discovered some loose floorboards beneath the stone altar. After compline that evening, she had Jane stoke the brazier in the bath and she burned all of la Condesa's letters, one by one, the smoke billowing darkly out of the barred window. When she had finished the immolation, Juana placed a rat trap in the secret compartment of her desk, hidden under a sheet of paper to surprise any interloper. Just before curfew, she hid Pandora's Box under her scapular and took it to the *beata's* chapel. No one went back there but she, terrified as her good sisters were of being near the graves. She would not be able to write every day, but at least the diary was safe out there under the altar, and she could, on occasion, scribble a few lines.

Three days later, a broadside announcing the escape of the daughter of Timón de Antillas from the House of San Jerónimo was posted on the convent's portal. It offered a reward for information on the whereabouts of the miscreant. For days, the *portería* was inundated with informants, all spinning different testimonies about an escape they had never witnessed. Rafaela recorded the stories and read them at Friday chapter. Only one made sense to Juana, reported by a gondolier who regularly traversed the canals between Mexico City and Chalco. He had seen, he said, a China Poblana accompanied by an Indian fellow, *amulatado* and a little *afeminado*, walking up and down the banks of the Jamaica canal. On the day in question, his wife, a clothier from the Thieves' Market, had sold a poncho, a pair of breeches, and two sombreros to a Poblana who had paid for her purchases with a full peso, not even waiting for her change. Juana had to smile. No doubt Concepción got the idea of dressing her friend in male clothing from my *Trials of a Noble House*, she thought.

A month after Concepción's escape, Jane gave birth to a sickly boy. Juana had been sitting up with Madre Catalina, reading aloud to her from the second volume of *Don Quixote*, savoring every word and the feel of the book in her hands, the smell of the bindings and the leather cover, so completely absorbed in the prohibited act of reading that she barely realized the curfew bells were ringing. She needed to get back to her cell.

"There's a letter for you," Madre Catalina whispered as Juana bent to kiss the old woman's forehead. "Somehow la Condesa always finds out when you're punished." Her old eyes gleamed.

"But how did she get a letter past the gatekeeper?" asked Juana.

"Didn't I tell you? La Condesa has been sending me herbals prepared by her own apothecary at the palace. So kind of her. A lovely girl page brings them to me, and she brought this letter for you today. It's here, under my pillow."

Juana lifted the edge of the lacy pillow cover and felt her heart lurch at the sight of the handwriting. She took the note and kissed Madre Catalina again. "Thank you for your discretion, Mother," she said, tucking the note between the pages of *Don Quixote*.

"*Cuídate*, Juana," Madre Catalina said. "You must be careful. Those are not women but witches you're dealing with."

"Rest, Mother. Don't trouble yourself. I know how evil they are."

"You must help Andrea," Madre Catalina insisted. "Promise me you'll help *las santas*, Juana."

Juana realized she had just been bribed. Old and ill as she was, Madre Catalina was still playing convent politics.

"Yes, Mother, I promise. Now close your eyes. Time to rest." She tucked Madre Catalina's arms under the blankets, blew out the candle on her bureau, and took her lantern and the book with her. Who would see at that hour that she had a book under her scapular anyway?

She was not expecting the congregation of maids she found filling the parlor of her cell, a lake of candles and praying bodies in the front room, a conflation of smells and chanting voices coming from Jane's room.

"Jane of San José is giving birth, Madre," a young girl kneeling by the door told her.

"Is Sor Gabriela here? Has anyone gone for the infirmarian?"

"It's too early," the girl said, then lowered her head and rejoined the praying.

"Too early for what?" asked Juana, but the girl would not look at her again. She managed to wind her way through all the candles without setting her habit on fire and pushed through the bodies that had crammed into Jane's room. The smell of boiling eucalyptus choked her in the kitchen.

Jane, naked, was writhing on the edge of the bed, her arms and legs held down by several maids, her belly sticking out like a huge eggplant.

"Jane!" Juana shouted over the din of chanting voices. "We have to get you to the infirmary. You can't give birth here!"

The woman kneeling between Jane's legs was Artemisa, the head cook, but she hardly resembled herself in that odd headdress of cowry shells, her black arms and face and neck painted in yellow spots.

"Silence!" hissed Artemisa. "Do you want to call the *abikú?*"

At the mention of that word, Jane let out a piercing scream and nearly pulled the women holding her down on top of her. Artemisa mumbled incoherent words to Jane while another woman—it looked like one of Agustina's maids under a veil of blue beads—sponged her down with a wet towel.

"The child is early, Madre" whispered a maid standing beside her in the doorway. "*Abikú* likes the early ones."

"What is *abikú?*" Juana asked.

"Bad spirit, Madre. Makes baby die. We pray to Oshún for protection."

Juana realized then that she had walked into a world that had little to do with her own, that she was an outsider here, though this was her own cell and Jane her own maid. The others, too, were all servants of the convent with whom the nuns shared living quarters and food, and yet they were strangers. All Juana could do was watch. She identified the smoky smell in the room as burning sugar and garlic and saw that a brazier had been placed in each corner of the room where the mixture smoked from clay censors. She saw that Jane's altar was alight with candles and offerings of pumpkin and coconut. Statues of Our Lady of Mercy, Our Lady of Mount Carmel, Our Lady of Caridad del Cobre sat on Jane's altar beside the Guadalupana, along with a bundle of twigs in the shape of a broom.

Another woman, this one wearing a veil of white beads, approached the bed with a white bowl and from it sprinkled Jane's belly with a white substance that looked like powdered eggshells.

"Here it comes!" Artemisa called out, and the women holding her arms raised Jane to a half-sitting position, her buttocks slipping off the edge of the bed, her legs opening wide, feet pushing against the floor. Juana saw the weird widening of Jane's womb, could almost feel the tearing of Jane's flesh, heard Jane's screams and the eerie chanting of the other women. She had not noticed that her hand was clamped over her mouth, as if to stifle the sudden nausea she felt. She began to feel faint and dizzy.

She heard someone knocking on the front door, knuckles rapping at the shutters in the kitchen, and went to see who it was, needing to remove herself from that horrifying scene.

"Sor Juana Inés?" called a voice from outside. "What's going on?"

"¿Quien grita?" called another voice.

"Open the door, Juana!"

She moved on straw legs to the entry and unlatched the door. Melchora, Rafaela, Agustina, and Gabriela crowded into the room. The maids' shadows swayed like ghosts on the walls of the parlor.

"Hail Mary full of grace," prayed the maids, "holy be thy name, and the name of Guadalupe, Yemayá, and Oshún."

"What manner of ungodly ritual is this?" said Melchora.

"Jane's giving birth, Mother."

"Virgen Purísima!" said Gabriela, promptly rolling up her sleeves and pinning them under her veil.

"Blessed are you among women, and blessed is the fruit of Olorún. Holy Mary, daughter of Obatalá, pray for your children, now and at the hour of their birth, Ashé."

Juana held back the infirmarian. "They have it all under control, Sister. They know what they're doing."

"Nonsense!" said Gabriela, shrugging off Juana's hand. "They'll suffocate the child is what they'll do. Look at all this smoke. Everyone, out!"

The litany of the maids grew louder. Gabriela tried to enter the room where Jane was giving birth, but a blockade of bodies in the kitchen wouldn't let her.

"This is madness!" yelled Gabriela. "Get out of my way!"

The woman in the blue beads scooped a gourd into the camphor-scented water that was boiling over the hearth and set it beside Artemisa.

"¡Basta!" Melchora raised her voice over the din. "Everyone back where she belongs! Immediately!"

No one listened. Melchora threw her hands in the air and walked out of the cell, followed by her minions. Only Gabriela remained, still trying to push her way through the bodies. Suddenly, they heard a final ear-splitting cry followed by the cry of a newborn. It was over. The maids in the parlor launched into another prayer, this one completely in another language.

Juana joined Gabriela and together they elbowed their way into Jane's room just in time to see Artemisa cutting the dark intestine that was winding out of the child's belly. It was a boy with gangly arms and legs and swollen blue genitals. Artemisa's assistants in the beaded veils held the child over the steaming cauldron while Artemisa brushed his body with the bundle of twigs she had seen on the altar.

"What in God's name is that?" asked Gabriela.

"Bitter broom, Sister," said Artemisa, "Sweep away the *abikú*."

"Beware you don't burn him alive," said Gabriela, looking disgusted as she left the room.

Jane had fainted from the strain of the birth and was not able to help during the passing of the afterbirth, which Artemisa had to massage out of her belly. Juana nearly vomited at the sight of that sack of blood and membranes. To think this would be happening to la Condesa soon. She shuddered and shut her eyes, then crept upstairs to her dormitory. The cold, quiet darkness of the room contrasted vividly with the bright, crowded heat downstairs, and she felt as though she were returning to her own world. She suddenly realized that she was still gripping *Don Quixote* against her ribs, and remembered she had a letter to read, thanks to Madre Catalina. The seal was broken, she noticed.

Dearest Juana,

It's been weeks since you've written, and now I know why. I wonder if you received my last letter, the one your girl was supposed to place under your pillow as I asked her to, to surprise you. Mother Catalina informed me of your punishment. When will it end, Juana? When will they stop tormenting us this way? What is a friendship like this supposed to become if there is silence between us? The babe continues to grow inside me and the oddest thing is that I can no longer tolerate it when Tomás touches me, not even when all he wants to do is stroke my belly. I have banished him from my quarters as I find it impossible to sleep with him beside me. Men, like God, I have decided, are the inventions of women like me; not knowing what else to do with them when they cease to be interesting, we store them around like the furniture filling the palace or the artworks in the

Cathedral. Poor Tomás. He's a good man and is as devoted to this child as I am, but I cannot help my revulsion, just as I cannot help this odd craving for ashes. My chambermaid collects ashes from the braziers and mixes them with lime juice and I drink it down as though it were the finest elixir. Don't think me mad, Juana. Perhaps it is the effect of not seeing you regularly, or the perpetual fear I have of losing yet another babe. Only three months to go now. I know that you pray for me. And now, I leave you with this: every night I read your poems aloud and know that the child is listening to the power of your love. I remain, not too far,

   your María Luisa
   27th April 1683

Chapter 19

"The Viceroy wants every able-bodied man to join the militia," Don Carlos said. "He fears the worst has already befallen Vera Cruz."

Juana stared at the broadside that her friend had smuggled in to her. *Lorencillo has attacked Vera Cruz under the very noses of the Spanish Fleet! The entire city is under siege! Pirates demand a ransom of 150,000 gold pesos to release the Governor!*

When the criers had run through Mexico City with the first news of the siege, Juana had asked every maid in the convent if she knew where San Lorenzo de los Negros was. Nobody had heard of it. Hadn't Concepción said it was a small village close to Vera Cruz? She had never heard again from Concepción. Nor had she received any news from her mother that the girl had gone to Panoayán. Now, Juana feared that Concepción had met her fate at the hands of those pirates. And yet who was to say that they had even reached their destination? Who was to say they had not already met their fate on the journey?

"I worry so for my assistant," she said in a low voice. "She was going that way, you know, to a village of refugee slaves near Vera Cruz."

"So it *was* she who freed that prisoner we read about," said Don Carlos.

"And I'm still paying for it with this ridiculous punishment of Melchora's," she said. "Do you think there's a chance she might be safe?"

"I don't know, Juana. Lorencillo hasn't limited himself to Vera Cruz; his pirates are ransacking the entire coast, threatening to burn down every settlement and kill every citizen unless they get their ransom. All Negroes and mulattoes have been taken as slaves, and the women are being raped inside the churches where they were held captive."

"They're not here just for slaves, are they?"

"Slaves are a lucrative enterprise, Juana, especially in the northern colonies of the English Crown where there are so few. But, of course, pirates are pirates, and they'll take whatever they can. I heard that all the gold and silver bullion that was awaiting transport on the Spanish Fleet was found in the dungeon of the Cathedral and hauled away. This is the worst attack New Spain has seen in decades. It's not going to look good on the Viceroy's record, I can assure you, Juana."

"Do you think the King would hold this against him?"

"Between this and the Indian uprisings in Santa Fe, how could he not, Juana? Pirates and uprisings take their toll on the Crown."

The Viceroy and his temporary militia set off toward Vera Cruz, leaving a garrison to protect the city and sentries posted along each causeway. By barge, he sent a coffer of gold in the amount of the pirates' ransom to be met in Puebla and transported by royal courier all the way to the coast. Special masses were held in all the churches for the safety and victory of the Viceroy's forces. Juana and her sisters climbed the *azoteas* of their cells where they could see what was happening. Women and children continued to ply their trades, but aside from the soldiers who remained on patrol at all hours, the streets grew eerily quiet.

Near the end of May, the militia returned. They had not yet reached Tlaxcala when they received the news that the pirates had gotten their ransom and fled the port. The Spanish Fleet, waiting in the harbor to do battle with the pirate ships, had not even heard the pirates slip away. The Viceroy dispatched the militia and the infantry back to Mexico while he and a troop of reinforcements went on to Vera Cruz to assess the damage.

After the Viceroy's return, the Widow Calderón printed his impressions of the devastations wreaked by Lorencillo and his French and English corsairs: the looted churches, the burnt houses, the stacks of bodies piled up in the main square. For several nights in a row Juana dreamt that Concepción's body had been found in one of those piles, raped and beaten and mangled, as were the ways of pirates.

Once the campaigns started for the new election, Juana had no more time to think about Concepción. Honoring her promise to Madre Catalina, she helped *las santas* to launch an indefatigable crusade against Melchora. They nominated the eldest among them, Brígida de San Ildefonso, for prioress, María Bernardina for *vicaria*, Andrea for chief *vigilanta*, Ana de Jesus and María Manuel for sub-*vigilantas*, Beatriz for headmistress of the novices, Lucía for portress, and Juana for both archivist and accountant. They organized daily visits to the older nuns and gave lectures to the younger nuns about the benefits of a more saintly administration that would see to their spiritual evolution as much as to the continued success of the convent's business.

In the priory, under pretense of working on her *villancicos*, Juana designed bulletins exhorting the sisters of Saint Jerome to follow in the enlightened footsteps of their patron saint and vote for the candidates of *las santas*. Every day after breakfast the bulletins were posted on the trunks of the trees in the patio, and every day after the noon service they were taken down by *las interesadas*, supplanted by bulletins of their own condemning their adversaries for their pride and deception, which were, in turn, pulled down by *las santas* before the evening meal.

It was during this time of limited mental stimulation that Juana indulged her students in the lessons of the natural world, herding them out to the gardens and the orchard to take note of the musical range of birdsong and the biological data encoded in bulbs and seeds. She taught physics using the pulleys at the well and constructed geometrical proofs to explain how ceiling beams could look like acute angles rather than parallel lines from a distance. It was impossible to stay in her cell and look at her boarded-up bookcases, the haphazard nails splitting the good walnut of the furniture. The leather trunks that held all the copies of her writings had been chained and locked. The tables were bare except for the ink marks that had soaked into the wood. The only books she had been allowed to keep were her prayer book and Padre Antonio's old *Guide for a Spiritual Life*; even her beloved *Book of Hours* that la Marquesa had given her so long ago had been locked away. They had not taken any of the instruments: her astrolabe, her telescope, her microscope, her harp, her magic lantern, her kaleidoscope, her compass. But she couldn't take one of these in hand or use it in any way without instinctively groping for a pen to scribble down her observations, and pens were nowhere to be found except in that locked box out in the chapel or under Rafaela's nose in the priory. With Concepción gone and Jane's newborn bawling at all hours, with no access to her books and her writings, her instruments serving no purpose other than decoration, Juana found her cell unbearable. She channeled the energy of her frustrations into the carols for Saint Peter: *Shepherd, if regret oppresses your heart, may your lament hurt earth, sea, air, and sky.*

Six days after the Apostle's *villancicos* were sung at the Metropolitan Cathedral, the Angelus rang from every belfry in the city announcing a royal birth at the palace. Buglers heralded the news from every corner. Criers ran through the streets, calling out the name Don José María de la Cerda, the first *criollo* son of the House of Medinaceli.

MY ONLY JUANA,

It's been three days since my son's birth and I have still to hear from you. Your Mother Superior sent an immense bouquet of sunflowers on the convent's behalf, but no personal gift or even a note from the one person whom I most miss. Are you ill, Juana, or still angry at me for being absent from your life for so long? Or is your punishment yet not lifted?

The day is hot and dreary, and I have grown sick of lying in childbed. My son is not beautiful, but the midwife tells me all newborns look like that, swollen and mottled and terribly fragile. The wet nurse has had no luck in getting him to feed and so I must hold him to my own breast, and his strong little gums pulling on my sore nipples repel me, make me imagine that he is a very old, toothless little man trying to suck the life out of me. Let me explain about birthing. It is a hideous event, made worse by the helplessness of its victim and all those who surround her. I know we, mothers, are supposed to preserve the secret forever and pretend that the birth of a child is a joyful occasion. Frankly, my breasts are so sore, my stomach so distended, not to mention other parts of my body that do not feel like mine any longer, that I have a difficult time understanding how this one secret has survived, passed on from mother to daughter, old woman to young, for eternity.

Perhaps you are right that there is no magic in children. True, we learn from them, we see our other selves in them, but I find little in them to recommend the agony of birthing. I have done my duty to my husband and country, this I do believe, despite how much you might not like my statements. But giving birth is not about bravery or cowardice. It is, I have come to believe, about blessing men, forgiving them, creating a place for them in history. I venture to say that I will never again endure the aches and annoyances of pregnancy. If Amazonia exists, as we Spaniards once believed, I am certain its inhabitants have found a cure for Woman's obsession with pain for Man's pleasure.

I miss your confections, your *aguas de fruta*, and most of all our conversations. It is only in your *locutorio* where I feel like an intelligent human being and not a cow with heavy udders as I do now. There was something in your eyes, in your spirit, when I saw you last that I did not like and could not define. It was, I think, disquietude and an impatience that seems like a thin shroud wrapped around you. I know that for nine months you have been cross with me, and if it's any consolation, know that at last I understand your argument about the narcissism of bearing children. I can say with expert certainty that there is nothing worse than birth pains. The doctors tell me I must remain abed for another month, but as soon as I am well again, as soon as all the aches and wounds have healed, I shall venture out into the city again and visit you. Sometimes I make myself irately jealous just imagining that you once lived under this very roof, at the beck and call of another Vicereine. How dare she have known you, have used you as her personal maid, while I cannot even communicate with you except through these wretched marks on a mute page.

I remain forever, your patrona and only sponsor,

M.L.

8th of July 1683

By way of the page who brought Mother Catalina's medication, Juana sent a message to the palace, informing Their Majesties of her continued inability to communicate with the outside world. The page was sent back from the palace, accompanied by a bugler, with a message from the Viceroy himself, and with orders to deliver the message orally, in the central cloister of San Jerónimo so that all in the community could hear. The bugler's clarion drew everyone out to the courtyard.

"Either the Reverend Mother restores Sor Juana Inés de la Cruz's writing instruments and her books and her visiting privileges," the page called out in a strident voice, "and any other right that may have been illegitimately revoked, or else His Excellency, the Marquis de la Laguna and Viceroy of Mexico, will cease his patronage to the House of Saint Jerome. Moreover, it is the Vicereine's special request that Sor Juana write a special laud in honor of the baptism of her son, to be held in the Metropolitan Cathedral on the Feast of the Assumption."

The envoys were to remain in the cloister until they received word from

Sor Juana herself that the Viceroy's orders had been obeyed. It was a Friday and the nuns had gathered for Friday chapter when they heard the bugling and the ultimatum. A vote was taken to overturn Melchora's punishment and submit to the Viceroy's will. Sitting at the executive table beside Andrea, Juana scribbled a note to Don Tomás thanking him for his intervention, which was the equivalent, she wrote, of rescuing her from being buried alive, and assuring him that she would be honored to write the baptismal laud for his son.

Las santas applauded vigorously. Andrea said Juana's victory boded well for their saintly campaign.

11 August 1683

MOST ESTEEMED MADRE JUANA INÉS, YOUR WORSHIP,

I trust you find yourself in excellent health and that God is once again smiling upon your quill and gracing you with His supreme inspiration. Knowing how taxed your schedule always is, and that you have only recently been released from a silence imposed by your Superior, I understand that you have been able to make little progress on *Trials of a Noble House*; however, perhaps it would be possible to complete the work in time for the Vicereine's birthday in October, as I would deem it a great honor to be able to present that *festejo* at my house at that time. I have secured the actors that you requested and they are all very diligently rehearsing Act One and most anxious to see Act Two. Last night they were actually casting lots for the parts in the prologue and the intermissions. Would it be possible to receive the rest of the play by the end of the month? That would give the actors two solid months to rehearse the different acts and *sainetes*. And, if it isn't too much of an audacity, may I request only one small change to the drama, which is more of an addition than a change, since your work is perfection itself: will you add a few lines to commemorate the official entrance of Aguiar y Seijas as our Archbishop? He has finally decided to make his stay in New Spain permanent, and it would behoove us all to acknowledge his entry as our spiritual ruler as well as the Viceroy's. You will, of course, receive the balance of the honorarium at the time of the performance. Thank you so much for understanding what an honor it is to be able to pay homage to our sovereigns with your brilliant work.

I remain your perpetual admirer,
Don Fernando Deza

QUERIDA JUANA,

Thank you for your poem celebrating the baptism. It is, like everything you write, beautiful and political at the same time. My husband does not like that you call the boy "Mejicano," but what else could he be when he was born, as you imply, on the ruins of the palace of Moctezuma? Your ability to weave the mythologies of Europe and America never ceases to amaze me. You compare him to Alexander, Aeneas, Julius Caesar, and yet he remains a Mejicano. Does this make him a descendant of the Plumed Serpent, or just a child of Spaniards in the New World? It's odd that we've never discussed this, Juana, but do you consider yourself a Mejicana or a *criolla*?

Still no hope of being allowed out of my entrapment. More and more I begin to see the true significance of the condition you have chosen, Juana, which, unlike mine, has no end. Why haven't you written? I so long to hear your thoughts. Always,

your Condesa
12th of August 1683

15 AUGUST 1683

DEAREST LADY,

How I wish I were able to leave the convent today and attend your son's baptism in the Cathedral. I can imagine how beautiful the ceremony will be, and how your eyes will glow with the reflection of your little prince. Unfortunately, we will spend most of the day in prayer, and it is customary that we fast from all meat in deference for the mother of God's corporeal ascension into Heaven. Actually, I'm looking forward to a day of rest, exhausted as I am from trying to finish the commission for your *festejo*. Little did I realize how difficult it was going to be to work without the aid of my assistant, whom, in case you have not heard, escaped from the convent several months ago. I didn't know how much I'd grown to depend on Concepción

258

until these last two weeks when I have had to recopy every page I write several times. I must be more careful with my first drafts. I cannot afford to hire an amanuensis at present.

Indeed, life seems to have taken a strange turn here in my cell. Jane, my slave, gave birth to a son, which was sickly from birth and was recently buried outside the convent walls. The Archbishop gave me license to sell her to my sister, Josefa, and so now I am alone until my niece, Isabel, comes to live with me, which she will do as soon as we can afford to pay her dowry. God knows I need help with my work, as well as companionship. Now I must leave you to attend prayers.

God keep you well,

Jidl†

JUANA,

The voice in your last letter sounds positively dull. I can tell that you are tired, or maybe the absence of our company from each other is making you morose. I detect, also, some melancholia at the loss of your assistant. If you would like, I can send you one of my own maids. I have two who know their letters, though neither of them would probably hold a candle to that *castiza* you trained so well. Josesito has grown pink and plump, and the doctors tell me he is ready, now, to venture with me outside the palace walls. After all of these months of being cloistered, first by my body, and then by the needs of this child, I would like nothing more than to spend an entire day visiting friends and shopping. I'll send the nursemaid back with the boy after we see you and spend the rest of the afternoon browsing in all the shops in the arcade. Tomás thinks I'm crazy, but I tell him that if he had carried a child for nine months and borne it from the most delicate part of his body he would want to reward himself with new things, too. I shall see you on Saturday, then, Juana. Do you think it would be possible to have you sit on the same side of the locutory with us so that you may hold José? I so look forward to seeing you with a babe in your arms, and even more so, to delighting in a slice of your incomparable *torta de cielo*.

In anticipation of our visit,

Your M.L.

11th of September 1683

MY DEAR CONDESA,

Here I am again apologizing for this foolish tongue of mine which long association with my good sisters has forked and poisoned. After not seeing you for so many months, I have become testy and unpleasant company, but that is no excuse for rudeness. And now I must clarify my statement, and fear that the clarification will bring even more scorn. Nonetheless, I must make the attempt.

When I said that the birth of boys is the best evidence God gives us of the imminence of the Apocalypse I was not saying anything specific about little José. Rather, I meant that the reproduction of the male gender, sui generis, with all of its tendency toward war and destruction, guarantees that the revelations of the prophets will come to pass. It seems to me that the world is run by an increasing battalion of men, bred from generation to generation to believe in their pervasive omnipotence just as you pointed out in a previous letter that women are bred to believe in the supposed joy of childbirth. The more men there are in the world, and the more they believe in their supremacy above all of God's creatures, the more probable seems the eventual doom and devastation of the human race. What, I wonder, will become of God if the creatures bred to believe in His or Her existence cease to exist? Those of us with corporeal bodies know we exist (though some of us have died to the world), but the Supreme Being exists only through our minds and through the faith we cultivate with our bodies. And so my question: if men lead us to the catastrophic ends predicted in the Book of Revelation, and if the end of the world brings the end of human existence, does it not also, then, bring an end to God?

Now, I suppose I have offended you even more in trying to explain the significance of my foolish statement. I should know better than to engage in philosophical jousting about the fate of our progeny with a new mother. I beg you to forgive me for my impropriety. You know that I would rather cut out my tongue than have anything it says affront you in any way. Please receive this copy of my "Philosophical Satire" as a token of my deepest apology. It is the last thing that Concepción copied for me before she left, and I think you will agree with me that she far exceeded herself in the quality of the calligraphy.

Always,

Juana

P.S. Don Fernando tells me that rehearsals for *Trials of a Noble House* are going well, though there is some rivalry between the actress playing Doña Leonor (who is the main protagonist) and the one playing Doña Ana (who insists that hers is the more important personage). It occurs to me that by the time the play is presented next month, it will have gestated nearly three months longer than your José did in you. I must admit that, were I a woman of the world, and as prolific in body as in mind, I would have an impossible brood by now. And yet they are all stillbirths.

QUERIDA JUANA,

Your last letter left me cold. What you say borders on heresy, Juana, and you must stop it or I fear that there will be serious consequences to pay. Please promise me, I plead it on my son's soul, that you will take more precautions with your beliefs. I send along these pages of perfumed parchment—if you hold a sheet up to the light you will see how tiny, translucent flowers have been embossed into the fabric of the paper—in the hope that they inspire you to write another poem, this one free, I hope, of political connotations and irreverent observations. I am having this letter and the parchment delivered directly to you. I know you say that the new gatekeeper is not an enemy, but nonetheless, I trust no one to keep the confidences that we share. I have, therefore, taken your example, and started burning your letters, as you should burn this and every one of my missives. Dare I visit you again, Juana, and risk another biblical dissertation?

Yours,

M.L.

22d of September 1683

P.S. Just because of the brilliance of your "Satire" I forgive you.

P.P.S. I forgot to tell you. The Archbishop is the laughingstock of New Spain. He wanders about in his unkempt cassock and ruined shoes as though he expected to be canonized by the Holy Spirit Itself. When I hear him called "the prelate with the golden hand," I am reminded that it is your money, along with everyone else's that he can cajole, that he distributes so freely. Don't give him any more, Juana. Even the apothecaries are going broke administering free medicines to the poor to comply with the wishes of our godly Archbishop. Now he's taken to burning books. He's established a ridiculous trade with the booksellers: in exchange for copies of some dull-witted religious guide he's penned for the masses, he takes good novels, romances, poetry, and plays, and then burns the literature outside the archiepiscopal palace. Can you imagine? Calderón, Góngora, Lope, Cervantes, Garcilaso, Quevedo—all in flames because of a presumptuous, fanatical prelate? I think he's dangerous; Tomás thinks he's just a cantankerous and credulous fool.

But you know the sayings, Juana: *más sabe el loco en su casa que el sabio en la ajena*; the fool knows more in his own house than the wise man knows in his neighbor's. Or, *más sabe el diablo por viejo que por diablo*; the devil's wisdom comes from age not from being a devil. That Aguiar y Seijas is no fool. If men are the sum of flesh and world and devil, as you say in your *redondilla*, then Aguiar y Seijas is the epitome of men.

I almost forgot: my husband and I spent the morning discussing Josesito's confirmation. We have decided that we want you to be his *madrina* and Don Fernando Deza to be the godfather. He should be confirmed in the Cathedral, as befits his status as son of the Viceroy, but I cringe at the thought of Aguiar y Seijas performing the ceremony. He smelled so bad at the baptism, and I'm afraid he will infect my son with a disease from one of those hospitals he's taken to ministering to. We have decided, therefore, to ask the Bishop of Puebla to perform the honor, in the lower choir of San Jerónimo so that you may stand by him as his godmother. Please say yes, Juana. We want him confirmed on the 12th of December, feast day of the Virgin of Guadalupe, whom I have grown to venerate with a native passion.

Oh, Juana, I can't stand not seeing you on my birthday! Won't you please send me a message through the play, one that only I will be able to interpret?

By the way, I dreamt that you had been elected prioress of your convent. What a nightmare that would be for one with your scorpion's temperament.

Filis de mi alma,

First, let me wish you the happiest of birthdays, and as many more as there are days in the year.

How I wish I could sit this evening in the courtyard of Don Fernando's house and watch *Trials* at your side. It is on the surface nothing but a light comedy, but you will, I'm sure, find certain resonances between my own trials in this house of intrigue and those of the protagonist. You're right, I could never be the Superior of this or any house that is filled with so many ignorant women. To our great fortune, it appears as though our faction will be able to checkmate Melchora and Rafaela in the upcoming election, and at last we can recover control of the convent from those duplicitious snakes. I look forward to returning to my normal existence. I know I owe you several compositions, and I shall begin with this *romance,* but a pale sketch of my adoration.

You know that I revere you like a goddess, idolize even your disdain, venerate even your severity, that, were I a moth, I should beat my wings against the lamp to reach the light you give, that I would hold my hand over fire for you, that I would run my finger down the blade of a knife for you. That you are a woman, that you are absent, neither of these impede my love for you, for the soul ignores gender and distance. To me you are the concave spaces in the air, the end of all intentions. How can I stop loving you when I am a happy captive of your excessive beauty, when I would pay with my own life (unless you give me credit) to be with you always. In truth, you work miracles or charms, for you turn pain into joy and torment into glory.

Enjoy the trials of my secret heart, and pay special attention to the way the characters change genders as they change clothes. To hide a man under a woman's dress is like hiding myself under a nun's habit.

Yours, as always,

Juana

"Mother Brígida de San Ildefonso has won the race for prioress by a margin of thirty votes," read Father Nazario from the other side of the grille, his baritone voice echoing in the nave of the church. "María Bernardina has displaced Rafaela de Jesús as *vicaria*. Andrea de la Encarnación steps in as chief *vigilanta*. Sor Juana Inés de la Cruz remains as treasurer. Sor Juana Inés de la Cruz, also elected archivist. And Sor Beatríz de San Esteban is the new headmistress of novices. The rest of the offices remain the same. Sisters, the votes have been recorded in the convent's Book of Professions and in the Archbishop's registry. May God give you grace to carry out your elected posts with humility and love."

The lower choir reverberated with the sound of clapping. *Las santas* had prevailed.

Chapter 20

In the dream she was falling, and the fall jolted her awake. She was out of breath, as though she'd been running in her sleep, and so thirsty. She reached for her water glass, but it was empty. Downstairs, she could hear Jane puttering around in the kitchen, working the bellows over the stove, but then she remembered Jane was gone, and yet there was definitely somebody down there. She sprang out of the bed and tiptoed down the stairwell in her bare feet.

"Good morning, Tía," said Belilla, rushing up to kiss her aunt's cheek with the bellows in hand.

"Oh my God," said Juana, heart still pounding. "I forgot all about you."

"Tía, this bellows doesn't work. I can't get the fire going."

It was the girl's first morning in Juana's cell, and Juana's first morning waking up to her exuberant niece. If only you knew what a foul mood your cheeriness puts me in, she thought, but held her tongue and looked down at the bellows.

"*I* don't know how to work that thing," she said. "Why are you asking me. Ask one of the maids next door. Is there any water?"

"Oh yes, Tía. I drew two buckets already. I'm going to do your laundry while you're at prayers."

"Can I have a glass, please? My head hurts. I keep having the strangest dream."

Belilla rushed to the kitchen and drew a glass of water from one of the buckets on the stove. "It isn't boiled," she said. "I hope it doesn't make you ill, Tía."

"I'll survive," said Juana, wondering if she would survive Belilla in the mornings.

"Shall I clean the cell after I finish your laundry, Tía, or should I just report to the infirmary?"

"Oh, please, dearest, don't torment me with these questions. I can't handle questions in the morning. What time is it? The prime bells haven't rung, have they?"

"I haven't heard any bells, Tía, but it's still dark out."

"Is there any bread? I've got to have bread or else I get dizzy at Mass, but you mustn't tell anybody, Belilla."

"I won't say anything," said Belilla, scurrying back from the kitchen with a hard bun on a plate. "I get dizzy, too, sometimes, especially when the incense comes around."

With no hot chocolate to dip it into, the bread was too hard to eat. "We're going to have to talk, *cariño*," said Juana, "about your different obligations. You're not here just to take care of your aunt, much as I would like that. You're a *beata* for the next two years. Your primary duties are to the convent, not to me. Just be sure I have hot chocolate before prime, and an edible piece of bread, and a good breakfast after Mass. That's all you have to do for me in the mornings."

"I thought I was going to be a novice. That's what Tía Josefa said."

"You'll join the novitiate after your two years of service as a *beata*. We thought this would be best. We knew how anxious you were to come to San Jerónimo."

"I was anxious to be a novice, Tía."

Juana's head started to ache again. She really couldn't engage in this much conversation without any chocolate to stir her senses. "You'll be a *beata* for now, which means that you're to behave like a novice and work like a maid. That's the arrangement we made to let you live here while we accrue the money for your dowry, since your father isn't anywhere to be found. Between what your mother can send and what your aunt Josefa and I can contribute, it'll take us two years to come up with the 3,000 pesos. Do you have an objection to that?"

The girl's cheeks tinged a fiery pink. "No, Tía. I just didn't know I'd have to wait."

"You will find, *cariño*, that life in the convent is about infinite patience. Might as well start learning that lesson now."

The prime bells tolled.

"I'm going to be late again," said Juana, rushing up the stairs to get dressed.

The decision to allow Juana's niece to live at the convent had been Mother Brígida's first administrative ruling, and it did not surprise anybody, least of all Juana, that it was taken in her favor. She expected as much after how loyally she had campaigned for *las santas*. The matter topped the agenda of Mother Brígida's first Friday chapter.

"My niece has volunteered to devote her labors to the convent for two years," Juana explained to the congregation, pausing just a second before throwing in her gambit, "in exchange for a reduction in her dowry."

"What?" she heard someone in the front row say.

"Who does she think she is?" came from the senior section.

"How much of a reduction?" asked Rafaela, forgetting that she was no longer the archivist.

"A thousand pesos, 500 per year," answered Juana.

"Five hundred a year?" Agustina yelled. "To do what? Hear confessions?"

"You want us to pay your niece for the privilege of joining the convent?"

"She's going to join anyway, Sor Melchora, it's just that with this arrangement, she can join sooner and work off some of her dowry. The girl is in sore need of a change of situation. The head of the family she's living with continues to insinuate himself on her person."

"Isn't she living with a sister of yours?" asked Andrea.

"Unfortunately, they are both victims of the husband's indiscretions. We really do need to get Belilla—I mean Isabel—out of there before she's harmed. She can live with me and, of course, I'll absorb the cost of her room and board. It won't cost the convent any more than it does to keep me."

"Which is plenty, no doubt, with all your extravagances."

"Plenty in terms of what, Sor Agustina? Do you have any idea how much my revenues contribute to the convent's investments?"

"Those are not matters to be discussed at Friday chapter, Sisters," interrupted Mother Brígida. "Rest assured, Sor Agustina, that Sor Juana's contributions to the convent deposit box are, indeed, substantial."

"Not to mention to the Archbishop's charities," added Juana under her breath.

"That does not, however," the Mother Superior continued, raising her finger at Juana, "grant her license to impose a member of her family upon this congregation with no clear indication as to her status. She is either a *profesa*, a boarder, a *beata*, or a maid. If the girl chooses to profess, she will have to pay the same dowry as everyone, Juana. I'm afraid there can be no arrangment. If she chooses to board, she will have to pay tuition, and since tuition is higher than our dowry, I think we can eliminate that option. Besides, I believe your niece is too old to be a student here. And we definitely don't need any more maids. Therefore, the only option left to her is to come in as a *beata*, and as such she will not be paid, she will not earn any credits toward her dowry, and she will not be allowed the privileges of either the novices or the boarders. She will be expected to work and to behave like a *beata*. If you're in agreement with this, Juana, we can take a vote on it. It's the only way."

Juana glanced over at Andrea, but Andrea did not meet her gaze. "If it's the only way to remove the girl from that perilous association and protect her innocence," said Juana, "then I agree."

"Sister Vicaria, you may call the question," said Mother Brígida, and María Bernardina stood up and took the vote.

As expected, the only dissenters were the Three Graces and their sycophantic little flock. Mother Brígida had shown she understood her role in the game. Though Juana had lost the gambit of a reduction in the girl's dowry, she had gained what she had most wanted: her niece's immediate entrance into San Jerónimo. Melchora hissed something to Rafaela, and they both gave her a slicing stare as she passed them in the courtyard. What else could they do? For the the next three years of Brígida's rule they were powerless, and Juana intended to make the most of her advantage.

In the priory, she wrote a note to her sister Josefa explaining that Belilla had been accepted, but that she should not arrive at the convent without a gift for the nuns, and recommended that the girl write her grandmother in Panoayán to ask for a shipment of something from the family's crops. She dispatched the gatekeeper's maid with the note at once.

Within the month, Belilla arrived with sacks of sugar and cacao for the Mother Superior and the rest of the administrative body, including her *tía* Juana, who as both archivist and treasurer, was entitled to a double share. The gift impressed Brígida beyond measure, and rather than be given the job of slopping the privies and the chamberpots of the older nuns, as was every new *beata*'s first task, she was assigned to assist in the infirmary, which would give her an edge over the others when time came to enter the novitiate.

At first it was difficult for Juana to remember Belilla's presence, and she kept calling her Jane or Concepción. "Jane, you're making too much noise in the kitchen," she would shout from her study, and the girl would run upstairs and apologize for a quarter of an hour. Or, "Where are you, Concepción? Didn't I tell you to get me those books?" and the girl would look up from the anatomical drawings and list of ailments that the infirmarian had given her to memorize and ask if she should continue with her studies or help Juana with her books.

Though sweet and sanguine by nature, her niece displayed an indecisiveness that irritated Juana even more than her good cheer in the mornings, and there were times when Juana caught herself on the verge of shaking the girl's shoulders. Her timidity, of course, would be a boon to her as a novice, so she was careful not to disturb that natural tendency in the girl, but sometimes she really missed Jane's impudence and Concepción's perpetual disobedience, though she had punished them both for those very traits. She was always such a tangle of contradictions.

At least she had help, she reminded herself, for in truth, in the eight weeks she'd been alone after Jane's departure she had almost volunteered to house boarders in her cell, if only to take care of the mundane tasks of cooking and cleaning. Though she enjoyed preparing repasts for la Condesa and her other guests, there was always the cleaning up to do afterward, and that meant getting a refectory maid to draw water from the well and to carry it up to Juana's apartments, but the maid would not wash the dishes or scrub the pots or sweep the floors unless Juana paid her for her trouble, which she could not afford on a regular basis. If she attended to the job herself, by the time she finished, the bells would be ringing for compline, and she would have lost another afternoon of study and would be too tired at night even to record the day's events in her diary. With Belilla around at least she could resume her regular writing schedule and her experiments in the kitchen, which included teaching the girl how to cook. Eventually, after her first year of service as a *beata*, she would train her to take dictation, to play chess and make copies of her work, and in that way she would be a bridge between Jane and Concepción.

The oddest thing about living with Belilla was that her niece loved her, a palpable feeling, like warmth or comfort, that stirred in Juana the strangest tenderness and desire to protect. She had never felt anything but antipathy toward her half-sisters when they had shared her cell those four years, but with Belilla, she found herself engaging in maternal talks about the most personal subjects of the sort she used to have with her aunt Mary. In the evenings, after curfew, after the embers had been banked in the braziers and the shutters were closed against the croaking of the frogs in the canal, she found herself braiding the girl's hair, the long blonde plaits gleaming like thick gold chains in the light of the candles. There was a quality to

the girl that reminded Juana so much of her grandfather—the furrowing
of her brow followed by a sudden smile, the habit of slouching over her
food—and this drew her even closer to the girl, so that she came to expect Belilla's kiss on the cheek in the morning and her soft hug at night.
Once, when the infirmarian told her how clever Isabel was with the mending, how she had renovated the worn linen by cutting the threadbare section in half and sewing the good outer edges together with the minutest
of stitches that left no bedsores on the patients, Juana gave her niece a hug,
right there, in public.

It was the first time since leaving her aunt Mary's that Juana felt like a
part of her own family, for suddenly she was receiving letters from both
of her sisters and visits from Josefa's children who missed their cousin and
brought regular news of her other nieces and nephews in Panoayán.

29TH OF SEPTEMBER OF 1684

JUANITA,

Sorry I haven't been by to visit. Villena is back from the mines and
doesn't let me out of the house. Every time he goes to Querétaro he
returns with an attack of jealousy. I'm beginning to believe the rumors
that he has another family there and that's why he comes back loaded
down with guilt which translates into jealousy. Felipe has been fighting
with him for a week now, every day, a yelling match, a battle of wills.
Anyway, the cobbler is now a full month behind in his rent, and I can't
even go and make a scandal in front of his door. I'm training Felipe to
sound threatening, but his voice breaks at the worst moments and
makes him so ashamed. *Pobrecito*, my Felipe. He so wants to be a man.
I'm praying that Villena goes back to Querétaro. Only then do we have
any peace in this house, and only then will I be able to get back to my
(sorry, *our*) business. By the way, has María written to you yet? She
says Mamá has contracted some disease of the lungs from one of the
maids who was hacking and running a fever for days before she finally
collapsed in the kitchen. Better close now, so that Felipe can drop off
this note on his way to work. Please tell Belilla that I miss her good
humor, it was the only sweetness to be had around here.

Cariños from all of us to both of you,
Josefa.

DEAR JOSEFA,

I've been terribly busy now that I have lost my assistant, so I've had no time to respond. María wrote asking for money to pay Mamá's physician, who's been waiting to be paid since last month. I don't have money, do you? I'm still waiting for the Archbishop to pay me back the 400 pesos I loaned him last May. And I've had to use the balance of what I earned for the *festejo* (talk about stretching out your funds!) to pay for the repair of the garden wall, which nearly toppled over into the orchard in the last rain. Have you managed to get the rent from the cobbler yet? I think he needs more than a scandal, at this point. Have Felipe investigate what recourse we have with the Audiencia. I'm giving him three onyx bracelets to pawn for me, and a garnet ring that an admirer gave me long ago. The setting on it is pure gold, so make sure he gets a good price for it. That should be enough to pay the physician and whatever medications Mamá needs. I don't see why they don't just sell some of the livestock.

Your loving sister,
Juana Inés

P.S. Villena should be reported to the authorities if you suspect him of bigamy.
P.P.S. Belilla says to tell you she sends hugs and kisses.

15 OCTOBER 1684

ILUSTRÍSIMA,

I beg Your Reverence to forgive my insistence, but I have just received word that my mother is ill and in need of funds to pay her physician. Moreover, the roof on the infirmary is leaking and needs repair, and the main doors of the church are riddled with termites and must be replaced forthwith. Indeed, they have already been taken down to prevent the spread of the termites, and now there is nothing to protect Father Xavier and the congregation from the cold wind that swirls freely into the church. Would it be possible to receive from Your Worship the 400 gold pesos I loaned you in the spring? There is some urgency to this matter. I trust Your Reverence is in good health and that you will see fit to spread the grace of your golden hand to your humble servant.

In service,
Sor Juana Inés de la Cruz,
Accountant, San Jerónimo

30 OCTOBER 1684

QUERIDA JUANILLA,

I write to tell you that Mamá has recovered. She is still weak and a little cough continues to bother her, but the medic says the infection is gone and she's out of danger. Now if we can only keep her in bed a little longer. She's already yelling at the maids and every night insists that I go over the accounts with her. Speaking of accounts, don't worry about the money. Mamá relented and we sold a few head of cattle, as you suggested, and that will get us through until the wheat harvest. Say hello to my daughter for me. Josefa tells me she has still not located Santolaya. Tell her to keep looking, especially in the *pul-querías*, which was always his favorite place. He has an obligation to honor, that's the least he can do for his eldest daughter. If he had no intention of keeping his word he should never have promised Belilla that he would pay her entrance into the convent. It isn't right that she should be working like a slave while her father squanders the money for her dowry. Both Josefa and I have been such fools, always falling for the worst of men. Of the three of us, you were the only smart one, not letting your life get tangled up with the likes of men. You don't know how grateful I am to the Virgin Mary that Belilla has chosen to follow your example rather than ours. For your birthday, Mamá sends you this lap blanket made of the wool from our first shearing.

Receive a tight hug from your sister,
María Ramírez, Panoayán

DEAREST JUANA,

We have just returned from Chapultepec and I regret to say that Josesito has come down with catarrh again. It was unwise to take him with us. Now I spend all day making sure he can breathe, and it breaks my heart when the medic cups his little chest, leaving angry red sores on his delicate flesh. Tomás is so angry he doesn't speak to me, but I remind him it was his idea that we spend the weekend in the woods. All he can think about is those ponies he had imported from Peru. I shall not be able to visit until the boy has recovered. Sorry to hear about your mother. It's the season for illness, I think. Please accept this latest edition of Kircher's *Corpus Hermeticum* as a belated birthday present. I remember you mentioning something about a strange dream involving mythological symbols the last time I visited, and thought this might be useful to you. I hope you don't already own it. Tomás says many happy returns and looks forward to visiting you next week. I guess this means we won't be alone.

With love,

M.L.

18th of November 1684 ·

20 NOVEMBER 1684

DEAREST CONDESA,

Thank you so much for the Kircher. No, I don't own it and it has already helped me discern the meaning of some of those arcane symbols in the dream. Actually, I've decided to work the imagery into a poem, nothing but a trifle at present that I'm calling First Dream (as I suspect there will be others). It's one of the few, if not the only thing, I've ever written (besides these letters to your beloved person) for my own pleasure. Its occasion is neither a commission nor a request, but my own inner struggle between the passions of a character I have deemed the Dark Queen and her nemesis, the Helios of reason. I am embroidering an intricate labyrinth of allusions and some fairly Gongoresque flights of fantasy that will take us from the pyramids of Mexico to those of Memphis, and for that reason I have chosen the simplest form, a *silva*, with its seven- and ten-syllable lines and free-flowing rhythm scheme. When I have completed a draft worthy of your perusal, I shall have my niece make a copy of it. Please kiss my godson for me. Belilla sends him this special concoction of herbs and honey that will help him recover.

yours, Juana

She knew she was dreaming, and the knowledge was a lucid one, like the awareness of being in a strange but familiar place. In the dream she was sitting across the chess table from the Onyx Queen, who had metamorphosed into human size with a human face, though she retained the form and color of an onyx chess piece. They were not sitting at her own small table below the arched windows in her study, but at an enormous board, carved of squares inlaid with a sun or a moon, each square larger than the span of her hand. The room had no floor, but there were windows, several pairs of arched windows all around them, and there were bookshelves between the windows, suspended in air and lined with ancient-looking tomes and icons representing pagan deities: a loom, a balance, a triangular harp, an owl, an oil lamp, an eagle with a snake dangling in its beak, a lion, a pyramid cast in silver, a pomegranate, a quetzal bird. The board was empty save for the shadow of the Onyx Queen, but if Juana's gaze lingered upon some object on a shelf, it would appear in the middle of the board for her inspection. The lamp felt warm, the harp played ethereal notes, the pomegranate oozed its red juice all over her hands, the balance weighed a tiny heart on one dish, a tiny clock on the other, on each face of the pyramid was inscribed one of the faces of the Moon: Virgin, Mother, Crone. She wanted to bring the owl down, but it flapped its wings and flew away, and just as suddenly a flock of other birds, dark and loud as crows though they looked like whippoorwills and had white plumes upon their crests, flew into the room and took their places on the shelves.

"You see, Juana," said the Onyx Queen, "that life is a dream."

"That is Calderón's conclusion," said Juana.

"Dare you live your dreams?" the Onyx Queen challenged her.

"I have no dream but time in which to do my work," said Juana.

"Close that hemisphere of light. Let the night have its way with you. Follow the owl to the source of all your dreams."

Unable to resist the Onyx Queen's words, she closed her dream eyes and felt herself spinning out of the room like a speck of matter in a great whorl of mist and stars and deepest night that, she realized, was the spiral of the Milky Way. On her shoulder was the owl, and she was robed in a white fleece that kept her warm as fur but felt light as feathers. Suddenly the spinning stopped and she found herself aboard a sail-festooned canoe in a dark sea flowing in four colors—crimson, black, yellow, and pale green—and she understood that she was sailing in a sea of humors, toward an unknown destination, marked only by a glowing obelisk in the distance. She saw that there was a sleeping crane perched at the prow and an esoteric symbol painted on the sail and backlit by the silver rays of the crescent moon. At once, the vessel picked up speed and skimmed the waves, leaving a wake of phosphorescent fish in the dark water. But then her stomach lurched—from fear or hunger, she knew not which—and suddenly she was awake.

Winter Solstice, 22 December 1684

2 A.M. Cannot sleep. The dream has woken me again. The cell is freezing, but I have no more wood for the brazier, so got dressed instead. My mother's lap blanket is such a comfort as I sit here shivering over my "Sueño" notebook. This poem is beginning to feel like an obsession.

2:15 A.M. Uncovered my telescope to look at the dark morning sky and found a full moon rising over the volcanoes, their snowcapped crests luminescent in the white light. Is it my imagination or do I see the cone of a shadow over the face of the moon? Could it be the shadow of the volcanoes? But how is that possible if there is no other light illuminating them from this side that would cause their shadow to be cast upon the moon? Perhaps it is the beginning of a lunar eclipse and perhaps that is why I have not been able to sleep.

2:30. It is definitely an eclipse. The earth's shadow begins to creep over the moon like a black orb swallowing the light of Athena crescent by crescent. I wonder if Don Carlos is watching this?

3:00. The moon is in full shadow now. I can hear dogs howling in the streets, and a wild hooting of owls in the yews that line the canal. It's getting colder and my hand trembles over the page, my fingers stiff on the quill. I am overwhelmed by the deepest melancholy. I think I know the meaning of that strange dream now, as though my sleeping mind, somehow cognizant of this eclipse, were feeding the symbolism of its imagery into my psyche. Clearly, the moon is Athena and the lunar eclipse is also her eclipse. If Athena's light is vanquished, and Athena represents wisdom, women's wisdom in particular, then the beacon of my existence has been extinguished on the horizon, and all that's left is a star-filled void, cold and empty of light. When Nyctimene, the lady of Lesbos, thought to gain knowledge by consuming the oil of the lamps burning in Athena's temple, she was punished by the goddess and turned into an owl, sentenced to a nocturnal existence. Am I, then, like Nyctimene, and have I been drinking of the sacred oil only to be punished with perpetual darkness? And yet darkness is the province of all secret wisdom. The moon is the goddess incarnate. To be sentenced to darkness is to live eternally in the presence of the goddess. Is darkness, then, a punishment or a reward? I see such a clear correspondence between this eclipse and my "Sueño." Must follow this line of thought. Have completely lost touch with sleep anyway.

4:00. The moon is still utterly dark, just the thinnest sliver of white light pulsing over the edges of earth's shadow. It has become my conceit for "Sueño," this lunar eclipse that has by now stirred up all the night birds, whose cries echo in the eerie stillness that surrounds the valley. If at this hour that the body is in full repose, but two hours away from daylight, the soul—my soul—were to take flight through the diaphanous spiral of the skies, it would be a footsoldier in Athena's army, its quest to uncover the moon and release her light again over the night.

5:30. Went back to the poem and got so caught up in the metaphor of war between the knowledge that Athena represents (the secret knowledge of women) and the knowledge of power represented by Apollo (the sun, of course, is the culprit behind the eclipse), that I didn't even realize the shadow had started to move away from the moon. But now there's an even odder development, as Venus has appeared in the east just before the sun, and it looks as though the sun will rise over the full moon. Covered first by shadow, now by light, the moon has lost the battle and the prime bells are ringing. If the moon represented passion rather than wisdom and the sun reason rather than power, it would make sense that the Sun God should triumph over the Moon Goddess, for she like a dark empress (or the Onyx Queen I gave to Concepción) tyrannizes my nights and I find relief from that tyranny only when the light of reason illuminates my heart. Otherwise I would go mad, and be plunged, like Phaëton or Lucifer from glorious heights to the cold currents of doom.

Now I must quit this fancy and rush to prayers. Good thing I'm already dressed. Just have to throw on my veil and scapular, buckle up my shoes, and pin the shield to my chest. This is my armor, and I find myself fighting on both sides. I defend and attack either side of myself, sun and moon, Apollo and Athena.

Chapter 21

"What I don't understand about that analogy, Don Carlos, is that, if the gardener is the symbolic husband of the earth, for he (or she) sows the seeds that make the earth productive, then the tree or plant that grows as a consequence of this sowing would be their offspring."

"Yes, precisely, Sister. That is the way of nature."

"Could we not also say, though, that the fruit produced by the tree or the flower by the plant is a consequence of the mating of the earth and its own offspring? Is that not also the way of nature?"

"The seed is inherent in the offspring, Sister. It is the wind that acts as husband when it pollinates the seed."

"True, and yet the fruit or flower springs from a source that once was the offspring of the earth and the seed, and then becomes host to its own pollination."

"I don't quite follow you, Sister."

"I am simply extending the analogy, my friend. If it is natural to think of he (or she) who sows the seed as husband and that which with the seed produces offspring as wife and mother, then is it not also natural for mother and offspring to reproduce?"

"But that is incest, Sister, an abomination of nature. Surely you're not suggesting that incestuous relationships are natural."

"And yet they occur in nature, as I have just described, and did you not say, Sir, when we began our exchange, that that which occurred in nature was natural and that which did not occur in nature was unnatural?"

"Indeed, Sister, but nature has no morality, and that is what distinguishes Man from nature."

"Listen to the dissolution of your own argument, my friend. If morality does not occur in nature, then morality must be unnatural."

"We were not speaking about human nature, Sister."

"And yet you made a human judgment about a natural occurrence. The synthesis of seed and progenitor occurs quite commonly in nature and yet you call it an abomination."

"That it is common in nature, Sister, does not make it common in human nature."

"Ergo, the sowing of seed and the producing of offspring need not be common or natural in human nature either, though it be a natural occurrence. And that, Sir, is precisely the point with which I opened our debate. Woman need not be wife or mother if it is not in her nature to be sowed or pollinated."

Don Carlos covered the bottom half of his face with the long, skeletal fingers of his right hand and shook his head. "I concede, Sister, that I have trapped myself with my own logic." He turned to face the other guests. "You see, once a week I do penitence at Sor Juana's *salón*. She never forgives a fault in logic."

The other guests applauded: la Condesa, Don Ignacio de Castorena y Ursúa, Rector of the university and Sigüenza's employer, and the Bishop of Puebla, Don Manuel Fernández de Santa Cruz, who had started to join the weekly *tertulias* in San Jerónimo after the baptism of la Condesa's son.

"Excellent debate, Sister, though a bit disturbing," said Castorena, wiping the chocolate foam off the fluffy tips of his mustache.

"I found the argument stimulating," said the Bishop, holding his plate out for a second helping of *huevos reales*. "Though based on a faulty comparison."

"Belilla," Juana called to her niece, who was rocking the three-year-old José on the wooden horse Juana had had made for him the previous Christmas. "Please attend to His Grace, the Bishop."

Belilla took the Bishop's plate to the sideboard and set another piece of custard on it.

"I want my dogs," said the boy to his mother.

Belilla handed the Bishop his plate and curtsied to him.

"If you'd like, Señora," offered Belilla, "José and I can play out on the patio with his puppies."

"Your niece is a treasure, Juana," said la Condesa. "Thank you, Isabel. But make sure he doesn't get into any water. He's just getting over a cold."

Belilla curtsied again and went to scoop the boy off the rocking horse.

"You were saying something about a faulty comparison, Your Grace?" asked Juana.

"The first rule of a comparison, Sister," said the Bishop, caressing his custard with the tip of his spoon, "if I may quote Aristotle, is that the two objects being compared belong to the same general species. Humans and plants do not belong to the same species, therefore any comparison between them would result in a faulty conclusion."

"I thought the argument was more general than that, Your Grace," said Juana. "I thought the topic was nature, not humans or trees."

"And yet you used them as examples, Sister, to illustrate nature. But you see, there is no comparison between what we call *human* nature and the nature of the environment."

Castorena and Don Carlos glanced at each other. La Condesa opened her fan and hid half her face behind it, tilting her head so that only Juana could see that she was yawning.

"But, Sir," said Juana, getting to her feet on the other side of the grille, "the science of medicine tells us that the four humors that guide human feelings and dispositions all come from the physical universe. Thus, those with a happy nature are said to be sanguine, and ruled by heat and moisture; those with an irascible nature are said to be choleric, and ruled by heat and dryness; those with a melancholic nature are said to possess an abundance of black bile, which is governed by cold and dryness; and those who tend toward sluggishness are said to be phlegmatic, and ruled by cold and moisture. Blood, bile, and phlegm, Sir, are not the exclusive domain of human beings."

"I think she's trapped you, Bishop," said la Condesa.

Don Carlos and Castorena applauded lightly. The Bishop blushed, his choleric nature beginning to show.

"Moreover," Juana added, unable to resist making a final point, "it is said that heat and dryness make better minds than wet and coldness, and though I do not subscribe to that view, as women in general are said to be either wet or cold, and thus are said to possess inferior minds, the argument, again, points to the use of physical qualities to describe human nature."

"Brilliant rebuttal, Juana," said la Condesa. "As always."

"Very well, then," said the Bishop, still flustered, "let us return to your disturbing analogy of the mother and offspring mating. Who, in that case, would be considered husband if there is not a seed sown to cause the reproduction of fruit or flower, for the seed is already contained in said offspring."

Juana smiled at the Bishop. "Nature, Sir."

"Aha!" said the Bishop.

"But what about the conceit of *Mother* Nature, Sor Juana?" asked Castorena.

"I believe she would say that nature is neither masculine nor feminine, Don Ignacio," said Don Carlos. "Am I right, Sister?"

"No," said Juana. "I would say that nature is *both* masculine and feminine."

The Bishop nearly choked on his chocolate. "You do like to tread on dangerous ground, Sor Juana," he said.

"But it makes perfect sense, Your Reverence," said la Condesa. "If nature contains both masculine and feminine qualities, there is no need for strict adherence to the laws of gender. Thus, it would be possible for the offspring to reproduce itself, and would be both mother and father to its own offspring."

"Are you suggesting, Madam," said the Bishop, blushing again, and looking mildly scandalized, "that there is no need for husbands?"

La Condesa fanned herself placidly. "Certainly not, Your Reverence," she said, feigning shock, "only that there is no need for gardeners."

At this everyone laughed, including the Bishop.

"Would anyone care for more chocolate?" asked Juana. "I can have my niece start us another pot. Another pastry, perhaps?"

"No, no, no," said the Bishop, getting to his feet. "It's getting late, and the Archbishop wants me to say Mass tomorrow. Gentlemen, shall we retreat?"

Don Carlos, clearly, was not ready to leave, but since the three men had arrived together, it was understood that they would leave together. He and Castorena rose and donned their feathered hats. Belilla came in from the patio to help the Bishop with his fur-lined cloak.

"Madam?" said the Bishop. "May one of us escort you back?"

"No, thank you, Your Reverence. My footmen are with me. There are still a few matters I need to discuss with Sor Juana."

"Please give my regards to the Viceroy then," he said, holding out his hand for her to kiss his episcopal ring.

"Won't you dine with us tomorrow evening?" she asked. "It could be the last time we shall have the privilege of entertaining you at the palace."

"*Muy agradecido*, Señora," he bowed his head. "Until tomorrow evening then. Sor Juana, thank you for illuminating us with your rhetorical skills."

"My pleasure, Your Grace," she said, curtsying to him.

Don Carlos and Castorena took turns kissing la Condesa's hand, then bowed to Juana.

"Again, happy birthday, Sor Juana," said Castorena. "The bookshop will send over the Kepler I promised in the morning."

"Thank you, Don Ignacio. My knowledge on astronomy would be nil were it not for the kindness of my friends."

"Good night, Señores," Belilla said at the doorway as the men passed her.

"Good night, Señoritas," said the boy standing beside her.

"José!" scolded la Condesa, but the boy giggled and went to bury himself under the azure canopy of his mother's skirts. The two shepherd pups he had brought from home to show his godmother traipsed into the locutory, leaving a trail of muddy prints.

"José, *hijo*, ¡ven acá!" said la Condesa. "Look at the mess your animals have made."

"Shall I clean it up, Tía?" asked Belilla, already gathering the plates and cups.

"Just take the dishes back to the cell, dearest," said Juana. "Wait for me there, and we'll walk to compline together."

Belilla piled the dishes neatly on the tray and left the room after bidding a polite farewell to the Vicereine. José peered out from under the folds of blue satin.

"Adios, Belilla!" he called.

"Behave yourself, *nene*," she said over her shoulder.

"That glutton," said la Condesa, referring to the Bishop. "He was just waiting for an invitation."

"I'm afraid we've scandalized him," said Juana.

"They're always ready to be scandalized by something," said la Condesa. "Whatever put it into Sigüenza's head to bring him along?"

"He makes it a point to join our *tertulias* whenever he's in the capital," said Juana. "He's even started to write to me from Puebla."

"What a bore," said la Condesa. "And now I shall have to draw up a guest list and think about the menu and hire a band."

Juana came up to the grille. "I can't believe you're leaving the palace."

"Nor I, actually. I've grown so used to it."

The boy crept out of his hiding place. "One of them bit me, Madrina," he said to Juana, holding out a dirty finger. The pups were now wrestling each other by the sideboard, and he chastised them in a mock angry voice.

"That should do it," said Juana, amused despite herself with the boy's antics. He was almost the exact duplicate of his mother, except that he had blonde curls rather than brown.

"Come, José, you said you were going to give one to your *madrina*."

"But we're not allowed to keep dogs anymore," Juana protested. La Condesa winked at her. It was only a game for the boy's sake.

"The yellow one," said the boy, sucking on his finger. "He's the mean one that bit me."

"Of course, it's out of the question that we leave New Spain before José is fully weaned," said la Condesa, resuming their conversation. "What suckling child would survive such a journey?"

"Where will you live after the Count of Montclova arrives?" said Juana. "Isn't he making his entrance next month?"

"Tomás has rented Castorena's residence behind the university. It's a lovely old house, a little pretentious but with good character. Castorena's going on the Flota to recruit masters in Madrid. Odd that he didn't say anything to you about it tonight. He'll be gone half a year."

"May Mexico be graced by your presence for many years, Señora."

"Oh, but I'm homesick at the same time. I miss my sisters and the Guadalquivir and the food most of all. Nobody knows how to make a good gazpacho here, Juana, and sometimes I dream of eating black rice with calamari. I'm sure I'll miss squash blossom quesadillas when I return, though, not to mention your desserts. Don't you just hate it when you can't make up your mind about something?"

"Indecisiveness is not a luxury I can indulge in, Condesa. In here you have to know exactly what you're going to do at all times or else someone is bound to pin you into a corner."

"Don't tell me you're having problems with the prioress again."

"No, not with Mother Brígida. She's very prudent and actually very good as an administrator, but Rafaela's back in her role as *vicaria*, which means, of course, that she's taking copious notes on everything I say and do, and the twins, María and Marcela, are still following me around like a pair of albino shadows. But at least we still own the majority of the administration. It's a matter of fund-raising now. We've invested a good sum of our holdings in real estate, and we're doing rather well, actually. As long as we continue to draw more money to the convent than Melchora's group, we can retain our popularity with the sisters."

La Condesa shook her head in amazement. "From poetess to financier, Juana."

"I do whatever it takes to survive, Condesa."

"José!" The boy had climbed up the sideboard and was about to topple the washbasin on his head. One of the puppies started to bark.

"He's getting restless," said la Condesa, pulling the boy onto her lap. "We'd better go. It was foolish of me not to bring his nurse with us."

"But it's so nice when it's just the two of us, Condesa."

"I know, it's just that he's a handful, aren't you, you rascal? Tell me, Juana, where is that girl of yours, that secretary? I never see her anymore, since your niece moved in with you."

Juana felt her eyes grow misty. "Concepción," she said in a low voice to mask the sudden melancholy that tightened her throat, "left three years ago, Señora. Don't you remember? To this day I don't know what became of her."

"That's right. I forgot about that petite scandal. What a pity," said la Condesa, retying the ribbon on the boy's ponytail. "I thought she'd returned. I was going to bribe her into going back with us when we return to Spain. José is going to need a good tutor. What better tutor, I thought, than the one trained in my dear Juana's image?"

"That *is* a pity," said Juana, "I fear that wherever she ended up her education has gone completely to waste."

"At least she served you well, Juana. But, look! You've gone somber on me. Do you miss her?"

Juana noted the edge of jealousy in la Condesa's voice and shook her head. "Such a shame to lose a good assistant," she said. "Belilla is a wonderful companion, of course, and my own flesh and blood, but she's just begun her novitiate, and has her own life to attend to."

"The girl did have better penmanship than yours, Juana," la Condesa teased, dark eyes glittering. "Masculine handwriting, isn't that how your good sisters described it?"

"Señora, please don't tease me. I do my best to impress you."

The dark eyes crinkled as she smiled, and Juana felt her breath catch, as always, when la Condesa looked at her so candidly. "It's the content that counts." The boy laid his head in the crook of his mother's shoulder, tucking his thumb into his mouth.

"To me the form is as important as the content, Condesa."

"I see only the form given by the content, Juana."

You are the form, she wanted to say, and that child cuddled in your arms is the content. "Then I suppose my purpose is achieved, despite my masculine penmanship."

The boy took his thumb from his mouth and began rubbing at his mother's breast.

"I adore everything you write, Juana."

Juana tried not to watch the boy's hand, now slipping under la Condesa's bodice.

"And I the audience for whom it is written."

For once la Condesa blushed at Juana's comment. "Stop that, José! We have to go now."

Juana felt pleased with herself, and almost thankful that the visit had come to a close, for she had lost her ability to breathe in the sudden warmth of the *locutorio*.

"Come, José," said la Condesa, pulling the boy's hand out of her cleavage. "Don't fall asleep. We've got to get you cleaned up before bed. *Vamos*. Find your dogs and let's go."

Juana stood up on her side of the grille. "*Hasta pronto*," she said.

"On Christmas Eve," said la Condesa, "after our ride through the Alameda. My husband wants to talk to you about Brazo de Plata. He's not a friend of the Medinacelis, you know."

"Tell him not to worry. As long as Your Excellencies are in Mexico, I shall give my allegiance to no other Viceroy."

"Only while we're in Mexico, Juana?"

"My loyalty is with you always, Señora."

"Can you imagine? A one-armed cripple for a Viceroy, only because my husband's brother has fallen out of favor with the King."

"Let us hope he can govern with one arm as well as Cervantes could write with one hand."

"We wouldn't want him to govern too well, Juana. How would it look if, incomplete as he is, he were deemed a better Viceroy than my husband, who is whole?"

"That could never happen, Señora."

"¡*Vamos*, Mamá!" the boy said, stamping his foot.

"Until Noche Buena, Juana?"

Juana bowed her head. "I shall not breathe until then."

Again, la Condesa's face colored. "You torment me, Juana. José! Don't forget to kiss your *madrina*'s hand."

Juana held her hand through the bars of the grille and the boy clicked the heels of his white boots together, took the tips of her fingers, and kissed her lightly on the knuckles. Both she and la Condesa laughed at the boy's seriousness. Heart pounding in her ears, Juana watched them walk across the gatekeeper's patio, the boy herding the pups out with his little cane. Sor Clara held the portal open and one of the footmen gave the old woman a tip. Juana took her lantern and rushed from the locutory before Sor Clara came over to talk with her about the visit. She was headed in the direction of the chapel in the cemetery. She needed to visit Pandora's Box before prayers.

12 November 1686

There is an odd silence in the convent today, or perhaps it's just that all I hear is the pounding of my heart and the racing of the blood in my veins. La Condesa has just left, thank God, for I could not have kept up the pretense that I was not thinking of Concepción while speaking with her in our private code. It was not Concepción so much as her body that I was thinking about, remembering the feel of her skin under my fingers. Would that I were the boy and it had been my hand massaging that royal breast. She felt it, too, I know she did, this sudden spark of desire as the boy acted out my thoughts on her body. Oh, to be jealous of a child and of the innocence with which it expresses its need for a mother's breast!

And yet, there was a shadow in the room, also related to Concepción. I *do* miss her and still worry about what may have happened to her. She's probably somebody's wife by now (if she lived), with a child clinging to her as José clings to la Condesa, in total ownership. Did I ever own my mother that way? I don't recall much of my childhood any longer. Just as well. Better to recall an absence than a presence that was never mine. Certainly, Mamá did not belong to me as she belonged to Josefa and María, and she never belonged to them the way she now belongs to her grandchildren. I hear Diego has a son now, born out of wedlock, as is the fate of all my family.

I still cannot believe the Count of Paredes has been replaced, but at least I shall be able to hold on to la Condesa for a little longer. She says they won't leave until the child is fully weaned. Not knowing anything about children, I have no idea what age that might be (though he looks old enough to be weaned already), but I thank God it's a reason to keep them here a little longer.

Now I must quit this diary. It's too dark and the wavering of the lamp is hurting my eyes. Need to remember to bring another ink pot when I return to the chapel. My poor Pandora's Box has gotten scratched and dented in its hiding place, and the scent of sandalwood that used to emanate from the wood has now been replaced by a mossy smell. I suppose I could have left the box in the hidden compartment of my desk, but having Rafaela installed in the priory again tells me it's safer out here. Must hurry. Compline bell is ringing.

"Tía, Mother Rafaela was here waiting for you," said Belilla when she got back to the cell.

"What did she want? She knew I had guests."

"She said she needed to look at the accounts, but I told her she had to wait for you. Here's your rosary, Tía. You left it on the bed."

"God bless your good sense, Belilla." She pinned on her rosary. "Let's go. No, don't take the lantern. It's a full moon tonight."

"No wonder," said the girl.

"No wonder what, *cariño?*"

Belilla shrugged. "Nothing important, Tía." The girl's face blushed. Juana knew exactly what her niece meant. Funny how, now that she had donned a habit, the girl would be pursued by "nothing important," a clandestine way of saying illicit thoughts. *Privatio est causa apetitus*, she wanted to say, but her niece was not fluent in Latin and it would be better that she found out on her own how to quell those pernicious appetites born of privation.

Chapter 22

16 December 1687

QUERIDA HERMANA,

I write to tell you that Mamá's health has taken another bad turn. This one, I fear, may be fatal. According to the medic from Chimalhuacán, her lungs never fully recovered from that old illness she contracted a few years ago, and she is now spitting up clots of blood. The medic says it is only a matter of time before she leaves us. I have written to Josefa and asked her to come be with me during this terrible time. Diego is here and so is Antonia, but Inés can't find it in her heart to leave her brood, not even to say good-bye to her own mother. I don't know if they'll let you out of there, Juanilla, but if it is possible at all, it will do Mamá much good to see you one last time, and if you can, bring Belilla with you. The thought of being orphaned makes me want to see my daughter again. Besides, there are matters of inheritance to discuss.

I remain your loving sister,
María Ramírez

20 December 1687

Belilla, Josefa and her four children, and I have just arrived at the inn by the lake in Chalco. It is the first time in eighteen years that I have set foot outside the convent and I felt, at first, oddly terrified of the filth and bustle of the city. I thought we would hire a coach since we had a heavy trunk to lug between us (mostly gifts for the family that I had Josefa buy, and of course, some books and my writing box), but la Condesa's own carriage was waiting to take Belilla and me to the Plaza Mayor. She sent one of her ladies along with a note that begs me to stop over at her house on my return from Panoayán. Who knows when that will be.

Belilla arranged for Josefa and her family to meet us on the bank of the

Jamaica. It seems Josefa is going with us without Villena's permission. I am traveling in my habit to afford us some protection from highwaymen. Josefa's eldest, Felipe, is tall and burly for his age, but his youth betrays him whenever he speaks. Once we reach Panoayán I will wear lay clothes again, if I even remember how to walk without this heavy veil on my head, without these sleeves weighing down my shoulders, without this scapular, escutcheon, rosary, cincture, and coif adding breadth to my bones.

Mother Brígida gave me permission to remain at my mother's bedside for as long as I thought necessary, veiled language for "until she dies." She had to request a special dispensation from the Archbishop to let me go (accompanied by a donation from me to His Ilustrísima's favorite charity at the moment, the Hospital de San Hipólito), but we were told that Belilla will have to repeat the last six months of her novitiate year when we return.

I don't know if it's my own state of mind or the general unruliness of the season, but the city I used to love, the beautiful city of my memory, is now a crowded, squalid, stinking cesspool. The streets surrounding the *traza*—Calle de San Agustín, Calle de Toledo, Calle de Aguila, Calle de los Plateros, Calle del Reloj—seemed narrower than I remembered, and the arches of the aqueduct looked like they would collapse in a strong wind. Several of the public crosses we passed seemed about to topple from wood rot or the weight of so many indigent *zaramullos* leaning against them. The public fountains, which I remember were among the Marquis de Mancera's most assiduous projects of reconstruction, are now choked with every form of detritus, and the stench of urine in the arcade of the *municipio* is overpowering. Even the palace has declined under Brazo de Plata; gone are the liveried doormen and helmeted sentries at the gates. Only the Cathedral, still awaiting its last towers, looks better than it did eighteen years ago, but it seems incongruous sitting there in its exaggerated ornateness, its mammoth stolidity and opulence, amid so much ugliness and squalor. If this is any evidence of the way Brazo de Plata is running the realm, it is no wonder the people want him deposed.

I was glad when Felipe finally arranged our passage on a *piragua* transporting textiles to the market in Chalco. I wanted desperately to get away from the noise and the stench, not that the canal smelled any better. Despite the floating flower gardens and the barges bearing fragrant woods and spices, dead animals floated in the water alongside other waste and sewage. Josefa's girls vomited from the smell and the motion sickness. It

wasn't until after we crossed the valley, passing fields of corn and sugarcane and cacao, and entered the shadow of the hills and the scent of ju-
nipers that we were all able to breathe normally. I had forgotten how cool
the air is at the foot of the volcanoes. My volcanoes, still so beautiful, welcoming me home after thirty-one years of living in the city.

I don't know if this is the same inn at which my uncle and I stayed back
when I was eight years old, but I seem to remember the building, the smell
of mutton cooking and the sound of the lake soughing on the nearby shore.
But there's a blooming rose of Castile climbing the wall outside our window which I don't remember, and the woman who runs the place seems
as young as Belilla, though she has three toddlers following her around
like ducklings. I have rented one of the private rooms for the womenfolk;
Felipe and his brother will share their bed with the other travelers in the
common room. Tomorrow I will hire an oxcart to take us all to Panoayán.
My back is not strong enough to sit on a mule for six hours.

All day I have vacillated between dread and joy; the latter because I am returning to Abuelo's hacienda after three decades, leaving the dark intrigues
and redundant ritual of the convent; and yet, dread is at the root of all my joy,
the knowledge in my heart that my mother's trial with death awaits.

"And you say, Sister Melchora, that during your term as prioress, Sor Juana
exhibited severely irreverent habits?"

"She did, Your Grace, as we can all attest, isn't that right, Rafaela?"

"I shall ask the questions here, Sister. Suppose you give us an example."

"She called me a fool once. Can you imagine, calling the prioress a fool?"

"To your face?"

"She cares not for protocol, never has. From the moment she entered
our community she caused problems of that sort."

"And what did you do, Sister, to reprimand this grave irreverence?"

"I reported her to Fray Payo."

"Naturally. And what did our beloved Archbishop do?"

"He didn't help at all. Told me to prove that I wasn't a fool and he would
take measures."

"Have you another example of something slightly more severe than a
fault of respect?"

"She failed to attend our sacred Offices for a week. And it was Holy

Week at that. She didn't even show up to the rosary on Good Friday or to the Mass on Easter Sunday. That should qualify as a severe irreverence."

"How long ago was this?"

"She just recently missed the evening and the morning services, also during Lent, Your Grace."

"Don't you find it fascinating, Your Grace, that while everyone else is refraining from their indulgences for forty days, Juana indulges herself in disobedience?"

"Write that down: the habit of disobeying the Rule during Lent. Now, Sisters, what else? And remember that these *diligencias* benefit from detail and not summary."

"She had the habit of staying up all night reading and working on her worldly commissions—"

"The *villancicos* and *loas* commissioned by the Cabildo? The triumphal arch? Those are legitimate commissions."

"Oh, no, Your Grace. She has many more than that. She writes all manner of secular poetry: sonnets, *décimas*, *endechas*, panegyrics, plays, satires—"

"Even love poems to a certain Vicereine."

"You seem quite versed in the variety of literary genres, Sister. Did you ever read these works?"

"Certainly not!"

"Weren't some of her plays performed in the cloister?"

"Yes, but—"

"So then you must have heard some of her verses."

"We were not required to attend performances of that nature, Sir. They were meant for the entertainment of our boarders and their families. Some of us do not believe in secular entertainment for girls whom we are training to be epitomes of obedience and humility."

"So you can tell us nothing about her secular verses?"

"Only that her own father confessor abandoned her because of them."

"They were always arguing about her poetry. That seemed to concern him more than her faults in etiquette."

"What manner of argument?"

"He wanted her to forbear her worldly commissions and her secular scribblings—"

"Particularly those love poems to la Condesa—"

"—and devote herself to reading Scripture. He also insisted that she change her manner of writing, her penmanship bore no feminine grace at all—"

"Did you get that?"

"I did, Sir, 'penmanship bore no grace at all.'"

"*Feminine* grace. This is an important point, Sister. Why have I never heard anything about this? Everything I've ever seen of hers is written in a graceful calligraphy."

"She's always had someone copy her work, Sir," said Melchora. "First that *castiza* Madre Catalina gave her, and now her uppity little niece who calls herself Sor Isabel."

"Can you procure an example of this penmanship, Sister? It would most benefit our case."

"There was a writing box where she kept her letters, Your Grace. Her cousins, when they lived with her, discovered it. But it has since disappeared from her cell. We've looked everywhere."

"I would like to leave you two in charge of locating this writing box, if I may?"

"We have tried, Excellency, to no avail."

"Please, Sisters, exercise the virtue of persistence."

23 December

We arrived late last evening. Josefa's children were starving and Belilla and I did not want to disturb Mamá's sleep; María says she sleeps no more than three hours a night and spends the rest of the time groaning and tossing from the pain. She must have sensed something, though, because as soon as I stepped into the room, her eyes opened.

"Juanilla," she said, "you're like an apparition." She wanted to hug me but could barely lift her arms from the bed; even the slightest movement hurts her lungs, but at least she is eating, María tells me, and she takes several naps during the day that give her a reprieve from coughing.

It was difficult not to weep in front of her. She looks so old, so fragile. Her skin has a tinge of jaundice, and when she coughs it sounds as though she had a fire raging in her lungs. She has the same starved look about her that Aunt Mary had the last time I saw her (does this disease run in my family?), and when she turns on her side, I see a pronounced hump to her back. We didn't want to tire her, so left her in the care of her physician while Belilla and I went to change out of our habits.

María loaned me a brown dress with a dark green bodice and matching *rebozo*. Haven't worn a corset since I lived at the palace, and forgot how painful it is to cinch the waist in so tightly it squeezes the air out of your lungs. And without their bindings, my breasts felt obscenely exposed. I must say I felt utterly ridiculous with all that crinoline under the dress ballooning out on either side of my hips. It's odd what you don't notice until you're wearing it. Belilla, too, looked peculiar in the red velvet dress María selected for her. Against her white habit, the girl's pale skin looks almost rosy; against that red velvet she looks blanched. When we rejoined everyone in the kitchen (nothing has changed in my mother's kitchen, but it looks much shabbier than I remember, and yet there are glass panes in the window now), I became the topic of conversation.

"Your hair is so long, Juana," said María, holding up the long braid I had woven. "I expected it to be short under your veil."

"I thought nuns were supposed to be *pelonas*," called out one of Josefa's girls.

I had to explain to them that the cutting of hair upon taking one's permanent vows was a symbolic act, meant to show that you were choosing to sever all connection to the world and to the person you used to be in that world.

"But it's allowed to grow back," I said, winking at the youngest of the children.

"I can't see barbers coming to the convent on a regular basis to keep the nuns shaved," said Diego, and Josefa's boys laughed at their uncle's joke.

"Isn't hair a sign of vanity, Juana," said Antonia, and for an instant I remembered how, when she lived at San Jerónimo, she could sit for hours staring into space, twirling her ringlets in her finger.

"A sign of stupidity, I used to think," I said. "Not the hair itself, but the passage of time it took to grow out a measured amount that marked how slowly or quickly I progressed from being stupid about a subject to learning something about it. There were many times when my hair grew long and I had not yet left the stupid stage, at which point I cut it off again and gave myself another chance."

"Do you cut your hair often, then, Tía?" asked one of Antonia's girls, clearly the only one of my nieces who understood what I was saying. "Otherwise it would be much longer than it is."

"And I wouldn't be any the wiser," I told her, and she chuckled.

"There *are* some nuns who are vain about their hair," Belilla interjected. "One named Sor Felipa used to wear curls under her veil, or so I was told."

"Sor Isabel," I said, cutting a glance at her, "those are matters of discretion. I hope you have not forgotten that as a novice you should practice modesty of the tongue, even if you're not in the convent."

Belilla stirred uncomfortably in her chair, then offered to help the maid serve our chocolate. The boys nudged each other's ribs. The girls sat up straight.

What amazes me about being here is not only that I am surrounded by little strangers who are my nieces and nephews and pretend to know me—one of Antonia's girls likes to lay her head on my shoulder and cuddle up against me, as if I'd known her all her life—but that, aside from being a nun, I am no one special in their midst. I am not the intimate friend of the Vicereine, the *comadre* of the Viceroy, and hostess of the most popular *salón* in New Spain; I am, simply, Juanilla, the one who left many years ago and who is now a nun in a convent. What a relief it is not to play the hostess, though even here I feel as though I must entertain everyone with stories of convent life.

later

The last Navidad I spent here with my sisters and mother I was eight years old, thirty-one years ago now. How is it possible that so much time can be condensed in the space of a few lines in a diary? I remember the pastries that Francisca used to bake, especially the pumpkin empanadas and fruit-filled *rosca* where she hid the miniature baby Jesus. Francisca passed away several years ago, my mother tells me, and Jane died in childbirth a year to the day after Francisca was buried.

"All that scandal you caused for keeping a slave as a novice," Mamá said. She tried to laugh a little, but it stirred up her lungs and made her cough until she wheezed. The doctor says we must keep her quiet, but Isabel Ramírez has always had a mind of her own and none of her children or her grandchildren will ever tell her what to do. We are leaving Mamá in Antonia and Belilla's care while my sisters and I take flowers to Abuelo's grave in the cemetery of the Sacred Hill.

Noche Buena

This is the last night of the Christmas *posadas*, and María is busy supervising the making of tamales and atole to distribute to the tenant farmers and their families. Belilla and I will attend *misa de gallo* in Chimalhuacán, in the same parish where I was baptized. María and Josefa don't want us to go, but I remind them that for more than half of my life I have been singing the midnight Mass on Christmas Eve and cannot easily forgo the tradition. I actually look forward to wearing my habit again and removing this terrible pressure from my torso. And, after all those years of longing to leave my enclosure, if only for a few hours, I find myself missing the convent. It is my books that I miss, my routine of quill and paper in the silent hours after curfew. Though I am able to write here, indeed I'm doing it now, I can only do so after everyone has gone to sleep. My nieces find this habit intriguing and want to read over my shoulder or sift through the pages in Pandora's Box.

Such innocence and sincerity about these girls. At their age I, too, wanted to read everything I could, despite Abuelo's scoldings. I could never understand his admonitions, for his favorite activity was for both of us to lie in the hammock under the jacaranda trees, each of us reading a book. Being here brings him back to me in my dreams, where inevitably we are playing a chess game.

29 December

Mamá is too weak to use the chamber pot anymore. She says it feels as though all her bones were breaking when we try to lift her out of the bed to clean her. Her face, her whole body, has shrunken and makes her look like a child, a tiny, withered child with deep hollows in her cheeks and sharp lines at her jaw and brow. She says she can feel Death sitting on top of her, not letting her breathe, filling her with so much cold. The five of us, Josefa, María, Antonia, Belilla, and I, take turns leading the novena. The children kneel quietly in the hallway, trying not to cry for their grandmother. Diego stomps in and out of the house, bringing firewood to stoke the braziers, going up and down the stairs with the doctor. Some nights he gets very drunk and falls asleep at the kitchen table, weeping into his arms. Of all of us, I guess he and María are the ones who spent the most time with Mamá. I feel like I have been mourning for her loss most of my life.

3 January 1688

Mamá died this morning. The house is filled with the crying of children. The oldest of the children understand what is happening, the youngest cry because their mothers do. Late last night when the wheezing fit started and a black glaze fell over her eyes, Diego went to call the local priest. The doctor wanted to cup her one more time, but she didn't let him. "I think I'm going now, Juanilla," she said to me as I held her up to keep the phlegm she's passing from suffocating her. She wanted us all in the room with her so that she could give us her last blessing. Then the priest administered extreme unction, and she fell into a kind of trance, from the fever, the doctor said. She never awakened. The priest says we should bury her ravaged body right away and the doctor agrees. We've decided not to hold a wake so that the infection of her body doesn't spread to any of the children. She'll be buried at Abuelo's feet in the cemetery of the Sacred Hill. I will wear my habit from this day forward, and keep the veil drawn over my face for a year. Soon I must return to my cloistered life.

Epiphany 1688

We have decided to return to Mexico at the end of the week. Dreamt there was an earthquake in the city and that Melchora and Rafaela had excavated Pandora's Box from the rubble of my cell, though the box is here with me. I must be more anxious about being gone than I realize. It would be easy for the Three Graces to get into my study. The thought of their snooping through my things makes my head throb. I must begin bidding farewell to Panoayán. After lunch today I'm going to take a walk down to the cornfields, from where I used to watch the volcanoes as a child. I want to fill my eyes with Popocateptl and Ixtaccihuatl. Somewhere in their shadow, in a cemetery in Tepeaca, lie the bones of Leonor Carreto, my Marquesa, who thought I saw in her a surrogate mother. Now Mamá lies in their shadow, too, and I must add another skull to my altar on the Day of the Dead.

"The Inquisition is not an autonomous body, Sister Melchora. Not in the colonies, anyway. There are the Audiencia and the Tribunal to consider, on both of which sit some powerful friends of the Marquis de la Laguna, not to mention, of course, that the Viceroy is the Presiding Officer of all the governing bodies here and would be able to override any judgments made against her. We must bide our time, Sister Melchora. Exercise the virtue of patience and collect more of these specimens of Juana's folly for this archive we're building. How goes your search?"

"Rafaela discovered a notebook entitled 'Primero Sueño' with some obscure poem she's writing."

"I'm not interested in her poems, I told you."

"It's what we found on the inside cover that you'll find intriguing, we think, Your Grace. She's taken notes on an eclipse of the moon (you know how she indulges her vision with that telescope of hers), filled with all manner of pagan references to the Greeks. And look at this! See! She's equating herself with Lucifer!"

"Is that not priceless, Your Grace?"

"You've done well, Sisters. I believe the Archbishop would want to grant you both an indulgence of ten years against your sins just for this document."

8 January

María has spent two days in Mamá's bedroom, scrubbing and weeping. She won't let any of us in to help her. On the other side of the locked door, we can hear her cursing at something through her grief and at times the brush slams into the wall or the door. Last night I heard her wailing like the woman who wanders the night calling out for her lost children. But now it is the child who is crying and the mother who is lost. Sleeping beside me, Josefa wept into the pillow. She wanted me to hold her, I know, but instead I got up to write. Only writing brings me solace. I believe the time has come for us to return to Mexico. We must all proceed with our lives.

10 January

Back at the inn in Chalco; it's been raining for two days so have not been able to find a barge back to the city. Josefa is anticipating an ugly row with Villena for having left without permission, and Felipe has promised to kill the man if he harms his mother. The girls are already crying at the thought. Such histrionics, and all for the sake of that bigamist. I don't know why Josefa doesn't leave him for good and bring herself and her four children to live in Panoayán. God knows María could use her acumen. I'm worried about María. She didn't shed a tear at our departure and barely said two words to Belilla. Even her embrace this morning felt forced. It's as though she's locked herself into her mourning. It's started to rain again, so we won't be able to leave until it clears. Belilla says she continues to dream about Mamá, so I guess her spirit is restless about something. I had that old nightmare about Uncle John and the genie of Aladdin's lamp. Must be this place and the memory of my first journey to the city that stirred those ugly images out of the catacombs of my memory.

11 January

Just found the note that la Condesa sent with her maid asking me to stop over at her house on my return to the convent. Dare I even contemplate this temptation? Dare I not take advantage of this opportunity to visit her for a change, see her in her own environment, sleep under her roof? I daresay I'll never leave the convent again. I'll have to take Belilla with me, but, given the temptations that could arise, this is a good thing. Good God. I should be flogged. I've just buried my mother and here I am worrying about temptations. Just have to remember to keep the influence of the Dark Queen at bay. Remember the veil of mourning over my face.

Chapter 23

They arrived after vespers in the city, and Juana hired a carriage from the Plaza for all of them, going first to the district of San Pedro y San Pablo to drop off Josefa and her children. Josefa wanted Juana to come in, afraid of her husband's retribution, but Villena was standing in the doorway of their *vivienda* with his shirtsleeves rolled up, his shirttails hanging loosely at his sides, and Juana had no desire to enter into any familiarity with him. Begging Josefa's forgiveness, Juana kissed her sister on both cheeks, hugged her nieces and nephews, and told the driver to drive on. She did not tell Belilla where they were going until the carriage stopped in front at the granite lions that guarded the mansion.

"La Condesa invited us to spend the night," Juana said simply.

"Here, Tía?" Belilla's eyes were wide with amazement. "Is it allowed?"

"You mustn't say anything about this to anyone at the convent, Belilla. It's our secret, understood?"

"If you say so, Tía."

She told the gatekeeper her name, and he called two footmen to unload her trunk from the carriage. "Follow me, please," he said, and he lit their way up to the main door of the house and pounded the lion head on the knocker. The veranda was lit with sconces, their soft light shimmering on the golden globes of the miniature orange trees growing in pots on either side of the double portal.

"Sor Juana Inés de la Cruz here to see la Condesa," he announced to the chamberlain standing in the door in a white doublet, white pants, and white gloves. The chamberlain opened the doors and bowed as they stepped into the foyer.

"Please," he said, motioning to a pair of gilded, high-back chairs, "sit down while I announce you. The Marquis and and the Countess are having dinner. May I take your cloaks?"

Belilla's gaze took in the tapestries on the wall, the silk hangings on the windows, the gold leaf on the furniture. "I've never been in such a rich house," she said in awe.

"Don't gawk, Belilla," said Juana. "Act as though you've seen it all before. It's rude to act too impressed."

"Yes, Tía," said Belilla, sucking in her cheeks and sitting up straight.

Two maids came in pushing a delicate cart with a washbasin and a stack of towels on it. Belilla imitated her aunt, dipping one of the towels into the basin and wiping the grime off her face, then rinsing her hands in the water and drying them with a fresh towel. When they were finished, the maids knelt down at their feet and wiped the mud off their shoes and hems, then hurriedly pushed the cart away and disappeared behind a side door.

"I'm unused to all this pampering, Tía."

"Think of it as a good way of keeping the floors clean," said Juana.

Belilla nodded, staring down at her clean shoes as though a charm had been worked over them. The huge clock tolled the hour before compline. Suddenly, the sound of small feet running.

"Belilla!" a shriek echoed beyond the door and in a moment the body of little José came bounding into the foyer and jumped into Belilla's lap. Behind him came the sound of heels walking quickly over the tiles. Juana held her breath and forced herself to remain seated.

"Oh, Belilla!" José chimed, throwing his arms around the girl's neck. "I've missed you. Where have you been?"

"Is he tormenting you already?" la Condesa said. Juana had to swallow before she could speak. María Luisa was wearing yellow damask with a low-cut black velvet bodice that accentuated the narrowness of her waist, and puffy black sleeves slashed with yellow satin. The bun at the nape of her neck was dressed in a fine gold netting and long gold hoops dangled from her earlobes. Behind her stood Don Tomás, beaming his gap-toothed smile.

"Sor Juana! What a surprise! Welcome!" he said.

"Señores!" said Juana, getting up and curtsying. "Forgive my imposition."

"Nonsense!" said Don Tomás, kissing her hand. "As they say in your country, our house is your house." He ordered the chamberlain to have her trunk taken to the guest wing.

La Condesa had not taken her eyes off Juana's face. "I can't see your eyes with that veil, Juana."

"Forgive me, Señora. I'm in mourning."

"Oh, Juana, I'm so sorry." La Condesa embraced her and then Belilla. "It must have been a great comfort to have both of you there with her," she said.

"I'm sure it was, Señora," said Belilla, "especially my aunt Juana."

"Come in, come in, you must be hungry after your journey," said Don Tomás, slipping an arm around Juana's shoulders. "José! Stop clinging to Belilla! You're going to suffocate her."

"I don't mind, Sir," said Belilla.

"He's too old to be jumping in women's laps like that, aren't you, son?"

"I'm almost five," said the boy, keeping his hand in Belilla's as they walked past the open-air solarium and then down a corridor toward the dining room. Belilla could not help staring at the ornately framed mirrors and portraits that lined the hallway, lit by brass sconces in the shape of lion claws.

Under a chandelier made brighter by the slim crystal panes hanging between the candles, two new places had been set at the table, which, Juana noted with some satisfaction, was covered in a lace cloth bearing the famous Hieronymite pattern.

"We were just having soup and an omelet," said la Condesa, "but if you'd like something more substantial—"

"No, thank you, Señora. Soup will be fine."

"Wine for the ladies," Don Tomás told the steward.

"None for me, Sir," said Belilla. "I've never had wine."

"Give her a drop," said Don Tomás, and the steward half filled both their glasses with claret. "It's the last of our Rioja stock," he said, holding up his glass for a toast. "Good thing we're leaving in a few months otherwise I'd die of dysentery from the bad wine they make here. Here's to the unexpected pleasure of your visit, Comadre."

Juana's pulse had stopped, but she held up her glass and toasted. Did he say they were leaving?

"Juana," said la Condesa, "do you intend to dine with your veil on? Can't you lift it? Just over dinner?"

Juana did as she was asked, rolling the gossamer cloth up and tucking it under the black wool of the outer veil.

"That's better," said la Condesa. "Now you won't get any wine on that pretty cloth."

Juana sipped the dry Rioja and let it slip down her throat, welcoming the sudden warmth it produced in her ears and face.

"Shall I serve the soup, Madam?" asked the steward.

"Please, Rogelio. And bring fresh bread."

"Excuse me, Don Tomás," said Juana, "did you say you were leaving in a few months?"

"With the Flota in April," he said. "I'm afraid our sojourn in Mexico has come to a close."

"We're devastated, of course," said la Condesa.

"When did you learn you were leaving?" asked Juana.

"With the last dispatch from the King," said Don Tomás. "He is appalled by the job that Brazo de Plata has done in New Spain, and tells me that the new Viceroy making his entrance in November is Melchor Gaspar Baltasar de Silva Sandoval y Mendoza, otherwise known as the Count de Galve. I remember him as a page for the Queen Mother and then as a gentleman-in-waiting for the King, but apparently he has inherited several important titles, Viceroy of Mexico now among them. How he managed that I'll never know."

"Either he or his wife must have bought the viceroyalty," said la Condesa. "Doña Elvira's family can afford it, I hear."

"I've checked into it, María Luisa," said Don Tomás. "Nothing of the sort happened. It's as much a mystery to my allies in Madrid as it is to us. In any case, I do know that de Galve and his brother plotted against my brother, the Duke, and had something to do with his fall from grace, and, concomitantly, with our own dismissal from the palace. I shall not be in Mexico when he arrives."

Juana stared down at the cream of carrot soup and knew she could not eat. She took a hot bun from the basket, a wedge of potato omelet from the platter, sipped more wine, listened to Belilla describe their journey, but all she could think about was another piece of her heart being carved away.

"—Papá said so," the boy was saying.

"No, young man," la Condesa was shaking her finger at José, "your Papá does not make the rules where you're concerned. Not yet. Off to bed with you. Go ahead and take him, Lupe."

"I want Belilla to take me," the boy pouted.

"Belilla's eating. Now stop being such a nuisance."

"I'll come up after dinner and tell you a story," Belilla told the boy, smoothing his hair back.

"Promise?"

"Promise," said Belilla.

"A long story? I want a long story."

"As long as you want," said Belilla.

The nurse helped the boy down from his high chair and led him away by the hand. "Don't forget or I'll cry," he said on his way out.

"Aren't you going to kiss us goodnight?" asked Don Tomás.

"No," said the boy, skipping out of the room.

"So spoiled," said la Condesa, shaking her head. "But you're so good with him, Belilla. Wherever did you learn your way with children? I have no patience for him when he gets petulant."

"I took care of my aunt Josefa's children, Señora."

"Odd that a girl who has such a way with children should want to be a nun," said Don Tomás.

"I love God more than children, Sir," said Belilla very quietly, eyes on her plate.

"She has a true calling," said Juana, stepping in to rescue the girl from more questions.

"Like her aunt, I'm sure," said la Condesa, catching Juana's eye.

"I hope not," said Juana. "She takes her final vows at the end of August, and I pray she will find the life of the cloth more suited to her nature than I did."

Belilla frowned, unsure of her aunt's meaning, but did not pursue the issue.

"Look, María Luisa. Juana hasn't touched her food."

"Forgive me," said Juana, pushing her bowl and plate aside, "the news of your departure took my appetite away."

"Oh, Juana, you knew we were leaving some day," said la Condesa.

"I prayed you would stay, Señora."

"If it weren't for this Galve," said Don Tomás, "we might have remained a few years more. I'm in no hurry to return to Spain, that's the truth, not with all those damned intrigues brewing at court."

"Would you consider going somewhere closer?" said Juana. "Remain in Puebla, perhaps, or go to Michoacán. I hear Morelia is quite beautiful, the Valladolid of New Spain, they call it."

"Remain in New Spain and be the subjects of the fop who betrayed Medinaceli? Honestly, Juana, be realistic! How would that look?"

"I'm afraid my husband is right, Juana. Much as I hate to leave . . . this country . . . we mustn't expose ourselves to ridicule."

Juana finished her wine. Suddenly, she felt like losing herself in the spirit of the vine, and why shouldn't she? She was free tonight. Who was to stop her? The steward refilled her glass, and she held it up for another toast. "Here's to the eight happiest years of my life," she said, her voice breaking, "thanks to Your Excellencies."

The three of them clinked their glasses against hers. Belilla touched Juana's shoulder, and impulsively kissed her cheek.

"Just promise me one thing," Juana said, turning to face la Condesa, her words already starting to slur from the effect of the spirit. "Promise that you won't die on the way to Tepeaca."

La Condesa's eyes watered. "You're just thinking about Mancera's wife," she said.

"I think we should retire now, Tía," said Belilla. "You sound tired."

"Tired?" said Juana. "I'm not tired, Belilla, just heartbroken."

"Here, here," said Don Tomás, "I've always wanted to have a few cups with you, Juana Inés de la Cruz. You know what they say, Juana: poets and drunks always tell the truth. Rogelio, more wine!"

"Are you suggesting I've lied to you, Señor?"

"I'm suggesting that this is our only opportunity to get to know each other sincerely, as equals."

"Oh, no," said la Condesa. "Here he goes. He's been getting drunk with every guest we've had since we got the King's letter. I think Mexico got under his skin as much as it did mine."

"Señora," Don Tomás said to his wife, "don't you have a child to attend to? And you, *doncella*," he looked at Belilla, "don't you have a promise to keep to a young man?"

"Come, Belilla," said la Condesa, pushing her chair back from the table. "It's time for us to retire and leave the *señores* to their bacchanal."

"But, Tía," Belilla protested.

"Obey la Condesa," Juana said to her niece, enjoying how la Condesa had placed her in the category señores, "she hates to be disobeyed."

"That's God's truth!" said Don Tomás.

Juana was sorry to see la Condesa go, but she looked forward to this exchange with the Viceroy—he isn't the Viceroy anymore, she had to remind herself—with Don Tomás, with her *compadre*. For the first, and no doubt only, time in her life she was going to know what it felt like to be treated as an equal to a man, not in the feigned equality of the *locutorio*, where she was nothing more than a performer for her guests (even Don Carlos at times treated her with a condescending deference), but in the true parity of friends conversing over a bottle of wine.

They talked on a variety of subjects: her mother's death, her abandonment as a child, her grandfather's library, the way she had stopped eating cheese because she had heard it made one torpid of the brain, the price of a passage to Cádiz, the difficulties he was going to encounter shipping his Peruvian ponies back on the Flota, the wasteland that Mexico had become under Brazo de Plata, the Queen's imminent death if she failed to produce an heir to the Spanish throne, the pride he felt for his son and the odd way that love had come back to him for his wife after his birth, and the even odder way in which María Luisa had withdrawn from him as a consequence of the same event. He told her of the time his older brother had struck him on the back of the head with a garden shovel out of jealousy at being their father's favorite, and insisted, fist pounding on the table, that he didn't care if he had no other children since all it led to, anyway, was sibling rivalry and resentment from his wife.

With equal emphasis, she told him of her commitment to make a fortune in the convent, even if it meant abandoning her studies for a time. She was convinced, she said, that the vow of poverty was a hoax, yet another artifice invented for the subjugation of women. Even the mendicant friars, she said, or the Archbishop who was always borrowing money from her and never returning it, hoarded coin and traded in relics. There was no such thing as saintliness through poverty, she insisted, pounding *her* fist on the table, only suffering and torture and injustice and one day out of 365 in which to be remembered for one's sacrifices.

"Come, Juana," said Don Tomás, "wouldn't you like to be canonized?"

"For what, Sir?"

"For your sacrifices. For your knowledge. For your rebellion."

"If rebellion were a holy thing, Sir, then I should certainly be a saint."

"Santa Juana Inés de la Cruz," he said, patting her on the back, "patron saint of women rebels. What day shall we make your saint's day, do you think?"

She took another deep swallow of the wine, which now felt to her smooth as milk. "Let us say the day of your departure," she said, "because saints are usually commemorated on the day in which they were put to death. Do you know the day you're leaving yet?"

The mirth went out of his eyes. "April 28th, if there aren't any delays."

She held her glass up. "Then April 28th shall be my day, day of *las rebeldes*, of women with brains and the freedom to use their brains any way they see fit. And at my death, may my limbs and head, my heart and liver and all internal organs save the sexual ones (which are to be burned and the ashes cast into the canal), be distributed to the best universities in the realm and used to prove that women are, indeed, like men. That anatomy is not destiny. That it is not biology but religion and the government of men that dictate the superiority of the male gender over the female."

Don Tomás had a look bordering on stupefaction. He toasted with her, never removing his eyes from hers, and she could see that his pupils had dilated. What an anomaly she made at this bacchanal, as la Condesa had called it: a Maenad in a black and white habit next to a noble Pentheus in a wine-stained collar and a crooked wig.

"And how, Santa Juana, would you prefer we commemorate your day?"

She stared down at the claret in her glass, then looked up, holding her glass out for another toast. "All men on that day shall wash the feet of every woman they meet, friend or stranger, pauper, prostitute, or nun."

"So it is humiliation that you seek, Juana?"

"Retribution, Sir, for an eternity of kissing the ground men walk on."

A shadow fell over his face. She heard the tolling of the curfew bells.

"Will you not toast with me, then?" she asked.

"I will toast with you," he said. "I will wash your feet. I will kiss the ground you walk on, but unfortunately, none of it will give you the equality that you seek."

"Perhaps that is for another age," she said, "and my life is but a brick in its foundation."

"I have a better idea," he said, motioning for the steward to open another bottle. "The commemoration you describe is meant for the benefit of all women, but there is only one way to pay homage to Santa Juana, who is not only a woman rebel but more important a woman scholar: by keeping her alive forever, by conserving that brain of yours, Juana, not in the foul liquids of science, but in the perpetuity of print." He held her hands in his own. "That our generation, and every future one which adds a brick to the foundation of women's equality, may always have access to your ideas.

Now that is fitting homage for the patron saint of women scholars, don't you think?"

She had started to weep, great deep sobs that rent her lungs and shook her shoulders. The steward poured them more wine and Don Tomás drank his in silence, listening to her cry. He said something to the steward, who left the room and returned with a lacquered box of cigars. Don Tomás took two, lit them with a taper on the table, and offered one to Juana. She had never smoked a cigar, though she had grown fond of cigarillos, but the smoke mingled easily with the taste of the wine and quelled the sadness that had been congealing around her heart for days.

After the second bottle of wine they proceeded to port and then to brandy. The cigars made her hungry, and Don Tomás ordered the steward to bring a platter of cheese and fruit, and they had quince and oranges and sugared dates and goat cheese and olives. For a time they argued over the true intentions of El Tapado, whom Juana remembered fondly as the artist Fray Payo had commissioned to paint the panels of her triumphal arch.

"He was found to be a Flemish spy seeking to infiltrate the Mexican court," Don Tomás said. "How could you expect me to be lenient, Juana?"

"But he didn't deserve the noosed fate you gave him," said Juana. "When Fray Payo brought him to the *locutorio* to meet me, I remember he had the kindest eyes and a disconcerting way of looking into my inner self."

"All spies are good judges of character," said Don Tomás. "They have to be in order to know who they're duping. Payo was always too trusting with foreigners."

"Such a pity," she said, "he was such a good artist."

Their conversation grew redundant, though neither of them noticed, and Don Tomás told her again of the incident with the shovel and his brother's glee at having nearly killed him.

"Did he damage you?" she asked, laughing.

"Just my head," he said, casting his wig to the floor. "See?" He turned to show her the back of his head. "See how flat it is? I could pass for an Indian."

They laughed, drank more brandy, ate more fruit. It was nearly daybreak when they finally stumbled from the table. Juana had to tuck her sleeves into her cincture to keep from tripping on them as the steward led her upstairs to the guest wing.

She had been given a separate room from Belilla, for which she was deeply grateful, as it would not do at all for her niece to see her in this intoxicated condition. As best she could, she pulled off the veil, lifted the scapular over her head, failing to remove the escutcheon first and scratching her cheek on the metal of the shield. She winced at the pain of the cut, but paid no more attention to it as she unpinned the coif, unbuckled the cincture, unlaced the stays of the tunic, and unwound the breast bindings. For a reason that she could not fathom in her current condition, she removed the Catherine-wheel medal she had not taken off for fourteen years, and laid it on the little bureau by the headboard. Still wearing her shift and shoes, she crawled into the draped shadows of the bed.

At first, she thought she was dreaming, she must be dreaming, for here was Concepción again, lying naked beside her, touching her through the shift. She wanted to push the girl away, knowing they would be seen and reported, but her limbs were so heavy, her head felt like wax, and she could barely open her eyes. She dozed again, comforted by the touch of those fingers stroking her back, and dreamt she was floating backward in a river and that a woman was waiting for her on the other bank. That old dream again, she thought, and let herself be wrapped up in the dark shawl and led toward the house made of glass. But then the dream changed, and she was walking up the stairs of la Condesa's house, and it was la Condesa leading her by the hand, not to a glass house, but to a bed surrounded in velvet drapes, and la Condesa was taking Juana's clothes off, and unbuttoning her shift and touching her breasts.

She awakened with a start.

"You smell like a *zaramullo*," said la Condesa lying beside her.

She tried to sit up. Surely this was a dream!

"Where are you going, Juana? I've been waiting for you all night." La Condesa caressed Juana's face in the dark.

"My God," said Juana, "I'm not dreaming."

"What's this on your face? It feels like a wound," said la Condesa, tracing the cut on her cheek with a moist finger.

"Just a scratch, Señora."

Suddenly she felt la Condesa's tongue on her cheek. "It's bleeding," she said.

The thought of la Condesa tasting her blood made Juana's belly contract, but she couldn't move.

"What took you so long, Juana?"

"But, Señora—"

"Sshh!" La Condesa covered Juana's mouth with warm fingers. They smelled of rose water. "Kiss me, Juana."

She forgot about the pain slicing through her head and sat up on an elbow, drawing la Condesa against her. She kissed her gently, letting her hand travel over the satiny curves of la Condesa's hips, the soft folds of her waist, the globes of those breasts that she had so often touched in her fantasies, the swell of her belly, the round, cool flesh of her buttocks. Hands and lips filled with tenderness.

"Your mouth is so warm," said la Condesa, yielding under the pressure of Juana's tongue.

"If I could feel your knee break the waters of my shame," Juana whispered, the words of an old poem rising hot on her breath. "If I could lay my cheek against the tender sinews of your thigh, smell the damp cotton that Athena never wore—"

She was aware of their united breathing, of la Condesa's fingers in her hair, of the smell of la Condesa's sex rising out of the sheets.

"If I could forget the devil and the priest who guard my eyes. If I could taste the bread, the blood, the salt between your legs—"

Juana climbed on top of her and kissed her throat, her shoulders, her earlobes, those tender lips again. She suckled each hard nipple until la Condesa arched her back and moaned as if it hurt.

"If I could turn myself into a bee and free this soul, nothing could save you from my sting."

Their hips were grinding hard now, and Juana was aware of how strong and young she felt, how the muscles in her arms flexed with their motion, how her thighs rocked them both to a sudden crescendo that felt like ecstasy but sounded like the deepest pain. She felt a ribbon of sweat down the middle of her back, and la Condesa's nails digging into her flesh.

After a moment, la Condesa started to hit her on the chest and belly, small but insistent jabs with the heels of her hands that, together with the sounds she was making, told Juana she was crying. Juana sat up and held her tightly, burrowing her face into la Condesa's lilac-scented hair. They wept together for a time, clinging hard to each other's arms, every surreptitious look and touch that had ever come between them transformed into this sweet embrace.

"After tonight I will never say I have no faith in miracles," said Juana.

La Condesa pulled back. "How did you know, Juana?"

"Know what?"

"What I wanted. What to do. Have you done this before?"

Even now she needed reassurance of Juana's faithfulness. "No," said Juana, "have you?"

"Of course not! It's just that it didn't seem unfamiliar to you. You seem quite practiced."

"You live in my dreams, Señora. That is where I've practiced."

She kissed her, pushing her tongue into Juana's mouth. Juana tightened her embrace, slipping a thigh into the moistness between la Condesa's legs.

"What was that poem you were saying? I've never seen it, have I?"

"Just a litany I wrote, Señora, of subjunctive dreams and desires."

"You've never called me by my name, Juana."

"María Luisa," she said. "*Te quiero*, María Luisa."

"And I, you, Juana Inés, my poet, my Sappho."

"Sappho loved men as well as women," said Juana.

"And you?"

"I love only you."

"And before me? You loved her, didn't you? That other Vicereine?"

"Not like this. I've never loved anyone like this. And I've never felt any desire for a man, only aversion at the thought of intimacy. I married my books, married the abstraction on the Cross, to keep myself chaste of a man's touch. Unlike you, Señora de la Laguna."

María Luisa stroked Juana's face with the back of her fingers. "I haven't slept with my husband since José was born."

"I guessed as much after what he said this evening," said Juana.

"You talked about me?"

"You're our common denominator." Juana lowered her face to taste again the bread and salt between María Luisa's legs. More sighs of agony and joy. No nails on the back this time, but a swift and violent pull of fingers in Juana's hair. She wiped her face with the sheet while María Luisa caught her breath.

"In all the years that Tomás has taken his pleasure with me," she said at length, "I have never known this feeling, Juana, this intensity that makes my legs tremble and my bladder feel like it's going to overflow." She held Juana's face and kissed her gently—cheeks, eyelids, mouth, nose, forehead. "You taste of olives, Juana."

"I taste of you."

María Luisa kissed her mouth again. "What else can I give you, my tenth muse?" she whispered.

Somewhere a rooster crowed. Juana realized that it was dawn and that she was finally, at the age of thirty-nine, waking up to her true self. When, at last, they fell asleep, Juana, still in shift and shoes, with her knee on María Luisa's thigh, taste of olives and rose water on her tongue, María Luisa with her fingers curled in Juana's hair, the bells of all the churches in the city tolled for High Mass.

It was midday before Juana stirred back to life, and by then the bed was empty, save for a few strands of María Luisa's hair on the pillow. She got up groggily, unsure except for the fragrance on her fingers, that she had been with la Condesa. Her ankles were swollen from having slept with her shoes on. She used the chamber pot, washed her face, washed her sex with a towel, then dipped her head into the basin to wet her hair. The coldness of the water penetrated her scalp, opened her eyes, took the edge off her headache. She dressed quickly, tucking a strand of María Luisa's hair into her breast bindings. The veil and scapular were wrinkled from the careless way she had undressed after her revelry with Don Tomás. The night had, indeed, been a bacchanalia. She understood, now, how it was possible for the Maenads to tear a man to shreds under the influence of the vine. Anything was possible in that condition.

On her way down the wide, spiral stairs, she unfurled the white gauze of the inner veil and let it drop over her face. She could not bear to look into María Luisa's eyes. La Condesa and Belilla were in the solarium sharing a pitcher of orange juice, José playing at spilikins at their feet. The sun glinting off the flagstones hurt Juana's eyes, but she noticed how the light accented the gold and auburn streaks in María Luisa's hair, how it cast a glow over the creamy texture of that beloved face.

"Good morning, Tía," said Belilla, bending down to tickle José. The girl looked flushed.

"It's late, Belilla," she said, "why didn't you wake me? Señora. I hope you slept well."

"The question is how did *you* sleep, Juana?" There was an erotic glint to la Condesa's teeth. "Rogelio tells me you and Tomás had a long conversation over several bottles."

"Please, Señora," she said, rubbing at her temples, "don't remind me."

María Luisa poured her a glass of juice and she drank it in thirsty gulps.

"Shall I ring Rogelio to bring you breakfast?"

Her mouth still felt dry and the headache was starting to spread its roots over the soft loam of her brain, but she declined, and said they had to leave. The trunk, she saw, was already waiting in the foyer.

"Tomás will be disappointed if you leave before he gets up," said María Luisa, "but then he probably won't get up the rest of the day. He usually doesn't after that kind of evening."

She walked them to the door, slipping her arm into Juana's like a *comadre* or a confidante. Juana longed to put her arms around her, feel her hands on that hourglass waist of María Luisa's again, but kept her hands crossed under her scapular. Little José clung to Belilla's veil.

"Thank you for everything, Señora," said Juana, not daring to turn her face for fear of being drawn by the magnet of María Luisa's lips. "Please explain to my *compadre* that it was impossible for us to stay longer. And thank him for an unforgettable evening."

María Luisa leaned over, lifted Juana's veil, and rubbed her cheek against Juana's. "Unforgettable, indeed," she whispered. "And thank you, Juana, for honoring my invitation. And you, too, Belilla, for keeping my little demon company last night." She turned and drew the girl into a tight embrace, then ordered the boy to kiss his *madrina* farewell. The boy threw his arms around Juana's waist. She bent down to kiss him, holding his slim little body for a moment against her.

The gatekeeper already had their carriage waiting, and two footmen strapped the trunk to the back of it. La Condesa stood at the door and watched them leave. It almost seemed to Juana as though she had been eager for them to leave.

"Remember, Belilla," she said as the carriage pulled away, "no word of our visit to anyone."

"I'll keep your secret, Tía."

Juana stared at her niece for a moment, perceiving a flare of arrogance to the girl's expression, and she was certain that the girl knew something of the night before. On their way down Calle del Reloj, Juana remembered how Belilla had impugned the memory of Sor Felipa in Panoayán, repeating hearsay about the novice's vanity with her hair.

"Don't think I've forgotten that immodest comment you made about Sor Felipa," she said coldly. "I'm sure your headmistress would be most displeased if she heard that you were maligning the dead."

"That was wrong of me. Thank you for correcting me, Tía." The girl's arrogance withered. Satisfied, Juana leaned back against the seat and took in the bustle of the *traza*. Outside the Cathedral, Indian women with babies slung to their backs balanced huge baskets of flowers on their heads. She called one of them over to the carriage and bought a stem of callas.

"Get out," she said to her niece.

"What for, Tía?"

"Go and take these lilies to the altar of Saint Jude in the Cathedral, and thank him in my name."

"Su Merced," said the driver, "the street here is too dangerous for a young woman."

"Your habit will protect you," said Juana, "just wear your crucifix over your collar."

Only then did she realize that she had forgotten her Catherine-wheel medal on the bedside table.

Chapter 24

13 January 1688

Back at San Jerónimo, and the citrus harvest is well under way. My cell is fragrant with the sweet tang of mandarins and yellow lemons that Andrea brought to welcome us home. I feigned fatigue so that she would leave me alone and give me some time to scratch out my thoughts here before vespers. Odd that I'd missed the sevenfold ritual of the canonical hours while I was away and now that I'm back can only sigh at the sound of the bells that regulate our daily lives with monotonous precision. But this is not what I wanted to write about. Need to record my feelings about last evening, and then burn these pages before going off to choir. Cannot risk exposure.

I remember how my mind seemed to separate from me, like a yolk from the egg white, and how in my imagination I watched my hands and mouth demonstrate the knowledge of my desire, as if I have always known what to do to another woman's body. Is it the harmony of our sex, the fact that we are both women, that gives me this knowledge? Or is it an epistemology long buried in my bones, a knowledge I was born with?

At first, it happened so quickly, I don't even remember how it started, and yet every second remains etched someplace deeper than memory, that place where time distends like liquid glass, losing its shape and all memory of its function, melting down into its most basic essence to be shaped again into anything, any form that the lips blowing air into the mold want it to take. Right now, the glass is still molten, still swirling hot and formless in my mind. I do not want to give it form, for that would mean making it tangible, fixing it with meaning. And for once, it isn't meaning that I seek, just the memory of it, and of her, ripening under my tongue.

after vespers

I sense that someone has been going through my things. No, I'm certain of it. Have been inspecting everything and I find that two of my quills are blunt and there's a different kind of ink, a cheaper variety that dries pale, in the inkwells. One could say that ink grows thin in the cold and that I forgot to sharpen my quills before I left, but the most flagrant evidence is the watermark on the ream of paper in my desk. It is a different watermark, which means the paper was not purchased at Don Lázaro's shop. Dear Mother of God, has someone been making copies of "Primero Sueño" while I've been away? Who would even understand it? And why would they use so much paper and wear down the quills so much? Also found all of my books moved; some of them are now in alphabetical order where they were all once organized only by category. Belilla says she cleaned in here before we left but doesn't remember moving the books off their shelves. Must ask Andrea if she knows anything about this.

25 *January*
Two weeks have passed, and still no sign of la Condesa. No messages, no letters, no visits. I guess this absence tells me everything I need to know. Were it not for this absence I would almost believe nothing happened, inebriated as I was, and capable of bringing any fantasy to life in my Dionysian state. Belilla watches me closely. I daresay the girl knows something. If ever you read these words, Belilla, know that I was weak and submitted to temptation, and I beg you not to think less of me for being what I am. But what, after all, am I? It is not the same as sodomy to love another woman. Adultery, perhaps, coveting the wife of my neighbor, but not the sin of the Greeks. Or is it? And why am I speaking of this love as a sin again? Long ago I resolved that there could be nothing sinful about my love for María Luisa. Was that the voice of abstraction speaking, the voice of chastity and innocence? Aristophanes would say I am a whole Woman now, having found my other half in body as well as mind. But what does *she* say, I wonder? Does she think of herself as whole or as sinful? As my other half or as an accomplice in an unspeakable crime?

"I'm so afraid, Sor Andrea. For her, I mean. For her soul."
"You mustn't exaggerate, Isabel. Leave the fate of your aunt's soul to God. It is none of your concern."
"But I feel like it is *my* sin. And if I don't confess it, I, too, will be damned."
"Then you must tell your father confessor, Sister, not me."
"I cannot. Don't you see? That would be like reporting her."

314

"Dear God, what has she done now?"

"Do you give me license to tell you, then?"

"This doesn't count as a confession, you understand?"

"And if you tell Padre Miranda, will that be a confession?"

"No. Not unless I feel that I have sinned by listening to you and indulging your weakness."

"We spent the night at la Condesa's house when we returned from Panoayán."

"Yes, Mother Brígida already knows this. News travels quickly among servants."

"Tía drank wine with the Marquis, lots of wine, I think. And then in the morning when I went to wake her up, they were asleep in each other's arms, and there was a strong smell of spirits over the bed."

"Mother of Mercy! Juana slept with the Marquis?"

"No, not him. It was—"

"What? Who?"

"La Condesa. La Condesa had no clothes on and they were holding each other like—like lovers."

"In the name of the Father, the Son, and the Holy Spirit. Did they see you?"

"Of course not. I was so terrified, at first, I just let the bed hangings fall back and sat down to wait. I didn't know what else to do. Then I crept back to the bed and touched my aunt on the leg (she didn't even take her shoes off!) and tried to wake her. But then I thought, how would she feel if she saw me standing there, witness to the intimacies of that chamber. And then, I thought, no, I better not wake her. So I went downstairs and sat with the little boy until they awakened of their own accord. La Condesa came down first, and acted like nothing had happened. About an hour later, Tía came down and she had her veil pulled down and we said good-bye and left. And then she bought this flower and made me get out of the carriage and go to the Cathedral so I could take the flower to Saint Jude."

"She made an offering to Saint Jude? Oh, Juana. What gall."

"What does it mean, Sor Andrea?"

"Do you love your aunt Juana, Isabel?"

"Of course I love her."

"Because if you do, then you have to understand that loving your aunt will require you to make certain sacrifices, commit certain sins. Are you ready to do that for her, Isabel?"

"But how can I do that and try to achieve perfection at the same time?"

"All you can do is pray for the grace to understand her."

Ash Wednesday

History indeed repeats itself. Here I am again on the eve of another Vicereine's departure, with ashes on my forehead and a vow of silence and solitude for Lent. It is the only way I can keep myself from falling apart. I ask again, God, why are You always taking away those I love? Have I displeased You so much that You must punish me over and over, in different degrees of loss, from my grandfather to la Marquesa, from my aunt Mary to my mother to la Condesa? I do not doubt that You exist, that You are my Savior, I believe entirely in Your Omnipotence; it is the priests that I disbelieve, the rules of men that I doubt and defy. Is this what You are punishing me for? Is this the unpardonable sin that will keep me forever in purgatory? I cannot continue like this. My heart can bear no more breakage. I must, once and for all, resolve to keep my emotions under control, never, ever, give my heart again, or even allow myself to utter the secret desires of my soul. Those, too, I must eradicate, pull them like pernicious weeds from the loam so that desire withers completely and fails to pollinate. I must make my heart sterile and plant only the fields of my mind. Enough, my God, enough of this perpetual pain.

Holy Saturday

Can barely write. The fever makes me shiver so. Have been ill all of Lent. Do nothing but sit in my chair with rosary in hand, pray for the loss of memory and the advent of death. Belilla reads to me. Spent two weeks in the infirmary, a bout of scarlet fever, says Gabriela. Caught it from Madre Catalina before she died. Another death. Let me die, too. I just want to die. No resurrection for me. Roll the stone over me. Take the pain away. The rash continues, itches like ants on my skin, and Belilla keeps the poultices fresh. Doesn't understand what the real disease is. Father Peter coming to confess me later, so I can take Communion tomorrow. Hope the host doesn't shrivel on my tongue.

JUANA, HEART OF MY HEART,

I hear reports of your recovery. I, too, have been ill, though mine has been more of a psychic malady than a physical one. But now there is no more time to indulge in sickness. Must get the house in Chapultepec packed and prepare for our departure at the end of the month. I want to take your writings with me, Juana, get them published, give them the audience they deserve. We know a publisher in Madrid, a Knight of the Order of Santiago, very powerful and influential, and my husband intends to have a favor repaid by getting him to publish your work. I want everything, even *loas* and *villancicos*, and the script to *Trials of a House*, even the drawings to *Neptuno alegórico*, if you can find them.

Can you get it all together for me, dearest, before the 28th? I cannot leave New Spain without you, and it's the only way I know of taking you with me, other than having you abducted. This will please me, Juana, as almost nothing else you've ever done. Write to me,

M.L.

4th of April 1688

(24 days before we leave)

18 APRIL 1688

MY DEAREST CONDESA,

Ten days away from your departure and I have yet to receive copies of my *villancicos* from Puebla. Perhaps I could send these to you if they do not come in before you leave. The Cabildo is tracking down the drawings to *Neptuno alegórico,* but I wouldn't count on them being found. Don Fernando Deza is having "Empeños" copied, and meanwhile, Belilla is copying everything in my possession for which I don't have duplicates. I would do it in my own hand, but as you know, my penmanship does not do justice to the work. Ever since Concepción left, I lost the habit of making copies. Some of the poems are incomplete, others we found buried inside books, but I think when everything is ready I will have enough to fill an entire trunk, certainly more than could ever make its way into a published volume. Why any publisher in Madrid would want to print the silly scribblings of a nun in the colonies is beyond me. Still I will honor your request, and leave the editing and choice of material up to you, as you are not only my sponsor and most beloved audience but also the owner of all my work, for the child borne by the slave belongs by right to the

slave's master. Therefore, I shall entrust you with the added labor
of giving a heading to the poetry.

In anticipation of seeing you again,

Jidl†

It took four maids and Belilla to carry the chest filled with Juana's writings down to the locutory, where la Condesa and Don Tomás were waiting to bid her farewell. She had not seen María Luisa since that night, first
because of her vow of silence, then because of the illness, then because of
la Condesa's preoccupations with the move and her own flurry to collect
her writings. In that time she had, she thought, managed to embalm what
was left of her heart in a shroud of rationality, not allowing herself to write
too much in Pandora's Box lest the temptation to express feelings creep
up on her unaware, and absolutely refusing to remember anything that had
happened at la Condesa's house or to dwell on la Condesa's departure.

In the main, the strategy had worked, until now that she realized it would
be the last time she would see María Luisa. She dabbed more sandalwood
oil on her wrists, pinched her cheeks to add color to her sallow skin, and
took three deep breaths before leaving her cell. It would not be a private
visit, she reminded herself, Their Excellencies were bidding farewell to all
the religious communities they had favored, and to all the abbots and prioresses whose houses they had championed in the course of their eight
years in New Spain. The entire administrative body would be at the *locutorio*, not to mention the sycophantic sisters who never lost an opportunity to rub elbows with aristocratic guests.

She took another deep breath in the vestibule and, upon entering, saw
that all of the sisters had joined their guests on the other side of the grille,
where already every seat had been divided among the two factions—
Mother Brígida, Andrea, María Bernardina, and Ana de Jesús on one side
of la Condesa, Melchora, Rafaela, Agustina, and the twins on the other
side of Don Tomás, with a body of supporters standing behind each group.
Everyone was drinking a pale green cordial out of tiny crystal jiggers.

She had not seen Don Tomás since the night of her visit, and though she
expected to feel uncomfortable around him, ashamed, at least, at having
transgressed against his hospitality, she found herself feeling a strong ca-
maraderie with him, as though he were like an elder brother, and almost
returned his wink.

La Condesa's eyes pierced her like darts. She was dressed in royal blue, and the peacock feathers in her hat set off her alabaster skin, the carmine blossom of her mouth, the emerald teardrops at her earlobes. Hanging over the crease between her luscious breasts—Juana dug her nails into her palm—was the Catherine-wheel medal that Juana had forgotten at her house. She felt a shiver run down her spine. A long time ago, she had given that medal to la Marquesa and now María Luisa was wearing it as a sign of her claim on Juana. And Andrea knew that it was hers.

"Forgive my tardiness," she said, curtsying, aware that everyone in the room was looking at her.

"Have some chartreuse," said Mother Brígida, and someone handed her a glass. "A gift from the Marquis, and the glasses are from Her Majesty."

"You're so thin, Juana," said la Condesa.

Don Tomás stood up and gave her his seat. "Please, Juana," he insisted when she refused. How could she sit that close to María Luisa and not lose her mind entirely? "In honor of a special saint that you and I once discussed."

Juana did not know what he meant, but she took the chair and la Condesa gazed openly at her with tear-rimmed eyes, taking hold of her hand.

"What saint are you referring to, Excellency?" asked Melchora.

"A saint whose day is the 28th of April, Mother," said Don Tomás, raising his eyebrows at Juana.

"I know of no special saints that we honor today," said Melchora, "how about you, Rafaela?"

"We celebrate Saint Catherine of Siena tomorrow," interjected Andrea, "but that's the 29th."

It was starting to come back to her, that drunken conversation with Don Tomás, about herself as the patron saint of rebellious women. Santa Juana, canonized on the day they left Mexico, the day of her demise. She decided to change the subject.

"Everything I could get my hands on is in the trunk, Señora," she said to la Condesa, pulling her hand out of María Luisa's grasp, "though there are still many pieces missing from commissions whose owners I have not been able to locate."

"Isn't it generous, Mother," said Melchora to Mother Brígida, "for Her Excellency to take Juana's scribblings and find a publisher for them in Spain?"

"Generosity has nothing to do with it, Ladies," said Don Tomás, sipping his cordial. "It's the least we can do for our tenth muse."

"Tenth muse?" said Melchora. "Is that what you're calling her, Sir?"

"That's what *I'm* calling her, Sister," said la Condesa. "After Polyhymnia, the muse of sacred poetry, Euterpe, the muse of lyric poetry, Erato, the muse of love poetry—"

"Melpomene, the muse of tragedy," Don Tomás stepped in, "Clio and Calliope, the muses of history and epic poetry, Urania, the muse of astronomy, Thalia, the muse of comedy, and . . . what's the name of that last one, María Luisa, I always forget her name."

"Terpsichore," offered Juana, "the muse of dance."

"That one," said Don Tomás, "the ninth daughter of Zeus and the goddess of memory."

"As I was saying," said la Condesa, "after the nine of them comes Juana Inés de la Cruz, the muse of *décimas* and, therefore, *décima musa.*"

Don Tomás laughed aloud, enjoying his wife's wordplay.

"I see," said Juana, "it's a pun."

"Partly it's a pun," said la Condesa, "but mostly it's the honor I wish to bestow on your work, which is worthy of the muses."

She was beginning to feel warm under her veil. Melchora's faction was exchanging glances at one another. Rafaela had moved over to the sideboard and was taking notes in the guestbook.

"There is already a tenth muse, Señora," said Juana, "according to Plato anyway." She sampled the thick, medicinal liquid in her glass, and it made her head shake involuntarily.

"Yes, I know, Juana, but she's the tenth muse of the ancient world and you're the tenth muse of the new one."

"I have a better idea," said Don Tomás, sketching invisible words in the air with his hand. "The Phoenix of América—"

"Please, Sir—" Juana objected, but he held up his finger to keep her from continuing.

"Indulge me," said Don Tomás. "The Phoenix is a mythological creature that is born from its own ashes, just as América is born from the ashes of Europe, and just as your poetry, Sor Juana, is born from the ashes of Greek verse."

Agustina made a face at one of the twins, who nearly laughed.

"We want to inundate Spain with your work, Juana," said la Condesa.

"Like a spring overflowing its banks," said Don Tomás.

"A Castalian inundation," said la Condesa, "from Delphi to Valladolid."

"Your Excellencies, please!" said Juana, setting her glass on the table next to her and turning her embarrassed gaze on Andrea.

"Look at how she blushes, Tomás," laughed María Luisa.

"I would die of shame," said Melchora, "if anyone gave me so much praise."

"Adulation is more like it," said Agustina.

"It's unhealthy for a nun to receive such accolades, Señora," Mother Brígida said to la Condesa.

"Forgive me, Mother," said Don Tomás, glaring down at the Mother Superior, "far be it from me to display any discourtesy to your Ladyship or to any of the good sisters here whom we have loved and sponsored for eight years, but you must understand, all of you, that my lady wife and I will praise whomever we want, as much as we want, and if your Ladyship does not wish to be privy to it, she and her flock of dead flies can leave us alone."

"It is Juana we want to spend time with, anyway," added la Condesa.

Juana closed her eyes. Good God! she thought. That's all I need, for them to create a scandal here in front of everyone and leave me alone to face the consequences. She heard her sisters getting up from their chairs, Melchora mumbling something about a report to the Archbishop. Chairs scraped the floor, bodies crowded around her and then dispersed.

"Adios, hermanas," called Don Tomás. "God keep you company."

"Señor Marqués," said Mother Brígida, "it is a sad day for me to see you and Her Excellency leave New Spain, but I must say, and please forgive the candor of an elder who sees things too clearly, that that was a very imprudent remark, a grievous error, for which Juana, I'm afraid, will have to pay."

Juana opened her eyes but kept them downcast.

"We shall expect you at chapter meeting, Juana."

"Yes, Mother," said Juana.

"On time, if you please."

"I'll be there, Mother."

Mother Brígida and Andrea left the locutory.

"Oh, dear," said la Condesa. "Now you've done it, Tomás."

He poured himself more chartreuse from the crystal decanter on the sideboard and plopped into a chair. "I'm sorry," he began, but Juana did not let him continue.

"There's no need to apologize. I've been paying for one grievous error after another since I came into this house. I'm quite inured to it."

"I'm glad they're gone," said la Condesa, taking Juana's hand again and kissing it. "I want to kiss you and hug you until we leave," she said. "Tomás, why don't you see about loading that trunk into the carriage."

"Ah," he chuckled, "now it is I who am being banished." He got to his feet. "*Muy bien. Os dejare solas.* But only for a few minutes. I want my eyeful of her, too, María Luisa, and we haven't that much time."

The minute he and his footmen stepped out with the trunk María Luisa bent over and kissed Juana on the lips, a rich moist kiss that tasted of chartreuse. "My heart," she whispered. "How I've thought about you."

"Señora," said Juana, looking over her shoulder, "this is not safe."

"Oh, Juana, what are we going to do? I can't live without seeing you."

Juana's eyes filled with tears. "Hear me with your eyes," said Juana, gripping María Luisa's hands. "Can you see through this liquid humor how you have torn my heart apart? How I have lost my soul to your love? You are the soul of this body now, and the body of this shade. Don't you see? Once you leave I lose my reason for living, I become a phantom with a pen."

"Juana, stop it!" María Luisa shut her eyes and tears streaked down the white powder of her cheeks.

"You take the best part of me. I don't care if it's published. I just want you to have it."

"Promise me you'll send me everything, Juana. I want what you've already written, what you're going to write, what you're writing now, everything, Juana. Even that litany of subjunctive longings."

"And will you promise not to die before I do? Will you promise not to forget me."

"I'm dying now, Juana."

She wanted so much to kiss her, to hold her again, inhale the scent of her skin and hair, lick the tears from her eyes. But she had to be strong, for both of them. It was the only way of keeping her sanity. She disentangled her fingers from María Luisa's. "There are two new sonnets for you in the trunk," she said. "I hope you like them."

María Luisa reached into her reticule and drew out a velvet box. "It's a ring," she said, "with my portrait on it."

Juana tapped the Catherine-wheel medal with her finger. "This is the symbol of my heart," she said, closing her eyes to keep from staring at the soft white flesh pushing up over the royal blue bodice. "I haven't taken it off in many years."

322

"I shall kiss it every night, then," said la Condesa, "and remember where you left it."

"I love you so much," said Juana.

"Promise you'll never love another, Juana."

"How can I love if you're taking my heart with you?" whispered Juana, just as Don Tomás returned to the locutory.

"The last favor I want to ask of you, Sor Juana, as your humble admirer and once upon a time protector," he said, swooping down on his knee in front of them, oblivious to the tear marks on their faces.

"Anything, Señor," she said.

"Recite 'Hombres Necios' for me. I want it fresh in my memory as we leave the city. It's the most ingenious use of irony."

"Señora," she said to la Condesa, "your husband is most unusual. I doubt that any man could find that *redondilla* tolerable, much less ingenious."

"Let me show you how unusual he truly is, Juana," said la Condesa, taking Juana's face between her hands and kissing her long and hard in front of him.

"You have always been fearless, Madam," said Juana, blushing.

"Now it's my turn," said Don Tomás, but la Condesa cut a glance at him that even made Juana shiver.

"May I at least touch her hand, then?" he said, taking Juana's hand between his own and kissing it very lightly, his mustache tickling her wrist.

"Recite the poem, Juana," said la Condesa, "for me."

She straightened her shoulders and recited the poem to them, the tears flowing freely down her face and over the images of the Annunciation on her escutcheon.

"Santa Juana," said Don Tomás after she had finished, "every year on this day I shall anoint my wife's feet in holy oil and kiss the ground she steps on, in your honor." He lifted Juana's foot and kissed the sole of her shoe.

"Señora," he said to his wife, "the time to leave is upon us. We still have Regina Coeli to visit and we must reach the Villa before sunset."

She walked between them to the gate, María Luisa with an arm around her waist, Don Tomás with an arm around her shoulders.

"Tell me, Juana," said Don Tomás, "when will Belilla take her permanent vows?"

"Her veiling ceremony is at the end of August."

"We should be in Cádiz by then," he said, taking from his pocket a leather pouch filled with coins, "but it would make us very happy to contribute to her *fiesta flórida*, in the name of our son, who has grown very fond of her. And in gratitude to his godmother who has loved him well."

"Señor, I couldn't," she said, shaking her head

"You must, Juana, I won't hear a rejection." He closed her fingers over the pouch.

"Say good-bye to Isabel for us," said María Luisa. "Tell her José will write to her when he learns his letters."

"And please kiss my godson for me, and for Belilla, too." Her chin had started to quiver. When Don Tomás held her, her throat felt as though she had a knife stuck in her vocal chords. She could not bring herself to hug María Luisa and stood stiffly in her tight embrace, inhaling the warm fragrance of rose water on her skin.

"I won't hear of any more sadness," said María Luisa. "We may never see each other again, Juana, but I won't vanish from your life, and I expect prompt responses to all my letters."

In front of the portress, she kissed Juana again on both cheeks and gave her hands one final squeeze. Juana kept her head bowed so none of them could see she had started crying again. As soon as the portal closed behind them, she hurried out of Sor Clara's patio before she was asked any questions. She spent the rest of the afternoon on her knees before the image of the Guadalupana, until the nones bell reminded her that she had missed chapter.

The Endgame
1689–1692

Chapter 25

My Dearest Juana,

Tomás and I have just returned from our *paseo* on the Guadalquivir to find four copies of the first volume of your works, delivered earlier by the printer. What better birthday present can I offer you than this, though it be several months late when it arrives there? These two are advance copies only; the printer has shipped off a crateful on the Flota to each of the bookshops of New Spain. Oh, Juana, I'm so proud. I hope that the speedy nature of the book's compilation does not detract from the depth and complexity of its content. I hope you approve of my editorial skills and that you not think my titles of your poems too simplistic. This, at least, has lifted my spirits, for I was quite morose on our excursion, remembering the canoe rides that Tomás and I used to take in Xochimilco, serenaded by musicians on orchid-covered barges and you not too far away in your convent. All year my heart has been heavy with missing you, Juana, made worse with the knowledge that I have your words, your poems and carols, and, of course, eight years worth of memories—I have all of this except you, your presence, your voice, those eyes of yours that had the capacity to see right through me.

Tonight, with this volume pressed against my breast, I glance up at the heavens and thank God that you were gifted with that special ability to put flesh into words, for at least the words can live on, like the stars that hover this evening over Sevilla. If I squint at Cassiopeia, I can almost see you sitting at your desk, quill in hand, burning the midnight oil to the rhythm of the spheres.

I have many more thoughts to share, but for now, I want to get these copies off to you. I regret that I cannot tell you with my eyes what I mean to say, but know that tonight our souls gazed upon one another in the wonder of a moonlit night along the Guadalquivir. Remember that you remain the gatekeeper of my secrets and closest friend. Many more birthdays to you, Juana.

Yours always,
María Luisa
12th of November 1689

Juana kissed the handwriting on the parchment, then tucked María Luisa's letter back into the leather-bound volume. What better birthday present, indeed, she thought, brushing her fingers over the embossed gold letters of the elaborate title la Condesa had composed. *Castalian Inundation of the Only Poetess, the Tenth Muse, Sor Juana Inés de la Cruz, professed nun of the Monastery of Saint Jerome in the Imperial City of Mexico, Which, in Various Meters, Languages, and Styles, Fertilizes Various Matters with Elegant, Subtle, Clear, Ingenious and Useful Verses: For Teaching, Delight, and Admiration.* Tenderly, she placed the book on the desk and opened Pandora's Box.

22 *February 1690*

After weeks of looking at my book I still cannot believe I'm an author. Now I understand a mother's pride in her firstborn, how she must hold it constantly, stare at it, caress it, wonder at its presence, for surely this is the product of the fertile loins of my own mind and la Condesa's persistence, which was, in truth, the instrument of delivery. I peruse these pages and still find it odd to see my work collected in a book, some of it I don't even remember writing. Gave the second copy to Belilla, with a special dedication to my favorite niece. She's not much of a reader, she says, but promises to read the book cover to cover. You're famous now, Tía, she said, her eyes alight with a kind of wonder.

"Tía, Sor Clara says your guests are waiting!" Belilla's voice seemed to resonate off the wood floors. Juana had still not gotten used to the sounds of the new cell, especially the way voices and footsteps echoed in the rooms. She had moved into Madre Catalina's cell as a gesture of renewal after la Condesa's departure. It was a two-bedroom flat with a small parlor and kitchen and a bathroom with a tiled bathtub large enough to lie down in. She and Belilla shared one of the bedrooms—barely large enough to accommodate their two beds and wardrobes—and the other she used as her study. It was not as large or as luxurious as old Mother Paula's cell had been, with those beautiful tiled floors and arched windows overlooking the volcanoes, but it was more practical and easier to keep clean between the two of them, and at least she didn't have stairs to climb. The stairs were wreaking havoc on her sciatica. She stowed Pandora's Box in the desk's secret compartment and went to get herself ready for yet another afternoon of visitors.

Since the release of *Castalian Inundation* in Mexico, she had received more guests in the locutory than when either la Marquesa or la Condesa reigned over the social life of New Spain. Those who had managed to get a copy of her book wanted her to dedicate it to them; those who had not thought maybe she had her own supply and would be willing to sell them a copy, for which they were happy to pay twice as much as those sold by the book-sellers. Disappointed and doubting her word that she had naught but her own personal copy, they insisted that she at least give a recital of her poems, applauding politely after each one, though it was clear from the glazed looks in their eyes that they were not really listening.

For today's guests she would have to be at her most guarded, for her visitors were none other than Brazo de Plata and his wife, Doña Elvira, who, unlike their predecessors, had chosen not to honor Juana with their unconditional friendship and protection. Also in tow was the Viceroy's ex-uberant and rather redundant elder brother, with whom, it was rumored, Doña Elvira had a passionate epistolary love affair, which won Brazo de Plata the epithet Royal Cuckold. The Viceroy had requested a private au-dience and a special performance of her poetry just for the palace and its retinue. Their Majesties, of course, had their own copy of Juana's book, brought to them from Spain by the brother, and they wanted Juana to write something personally meaningful in her dedication. In a roundabout way, they let her know they were displeased that none of the poems she had written for them was included in the publication, but she reminded the sovereigns that the book had gone into production only a few months after their entrance into Mexico, and that the book had been circulating in Spain for all of a year before arriving in the colonies. She assured them that they would have their own section in the second edition, which la Condesa de Paredes had already submitted for publication.

"And to whom will you dedicate this second edition, Sor Juana?" asked the Vicereine. Doña Elvira had the most annoying habit of covering her mouth with her fan whenever she spoke.

"The dedication does not typically change, Señora, in a revised edition of the same text. Besides, la Condesa would never allow it. She tends to be quite possessive of dedications."

"I can see her point," said Doña Elvira, pouting at her brother-in-law.

"Perhaps we shall merit a dedication of a future volume," said the Viceroy.

"You should see, Gaspar," said the Viceroy's brother, "what an admiring audience our 'tenth muse' and only poetess of the imperial city of Mexico here has generated in Madrid."

"Please, Sir," Juana interrupted. "I know those are la Condesa's subtitles and not your own epithets, but I am not allowed to listen to such flattery. It compromises my vows, you see."

"But it's true, Sister. You're quite famous over there," insisted the brother.

"Much to my chagrin, I assure you, Sir," she said.

"Come, Sister," said the brother, "from what we have heard, your prodigious intellect has been the toast of New Spain for several decades. Seems the colony hasn't produced any other *criollo* offspring to outwit you."

"You're forgetting Sigüenza, my love," Doña Elvira said.

"Sigüenza is a pompous ass," retorted the brother, "who couldn't write himself out of a corner."

"Don Carlos," said Juana, "is my dearest friend, if you don't mind, Señor. I cannot listen to any criticism of him without becoming choleric, if you understand what I mean."

"Indeed, Sor Juana," said the Viceroy, his voice as icy as his eyes. "If a lowly canon can elicit such devotion for which your viceregal guests find no counterpart, then perhaps our visit has come to an end." He turned to his wife and brother. "It seems we have been dismissed. Shall we retire?"

"I guess we shan't be having our Easter dinner at San Jerónimo this year," said the Vicereine. Juana knew exactly what she meant. Due to the perceived offense, the convent wouldn't be receiving any special alms from the Viceroy this Easter.

Juana watched them leave without attempting to explain her comment or make excuses for her candor. Enemies of the Medinacelis, as she had sworn to la Condesa, were her enemies as well. It was foolish to alienate the palace, she knew, but she would permit herself no more attachments to any Vicereine or Viceroy. Still, she knew she had better repair the damage if she expected any patronage at all from the palace. She would write a ballad for Doña Elvira's birthday, and a *loa* for the Count's.

"Go in peace. The Mass is ended," the Archbishop intoned in Latin, arms spread wide over the altar. He brought his hands together in a brief prayer, then kissed the altar cloth and, followed by his six acolytes, led his flock out of the Cathedral. By the stone benches that flanked an entire side of the atrium, dozens of *zaramullos* in tattered breeches and matted hair stood in line, waiting for the Archbishop. It was Maundy Thursday, and they were going to get their feet washed by the highest pontiff of the colony. Such was the ritual that Aguiar y Seijas had established eight years ago. Before he could begin, however, another prelate had to perform the humbling service on His Ilustrísima.

This year, it was the Bishop of Puebla's duty to wash the archiepiscopal feet, but the Bishop had delegated the honor to one of the *léperos* in the Plaza, promising him a handful of ducats for his trouble. Dutifully, the poor man knelt at the Archbishop's feet, unbuckled the cracked leather straps of his sandals, and removed the torn stockings from the pontiff's feet. Those closest to them pinched their noses. Between the stench of sour pulque issuing from the *lépero*'s pores and the rancid, goat-cheese smell of the Archbishop's feet, the spectacle was an insult to the senses.

The Bishop held his breath, horrified by the black clay between the Archbishop's toes, the dark crust of his overhanging toenails, the thick bunions and calluses. With a cake of soap, the *zaramullo* lathered each malodorous foot, scrubbing hard between the toes, the grime of his own hands mingling with that of the pontiff's. When they emerged from the towel, rinsed and dried, the feet did not look any cleaner except that they reeked now of lye soap rather than spoiled cheese. The Archbishop slipped on his fetid stockings again, buckled his shoes, and exchanged places with the *lépero*, who had no shoes and whose feet, though black with filth, at least did not stink up the atrium.

"A new commandment I give unto you," quoted the Archbishop before plunging the fellow's feet into the soiled water, "that you love one another as I have loved you."

"Your sermon, Ilustrísima," the Bishop heard himself saying aloud, "was Vieyra's Sermon of the Mandate, was it not?"

"It is the sermon I always deliver on Maundy Thursday," the Archbishop responded, scrubbing away at the man's crusty toes.

"A difficult question he poses."

"The man is a genius," said the Archbishop.

"What do you believe, Ilustrísima?"

The Archbishop finished drying the first pair of feet and signaled for the next man to sit down.

"If you don't mind, Manuel, I have—" he gestured to the long line of dirty feet waiting to be washed "—a few matters to attend to. Could we please postpone our discussion of Vieyra until after vespers?" He took the second man's feet and scrubbed vigorously at the mucky soles with the soap. "A new commandment I give unto you, that you love one another as I have loved you," he muttered as he washed.

"I see there are no women in the line, Ilustrísima," said the Bishop.

"Do not mock me, Señor."

"If I remember correctly, Ilustrísima, it was Mary Magdalene, the prostitute, who gave Christ the example that you are following here today. Did she not bathe his holy feet with her tears and dry them with her own hair?"

The next wretch took his place. The water in the basin took the odor and color of the canal.

"A new commandment I give unto you," the Archbishop began, but the Bishop interrupted. The stench was turning his stomach and he was tired of the charade, which was not humility but its opposite.

"Perhaps, Ilustrísima, in honor of your friend, Vieyra, you would consider extending your beneficence to womankind, since it was a woman, after all, and a renowned sinner at that, who demonstrated to our Lord the humility of love."

"This is no place for a theological discussion, Señor. If you do not care to help me, then at least remove yourself from my side and let me concentrate on my work. You!" He called to the acolytes. "Bring more water, more soap, more towels!"

But the Bishop was not easily dissuaded. "He did, after all, die on the Cross for Mary Magdalene as much as for these fine specimens of manhood," he persisted, smiling at the small audience that had gathered around them.

A vein in the Archbishop's forehead started to palpitate. "What is your point, Sir?" he demanded.

"Would you, Ilustrísima, be capable of demonstrating a similar *fineza* toward a daughter of the Church? Sor Juana Inés de la Cruz, for example."

The Archbishop sat back on his heels and glared at the Bishop. "Are you suggesting I am not capable of washing that sinner's feet?"

"Clearly, you are capable of washing anyone's feet, Ilustrísima," the Bishop nodded at the line of beggars and vagabonds. "The question is, could you love her as you love these men? As Christ loved the whore of Magdalene? Now that Juana's book is the toast of Madrid, surely she merits a spiritual scrubbing in your eyes, Ilustrísima."

The Bishop's face grew mottled in different shades of crimson. "In my eyes, Manuel, I see one thing very clearly."

The Bishop cocked an eyebrow and waited for him to proceed.

"I see that you were not named Archbishop of Mexico because of your persistent traffic with women. Don't think that news of your behavior has not reached the Holy See."

The Bishop felt his neck burning with the humiliation. "That is a libelous accusation," he said.

"Report me to the Audiencia, if you wish, but do me the favor of getting out of my sight."

The acolytes reappeared, hauling two more basins of clean water between them. The Archbishop resumed his ablutions. "A new commandment I give unto you, that you love one another as I have loved you." Without another word, the Bishop strode out of the Cathedral and took a carriage to the House of San Jerónimo.

"Why vex yourself, Your Grace?" asked Juana. "Your slate is clean."

The Bishop dipped an empanada into his chocolate, and ate half of it in one bite. "In public he says this to me."

"But didn't you also embarrass him in public?"

"He deserved it, the hypocrite."

"No doubt he thinks you deserved it, too. An odd argument to have over dirty feet."

"It was Vieyra's Sermon on the Mandate that started it all," said the Bishop. "I wanted to discourse with him about the choice he poses as to which was Christ's greatest act of love, and reminded him that it was Mary Magdalene who gave our Lord the idea for the bathing of the feet."

"But Vieyra's purpose is not with Mary Magdalene," said Juana.

"I know that, Juana, but the Archbishop had just delivered Vieyra's sermon, and I thought it hypocritical that he should so blatantly despise womankind and yet be willing to practically kiss the feet of those filthy, abject men. He understands nothing of Christ's humility, and yet he pretends to be so charitable. Anybody who shows off humility the way he does, knows nothing about the meaning of the word. And you should have seen his feet!" He grimaced. "So disgusting! I don't understand how that man can live with himself."

"He likes to affect the trappings of humility, I'm told," she said.

"I don't pretend to be humble, Juana. I believe in cleanliness and in setting an example for the poor. But the Archbishop! He considers himself the canon of humility. The man thinks he understands Vieyra just because they're friends."

"And what is your understanding, Your Grace? What do you think is Christ's greatest beneficence? The sacrament of the Eucharist through which we can become one with Christ, as Saint Thomas believed; His washing of the feet to show us the humility of true love for mankind, as Saint John Chrysostom believed; or His sacrifice on the Cross to redeem our sins, as Saint Augustine believed?"

"Frankly, I disagree with Saint John. I don't believe the feet thing compares to the other two. It's a difficult choice between the Eucharist and the Crucifixion, though. Don't you agree, Juana?"

"I don't really think it matters which was greatest. Can one perfect action be greater or lesser than another?"

"The consequences of the action can vary in degree of beneficence, wouldn't you say, Sister? Does mankind benefit more from the sacrament of Communion, in which he can participate on a regular basis and prepare for daily, or from the abstract redemption of Christ's sacrifice?"

"I see you believe in practical rather than spiritual beneficence," she said.

"Not necessarily, Juana, but men are a practical lot and tend to benefit more from something that they can sink their teeth into. Literally."

"And yet Vieyra's point, I believe, has nothing to do with mankind. His question is not about the consequences of Christ's actions but about the motive of each action, and even more than that, about the *fineza* of the beneficence. Which one is a greater example of Christ's love is Vieyra's question, not which one benefits mankind more. There's a difference between cause and effect, wouldn't you say?"

"I see your point, Juana, but what would be the point of an action if not its effect? Christ is called the Divine Verb because through Him God acted out His commandments, one of which was for men to love each other the way Christ loved us. To prove His love, He sacrificed His own Son on the Cross to redeem our sins, and left us the sacrament of Communion with which to cleanse our souls. You see, Juana, every divine action had an earthly purpose—to redeem our sins, to cleanse our souls—and it is because our sins needed redeeming and our souls needed cleansing that He acted."

"Are you saying, then, Your Grace, that our sinful souls were the cause of His actions or that His love for us caused Him to redeem and cleanse our souls? If we are the cause of God's actions, then His actions are but the effects of our sins, and we can say, according to that argument, that it was not God but we, ourselves, who begat Christ through our sins. Don't look so scandalized, my friend. It is your argument, after all, not my own."

"And what is your own argument, then, Juana?"

"Well, we have come so far from the point, Your Grace, that we'd have to backtrack quite a way to find my argument. I began our exchange by stating a general premise: that one perfect action cannot be greater or lesser than another. It goes without saying that, as the Son of God and also the son of Mary, who was conceived without sin, Christ is perfect. Thus it follows that both Christ's death on the Cross and the sacrament of the Eucharist that he initiated with the Last Supper are perfect actions (as was His washing of the feet, which was but a demonstration of perfect love), and therefore, equal to each other in terms of beneficence and *fineza*. My intention was to refute Vieyra's premise that one of Christ's *finezas* can exceed another, which I find to be an invalid premise based on the perfect nature of the agent as well as on the etymology of the word *fineza*."

The Bishop leaned over and said in a low voice: "Do proceed, Juana. This is fascinating. Nobody has ever challenged Vieyra's premise in the forty years since he first delivered that sermon, much less engaged in a semantic argument with him."

"It could be that, being Portuguese, he has mistranslated the Latin root of *fineza*," said Juana. "For Vieyra, *fino* in relation to love means love that does not seek reciprocity, love for love's sake. Based on such an interpretation, it isn't difficult to see why he would make a distinction between the Eucharist, the washing of the feet, and the Crucifixion, for, if taken out of context, one action would seem to be more *fina* than the other, more motivated purely out of love and without hope of reciprocity, for, indeed, how can mankind reciprocate Christ's sacrifice? Men can become priests and wash the feet of the poor and administer the Eucharist, but they do not give up their lives on a Cross."

"We give up a large part of our corporeal existence, Juana. Our vow of celibacy, if you will excuse my candor, is as close as we get to sacrificing ourselves on the Cross."

"True, but your celibacy does not redeem our sins, Your Grace. It may redeem *your* sins, but not those of mankind. Thus, your celibacy is not a *fineza*, because the etymology of the word means the demonstration of perfection. In its adjective state, something that is *fino* is something that is perfect and pure. As a noun, *fineza* is a demonstration or an example of perfection, an imitation, if you will. Think of Plato. Plato says nature is the imitation of reality, for reality exists in God's mind, and what is in God's mind is perfect, and what we have in nature is an imitation of the real thing. The reality we are talking about here is Christ's love, which is perfect, and therefore *fino*, but the imitation of His love, the action itself through which God demonstrates His love, is the *fineza*. Thus, when Vieyra calls Christ's love a *fineza* he is confusing the reality with the imitation. Furthermore, when he asks which action—the Eucharist, the washing of the feet, or the Crucifixion— is a greater example of Christ's love, he is forgetting that what is *fino* is already perfect, and that, if they are all *finezas*, then they are all examples of perfection, and therefore are all equally perfect examples of Christ's love."

The Bishop's eyes glittered. He chuckled heartily at Juana's discourse.

"Are you laughing at me, Your Grace?"

"On the contrary, Juana. I am completely delighted by your analysis. Given time, no doubt, you would be able to refute even Saint Paul."

"Invalid arguments aren't difficult to refute. Vieyra gives plenty of examples that contradict his own premise and elucidate my own."

"You need to write this down, Juana. This is too . . . *fino* of a critique to not be recorded on paper. Somebody needs to really humble Aguiar y Seijas."

"I doubt it would behoove me to provoke the Archbishop's wrath. We both know what an extremist he can be."

"Then let me do it, Juana. Let me rub his hypocrisy in his face. He thinks Vieyra's a genius and beyond critique. Your analysis will give him apoplexy, I can tell you. Do write it down for me, Juana. I know just the right group in which to share your views."

"I want no problems with the Archbishop, Your Grace."

"Don't worry, Juana. If you will permit me, I will claim this critique as my own. But I need to see it in writing. I need to see these examples that you're referring to. Logic is nothing without examples."

"But what could I possibly gain from this exercise?" she asked.

"What else? Revenge against the Archbishop's hatred of you. You don't deserve such hatred. Not to mention the satisfaction of having jousted with one of Aguiar y Seijas's favorite knights."

Juana frowned, unable to make up her mind if she should do this. What would the repercussions be if the Archbishop discovered it was her argument rather than the Bishop's? Surely, he would put an end to Juana's writing privileges. And she had no more friends at the viceregal palace to stand up for her. De Galve had his hands full quelling the *castas*, and the Vicereine, Doña Elvira, it was said, was too busy writing love letters to her brother-in-law. And yet it was such an opportunity to get back at Aguiar y Seijas for all of his abuses, all of his ridiculous edicts and punishments, all of the money he had no intention of paying back, all of his miserliness and misogyny. With her logic and the Bishop's connections, Aguiar y Seijas would, at the very least, lose some of his pontifical arrogance.

"If I were to concede, Your Grace, it would have to be under the strict condition that nobody know the true author of the critique."

"But of course, Juana. Do you think it would look good for me to be in league with a nun, much less you, Sor Juana, on something like this?"

"And that it will not be made public."

"Of course not."

"It will not be published."

"No, Juana."

"Nor circulated throughout the realm."

"Just my friends will read it. I promise."

"Very well, then. I shall write down my critique, but I cannot send it to you. I must deliver it to your own hands."

"How much time will you need, Juana?"

Outside the bells rang for the midday Office.

"I have to finish the *Divine Narcissus* to send to la Condesa first, and then I have the *villancicos* for the Assumption to get to, but I can do those with my eyes closed by now." She counted the months on her fingers. "Let's say July. The feast day of Mary Magdalene."

The Bishop's eyes creased. "Very appropriate," was all he said. "Now, I must leave you, Juana, before His Ilustrísima finds out that I was here. I wouldn't want him to think that I came to bathe your feet." He bowed low to her and donned his red hat.

She watched him walk out of the *locutorio* and pause to say a few words to Sor Clara. Something in her chest began to tick.

Chapter 26

For two weeks after she had finished her critique of Vieyra, Juana did not want to tell Don Carlos about the work, fearful of letting the truth out into the world, but her desire to impress her friend with her powers of rhetorical refutation had gotten the best of her and she had shared her views with him at their last workshop. She would not let him take her copy home with him as that would certainly increase the risk of it getting to the Archbishop, who was, inexplicably, a good friend and champion of Don Carlos, and so he had sat for an hour poring over her argument while she prepared an onion and cheese omelet for him in the refectory.

He was pacing in front of the door when she returned to the locutory, followed by a maid with the tray. Don Carlos had developed a pain in his side that he diagnosed as a gallstone, and could drink nothing but milk and eat nothing but the blandest food.

"Well?" she asked.

"Are you thinking of sending this to la Condesa for the new volume?"

"It had occurred to me, though, of course, the subterfuge is that the Archbishop never find out it was I who authored the critique."

He continued to pace.

"Your omelet is getting cold, my friend."

He paused at the tray, pulled a stray slice of onion off the plate, and chewed it slowly. Juana was getting annoyed with his silence.

"Is it any good? Does it convince?"

He turned to look at her. "Dear Juana. When have you ever written anything that does not convince? It is precisely because it's so brilliant that I worry."

"Worry? About what?"

"What are the Bishop's intentions here? Do you have any idea?"

"I'm sure he's still harboring resentments against Aguiar y Seijas for having received the Archbishopric rather than he."

"So why is he using you to get back at the Archbishop?"

"He's not the only one with an archiepiscopal bone to pick."

Don Carlos folded the omelet and picked it up. He resumed his pacing, eating as he walked and leaving a trail of egg and onion on the floor.

"There's something suspicious about all this, Juana, but I can't pinpoint what it is," he said, the food bulging in his cheek. "Delicious omelet." He licked his fingers. "Don Manuel is going to pass off this critique as his own, and circulate it only among a select group and somehow this is going to afford him retribution? How is that going to work, Juana, if the Archbishop doesn't know anything about it?"

"I'm sure the Archbishop is among the group, Don Carlos."

"But don't you see, Juana, that in order for it to serve its purpose, which is a minor revenge for both of you, the Archbishop needs to know that you had a part in it?"

"My revenge has come just in writing the critique. He need not know it was me in order for me to feel vindicated."

"But Juana, my friend, you're above such pettiness. Since when must you engage in subterfuge when your life has been an open book of brilliant defiance? This critique needs to be published, and let the world see what an illuminated mind can do with outdated theology. To the devil with the Bishop's intrigues and resentments. Let him find somebody else for his ventriloquism!"

"Is it because the Archbishop is your friend that you object?" she asked.

He drained his milk, rinsing his mouth lightly with the last swallow. "The Archbishop has been good to me, Juana. He has helped me secure important posts without which I could never have provided for my family or paid my debts. But my objection has nothing to do with the Archbishop, and moreover, this Vieyra is no prophet. He is a scholar, just as we are, and scholars refute one another. That is what keeps our scholarly discourse alive. But you see, what I have always admired about you, Juana, was that you were never afraid to speak your mind, and now you have allowed the Bishop to drag you into this silly deception. You have transferred your authority over to him, and have given him the right to claim your most ingenious piece of theological scholarship. That, my friend, is a tragedy."

He had never spoken anything but praise to her, for which she looked forward to their weekly gatherings like one in need of air and light. Even when they disagreed in their interpretations of a certain text, he never failed to admire the acumen of her argument, though it did not convince him to alter his opinion. Here, again, he was admiring her critique and yet critiquing the occasion for which it was written. More than a critique, though, he was expressing something altogether new for her: his disappointment with something she had done. She could not bear his disappointment. In a way it was like being betrayed, and yet she realized he was right. She had never resorted to subterfuge before, and in doing so she had betrayed herself. She felt a sudden nausea well up in her throat.

"Juana, you've gone pale," said Don Carlos, approaching the grille. "Please forgive me. I didn't mean to be so harsh."

She took a sip of pineapple water to wash down the queasiness. "You're right," she said, shaking her head. "I didn't think. I allowed my emotions to make the decision for me." She shook her head. "All of them make me so indignant."

"You have a right to be indignant, Juana, and a right to critique any scholar you wish. It is the deception that I don't think was wise."

"I agree with you, my friend. I made an error in judgment."

"And now I've succeeded in making you melancholic," said Don Carlos.

"I'm angry at myself," she said. "You'd think that someone who's dedicated a lifetime to developing her intelligence wouldn't give free rein to her emotions, especially base ones like revenge."

"It's a hard battle, Juana. And who am I, anyway, to criticize your actions? I know nothing of what it feels to be hated for my gender, but if it feels anything like what I feel when my work is disparaged as the difficult judgments of a criollo, then I imagine it must provoke the deepest ire, the deepest wish for revenge."

She shrugged. "What difference is it going to make, anyway? The world is ruled by misogynists."

"You do not count me among that lot, do you, Juana?"

"If I did, my friend, you would not be sitting here showing me the error of my ways. You would be gloating as the Bishop must be doing now over the fatal flaw in my nature."

"And what is that?"

"Vanity, what else? Egotism. Witness the immodesty I feel when I look at my own book."

"It's difficult for an intellect of your caliber not to be vain, Juana. Especially when surrounded by fools."

"Fools live longer and happier lives, I think," she said.

"Any fool who cannot read the lyricism and perspicacity of your words should count himself wretched."

"You are always so forthcoming with your praise, Don Carlos."

"I just wish this magnificent analysis could have more of an audience than the Bishop of Puebla and his cronies. Especially now that so many people have bought your book. The Bishop himself purchased three copies of it."

"Yes, he said he had some business at the Widow Calderón's."

"So you've seen him recently?"

"He was here yesterday, to pick up his copy of the critique."

"You gave it to him before showing it to me?" His eyes bulged behind his lenses.

"We had an agreement," she said.

Don Carlos shook his head. "Oh, Juana."

"What is it?"

"I don't know if I should tell you this, but maybe it'll help you understand my suspicions of our beloved Bishop." He paused to clean his spectacles on the hem of his cloak.

"Well?"

"I was at the Widow Calderón's when the Bishop came in, with Padre Antonio. The Bishop bought his three copies and gave one to Padre Antonio."

Juana frowned at his ambiguity. "So?"

"So isn't Padre Antonio still a censor for the Inquisition?"

"Are you saying he's going to censor my book?"

"All I'm saying, Juana, is that the Bishop and Padre Antonio came in together. I never knew them to be close friends."

Juana closed her eyes, remembering the conversation she had had with the Bishop about her father confessor.

"He's been quite ill, you know," the Bishop had told her. "Padre Antonio, I mean. A strange affliction of the eyes."

"He must be very happy. Padre Antonio relishes in self-punishment."

"I've been told that he asks about you all the time. I think he misses you, Juana."

"I wouldn't be so sure, Your Grace. Padre Antonio is a man of deep conviction, and he convicted me ten years ago to the perpetual penance of his absence."

"The word is *you* renounced him, Juana."

"I gave him a choice."

"In the mind of an old priest like Padre Antonio, I would venture to say, a nun does not give her father confessor a choice. It is the other way around."

"Free will is free will, yet another of God's *finezas*, Your Grace."

"You never give up, do you, Juana?"

"Rarely," she said.

"Which makes you very dangerous, Sister."

"I don't think any woman can be dangerous, Your Grace. That would imply she has power, and if a woman cannot even aspire to an education, how can she pretend to have any power?"

"I'm not speaking about *any* woman, Sor Juana. I'm speaking about you."

Ten days after the Feast of Saint Jerome a scandal overtook the city. Word of a new publication in Puebla was printed in the Mexico gazette: a bold critique of a learned Jesuit's Sermon on the Mandate, entitled *Carta atenagórica, Letter Worthy of Athena by mother Juana Inés de la Cruz, professed religious of veil and choir at the holy convent of Saint Jerome,* was hot off the press and making its way to the capital by coach, to be sold exclusively by the Widow Calderón. Dedicated to Sor Juana, its publication had been sponsored by one Sor Filotea de la Cruz of the convent of the Holy Trinity in the city of Puebla.

Structured as a letter to an anonymous "señor," *Carta atenagórica*, read the gazette, "was an ingenious if brazen semantical discourse upon a theological debate concerning the greatest example of Christ's love, to which the world-renowned Sor Juana was adding her mark, alongside that of not only the honorable Portuguese, Father Antonio de Vieyra, but also the greatest doctors of the Catholic Church: Saint Thomas, Saint Augustine, and Saint John Chrysostom."

The same day that the announcement appeared in the gazette, Don Carlos brought Juana a copy of the pamphlet. Andrea joined them in the *locutorio*, looking as ashen as Juana. It was the first scandal of Andrea's tenure as Mother Superior and she was not happy that it involved her friend.

"I've just returned from Puebla," said Don Carlos, handing the pamphlet to Juana through the bars. His face and cloak were still grimy from the journey, his hair awry under his dusty hat. "I knew it, Juana. I knew the Bishop had an ulterior motive for getting you to write down your critique. It was you who were supposed to remain anonymous, and it is he who has taken the pseudonym. That coward!"

Juana opened the text at random and started to pace, alternating between rage and despair as she reread her words. Sigüenza's admonitions kept ringing in her ears.

"She doesn't really refute the saints, does she, Don Carlos?" asked Andrea.

"Mother, it's a theological argument. It is the nature of such treatises to analyze all sides of a particular question."

"But the saints, Juana," said Andrea, turning around, "you've contradicted the saints!"

"He swore to me," said Juana, her voice squeezing through the tautness of her vocal chords. "He swore this would never get published. He was only going to circulate it among a select group."

"How could you trust him, Juana?" asked Andrea.

"I had no reason not to. He was a friend, I thought."

Don Carlos shook his head. "It was a trap, Juana. Don't you see?"

"Of course I didn't see!" she raged, casting the pamphlet on the seat of the bench. "What antecedents had I not to trust the Bishop?"

"Between your book and now this," said Andrea, picking up the pamphlet, "we'll never live this down with the Archbishop."

Juana rubbed her throbbing temples.

"That's not the worst of it, I'm afraid," said Don Carlos, his eyes like black puffs behind his lenses. "You haven't seen what precedes your analysis, Juana. A letter to you from this Sor Filotea."

Juana snatched the pamphlet away from Andrea and turned to the opening page, her mouth dropping open as she read.

"He censors and applauds your intellect at one and the same time," said Don Carlos, quoting verbatim one of Sor Filotea's injunctions: "'Literary learning that engenders pride God does not wish in a woman, but the Apostle does not criticize letters as long as they do not lead a woman from a state of obedience.'"

"'You have spent much time in the study of philosophers and poets,'" Juana read aloud, "'now it would be well for you to better your occupation and improve the quality of the books.'"

"It seems Sor Filotea doubts that you read Scripture, Juana," said Don Carlos.

"God have mercy," said Andrea.

"Read on, Juana," said Don Carlos.

"'What a pity that such a great intellect should so lower itself by unworthy notice of the Earth as to have no desire to penetrate what comes to pass in Heaven; and, having already stooped to the Earth, may it not descend farther to consider what comes to pass in Hell.'"

Juana looked up at Don Carlos. "Is he threatening me?"

"He's telling you you're on your way to perdition, Juana," said Andrea, sitting with her rosary beads clenched in both fists.

"Don't you hear it?" asked Don Carlos. "Don't you hear the envy in his tone? It's your book, Juana! Your book has engendered much fame, both here and abroad, and fame is the 'unworthy notice of the Earth,' which in turn engenders pride and disobedience and leads to a life of vanity and to an afterlife in Hell. That's what he's saying!"

"Sweet Jesus!" said Andrea, crossing herself with the crucifix.

"¡Víbora!" hissed Juana. "That duplicitous snake! No wonder I haven't heard from him! The liar! He promised he wouldn't publish it!"

"The Bishop may have intended to keep his word, Juana, and your book probably sent him over the edge," said Andrea. "Dear God. What will the Archbishop do to us now?"

"Forgive me for contradicting you, Mother Andrea," said Don Carlos, "but I don't believe the Bishop ever intended not to publish Juana's critique."

"How could you, Juana? Knowing how precarious your relationship with the Archbishop is—"

"It was a matter of honor, Andrea," Juana said coldly. "Don't you think I've suffered enough abuses from the Archbishop?"

"But you're in no position to take on an Archbishop, Juana," said Andrea.

"I thought I had the protection of anonymity and the promise of a Bishop."

Andrea pressed her fingers to her temples and moaned under her breath.

"I'm afraid, dear Juana," said Don Carlos, shaking his head, "that your protection ended with the departure of the Count of Paredes. Your only friends, now, it would seem, are myself—a lowly *criollo*—and your Mother Superior. All your other friends are in Madrid."

A side of her face had grown numb while the other raced with pain as the blood shot through her temple and into her skull just behind her right eye. She lowered herself on the edge of the bench beside Andrea and said a slow Hail Mary, inhaling and exhaling as she concentrated on the prayer.

Ave María, llena eres de gracia, el Señor es contigo.

She heard the panic in Andrea's voice on the perimeter of her awareness and Sigüenza's quiet drone as he tried to soothe Andrea's fears.

Bendita eres entre todas las mujeres, y bendito el fruto de tu vientre, Jesús.

The rain outside sounded like nails against the shutters, nails pounding into her temple, nails in her palms and feet, nailed to the Cross of her gender, that man nailing her to her fate by betraying his promise.

Santa María, madre de Dios, ruega por nosotros los pecadores ahora y en la hora de nuestra muerte. Amen.

"Juana?" Andrea was touching her shoulder. "Are you ill?"

The pain hovered just behind her eye now, so that even blinking sent tremors into her skull. "I'm fine. I just got a little dizzy."

"What are we going to do about this, Juana?" asked Andrea.

"She has to respond, of course," said Don Carlos. "A rebuttal is in order."

"Not another missive, please," said Andrea.

"What choice do I have, Andrea? If I don't rebut this injunction I'll become the laughingstock of New Spain. Everyone will think that I was cowed by the Bishop, when it was his idea in the first place that I put my thoughts into writing."

"It's your perpetual thoughts that are the root of the problem, Juana. Once and for all, will you not curb these thoughts, for the benefit of your own soul? You were supposed to leave the world when you took your vows, Juana, and yet you have brought the world into the cloister."

Juana took a deep breath to keep her anger in check. "I believe the best thing to do," she said, "will be to take a vow of silence and solitude. I need time to think about my strategy. I have to be very careful with my response, very thorough, and I mustn't have any distractions whatsoever. Will you allow me to do that, Andrea, as Mother Superior and as my only friend in the convent?"

Andrea looked at Don Carlos. "I trust your judgment, Don Carlos. What do you advise?"

"Do you remember bullfights, Mother? The way the bull charges out of its pen, ready to do battle, nothing but its own natural attributes to defend itself against an onslaught of *banderilleros, picadores, rejoneadores,* and a matador whose sole purpose is to dance that bull to its death, to stab its heart with his sword. That is what I see happening here, Mother. Juana is the bull and the Bishop is the matador. She has been thrust the last *banderilla* and now she is bleeding and enraged and afraid all at the same time. Would the bull be allowed to march back to its pen and forfeit the match? Would it lie down in the sand and wait for the sword to touch its heart? Juana must play her part in the *faena,* Mother. She must try to gore the Bishop with her response."

"But first a month of atonement, Juana, please," said Andrea. "For your arrogance."

DEAREST CONDESA,

I write this on the eve of my 42d birthday as I prepare to embark on what Don Carlos has called a "faena" with the Bishop of Puebla. Once you read the enclosed pamphlet you will understand what he means. I have spent all of a month atoning for my arrogance (for Andrea's sake) and trying to decide how to begin my response to this duplicitous Sor Filotea. How does a bull prepare to confront the matador? Where do I find the testicles to match the horns that Don Carlos says must gore this cowardly pontifical bullfighter? It's not as though I have nothing to say; I have more than enough for reproaches and recriminations, but I want to do more in this response than simply react to the Bishop's prodding. If, indeed, this is to be my last *faena* in the bullring of intellectual debate, then let it be a testimonial as well as a response in which I advocate for a woman's right to discourse on any subject she pleases. I am sick to death of this notion that women must remain obedient and ignorant, as though we were servants or dogs. Suffice it to say, of course, that we are chattel, but at least we may be thinking chattel, reasoning chattel, chattel with voices and thoughts, and not the mute fishes that Neptune is said to favor or the dull oxen that Isis would not permit into her bovine fold. Don Carlos tells me that already there have been two lectures delivered at the university by impugners attacking my views, as well as a sermon in the church of San Pedro y San Pablo slandering my reputation. The web of persecutions has widened. How I miss you! An enlightened mind to illuminate the shadows of my despair. Please write soon.

Your despondent,

Juana

She sealed the letter and had Belilla deliver it to the priory. When Belilla had gone, she made a tour of all the bookshelves in the cell and anything that might serve as ammunition for her defense came down: from the kitchen came the the *Lives* of Saint Jerome, Saint Thomas, and both Saint

Theresas, of Avila and of Jesus; from the parlor came *The Vulgate* and Juan Diaz de Arce's four books on the exposition of biblical text; from her bedchamber came Bocaccio's *Concerning Famous Women,* Christine de Pizan's *The Book of the City of Ladies*, and Baltasar Gracian's *The Art of Worldly Wisdom;* in her study she found Kircher's *Nature's Magnetic Realm* and Quintilian's *On the Education of an Orator*, several books on astronomy necessary to deconstruct allusions to constellations and myths in the Bible, treatises on music to decipher musical code, books on mathematics, physics, medicine, history, architecture, law, even astrology—for all of these, she was going to argue, were minor sciences compared to the Queen of Sciences, which is Theology. She wanted to prove that not only did she read Scripture, she read what was necessary to understand Scripture, for Scripture was filled with references to these sciences and many others, none of which made any sense if one did not have a grasp of the referents; thus, she was going to conclude, to truly read Scripture, to truly be enlightened by Holy Writ, it was necessary to master the minor sciences. Only then could one say one had understood the Prophets and the Apostles. And she wanted to prove that she was not the only woman in history so inclined toward letters and learning, but only a daughter in the genealogy of learned women, among them Santa Paula, lifelong companion of their own Saint Jerome and founder of the first nunnery of the Hieronymite Order.

She read and took notes for months, sketching the different parts of her argument on separate sheets that she gradually filled with layers of citations and several levels of analysis. She spread these sheets on the floor so that she could look at everything at once and see what needed developing or reducing or moving around, and at the same time maintain coherence in the whole. The sheets multiplied, and the floor of her study became a tapestry of proofs and refutations.

Andrea exempted Juana from teaching but did not allow her the vow of solitude, and so she was forced to attend chapter meetings and the daily Offices. She tried to work as much as possible between the bells that summoned them to choir, but she never knew if it was tierce or nones or vespers or compline, and while her sisters chanted, while her own lips formed the syllables of the chant, her mind stitched at the fabric of the response. At chapter she would sit with her notebook in her lap, completely oblivious to the issues under discussion, even to the complaints lodged about her lack of attention and participation. Usually Belilla would tap her shoulder to signal that a meeting or a service was over, and she would get up and follow Belilla across the cloister and again immerse herself in her work. Don Carlos waited for her in the locutory several times, but she never appeared at their weekly workshop, so he stopped calling.

She ate little during this time, preferring not to break her fast when she awakened for she was always more lucid in the morning and eating tended to slow her mind. Fruit and Turkish coffee were her main nutrients, and she smoked whatever tobacco the refectory maids managed to procure for her at the market. At times the smoke was harsh and bitter and scalded the roof of her mouth, other times it felt like cool silk flowing down her throat—regardless of its taste, the tobacco mixed with coffee gave her an unparalleled acuity. And suddenly it was the beginning of Lent and she realized that she had missed Christmas and Epiphany and the Feasts of Saint Paula and Saint Agatha. Her study was pure anarchy. Heaps of books cluttered every inch of the floor, papers strewn from her desk to the dormitory and the parlor. Her hands were mottled with ink and ink streaked the sleeves and skirt of her habit.

It was Shrove Tuesday, and outside the city blazed with fireworks. Processions filled the streets—huge clowns and effigies on stilts, *zaramullos* dressed as priests, *castas* dressed as *criollos*, men dressed as women and women as men. A good day to restore order, she thought, and set about reshelving her books and organizing the different sets of notes she had taken. Afterward she asked Belilla to collect eucalyptus leaves, lavender flowers, and rosemary twigs for a bath. Two *criadas* hauled buckets of water from the well. Juana heated the water on the brazier and poured it scalding into the tub, save one that she would use later, for rinsing. She let the herbs soak in the hot water and waited for the steam to rise into the bathroom before taking a candle in and latching the door behind her.

"Are you quite sure you don't need me, Tía?" Belilla called from the other side of the door. "I don't want you to fall asleep in there."

"Leave me alone, *cariño*," she said. "I know what I'm doing."

"But, Tía, you haven't been exactly aware—" the girl protested.

"Go on up to the *azotea* and watch the fireworks," said Juana. "I need to be alone. Don't worry. I just need to be alone and clear my mind."

She removed all of her clothes, even the shift that they were supposed to leave on for a bath, and inhaled the scent of the herbs rising out of the water. She stepped into the tub and immediately felt the sweat rise on her skin. Her scalp and armpits grew moist. The tile felt clammy under her feet. Her lungs labored in the thick, damp air.

It was a ritual bath, like those of the Indians from the north that Don Tomás had told her about many years ago, a sweat bath, it was called, for purifying the soul before a quest or a battle, only the Indians performed them in a round adobe room with hot stones in the center and an elder of the tribe chanting songs to the initiates. Here she would have to be both elder and initiate and, as she knew no chants other than the plainsong they sung seven times a day, she would talk, instead, not to the Virgin or Saint Jude, but to the spirits of her mother, her aunt Mary, her grandfather, and la Marquesa. She would ask them to bless her and give her courage for this *faena* with the Bishop. She would steep in the water and imagine every doubt and weakness melting from her like sweat. From her grandfather she asked protection and guidance; from her mother she asked clarity of purpose; from her aunt Mary she asked devotion to her task; from la Marquesa she asked subtlety, for her words had to be shrewd and delicate at the same time. In the distance she heard the fireworks going off in the Plaza Mayor.

She sat in the tub speaking to her spirits until the water grew cold and her skin smelled of an herb garden in the rain. Before stepping out, she washed herself well with the Castile soap, lathered her hair and genitals, rinsed herself with the remaining bucket of clean cool water, which ran down her legs and into the channel that served as a drain in the floor. The bedroom felt frigid on her wet skin, but she walked over to the brazier and dried herself in the warm glow before binding her breasts again and donning her night shift and her short veil and a clean writing smock. She was ready, now, to sit at her desk (take a deep breath, Juana) and write her response to this transvestite Sor Filotea, who was none other than the Bishop of Puebla cross-dressed as a nun and, therefore, her equal.

Chapter 27

The wicks flared in her study and the smell of tallow filled the room. For an instant she imagined that someone was contemplating her from the other side of the room, and a shiver climbed up her spine. This could be a play, she thought, and saw herself sitting in a theater watching the stage come to life under the steady glow of the candles: the crammed shelves, the telescope and astrolabe and mandolin, the chess table, the map table scattered with books and papers, the Aztec headdress suspended above an untidy desk. No doubt Don Carlos would think this an odd arena for a *faena*, she mused. She felt cold but did not want to take any time lighting the brazier, so she took the woolen blanket off its hook behind the door, wrapped it around her shoulders, and sat down in la Marquesa's chair.

Another deep breath, Juana. Yes, her spirits were with her. Exhale. She opened the inkwell (this is my blood), selected her best goose quill (this is my sword), and stirred the ink until the nib grew black and spongy. Then she took a clean notebook from the bottom drawer of her desk and inscribed the cover: *Response to the Illustrious Sor Filotea*. Inhaling and exhaling once more, she opened the notebook to the first page and, resting the feather in the crook of her hand, the quill stem pressed against the callous of her middle finger, she began to write.

1 March 1691

Most Illustrious Lady, my Lady:

It has not been my will, but my scant health and a rightful fear that have delayed my reply for so many days. Is it to be wondered that, at the very first step, I should meet with two obstacles that sent my dull pen stumbling? The first (and to me the most insuperable) is the question of how to respond to your immensely learned, prudent, devout, and loving letter.

She was going to add two or three other descriptors, but decided against it as excess was a facade for mockery and it was too early in the letter to give free rein to a vexed ethos. Still, she could not avoid all sarcasm.

The second obstacle is the question of how to render my thanks for the favor, as excessive as it was unexpected, of giving my drafts and scratches to the press: a favor so beyond all measure as to surpass the most ambitious hopes or the most fantastic desires, so that as a rational being, I simply could not house it in my thoughts.

She turned to the first pile of sheets she had arranged on her desk earlier, the pile labeled "Introduction," and copied several biblical citations about personages who questioned their worthiness in the face of divine favor.

It is not false humility, my Lady, but the candid truth of my very soul, to say that when the printed letter reached my hands—that letter that you were pleased to dub "Worthy of Athena"—I burst into tears (a thing that does not come easily to me), tears of confusion.

She wove more citations into the Introduction, taking her argument now into the domain of silence, which does not always signify an inability to speak, she wrote, but rather a muteness brought on by humility and stupefaction.

I confess with all the candor due to you and with the truth and frankness that are always at once natural and customary for me, that my having written little on sacred matters has sprung from no dislike, nor from lack of application, but rather from a surfeit of awe and reverence toward those sacred letters, which I know myself to be so incapable of understanding and which I am so unworthy of handling.

She added a quotation from Saint Jerome, another from Seneca, to insinuate that, as a lowly nun with an underdeveloped mind due to her age and sex, Scripture posed difficult challenges that were best left alone. For that reason, she argued, did she turn to secular subjects rather than sacred, but then only at the behest or commission of others (including yours, she wanted to add, but resisted the temptation). The only thing she had ever written for her own pleasure was her First Dream; everything else, she emphasized, including homages to the palace, *villancicos*, and spiritual exercises (her private letters and verses to la Condesa did not count, as what the Bishop was objecting to were her public verses)—all of them had been ordered by others.

> . . . truth to tell, I have never written save when pressed and forced and solely to give pleasure to others, not only without taking satisfaction but with downright aversion, because I have never judged myself to possess the rich trove of learning and wit that is perforce the obligation of one who writes.

Why shouldn't she lie and exaggerate? These were but rhetorical devices, such as the Bishop's pseudonymous voice as Sor Filotea, as well as her use of the nun's confession to structure her polemic against intellectual repression for women.

> For ever since the light of reason first dawned in me, my inclination to letters was marked by such passion and vehemence that neither the reprimands of others (for I have received many) nor reflections of my own (there have been more than a few) have sufficed to make me abandon my pursuit of this native impulse that God Himself bestowed on me.

She narrated several examples of this "native impulse" that had compelled her since childhood—since the day her three-year-old self had followed her sister to school and begged the teacher to instruct her in the art of reading—to live solely for the purpose of learning, forswearing friendships and activities and even foods that might interfere with her studies.

> I took the veil because, although I knew I would find in religious life many things that would be quite opposed to my character (I speak of accessory rather than essential matters), it would, given my absolute unwillingness to enter into marriage, be the least unfitting and the most decent state I could choose, with regard to the assurance I desired of my salvation.

She clarified those repugnant things about living in community that kept her from finalizing her decision to profess—lack of solitude, a daily schedule of obligations, the noise of so many others living close by—only to discover, once enmeshed in convent life, that her inclination *when snuffed out or hindered with every exercise known to Religion, exploded like gunpowder; and in my case the saying "privation gives rise to appetite" was proven true.*

Once having established the character of the speaker, she launched into the first justification for her defense: that, as a Hieronymite nun, daughter of Saint Jerome and Saint Paula, she felt obliged to match the erudition of her religious "parents" by turning her inclination toward the study of Theology. Here she would incorporate one of her main arguments: that to truly study this Queen of Sciences, she had, first, to learn from those other sciences that were its ancillaries.

Without Logic, how should I know the general and specific methods by which Holy Scripture is written? Without Rhetoric, how should I understand its figures, tropes, and locutions? Or how, without Physics or Natural Science, understand all the questions that naturally arise concerning the varied natures of those animals offered in sacrifice . . . How should I know whether Saul's cure at the sound of David's harp was owing to a virtue and power that is natural in Music or owing, instead, to a supernatural power that God saw fit to bestow on David? How without Arithmetic might one understand all those myterious reckonings of years and days and months and hours and weeks that are found in Daniel and elsewhere, which can be comprehended only by knowing the natures, concordances, and properties of numbers?

Geometry, architecture, history, law, music, astronomy—each science had its rationale, its application in the reading of the Holy Book, which was the sum of all books ever written just as Theology was the sum of all the arts and sciences.

And so, to acquire a few basic principles of knowledge, I studied constantly in a variety of subjects, having no inclination toward any one of them in particular but being drawn rather to all of them generally. Therefore, if I have studied some things more than others it has not been by my choice, but because by chance the books on certain subjects came more readily to hand, and this gave preference to those topics, without my passing judgment in the matter . . . Thus almost at one sitting I would study diverse things or leave off some to take up others. Yet even in this I maintained a certain order, for some subjects I called my study and others my diversion, and with the latter I would take my rest from the former. Hence, I have studied many things but know nothing, for one subject has interfered with another.

She went on to illustrate the faults and benefits of this method, concluding that perhaps she would have had more depth and less breadth in her education had she, on the one hand, had the advantage of a school environment with teachers and schoolmates, and on the other, a life of less interruptions as those posed by the Rule or by the needs and requests of her loving (she could not resist the irony) sisters in religion. And there were other problems that got in the way of a more advanced education, rivalries and persecutions that she had been enduring for twenty-two years.

> And the most venomous and hurtful to me have not been those who with explicit hatred and ill-will have persecuted me, but those persons, loving me and desiring my good . . . who have mortified and tormented me more than any others, with these words: "All this study is not fitting, for holy ignorance is your duty; she shall go to perdition, she shall surely be cast down from such heights by that same wit and cleverness." How was I to bear up against this? A strange martyrdom indeed, where I must be both martyr and executioner!

Remembering these inanities, she felt a choleric fever rising in her blood, moving her to an analogy that she might need to remove later, lest her audience accuse her of sacrilege, but that here fueled an ethical proof for her argument. The Machiavellian hatred against her, she wrote, was due to her significance, for in growing significant as a scholar and a writer of verses, she roused the envy of those who felt themselves superior and therefore displaced by her superior achievements, just as the Pharisees felt displaced by Christ's achievements and scorned His kingly attributes with a crown of thorns, for *the head that is a treasury of wisdom can hope for no other crown than thorns.*

Vaguely, she was aware of the curfew bells, the sounds of reveling dying out now in the Plaza Mayor. She heard Belilla washing out the bathtub, the bucket scraping against the tile, the splash of water on the floor, the swish of the broom. I must have missed compline, she thought, and prepared herself for a visit from Andrea, but the visit never came and soon the cell was quiet and she knew that Belilla had at last gone to bed.

She got up from the desk and stretched her back, bending first backward with her palms against the small of her waist and then doubling over to touch her fingertips to the floor, feeling the tingle of pain up her legs and spinal cord. She straightened again, rotated her shoulders in both directions, turned her head from side to side to stretch her neck muscles and finally reached her arms over her head and pretended to be scaling the rungs of a ladder with just her hands.

The exercise refreshed her and she sat down again, inked the quill, and continued writing, ignoring the rumbling of her stomach.

> I confess that I am far indeed from the terms of Knowledge and that I have wished to follow it, though "afar off." But all this has merely led me closer to the flames of persecution, the crucible of affliction; and to such extremes that some have even sought to prohibit me from study.
>
> They achieved this once, with a very saintly and simple Mother Superior who believed that study was an affair for the Inquisition and ordered that I should not read. I obeyed her (for the three months or so that her authority over us lasted) in that I did not pick up a book. But with regard to avoiding study absolutely, as such a thing does not lie within my power, I could not do it.

She recalled how Melchora had punished her as a result of Concepción's escape, boarding up her bookshelves and confiscating her writing instruments, and how she had learned empirically from the open pages of the natural world and from the scientific laboratory of the kitchen.

> I often say, when I make these little observations, "Had Aristotle cooked, he would have written a great deal more." And so to go on with the mode of my cogitations: I declare that all this is so continual in me that I have no need of books. On one occasion, because of a severe stomach ailment, the doctors forbade me to study. I spent several days in that state, and then quickly proposed to them that it would be less harmful to allow me my books, for my cogitations were so strenuous and vehement that they consumed more vitality in a quarter of an hour than the reading of books could in four days. And so the doctors were compelled to let me read.

She turned to her sheets again and sought the lists she had made of wise women in Scripture as well as in ancient texts who she was claiming as her intellectual foremothers: Deborah, Esther, Rahab, Hannah, the Queen of Sheba; Minerva, Zenobia, Hypatia, Gertrude, Catherine of Alexandria. History was riddled with famous women, women who wrote and ruled and governed and lived their lives as they pleased. She included the Duchess of Aveyro, Christina, the Queen of Sweden, Sor María de Agreda, even the lieutenant nun, Catalina de Erauso, who lived a large part of her life as a man, a soldier, a lover, even, and who was ultimately not put to death when her imposture was brought to trial because she had aspired toward perfection—the masculine gender—and been such an excellent Spaniard. She omitted Sappho, Joan of Arc, and Santa Librada on purpose, the first because she wanted no sexual allusions and the last two because they had both been put to death as a result of their respective rebellions against the Church.

And seeking no more examples far from home, I see my own most holy mother Paula, learned in Hebrew, Greek, and Latin tongues and most expert in the interpretation of the Scriptures. What wonder then can it be that, though her chronicler was no less than the un-equaled Jerome, the Saint found himself scarcely worthy of the task, for with that lively gravity and energetic effectiveness with which only he can express himself, he says: "If all the parts of my body were tongues, they would not suffice to proclaim the learning and virtues of Paula." Blessilla, a widow, earned the same praises, as did the lumi-nous virgin Eustochium, both of them daughters of the Saint herself; and indeed Eustochium was such that for her knowledge she was hailed as a World Prodigy.

She was coming now to the other axis of her argument: her refutation of Saint Paul's injunction to women, which the loving Sor Filotea had used as one of her own premises in exhorting Juana to curb her intellectual pursuits: "Let women keep silent in the churches; for it is not permitted them to speak." Using Juan Díaz de Arce's exposition on this issue in *For the Scholar of the Bible*, she concluded:

Arce at last resolves, in his prudent way, that women are not al-lowed to lecture publicly in the universities or to preach from the pulpits, but that studying, writing, and teaching privately is not only permitted but most beneficial and useful to them. Clearly, of course, he does not mean by this that all women should do so, but only those whom God may have seen fit to endow with special virtue and prudence, and who are very mature and erudite and possess the necessary talents and requirements for such a sacred occupation. And so just is this distinction that not only women, who are held to be so incompetent, but also men, who simply because they are men think themselves wise, are to be prohibited from the interpretation of the Sacred Word, save when they are most learned, virtuous, of amenable intellect and inclined to the good.

"Tía! Still awake?"

Belilla's words startled her. Her neck jabbed sharply to one side, sending an arrow of pain down to the middle of her back. She felt her face freeze in a silent wince of agony.

"Oh, Tía, I'm sorry," cried the girl, rushing to her side. "I thought you'd heard me opening the door. I knocked several times."

"You know I don't hear anything when I'm writing," she said, holding her head stiffly while Belilla rubbed at the strained muscle in her neck.

"It feels like a rope with knots in it," said Belilla.

"What are you doing awake? You're taking charge of my morning class."

"I was having such a bad dream, Tía. I dreamt you had drowned in the fountain in the courtyard and your body was just floating there and there were all these people walking by, some were throwing rocks, others rose petals into the water, and you had two gold pesos on your eyes and a black feather coming out of your mouth and your hands were crossed over your chest and you were holding your book instead of a rosary—"

"Gently, cariño!" said Juana. "Don't squeeze the muscle like that."

"Forgive me, Tía, just thinking about the dream makes me nervous. What do you think it means? It feels like a bad augur."

"You were just worried about me in the bath," she said.

Juana moved away from her niece's hand. She would have to pace now, to work the kink out, otherwise she couldn't hold her head up and wouldn't be able to continue with her response.

"Why don't you go make us some chocolate," she suggested. "Make it nice and frothy, the way I like it, and bring me some dry meat and bread. Go on. I'm suddenly so hungry."

"We have some leftover arroz con leche," said Belilla.

"That would be nice, too, as long as it hasn't soured."

"Don't you want to go with me to the kitchen, Tía? Don't you need to take a rest? You've been working since before compline and it's almost three in the morning."

"You go on," said Juana. "I'll just walk and do my breathing exercises until you return."

"Promise you won't work?"

"I have to finish this tonight. I've decided to give up writing for Lent."

"But, Tía—"

"Belilla! Do as I say!"

"Yes, Tía." The girl hurried out of the study and Juana did her exercise, taking a deep breath as she paced in one direction and exhaling it slowly in the other. Her lungs hurt, she noticed, as though she were afflicted with catarrh, though she had none of the other symptoms, yet. It was probably the bath, she thought, and slipped her hand under the veil. Her scalp felt a little damp still. She had forgotten to dry her hair before sitting down to work.

Belilla returned with a large clay platter that held the chocolate pot, the cups, the bread and strips of meat and rice pudding. In one of the cups she saw some dried linden blossoms that Belilla intended to steep in her chocolate to help her sleep without nightmares. They sat at the map table eating and drinking in silence. When they had finished, Juana lit a cigarillo and smoked it while Belilla built up the fire in the brazier. For the first time Juana noticed how gaunt and pale her niece looked. She had lost more weight, and she barely had the strength to work the bellows.

Juana felt a shiver run down her spine and drew the blanket more tightly around her. "I want you to go to bed now, cariño," she said. "You look like you haven't slept in weeks."

"I've been keeping a vigil for you, Tía."

"Don't be ridiculous, Belilla. Look to your own health."

Suddenly the girl was squatting in front of her, gripping her knees and looking up at Juana with teary eyes. "That dream frightened me so much. What if it means something's going to happen to you? What will I do without you?"

She stroked Belilla's cheek with the back of her ink-stained fingers and sighed so deeply it hurt her back. She felt so old for a moment and burdened with the knowledge that her life was an example for this girl and for all girls who sought to rise above their biological destinies. "Something is always happening to me, *cariño*, and somehow I resist it or fight it or survive it. The *respuesta*—" she gestured toward the papers littered all around them "—is meant to achieve all three. Now, go on. Get to bed."

The girl nodded and wiped the tears off her face with the collar of her night shift. "I think I'll wash the dishes tomorrow, after Mass," she said, eyelids quivering as she gathered up their plates and cups. "It's Ash Wednesday, don't forget."

Juana glanced up at the clock. In another two hours it would be time for prime. "Go and rest."

"I wish I could keep you company, Tía," Belilla yawned, and Juana watched her carry the platter out of the room as though she were a student taking reluctant leave of her teacher. This is what Juana had needed more than anything as a girl, to have been taught by an older woman how to use her intelligence to shape her life. Instead, Juana had learned that lesson on her own, through repeated struggle and persecution. The only teachers she had had were men like her uncle and the Bishop of Puebla and her own father confessor, Padre Antonio, whose intent was not to edify but to own and oppress.

She turned to a fresh page in the notebook and began a new passage extolling the virtues of women teachers. She had not thought about this earlier, but it made absolute sense that educated women should teach young girls.

For what impropriety can there be if an older woman, learned in letters and holy conversation and customs, should have in her charge the education of young maids? Better so than to let these young girls go to perdition, either for lack of any Christian teaching or because one tries to impart it through such dangerous means as male teachers. For if there were no greater risk than the simple decency of seating a completely unknown man at the side of a bashful woman (who blushes if her own father should look her straight in the face), allowing him to address her with household familiarity and to speak to her with intimate authority, even so the modesty demanded in interchange with men and in conversation with them gives sufficient cause to forbid this. Indeed, I do not see how the custom of men as teachers of women can be without its dangers, save only in the strict tribunal of the confessional, or the distant teachings of the pulpit, or the remote wisdom of books; but never in the repeated handling that occurs in such immediate and tarnishing contact.

By the time the Angelus announced the first Office of the day, she had finished the *narratio* of her defense and needed only the conclusion. Having missed compline the night before, she knew it would be in her best interest to attend the service, but she could not pull herself away from the response. She would just have to abide Andrea's anger and suffer the grievances lodged against her at the next chapter meeting: insubordinate, they would call her, impious, incorrigible. What did it matter, anyway? When she was dead and buried her rebellion would mean nothing in comparison to the import of this treatise.

She wrote a hasty note to Andrea begging her indulgence one more time while she concluded the last pages of the response and sent it with the groggy Belilla. When the girl had gone, Juana changed into her regular habit, her back straining under the weight of the veil, then went to the kitchen to boil some coffee and fix herself a fried egg. All that was left was her defense of poetry as both a sacred and a scholarly form and her closing remarks to her beneficent sister, Sor Filotea. She marked her own forehead with soot from the stove.

"I was wrong, Juana," said Don Carlos, closing the notebook that contained her *Respuesta*. "*Carta atenagórica* was a child's rhyme compared to this magnum opus."

She coughed into her kerchief and nodded her gratitude. The inflammation in her larynx had taken her voice away and she found it supremely ironic, if not poetic justice in the extreme, that her rebuttal of Saint Paul's dictum for the silence of women in religious matters should be followed by this infection in her throat that left her voiceless.

Don Carlos opened the notebook again, near the end, and read aloud: "'Is it bold of me to oppose Vieyra, yet not so for the Reverend Father to oppose the three holy Fathers of the Church? Is my mind, such as it is, less free than his, though it derives from the same source? Is his opinion to be taken as one of the principles of the Holy Faith made manifest, that we must believe it blindly?'"

His dark eyes were glittering with triumph when he looked up. "You are a genius of the rhetorical question, Juana. I take my hat off to your brilliance!"

Since she could not speak she made a face at him and he burst into laughter.

"And this—" He stood up to read. "'And so, with the few things of mine that have been printed, the appearance of my name—and, indeed, permission for the printing itself—have not followed my own decision, but another's liberty that does not lie under my control, as was the case with the 'Letter Worthy of Athena.'" A completely lucid and fearless rebuke, Juana, which I'm glad to see repeated several times throughout the text." He turned quickly to the last page. "But this, of all, is my favorite passage: 'If the style of this letter, my venerable Lady, has been less than your due, I beg your pardon for its household familiarity or the lack of seemly respect. For in addressing you, my sister, as a nun of the veil, I have forgotten the distance between myself and your most distinguished person, which should not occur were I to see you unveiled.'"

He laughed again, and she heard a vindictive reverberation in his throat.

"You have, in effect, unveiled the Bishop, Juana," he said, gray teeth showing through his mischievous smile, "and also turned his little masquerade in on himself, for now he is a gelded bishop, your sister, with whom you share the household familiarity of equal status. He sought to reprimand you in the manner of other bishops set on correcting errant nuns, and your response takes him at his word and completely assumes the feminine gender of your correspondent, thus, as you say, removing any distance between the real nun and the false one. He is no longer your superior. Bravo, Juana! Bravo!" He started to applaud, and the sound echoed in the silence of the locutory. "Or is 'Ole!' more appropriate?"

She smiled at him but could not share in his glee. She knew that a particularly fierce and courageous bull could be pardoned in the ring, but not if he had gored his matador.

Would you do me the favor of delivering a copy to the Bishop? she scribbled on the slate she had brought.

He frowned at her request, stroking the stubble on his chin.

"I would be honored to serve as your messenger, Sor Juana," he said.

She shook her head. That's not what she meant.

"But I would feel forced to inform the Archbishop of its contents."

WHY??? she wrote.

"In my new capacity as assessor for the Inquisition," he said, biting his lip. "It seems Padre Antonio can no longer perform that task without help, and the Archbishop has named me as his assistant."

Juana closed her eyes. The vein in her neck started to throb. Why hadn't he said anything before? Why had he blithely allowed her to show him this document when it was clear it would compromise his post, if not their friendship?

Have I lost my friend? she scribbled.

"You would never lose my support, Juana, and I would never do anything to harm you. It's just that if the Bishop were to inform Aguiar y Seijas that it was I who delivered your response, he would remove me from every post he's seen fit to give me, and then what would I do, Juana? You know the bills I have to pay."

They stared at each other across the grille.

"You must believe me, Juana."

Her eyes raked across his face.

"What if I ask one of my students to deliver your response the next time the Bishop is in Mexico? Is that to your liking?"

Promise me you will not share this with anybody. Please, please, please.

He knelt before her, took one of her hands through the grille and kissed it just above the knuckles. His lips felt cold and sticky on her skin, like oysters, but in his eyes she could read his loyalty and felt comforted, for the moment.

That night and for many nights afterward she could not sleep, besieged with worry over the fate of her response, over her own fate as a consequence of having sent it with Don Carlos. There were measures she had to take to protect herself—and Belilla, too—if she were condemned by the Inquisition. But why should the Holy Office condemn her? She had written nothing sacrilegious, nothing against the faith or against her vows. It was nothing but a nun's atonement, prompted by the unauthorized publication of a private letter. Surely the wise officers of the Inquisition could distinguish between heresy and confession. But what if they couldn't? The best thing she could do, for now, was protect herself economically.

She had 1,400 pesos saved from her commissions, and she would ask license to place this money into the convent's Deposit Box, to be invested in the purchase of some houses near the convent of the Capuchins that Andrea and her administration wanted to add to San Jerónimo's real estate.

She would ask a modest yield from this investment, 5 percent of it, or 70 gold pesos, to be paid to her annually until the time of her death, at which time the same amount was to be paid to Belilla for the rest of her life. As part owner of said real estate, her name would be placed on the title of the property and a copy of this title would be kept in her possession.

Only after she had executed her idea, after all the petitions were written and approved in the convent's Book of Profession, the notes signed, and the transaction witnessed by royal scribes—including a clause about punctual quarterly payments of her annuity beginning the following year—was Juana able to sleep again, resting in the knowledge that, no matter what the consequences of la Respuesta, she and Belilla could never be removed from the convent without breach of contract.

Chapter 28

Dearest Juana,

A month has passed since the *auto de fe* in the Plaza Mayor, and I
am still sickened by the stench of burning flesh and hair. I still hear
the lamentations of the condemned in my dreams. Thank God I did
not allow Tomás to take Josesito, for that would have been a most
cruel way of observing the Feast of the Immaculate Conception. How
can a city as advanced as Madrid be so barbaric in its punishment of
supposed criminals, whose only crime, in truth, is their disaffection
from an impotent Crown and a barren faith. Tomás reads over my
shoulder and warns me to curb my words, for the familiars of the
Inquisition are everywhere and royal seals matter very little in this
time of suspicion and turmoil. But I am not worried about my own
fate; it is yours that concerns me, Juana. That rebuttal against Vieyra
is one of your scholastic masterpieces, no doubt, but that alone is
cause for great consternation. Vieyra is revered by many, not the least
of which is Aguiar y Seijas, and I worry that you will antagonize him
beyond all measure and that he, in turn, will bring down the heavy
hand of the Church upon you. Tomás, dear heart, despite his illness,
reads your work avidly and in those moments I see the light return to
his eyes, and yet, even he is worried about the consequences of this
rebuttal. I will, of course, include it in the new volume, along with
"Primero Sueño," but first I shall seek the approval of some good
friends—theologians, all seven of them—and publish their views
with your text. Perhaps this will afford you some protection. Now
that Mancera has withdrawn as one of your protectors, it is up to
Tomás and me to do what we can for our Juana. And now I must
return to my editorial tasks. Your fame, my *décima musa*, is like a
bridge between Spain and her colonies. You should see the inundation
(couldn't resist that pun) of purchase orders we've received for

Castalian Inundation from booksellers in Barcelona, Santiago, Lima, Havana, Oaxaca, Puebla, even Santa Fe, not to mention your own fair city.

Please don't forget to send the prologue to the second volume as soon as you finish it. The Flota is late this year. Who knows when you will get this?

Anxiously yours,
Maria Luisa
Epiphany 1691

18 JUNE 1691

MY DEAREST CONDESA,

This is the last letter I shall write for a while, for I have agreed, as a special favor to Andrea, who is now our new Mother Superior, to give up my writing until such time as these relentless rains cease their hold upon the city. Every little sacrifice counts, she says. The gazette reports that the wheat and corn crops are ruined, and this will, no doubt, have dire repercussions on the *castas*. Our gate is besieged by those begging for bread at all hours. Several of our eldest sisters have died, for the rain brings much cold and damp, and, now that even our firewood is being rationed, there is not enough fuel to keep us warm through the night. Much has changed since your and Don Tomás's departure. I hear it said that the people blame de Galve for these rains and devastations.

Still no word from the Bishop about la Respuesta, though it's been over three months that I sent it to him. Indeed, in my own small world, these rains are a compensation for the drought of visitors that has befallen my afternoons. Not even Don Carlos comes for our weekly *tertulia*, and I can only imagine that his absence has something to do with the Respuesta. I find it terribly eerie that while *Carta atenagórica* received almost immediate (though negative) responses from clerics and professors and scholars all over the realm, the Respuesta has generated complete silence. Of course, the Respuesta has not been published, and that probably accounts for some of this silence; and yet I know that the Bishop has circulated the manuscript to his usual cronies in Puebla and Mexico. I know the Archbishop has read it, for Father Nazario told me the Archbishop had sought his counsel regarding my spiritual life, he said, after having read something exceedingly disturbing that I had recently written. Once this penance is over and I can find a way of purchasing more paper, I will have Belilla make a copy of la Respuesta to mail to you.

The chill feels like a knife in my bones. I must stop now and get back to balancing the accounts before my fingers go numb. Will write again tomorrow.

24 JUNE 1691

Forgive my long absence, Señora, but we have been in mourning for Mother Brígida, who died of a severe inflammation of the lungs. Today's procession in honor of Saint John's Day was filled with flagellants in *penitente* hats clamoring to Heaven for delivery from this watery punishment. All classes have been suspended and the boarders sent home to their families, as it is getting more and more difficult to feed everyone.

7 JULY 1691

Here again, Lady. There is no hurry, now, to get this letter to the post since de Galve has not had the causeways repaired and there is little traffic to or from the city. The rain ceased yesterday after nearly a month of continuous downpour, but now an ungodly heat inundates the city and a horrific stench rises up with the steam that issues from the flooded ground and mixes with the smell of rotted flesh from the meat market down the street. I can barely breathe without wanting to retch. Belilla has volunteered to help in the infirmary and I pray to the Virgin that she not become ill. Her body—slender as it is—is of a much stronger mettle than mine, but none can escape the effect of those putrescent fumes. Forgive all of these sordid details, Lady, but this letter is now both missive and chronicle.

12 JULY 1691

A new calamity has befallen us, an infestation of the *chahuixtle* weevil that has now spoiled the stores of the granaries. Famine reigns over the city and we have had to let go most of our servants, save the slaves and *beatas*. We are on a diet of a cup of beans and one yam a day, supplemented by two eggs every Friday. Andrea has posted a guard on the chicken coop to ensure that none of us is tempted out of hunger to steal one of the hens. I dreamt the taste of pineapple water and squash blossom quesadillas.

29 JULY 1691

A bruised and myopic Don Carlos appeared in the locutory yesterday. It seems he and the Archbishop got into an argument about my Respuesta and the Archbishop attacked him with his cane, shattering Don Carlos's spectacles on his face. It's a wonder the glass didn't damage his eyes, although the flesh is completely swollen and purple around them and he has intense headaches, he says, that feel like coagulated blood pulsing between his eyes. Aguiar y Seijas is a brute!

Don Carlos begs my forgiveness for his absence, but the rain and his increased obligations and then this attack all prevented him from visiting. When I asked him what news he had heard regarding the Respuesta he changed the subject, and only just before leaving did he tell me that the Bishop and the Archbishop are plotting some form of retaliation against me. He says I've scandalized them so much they're afraid of making the manuscript public for fear of stirring up the Inquisition. Why does that specter haunt my life like a malevolent shadow?

I have Belilla making a copy of the Respuesta so that I can include it with this letter and send it out as soon as the post resumes. Perhaps you would be so kind as to circulate it to Fray Payo and the Marquis de Mancera, and perhaps they will write apologies in defense of it. Belilla does not have Concepción's calligraphic skills, but she works more efficiently without all those fancy flourishes that used to take Concepción so much time. I hope you like it, Señora, well enough to include in a future volume. All my best to Don Tomás and my godson,

I kiss your feet,
Juana

"You mentioned earlier, Sor Melchora, that Padre Antonio and Sor Juana were always arguing about the love poems she wrote to la Condesa."

"Yes, Sir. He said that it was not only irreverent for her to be writing secular poems, and exchanging gifts with la Condesa on a regular basis, but that the passion displayed in those poems was anathema to her sex and her vocation."

"Rafaela, why don't you show the Archbishop those fragments you copied from her correspondence with the Vicereine."

"I daresay, Sister, you spent a good part of your time copying."

"Their correspondence has always been prolific, Sir, what we've seen of it anyway. There are many things we didn't see, things that arrived with a royal seal that we dared not break, things that were delivered in secret by that assistant of hers or by a royal page, ordered to stand by the gate to await Sor Juana's response."

"So the letters go back to the time when Don Tomás was still Viceroy?"

"Sadly, no, Your Grace. As Sor Rafaela said, there was much of their correspondence that we didn't see, either because she burned it or hid it in that box that no one has been able to locate. This has all been taken from la Condesa's letters since she returned to Spain."

"'That you are a woman, that you are absent, none of this is important, for the soul ignores gender and distance.'"

"Aren't you going to read any more, Your Reverence? There is one letter in particular that you're going to find very *illuminating*, shall we say."

"Not now, Sister. I'll read everything you've given me in my own time and return the whole bundle to you when the case is closed."

"But it's the only documentation we have, Your Grace."

"And it's in good hands, Sister. I commend you both for your foresight. I daresay you've earned yourselves another decade's worth of indulgence from His Ilustrísima. Of course, you could both eschew purgatory altogether if you could produce that famous letter box of hers."

"We're still looking for it, Your Grace."

"Now, then, Sor Agustina, what can you tell us about Sor Juana's relationship to the Vicereine?"

"Which one?"

"La Condesa de Paredes, of course. You do remember that friendship, don't you?"

"I remember it perfectly, if that's what you want to call it."

"What would you call it, Sister?"

"An abomination, what else? Two women kissing on the lips!"

"What did you say?"

"Oh, yes, Your Grace. It's not an invention. I saw it myself. On the day they came to say good-bye, her and the Viceroy. They didn't want any of the rest of us around. Don Tomás said something offensive to Mother Brígida and all of us got up and left the locutory, all except Juana, of course."

"I took notes, Your Grace."

"You are an archivist at heart, Sor Rafaela. Proceed, Sor Agustina."

"Melchora asked me to stay behind, and keep my eye on them, so I left the locutory door cracked and watched them. La Condesa sent her husband out to deal with the trunk of Juana's writings and when he was gone, she—"

"Who? La Condesa or Sor Juana?"

"La Condesa, Your Reverence. She took Juana's face between her hands and kissed her."

"On the lips? Are you sure?"

"Like a lover."

"Did Sor Juana pull away?"

"Didn't look that way to me, Sir. To me it appeared she kissed her back."

"But you're not sure?"

"I don't know anything about kissing, Your Reverence, but I do know that la Condesa kissed Sor Juana, not once, but twice. And the second time was right in front of her husband."

"And what did Don Tomás do?"

"He picked up Sor Juana's foot and kissed the sole of her shoe."

"This is no jest, Sister! You might be impugning a good man."

"It's what I saw, Your Reverence. Like I said, I'm not inventing things."

"I've always known there was something sinful in that friendship. But for Don Tomás to be involved! Who could believe such a thing? The Viceroy of New Spain kissing the sole of a nun's shoe!"

"Looking on as his wife kisses the lips of another woman."

"A religious woman. Supposedly."

"You see, Sisters. It's the degeneracy of the Spanish court. Is it any wonder that we, the subjects of that corrupt Crown, are being punished with these rains? Is it any wonder that Juana has not only gotten away with every transgression but is actually celebrated for her willfulness and disobedience?"

"Did we mention, Your Grace, that Sor Juana and her niece spent the night, illicitly I might add, at la Condesa's house upon their return from the mother's funeral?"

"I don't remember hearing that story, Sister."

"One of their footmen was a close friend of Mother Brígida's personal maid, and he told her all about it. Good girl that she is, she immediately reported it to the Mother Superior, but Brígida didn't seem very interested in the information, and never questioned Juana about it. Except for myself, none of the other prioresses has ever known how to discipline Juana."

"What did the girl report?"

"It seems Sor Juana and the Count made an evening of it, Your Grace. They smoked cigars and drank several bottles of wine and all manner of liquor until daybreak. Like *compadres*, according to the footman's description."

"The woman has no respect, no sense of propriety whatsoever."

"Never has, Your Grace, especially not when encouraged by the palace."

"Those days are certainly finished, Sisters."

Feast of the Assumption

Don Carlos brought me two of his publications today: his anthology on the Spanish Armada's victory over the French in Florida (to which I contributed a poem) and that old *relación* of his concerning the Caribbean youth Alonso Ramírez, which none of our local publishers had ever been enthusiastic about printing. I guess his association with the Archbishop is proving a boon to his writing career. He and the Widow Calderón seem to have renewed their friendship. I wondered how, in the midst of all of this turmoil with the rains and the heat, any printing can be going on, but I didn't ask. Don Carlos is exceedingly sensitive of late and he would, no doubt, be vexed by my question. He says he's heard that the second edition of my book is now circulating in Madrid. I guess I'll have to wait until the next Flota to see it.

23 August

It is just after tierce and yet the city is cast in darkness. I write by the quavery glow of a rancid oil lamp. Outside the convent, an incessant howling of dogs and braying of donkeys and tolling of bells and everywhere people screaming. The rains ended only to give way to a solar eclipse and this, more than the flooding, will invigorate the superstitious talk that has spread like the *chahuixtle*. Even Don Carlos believes that God is punishing Mexico.

"We are an impious lot, Juana," he said when I saw him last.

"Blighted crops for blighted souls?" I asked.

"It would seem just, Juana. Aren't you guilty of grave sin? I know I am."

"Are you saying, then, that we must feel responsible for these devastations? You surprise me, Don Carlos. What happened to the mathematician who trusted only the truth of numbers or to the scientist behind his telescope who used to thank God for the opportunity to study natural phenomena?"

"Even the Aztec astronomers believed in signs, Juana. God, of whatever denomination, has always worked in mysterious ways."

"I see that association with the Archbishop is taking its toll on you, Sigüenza," I said, unable to avoid the sarcasm in my voice.

"And I see that lack of association with the same person has produced a disbelief beyond all Christian measure, Sor Juana." There was no sarcasm in his statement.

I knew it. I knew I would lose Don Carlos eventually, and it seems so odd that, despite that beating which nearly blinded him, he has grown so fond of Aguiar y Seijas that he has actually sold part of his library at the Archbishop's request, and donated the proceeds to the Brotherhood of Mercy. But I suppose that is the way of men, to bond with one another and forget their friendships with women. But I fear in my heart that Don Carlos may be right, that this darkness is a sign in my own life of the eclipse of my influence in the world. It has been five months since I wrote the Respuesta and it is as though it had fallen into a void where only silence and darkness prevails. No comets or constellations to offer respite from the dark. No sound except the ticking of my feeble heart.

curfew

Andrea announced after sext (an eerie Office it was with our lamps lighting the lower choir at midday and the empty church like a black pit illuminated only by votives) that the Viceroy had sent a petition to all the convents and monasteries entreating the religious to do what we can to remove this curse of darkness from Mexico. Andrea ordered that we were to walk around the cloister in our short veils and scourges until vespers. Walking in pathetic circles in that turgid twilight, we prayed the fifteen mysteries of the rosary, and after each Hail Mary we had to discipline ourselves with one lash and after each Our Father we administered three lashes. I counted each one, it was the only thing that kept me from yelling at Andrea, and we gave ourselves a total of 195 lashes. Only the sickest and the eldest were excused from this exercise. Even the *beatas* and the children of the maids had to join us, though Andrea at least limited the whipping to the professed. I shudder at this grotesque display of ignorance and superstition that we call faith. Now I sit here with comfrey compresses on the welts and pray they don't become infected.

1 September

Whether or not our penitence had any effect (the superstitious would say that the sound of the wailing and the praying and the whipping, combined with similar sounds from the other religious communities, congealed into one piercing note that spiraled up into that black snail shell of the spheres and released the earth's shadow from the sun) the eclipse lifted and five days of a strong wind have cleared the air of its humid stench. There is still no corn or wheat or fresh produce, but the city seems to have awakened from its stupor and the streets are filled with the sounds of hammering and hauling as roofs and bridges get repaired. The gazette reports that the Viceroy has the Indians cleaning the aqueduct, for it is impossible to get fresh water into the city, choked as the aqueduct is with debris from the flood. Though the streets of the *traza* are still muddy channels, the Plaza Mayor has been drained, and Mass will resume in the Cathedral. From my bench in the *beata*'s chapel I hear the singsong rhyme of vendors and the shouting of children, and feel grateful that our world is returning to order, though there is still much hunger to appease.

10 September

Have received a missive from the Archbishop—terse and succinct—in which he forbids me to take up the pen unless it is for a religious purpose: a *villancico*, a spiritual exercise, or the like. If I should disregard his command and write anything of a secular or personal nature, he will take the matter to the Inquisition. Moreover, he has closed my accounts with the booksellers and requests that either I return all my books or pay off the balances immediately. Finally, he orders me to sell a part of my library and donate the proceeds to the College of San Juan de Letrán, which was almost completely devastated by the rains. He will send two of his friars with a trunk to collect the books I'm going to sell tomorrow morning. So this is it? This is the response to my Respuesta? They are severe measures, to be sure, but nothing in comparison to what I expected. Was it my imagination that the Respuesta was such a dangerous document, or is this just the beginning of a much greater censure? Now I must select the books I can live without and decide which others to give up. And I shall have to ask the booksellers if they can wait until my sister's return to pay off my balances. She has three months of rent to collect from that cobbler and I have more jewels for her to sell. I am not solvent now with my most recent investment.

20 October

A cold wind rattling at the shutters, piercing my tunic as I returned from music class. The poor girls are tired of singing the same *villancicos*, repeating the scales, but I have no desire to do anything new. No will to read or write for over a month. Didn't even send la Condesa a letter for her birthday on the 3d. Belilla tells me I look like a scarecrow in a habit since my appetite left with that trunk of books the Archbishop forced me to sell. Still no word from the Bishop of Puebla or Sigüenza.

Day of all Souls

Dreamt I was living at palace again eating the sweetest *mameyes* and debating with the Marquis de Mancera over the saintliness of Catherine of Alexandria. He kept calling her a mystic, and I kept insisting that she was a scholar of the highest caliber and used the example of her examination by those fifty philosophers as my evidence of her advanced learning. And then suddenly I was reliving my own examination that the Marquis himself had arranged with those forty professors from the University of Mexico, and I realized whilst still dreaming that Saint Catherine and I were victims of the same persecution, for she was persecuted for her faith in Christianity and for refusing to submit to the will of that libidinous pagan emperor, and I am persecuted for my faith in education and my failure to submit to the will of the Church. I think I have found a solution to my ennui and inertia. Since *villancicos* are on the Archbishop's list of approved writing, I'm going to write a set of *villancicos* in honor of Saint Catherine in time for her feast day on the 25th and offer it to the Cabildo to be sung in the Cathedral.

12 November

Don Carlos was the only one who remembered my birthday today. He brought me a copy of the second edition of the first volume of my book, wrapped in brown vellum and tied with a velvet ribbon, procured in secret from the Widow Calderón. The shipment arrived on the Flota, but the Archbishop is preventing its sale until my punishment is lifted. Don Carlos says the booksellers are furious with him. My friend looks warier than usual and a bit like he's dragging his tail between his legs. I showed him my *villancicos* and he balked at the idea of offering them to the Cabildo. He says he's certain the Archbishop would censor them and send the Inquisition to my door.

"But they're *villancicos* in honor of a saint," I protested. "It's not secular poetry."

"Yes, Juana, but look at the saint you chose to eulogize. You don't think the parallels between you and Saint Catherine would escape Aguiar y Seijas, do you?"

To make amends for his recent intolerant and ridiculous behavior, he says, he will take them once they're finished to the Cathedral in Oaxaca where he is sure the Church Council will happily accept and perform the carols. Is it his Aquarian nature that makes him change direction so easily, like the wind changing its course? But what does it matter as long as he's returned to his senses? And I agree that the Cabildo and the Archbishop would probably censor the *villancicos* anyway, since they speak too clearly of my own affront to male authority. Let Saint Catherine's praises be sung in Oaxaca! *Victor! Victor!*

27 *November*

Scribbling this. Just returned from confession. Father Nazario says the Archbishop is removing him as my confessor, and he's ordered Andrea to lock up my pens and my notebooks. *Villancicos* to Saint Catherine were a colossal mistake, Father Nazario says, made him look like a fool in front of his superior. Rubbing the Church's face in the excrement of my effrontery, is what the Archbishop called it. Where is la Condesa? Why hasn't she written? Has everyone abandoned me to this torture of silence?

Chapter 29

Querida y entrañable JUANA,

Forgive me for not having responded sooner, but I have been at the bedside of my poor Tomás for several months now and I regret to say that his health does not improve. His condition is one that the medics do not discuss with a woman, not even a wife, but whatever it is it causes him horrific pain, despite the heavy doses of laudanum he's given. And now a strange dementia has overcome him and he does not recognize me anymore, keeps calling me by a name he used to call his mother. By the time this reaches you in Mexico he may, God willing, be gone. It's not that I want him dead, Juana—and you are the only one I dare to trust with these thoughts, knowing that you understand me—it's just that he's in so much pain and it seems a grave injustice for a man who was such a good man to have to die in this ignoble way. Tomás dead! Just the thought of it makes me feel so desperately alone, and I begin to understand the sense of perpetual loss that you describe in your letters. The medics are quite certain that Tomás will not last another month. And what will I do then? Were it not for José (your godson has grown quite handsome and, though he is only nine, has already fetched the hearts of several of my ladies) I would lock myself in a cloister or brave the sea again and return to New Spain. But I have the boy's future at court to think about and the Queen Mother—whom Tomás was serving as Mayordomo—says she likes to think of José as the grandson that another María Luisa (may our French Queen rest in peace) never gave her. Now that the King has married again, who knows how long our favor will last. I must cultivate this affection of the Queen Mother's for my son, though of course there are those who sneer at him behind the Queen Mother's back for having been born in New Spain, and I am reminded that the only court for a *criollo* is in the colonies.

As you can imagine, Juana, with Tomás's illness I was not able during the summer and autumn to devote much time to the second volume of your works, but I am happy to report that I completed assembling all of the pieces after Christmas and the book is now at the publishers with publication set for July or August. With any luck you will see a copy before the end of the year. I think you will find that volume surprising for several reasons. The first, of course, is that it contains some of your finest work—that intricate, mystical "Sueño" which opens the poetry section and that bold, brilliant critique of Vieyra (which I've retitled, with your permission, as "Crisis of a Sermon," since I do not like using anybody else's titles but my own)—which opens the book, followed by the endorsements of my good friends. That should make an impact upon Fernández de Santa Cruz and Aguiar y Seijas, don't you think? That peninsular theologians should agree with the work of their female nemesis and denounce the work of their Portuguese idol!!! It is such a victory for you, Juana, and I wish I could be there to witness the effects of these responses on your superiors. Speaking of responses, I did not include "Response to Sor Filotea" in the volume, though I did receive it in time, because I believe it deserves to be published on its own. It is much too perfect and complete of a text to be bundled up with so many others. What reactions have you received, I wonder? And did Fernández de Santa Cruz take it upon himself to get this printed, as well? Somehow I don't think so. It would not be to his advantage to publish a work that so thoroughly disproves the allegations of this country bumpkin, this Sor Filotea. I shall, therefore, hold off on the publication of your Respuesta until the situation is clearer there with you.

Dearest Juana, you have no idea how I ache to see you, what I would give to be close to you again and touch your ink-stained hands and look into the dark inkwells of your eyes to read the words that your pen no longer writes to me. I pray to the Virgin of Guadalupe (our own dark Madonna for whom the one in Tepeyac was named) that you are well and holding up under the stress of these puerile attacks against your intellect. Those priests may be superior in gender and station, Juana, but they know perfectly well that they don't come up to your heels in intelligence. Receive all of my love and many kisses from your godson,

María Luisa

21st of February 1692

It had been more than three months since la Condesa had written the letter, which only last week had arrived in Vera Cruz on the Flota and just today been delivered in Mexico. The Count of Paredes was gone, no doubt, and Juana wept at the thought of his illness and his pain, at the loss of another protector, and offered mute prayers to his memory while her sisters chanted the evening Office. After compline, she bought a candle from the Sister sacristan and added it to her altar. Now, she would have to light eight candles—for her grandfather, la Marquesa, Aunt Mary, her mother, Mother Catalina, Sor Felipa, Mother Brígida, and now her *compadre*, Don Tomás.

She prayed a decade of Hail Marys and three Our Fathers to the memory of the Count and spent a time—she knew not how long—in silent mourning. She had been silent for nearly six months, since the end of November when the Archbishop had ordered that every writing tool of hers be taken away. Watching Melchora and Agustina throwing her quills and inkwells into a box, she had vowed not to speak again until those instruments were returned, and if they were never returned, then she would never utter another word. Her speaking voice, after all, was but the echo of her true voice, which flowed from her pens and spoke in solid, measured tones on the page.

At first Andrea and Belilla had both begged her to give up her vow. Belilla said it was like living with a ghost, and that it frightened her so much she preferred to stay in the infirmary and the classroom all day. Andrea went so far as to call it an indulgence of self-pity rather than what others mistakenly interpreted as penitence. It was neither penitence nor self-pity, but a rage and an indignation so profound, so unbearably loud that it almost deafened her from within.

At night in her sleep she could feel herself ranting in fury, mouthing all the words she had repressed during the day: How dare you remove my voice? Why don't you cut into my throat and pull out my vocal chords, yank out my tongue, pluck out my eyes, fill my nose and ears with tallow, slice off the tips of my fingers? Each one of my faculties is tied to my quill. Without it I am blind and deaf and mute and insensate. My thoughts twist around like worms in my head. My mind rots in this silence, my spirit becomes ash. I'm completely empty. I'm completely alone without my voice.

And she would dream images of a sacrifice in which she was the victim laid out on the sacrificial slab, with the Bishop and the Archbishop as High Priests and Andrea and Melchora and Agustina as their minions handing them the instruments of her torture: a rosary noose, a veil of thorns, a bit for her mouth, and a crucifix with sharp points that folded into scissors.

She would wake up just as the Archbishop, invoking the names of Abraham and Saint Paul, stabbed the shears into her neck, and find Belilla sitting up in her bed, huddled under her blankets, the whites of her eyes phosphorescent in the moonlight pouring through the window.

"This is terrifying me, Tía," Belilla would say. "Won't you please say something? I won't tell anybody that you spoke."

But Juana could not speak. She would get out of bed, go to her study, bring Pandora's Box out of hiding, and stare at the watermark on a blank page imagining her hand scribbling in illegible scrawls. She had made the mistake of leaving the quill that she always kept in the box out on her desk the last time she'd written and it, too, had been found, marking a page in a book, and taken away. For a few weeks she had picked up every stray feather she found in the courtyard or the orchard, hoarding them like precious coins in the pockets of her tunic, until somebody reported her. She had no ink anyway. The soot she scraped from the braziers and mixed with water made a thin, unstable concoction that the brittle pens could not absorb.

She started forgetting things: the words to a prayer or a chant, the names of her nieces and nephews (even Belilla's name, for a day, was lost to her), the titles of her favorite fictions. Once, she picked up her copy of *Castalian Inundation*, read her own name as the author, and could not remember having written anything in the book, much less having felt any of the emotions that blossomed on every page. The bravado in those last lines of her prologue to the reader: "And so, Godspeed, this is no more than a sample of the fiber: if the fabric pleases not, do not unfold the bundle." The ironies of that poem to the Peruvian who had sent her those clay pots. Castaño's humor in *Trials of a Noble House* as he dressed himself in the blue skirts and shawl of a lady and was taken to be Doña Leonor, wooed by Don Pedro. The cunning wordplay of her satire on stubborn men. The sorrow in those requiems to la Marquesa and those boldly rendered passions in every poem to la Condesa.

A passageway to Venus' gardens,
your throat is an ivory organ
whose music melodiously ensnares
the very wind in bonds of ecstasy.

Tendrils of crystal and of snow,
your two white arms incite desires doomed
to barrenness, like those of Tantalus:
thirst unslaked by water, fruitless hunger.

Who had she been then? And how had she come from that proliferation of verse and feeling to this barren wasteland of worms?

When she received la Condesa's letter she did not know who could be writing her from Spain, but after the first few sentences the waters of her memory were unloosed, and for several days she felt like Noah's Ark adrift in a deluge of remembrance.

She remembered *Neptuno alegórico*, and how she had fretted over finding the perfect mythological conceit for the arch; with a luxury of detail, she recalled long conversations in the locutory, the arguments with la Condesa about the comet, the Viceroy's chronicles of the northern territories, of the pueblos that had revolted against their missionaries and held off the Church for several years, of the giant, man-eating catfish in the limpid rivers of Paso del Norte, of the green twilights along the Camino Real. The last memory came in a torrent of awareness: the bacchanalian evening she had spent as their guest, and the double-edged pleasures that she had allowed herself.

Her lips, the silk of her flesh, the taste of her sex, the scratch of her nails, the words: *What else can I give you, my tenth muse?* The way they had wept together in the fragrant chiaroscuro of that bed. The calla lilies she had offered to Saint Jude both to thank him for granting her that one impossible night with la Condesa, and in memory of la Marquesa's painting, "Athena Among Calla Lilies," which for Juana had been the earliest sign of her true nature.

Dearest Juana, she reread la Condesa's letter, *you have no idea how I ache to see you, what I would give to be close to you again and touch your ink-stained hands and look into the dark inkwells of your eyes to read the words that your pen no longer writes to me.*

It was her first lucid week in months, though the lucidity came in stages, and made her aware first of her body and then of everything that surrounded her. When the memories of the Count and la Condesa subsided, she noticed that her habit had grown much larger, or she had grown smaller, for the sleeves of the tunic hung lower than normal and the coif felt almost loose around her head. She let her hands explore her ribcage under the scapular, move down to the bone of her pubis and further down, to the sharp angles of her knees, and realized she had lost much weight. Carefully, noticing at last that she was in the choir and that they were singing one of the Offices, she raised her hand to her face and explored her chin and cheekbone and temple, her forehead bonier than ever. Her mouth moved of its own volition, though no sound came out that anybody but she could hear.

And suddenly the silence changed and instead of hearing the worms of her unspoken thoughts sifting incessantly through her brain, she heard voices. *Beatas* talked about the lack of bread in the market. Characters spoke to her from her plays. La Condesa conversed with la Marquesa. Each time she sat at the chessboard, her grandfather said, "Protect your castle," until finally she understood that she had to buy this cell. Talk to Andrea about getting the paperwork started. A crier in the streets called out the Viceroy's name, el Conde de Galve. And in the background the constant noise of children shrieking and crying. Sounds of brooms and kitchen utensils and footsteps. And somewhere a pealing of bells, more persistent than the bells of the Rule.

"Tía!"

It was difficult to pay attention to everything going on, to distinguish all the different voices clamoring for recognition in her memory.

"Tía! Come, quick! There's a mutiny!"

Was that Belilla? Why did Belilla talk so much? Didn't she know Juana needed silence? Between Belilla and Jane and Concepción—the name struck her like a fist on the heart. *Mea culpa.* Concepción, for letting you go into a wilderness. *Mea culpa.* Concepción, for not protecting you. *Mea culpa*—

"Tía! The Indians! They're rioting against the palace!"

"What Indians?" Her first words in over half a year.

"Come with me, Tía! We can see the Plaza from the roof."

Belilla tugged at Juana's hand and pulled her up to the *azotea* of their cell. It was nearly sunset and a red haze seemed to be rising from the Plaza Mayor. She noticed the smell of charred wood and saw that the other roofs of the convent were already crowded. Everyone was gazing north toward the Plaza where clouds of dark smoke rose into an orange sky and torches moved like a body of bees in the darkening square.

"*¿Pero qué sucede*, Belilla? What is this?"

"It's a riot, Tía. The Indians have set fire to the market and the palace. The Viceroy's in hiding and the Cabildo's house is under siege. Didn't you hear the crier? The bells have been tolling for hours."

"But why?"

"It's the famine, Tía! The Indians are starving. The other day the soldiers beat an Indian woman who was complaining about the price of grain. I think they killed her, or the child she was carrying died. And they've beaten several more, just because they want food. They can't afford the prices they're asking. Now the *castas* have taken to the streets and have been demanding that the Archbishop or the Viceroy give them corn."

"But how can they benefit if they burn down the palace?" said Juana, thinking of the nests of pigeons that gathered under the balconies of her old home, of their gentle cooing that la Marquesa used to love so much she forbade anyone to kill a single bird on palace grounds.

"What good is the palace, Tía, if the people are allowed to go hungry?"

Juana looked long at her niece. In the growing twilight, with the sky streaked orange and black and a smoke-tinged breeze powdering her angular face with a light soot, the girl looked like a mendicant.

"Have you been starving yourself again? You look terrible, Belilla."

"Oh, Tía! I knew there was something wrong with you! You were sitting at chapter along with the rest of us when Sister Melchora announced that our rations had to be cut back. We have bread only twice a week now, and meat once a month. We have to live on broths and soups."

She could barely hear what Belilla was saying, though they were both shouting over the great din emanating from the Plaza. She closed her fingers over her palm and tried to make her hand into a telescope, half-tempted to send Belilla down to her cell to get the real thing. Suddenly the gallows in front of the Cathedral burst into flames, like a great blazing crucifix. All around her, her sisters cried out in panic. From her vantage point on the *azotea* of San Jerónimo, it seemed to Juana that the entire city had lost its mind, and she, in her silence, had been oblivious to it all. She wanted to ask her niece more questions about the riot, but she could not bring herself to speak loud enough. Instead Juana just watched. She felt like she had just awakened after a long illness and didn't know the day or the season, though the warm wind and the late angle of the sun told her it was summer.

They stayed on the roof until the haze died out in the Plaza and the moon rose behind the volcanoes to the east. The bells rang for compline and everyone filed down to the courtyard, eighty black-veiled figures descending the stairwells and winding across the cloister without a word or a whisper, just the noise of their footsteps on the flagstones.

In the choir, they sang the opening hymn, examined their consciences in silence, and began with the usual penitence of the evening: "I have sinned in thought, in word, in deed and by omission: through my fault, through my fault, through my most grievous fault." Then came the fourth psalm followed by the ninetieth, which seemed particularly appropriate for Mexico that evening: "You shall not be afraid of the terror of the night, nor of the arrow that flies by day, nor of the·plague that stalks in darkness, nor the destruction that lays waste at midday." By the last psalm of the service, Juana had started to weep and could barely sing the hymn and the closing antiphons. Her shoulders shook while she prayed the Paternoster in silence. The Salve Regina brought her voice back in full crescendo:

"Hail, holy Queen, Mother of mercy, our life, our sweetness and our hope," she sang, feeling her voice gather strength.

Andrea, Melchora, and the *vigilantas* all turned to look at her.

"To thee do we cry, poor banished children of Eve. To thee do we send up our sighs, mourning, and weeping in this valley of tears." The numbness of the silence was lifting, and she could feel the blood moving through her veins again, a tingling down the back of her arms and a warm pulsing in her solar plexus.

The ringing of the Angelus closed the Office, but before anybody could leave the choir, Andrea called everyone to her knees to begin the fifty-four–day devotion to the rosary.

"Tonight and for twenty-six more nights," she said, "we will pray five decades of the rosary to petition the incarnate heart of Christ and his Holy Mother to rescue Mexico from these disasters that continue to befall us. For twenty-seven nights after that we will pray five decades of the rosary to offer our gratitude for their divine intervention."

Andrea turned to Juana. "Sor Juana," she said with an almost maternal inflection, "now that your vow of silence is over, may I ask you to lead tonight's rosary."

Juana unpinned the rosary from her shoulder, swallowed the knots that had formed in her throat, and asked what day it was.

"Sunday," said Andrea, "the Glorious Mysteries."

Juana cleared her throat, made the sign of the Cross over her face with the crucifix of the rosary, and began the Apostle's Creed. The first Glorious Mystery was the Resurrection and for a moment she imagined that they were all praying for her, for her own resurrection from that tomb of silence in which she had wallowed for seven months.

"The real hero of the evening," Don Carlos said over his steaming cup of watery chocolate, "was the Archbishop. While the Viceroy and his lady wife were hiding in the monastery of San Francisco (the Corregidor and *his* wife were hiding in San Agustín, I think), His Ilustrísima said a Mass in the Plaza and walked around amongst the rioters, completely fearless. The poor acolytes were terrified, visibly quaking in their little cassocks, but His Ilustrísima, in his miter and his crook and his Corpus Christi robes, followed by two priests carrying the tabernacle on high behind him, looked exactly like a kind of messiah in the wilderness."

Juana wanted to roll her eyes at somebody, but they were all entranced with the story. Andrea had asked Juana if the administrative body could attend the visit with Don Carlos for all of them wanted to hear his report on the mutiny. They had each contributed a piece of chocolate, which the refectory maids had beaten with water rather than milk to make enough for everyone, and the last of the sugared fruit was brought from the larder.

"The pagans were drunk on pulque and intoxicated with their own hatred, looting and burning and shouting like savages, but as soon as they saw the Holy Sacrament—" He hit his forehead with the palm of his hand. "You should have seen them, Sisters. As if by a miracle, they quit their destruction and knelt before His Ilustrísima like a flock of obedient sheep. Of course everything was burning all around them—the marketplace, the Cabildo, the palace."

"We saw the gallows burn," said Rafaela.

"To the ground," said Don Carlos, "but it's been rebuilt now and used to hang some of the leaders of the insurrection."

"So the bastards have been found?" asked Agustina, not even bothering to cover her mouth at her obscenity.

"The officers of the Audiencia have been making tireless inquiries, especially of the Indians who had stalls in the market, and they've turned up three or four *cabecillas*. The strange thing is that most of them were women."

"The leaders were women?" asked Juana.

"The ones who started going back and forth between the granary and the Cathedral demanding food, pretending they'd been injured by the soldiers."

"So they were not beaten? A woman did not miscarry?"

Don Carlos scowled. "Pure lies. You know how good those Indian women are at spinning fantasy into truth."

"What fantasy can there be if people are hungry?" said a meek voice from behind. They all turned to look at Belilla.

"Rude and argumentative, just like her relative," Agustina said to Melchora.

"Belilla makes a good point," said Juana. "It would make sense that women would lead the riot when the issue is hunger, since it is the women who must feed their families."

"We hear there were many dead, Señor," Andrea changed the subject.

"The Plaza was filled with bodies, Mother," said Don Carlos. "Most of them had been trampled by the throng—there were tens of thousands of them, every Indian and *casta* must have crawled out of the woodwork—and others were shot by the soldiers. They kept climbing the balustrades of the palace with flaming reeds they'd pulled off the stalls in the market. And the municipal building—" he shook his head dramatically "—completely devastated. They set fire to the Corregidor's carriage and dragged it flaming around the Plaza, the poor mules pulling it were in a complete frenzy and had to be shot. The prisoners in the dungeon nearly choked to death from the smoke. I don't know how I managed to save the archives."

"You were right in the melee, then?" said Melchora.

"If it hadn't been for the students who went in with me, we would have lost it all. Can you imagine, Juana? An entire century's worth of documents up in smoke thanks to those ignorant Indians! As it is, we couldn't save everything, but we got a good part of it out before the roof timbers came flaming down."

"What a tragedy!" said Rafaela.

Juana had been listening to her friend's description and wincing at his choice of words. Since when did Sigüenza y Góngora refer to the Indians—the subject closest to his heart, she thought—as ignorant and pagan and savage?

"Have the fires been stopped, then?" asked Andrea. "We still see smoke."

Don Carlos shook his head. "The *municipio* is still burning, I'm afraid. And the palace is ravaged. Some good-for-nothing tacked a notice on one of the doors that read: This corral for native cocks and Castilian hens is for rent."

Agustina gasped. "Ungrateful sons of bitches," she said. "Excuse me, Mother."

Andrea raised her eyebrows at Juana.

"That notice, Don Carlos," said Juana, "could not have been written by the Indians."

"The College of San Juan de Letrán is for the *castas*, Juana. They're not all illiterate."

"I wasn't suggesting that," she said. "But the description of 'native cocks' refers, I think, to the Indians, don't you agree? And don't you find it highly implausible that they would refer to themselves that way?"

"Are you suggesting it was *criollos* who wrote that, Juana?" he asked.

"Yes, I think it *was* written by *criollos*, who are as disgruntled with the government as the native peoples. If *you* were in the crowd, Don Carlos, don't you think it's safe to assume there were other *criollos* there as well?

"Yes, but we weren't setting fires, Juana, or sacking the market."

"Still, I don't think it's fair to blame all of this ruin just on the Indians."

"Since when are you an apologist for the *castas*?" Melchora asked her.

"Don't you remember that little ditty she wrote for the Feast of the Immaculate Conception? That silly verse in the Indian tongue?" said Agustina.

"It's called a *tocotín*, Sister," Juana clarified, "and the tongue is Nahuatl."

"I don't think I've seen that, have I, Juana?" asked Don Carlos.

"It's an old piece, my friend. I think you had just started your affiliation with the Archbishop and weren't coming around here very much."

Don Carlos shrugged. "I'm not disagreeing that we are all unhappy with de Galve, Juana. But this was, I assure you, an incident created by the *castas*."

"Created by the *hunger* of the *castas*," Belilla interjected.

"And just who do you think is responsible for that hunger, Sor Isabel?" snapped Rafaela. "Or will you, like your aunt, blame the *criollos* for that as well?"

"*We* are to blame," said Belilla. "All of us. With our sins, and our arrogance, and our lack of contrition. We brought down the rains and the blight and the famine, and all of that produced the hunger that produced the riot."

Juana bit her tongue. Though she disagreed with the analysis, she was impressed; she had never heard Belilla stand up to her superiors. I have to stop thinking of her as a girl, she thought. She has her own mind, her own convictions.

"I agree completely with Sor Isabel," said Andrea. "For a week now, we've been praying the devotion to the rosary and we're being extra diligent with our discipline and our meditations. In fact, if you will forgive the imposition, Don Sigüenza, may we prevail upon you to ask the Archbishop for his blessing? He need not administer it in person if he's occupied with other matters, but perhaps he would send us Padre Miranda to say a Mass of Redemption."

Something clenched in Juana's throat. The thought of seeing Padre Antonio again induced a sudden queasiness in her stomach. Almost ten years had passed since she'd seen him, since she'd rebuked him for his lack of charity toward her. He was so incensed by her criticism that he not only resigned as her father confessor but also punished the entire community for failing to tame her rebellious spirit, vowing never to set foot in San Jerónimo until the bad apple was removed. Would he agree now, under the current circumstances, to return to the daughters of San Jerónimo?

"Sor Juana?" Don Carlos broke into her thoughts. "Our workshop at the usual time next week?"

"I think not, Sir," Andrea said before Juana could speak. "At least not for the time being. Sor Juana is undergoing a process of purification."

Juana lowered her eyes so that Don Carlos wouldn't see the perplexity in her face. She had no idea what Andrea could be talking about.

"I see," said Don Carlos. "In that case, Godspeed to you, Sister."

Juana nodded, eyes still downcast.

"Thank you for your report, Señor," said Andrea. "And please forgive us that we were not able to offer you anything more substantial."

"At your service, Mother. Sisters. *Buenas tardes les de Díos.*"

On their way from the locutory Andrea invited herself to Juana's cell. They had matters to discuss, she said, concerning Padre Antonio and the progress of her spiritual exercises. Only when they were in her parlor with the door and the shutters drawn did Juana speak.

"What are you setting me up for, Andrea?" she asked directly. "You know perfectly well I'm not engaged in any spiritual exercises, and I resent that you told Don Carlos not to visit."

"I'm sorry I didn't discuss this with you before, Juana," said Andrea, sitting down on a stool, "but we must talk about it now. We're running out of time."

"Do you need me for anything, Tía?" asked Belilla, yawning behind her hand. "If not I'd like to take a nap before vespers."

"I was very proud of the way you held your ground," said Juana.

"Don't encourage her impertinence, Juana."

Belilla hung her head. "I beg your forgiveness, Mother."

"Can we offer you something to eat, Andrea?" said Juana. "If we have anything."

"Thank you, no," said Andrea. "I have to go over the accounts again with Rafaela. She's an excellent secretary, but as treasurer she will have us denounced by the baker for failing to pay our debt."

"Go lie down, *cariño*," Juana told her niece. "You did nothing wrong."

Belilla gave each of them a kiss on the cheek and retreated quietly to the bedroom. "She's working too hard," observed Juana.

"Yes, she's quite an inspiration for the novices," said Andrea.

Juana dug a cigarillo from her pocket and lit it with a candle.

"I'm going to pretend you're not doing that in front of me, Juana."

"Thank you." Juana inhaled and immediately she felt the tobacco clear her mind. "Now tell me, what's this all about? I've never known you to lie before."

"We've got to get you back in the good graces of Padre Antonio. Your Silver Jubilee is coming up, Juana, and you need him back."

Juana squinted at her through the smoke. She could always tell when Andrea had something to hide. "What do you know that I don't?" asked Juana.

"This vow of silence of yours had you so out of touch with reality that I didn't think it would do any good to tell you before, but the Bishop of Puebla has riled up all the prelates of New Spain and they're going to draft a complaint against you to present to the Inquisition."

"A complaint about what?"

"Need you ask, Juana? Are you really so naive?"

"About my Respuesta to Sor Filotea?"

"That was the catalyst, yes, but their complaint is about you, specifically. They plan to make an example of you—negative, of course—to prove that the Church must not permit, ever again, a woman of religion to reach the height of notoriety that you've gained. They say that the Church Council itself has contributed to your ignominy by offering you so many popular commissions, and that the lax rules of our house are also to blame. They are going to argue for closing down the *locutorios* in all the convents since it is clear that women are too weak of faith to be permitted worldly associations. In short, Juana, though you are the example and the true target of their wrath, all the nuns of New Spain will have to bear your punishment. And don't think they're not going to use everything that's happened in Mexico since last summer as more fuel for their fire—"

The cigarillo had turned to ash between her fingers. She could not meet Andrea's gaze and stared instead at the image of Saint Catherine that hung near the door. *Victor! Victor! Victor!* She remembered how triumphant she had felt writing those *villancicos*, the only form in which she had been permitted to write, and it occurred to her that she would never again write another carol for the Church.

"—nothing else we can do," Andrea was saying. "I think the best strategy is to win back one of your protectors, the only one who can really intercede for you with the prelates and with the Archbishop."

"This is an outrage," said Juana.

"I know," said Andrea. "You've outraged everyone. But there's more, I'm afraid." Andrea bit her lip and glanced down at the floor, her hands twisting at the cloth of her sleeves.

"Tell me!" Juana yelled.

"At Friday chapter. You were there, but I guess you didn't hear it. The community voted against accepting you back into the Order unless you undergo a severe purification."

"They what? With what right? I've taken perpetual vows."

"The Silver Anniversary, Juana."

"But that's a formality."

"Yes, it's a formality, but you still have to sign a new testament of faith and wait the required year of approbation before the permanent vows can be renewed. The others say they find you unworthy to continue in the service of God."

Juana had started to pace. "How dare they, Andrea? How dare they? When I have brought such prestige to this house! They could tolerate me as long as I had protectors in the court, but now that I've been abandoned I've become anathema? Do they mean to turn me out into the street like some errant Jew?"

"It's not entirely up to them, Juana. That's why I want you to win back Padre Antonio. It'll help us kill two birds with one stone."

"He won't listen to me. He's old and stubborn as a mule!"

"That's why I've appealed to him myself, and hopefully, with the Archbishop's help, he'll come back as one of our confessors. And if he does, Juana, you must approach him with great veneration, on your knees, licking his shoes, if necessary, whatever it takes to make amends."

"And what am I to do in the meantime, Andrea? Practice crawling and licking the shoes of *las santas?*"

"You amaze me, Juana. What makes you think you can afford any sarcasm with the way things are now?"

"I'm sorry. That remark was out of place. I know you're trying to help me, but I don't know why. If the Inquisition is to be involved, I'm done with."

"The Inquisition may or may not get involved. It depends on the gravity they assign to your case. I've started the rumor about your purification, as you heard, and now it's up to you to make it manifest. And if I want you to practice crawling and kissing the soles of my shoes, that's exactly what you're going to do because I will not permit our house to be maligned or our privileges to be revoked because of the liberties you have taken with your scribblings."

Juana shook her head. "I can't believe it, Andrea. Was it a unanimous vote? Have even *las santas* turned against me, after everything I did for them?"

"Suffice it to say, Juana, that Belilla and I were outvoted."

The tears welled up in Juana's eyes and she wiped them impatiently with her sleeve. "What am I to do then, Andrea?"

"The best way to protect yourself, Juana, is to resort to your vows, to live the life you were intended to live when you took this veil twenty-four years ago. Show them a different Juana. Show them it's possible for you to change."

Juana suddenly felt exhausted. "I'll try."

"You'll begin tomorrow with a five-day fast and vigil. I've ordered the kitchen maids to collect everyone's food because from now on, we are all breaking bread together, as they do at Saint Joseph's. No more of this catering to private appetites. We will all take our three meals together in the refectory, and for the first month after your fast I'm going to ask that you read Scripture to us while we eat. You can eat with the maids later."

"I'm sure there's more to my purification than a fast and a month of reading to you at mealtimes," said Juana.

"I can't take you away from your students or else I'd hear it from the others, favoritism, they'd say, removing rather than adding to your obligations. But I can ask you to resume your duties as treasurer. Rafaela has made a riddle of the accounts, and you're the only one able to decipher them, Juana."

"Does this mean that my writing privileges get restored? That I get my pens back?"

"I can't be indulgent with you like Madre Catalina was, I'm sorry. You won't be given back your pens. You'll come to my office every day between nones and vespers and work on the ledger books there. And another thing: there are to be no more books by you, Juana. No more letters to anybody. No more commissions of any sort."

Juana swallowed hard. Andrea must not have read la Condesa's last letter or else she would know that the second volume of Juana's works was to have been published by the summer and was probably at this moment circulating in Spain.

"Is that all?"

Andrea got to her feet. "One more thing."

"I thought so."

"I want Belilla to witness your daily disciplines and report at Friday chapter the number of lashes you've administered during the week. Meanwhile, I shall do everything in my power to bring Padre Antonio back as our shepherd."

"Please, Andrea. Don't ask me to do that."

"I hope Belilla reports an incremental number, Juana. Our purity increases with every lash. I know I can trust her to tell the truth."

"But Andrea, this is beyond humiliation. This is mental abuse—"

"Perhaps, Juana, but then look at how you have abused your vows, look at how you have abused the trust of the Church and the love of your sisters. And besides, what is humiliation and mental abuse to one who died to the world so many years ago and who wishes nothing more than to die again?"

Andrea's eyes were like ice. Juana held her stare, but only for a moment. She had to admit—if only to herself—that she truly had no other options.

"How will any of this benefit me if the Bishop brings my case before the Inquisition? You know how much Aguiar y Seijas would like to see me doomed to the Quemadero."

"That you have gone astray, that you have sinned, that you have over-stepped the boundaries of your sex and your calling—we can deny none of that, Juana. But we can deny the charge that you are a deserter of your faith. We have to prove that you are not a heretic, Juana."

"They accuse me of heresy, as well?"

"Disobedience. Defiance. Notoriety. Illicit visits. Physical contact. They say they have proof for every one of their charges, and they all amount to the same thing: that you are not true to your vows and, therefore, are living in apostasy. Someone has done a very good job of procuring evidence against you, and they say it's irrefutable evidence, some of it written in your own hand."

It did not surprise her that they had found out about her overnight visit to la Condesa's house—had Belilla told them?—but what did they mean they had proof of physical contact? The only one who could have said anything, other than Concepción, was Jane, the night she had seen her struggling to keep Concepción from losing control over her mother's defection. Hearsay was not proof, however, and surely her word would outweigh the gossip of a maid.

"It's bad, Juana. That's why we have to take extreme measures."

"What if Padre Antonio refuses to return?"

"I shall send him monthly letters, if I have to, begging for his mercy on your behalf."

Andrea squeezed Juana's shoulder and left her sitting alone in the parlor, dread pulsing through her skull. They don't know anything, she thought. They're just trying to batter me into submission. She got up, cleaned the dust off the chess pieces with her scapular, and challenged her grandfather's ghost to a long game. It was the only way she could keep from yielding to her fear, the only way to think strategically.

Check

JANUARY–AUGUST 1693

Chapter 30

25 January 1693

My daughter,

I have received all the petitions of your prioress and failed to respond on purpose, for I am an old man, and infirm. I do not have the sanguinity of my youth nor the patience of my middle years. I have gained wisdom, that is true, but my wisdom pales next to the wretchedness that your actions continue to inflict upon my soul, and I could find no compassion in my heart that would bring me back to the House of San Jerónimo to resume my duties as spiritual adviser. I must admit that at first I was shocked by the insolence and the audacity of your request, knowing that your Silver Jubilee is at hand and that you have need of my guidance. How dare she, thought I, after all this time, after her rude and belligerent treatment of one who loved her as dearly as I, how dare she believe that I will come to her rescue?

More than a decade has passed since you renounced me as your father confessor, and, during that time, I have watched the foundation of your sins grow to rival the pillars of Tepeaca. Since your days at the palace you have been vain and proud, a *marisabia* of flagrant dimensions. All your life in religion, you have defied the counsel of your superiors. The monstrance of the Host, symbol of the laws that govern our Holy Mother Church, has served as your chamber pot. Rather than cultivate the fame of piety you have secured the notoriety of the world. Why then, I can only wonder, when you have been so recalcitrant and vainglorious, do you now seek the discipline of my guidance?

In truth, though I have spent many nights prostrate before the Cross praying for the grace with which to forgive you, the bitter taste of resentment still poisons my palate, the chancres of indignation still plague my flesh, the dark orb of anger still clouds my vision.

I would like nothing better than to burn these petitions that Mother Andrea has been sending me since last summer, and to carry on with my life's work, knowing that you are an ingrate and completely undeserving of my mercy, and knowing, also, that it is only the threat of banishment from religious life that leads you to solicit my protection. Mother Andrea and Father Nazario both have assured me of the sincerity of your appeal. They say that for half a year you have been constant and genuine in every effort of your purification, and yet I remain a disciple of the doubting Thomas.

But today is the feast of the conversion of Saint Paul, and if Christ Himself could forgive the foul heresies the saint committed under the name of Saul, blinding him with the light of the true faith, then who am I to harbor such grievances against a lowly woman?

I realize, now, that this is a test of my profession, perhaps the final test. God has put you in my path again because, of all the sheep in all the flocks that I have tended these thirty years in religion, you remain the only stray, the only one who not only refused the bidding of her shepherd but rejected the fold altogether. Therefore, I know, Daughter, that God will not clear my sight until I have done right by you, and gathered you unto the fold of the pure and the holy. Though my vigor is tempered by rancor, I am reminded of Saint Paul's counsel to the Corinthians: "Charity beareth all things; believeth all things; hopeth all things, endureth all things." Thus, in the name of charity, shall I reappoint myself as your confessor.

All I ask, Daughter, before I return as the guardian of your spiritual life, is that you take a vow of silence for the forty days and forty nights of Lent, fixing Christ's example in Gethsemane to your heart. During that time take as little food as that required to keep you hale, and do naught but meditate upon your sins and pray for forgiveness. In this way, and with your continued discipline and purification, shall you prepare yourself for a general confession which is the first step toward a renewal of your vocation. I exhort you to purge your memory, as you will purge your heart and mind of the vile humors of worldliness, disobedience, and pride. No doubt the Archbishop will expect you to make a public demonstration of repentance and renewal in Christ; thus, I will add your name to the list of sinners who take part in the *octava* processions of Corpus Christi wearing the sackcloth gown of the penitent, that it may help you atone for the shameless infractions you have committed against the Rule since you entered the convent. Moreover, I will ask you to add twenty lashes to your daily discipline, as it is only through diligent mortification, genuine abdication, and perpetual penance that you will bury your worldly name and indecent reputation forever. If you let blood in your discipline—as well you should, in memory of He who shed His own sacred blood to redeem you—think of it as a letting of sins, for sin is the most perfidious manifestation of spiritual illness. On the Monday after Easter we shall begin to undertake the difficult task of your salvation.

I remain your spiritual Father,
Antonio Nuñez de Miranda of the Society of Jesus

Juana removed a cigarillo from her case and lit it with a twig from the stove. Her hand was unsteady, and she had to squint to guide the flame to its destination. Her brain felt like shattered glass inside her skull.

"What will you do, Tía?" asked Belilla, sitting at the kitchen table, folding the letter into squares. Juana took a puff of the cigarillo and let the smoke out slowly, her eyes stinging as they always did when she first inhaled.

"He wants to make me a laughingstock!" she said, beginning to pace between the door of the kitchen and the parlor. "Some guardian he is!"

Belilla unfolded the letter again and reread it. "Would the Viceroy help?"

"The Royal Cuckold, as they call him? Please, Belilla, be reasonable. His help would only quicken my demise. I am finished relying on viceroys."

"At least Padre Antonio hasn't rejected your petition, Tía."

"Yes, but look at the solace he offers. Fasting, bloodletting, public humiliation. He means to make a mockery of me, mark my words." She took a series of small puffs to ease the sudden tautness of her throat. After all these years, she thought, all this subterfuge, to end in a public scandal! She finished the cigarillo in another series of puffs, then cast the tail of it into the brazier.

"What can I do to help you, Tía? I hate to see you so distressed."

Juana shook her head, fighting back the desire to yell at her niece to stop asking her so many questions. She had to think, plot out her strategy, regain her confidence. Already she had made the mistake of submitting to her fear and allowing Andrea to write to Padre Antonio. Now, as a consequence, she had to bear this invective, this threat to her very existence. Rather than save her from the disgrace of expulsion from San Jerónimo, Padre Antonio was suggesting a public purging in a *sanbenito*, along with perverts and *zaramullos*. She lit another cigarillo and resumed her pacing.

"—from la Condesa," Belilla was saying.

"I can't involve la Condesa in this. Don't you see? Had she not had those books published none of this would have happened. I only gave her the material she asked for because I doubted any publisher in Spain would want to waste his time on the scribblings of a nun in the colonies. And now there are two volumes and a third edition of the first! No wonder they hate me!"

"It's not as if you haven't published other things, Tía."

"But none of them is a book of collected works, none of them is published in Spain. Those are just carols and *loas*, published locally, nothing of real substance, except in religious circles."

"Don't forget the *villancicos* to Saint Catherine and the 'Letter Worthy of Athena' and that comedy you wrote for Don Fernando. Those didn't help."

Juana stamped her foot. "'Letter Worthy of Athena!' 'Tenth Muse!' No wonder they're saying I'm more pagan than Catholic. All those Greek allusions! They're not even my own titles!" She crushed the tail of her second cigarillo into the brass lip of the brazier. She could hear the bells ringing for sext.

"So what will you do?"

"There's only one thing *to* do for now. Go to prayers. Come along, Belilla. Afterward I'll come back and make lunch. You know I always think more clearly when I cook."

"But I promised to eat with Sor Melchora. She thinks I should take over the infirmary since Sor Gabriela seems to be forgetting everything."

Just as well, thought Juana, I can concentrate on what to do about Padre Antonio instead. "Just be careful what you say, *cariño*. That Melchora always has some ruse up her sleeve. Don't mention anything about Padre Antonio's letter. I'm sure she's already read it anyway."

They pinned their escutcheons to their scapulars and rushed out. Juana had gotten into the habit of locking her cell seven times a day. Ever since she had sold Jane, she had not allowed another live-in servant for fear of admitting one of Melchora's minions, and still she found things missing, signs of someone rummaging through her notes and papers. It was a conspiracy, no doubt. At times she even suspected Belilla.

In the cloister, they tripped over a gaggle of geese roaming freely amid the trees now that even the cats had been banned from the convent by the Archbishop's latest decree. Sisters joined them from all directions; some came from the schoolrooms, some from the refectory, the infirmary, and the music room, many from the sewing room, the novices from the garden and the laundry, Melchora, Agustina, and their cluster of sycophants from the chapter room—all scurrying past her as though she were painted on a wall. Only old Clara, the portress, bothered to address them as she hobbled behind, leaning on her cane. Juana let Sor Clara enter the church ahead of them.

"Will you obey Padre Antonio?" Belilla whispered.

"I have no choice but to obey," Juana whispered back. She craned her neck back to make sure nobody was behind them, but they were, as usual, at the end of the line. "But there's a way of subverting even as one submits, Belilla."

Belilla gripped her hand. "Oh, Tía, I fear for your life when you speak so."

"Nonsense. Fear for me if I submit to anything without a struggle. That is the true measure of my defeat. Now be quiet before we're reported."

Belilla took her seat at the back of the choir among the younger nuns, and Juana went to hers in the second row behind the administrative body. It was one of the few advantages to having served as accountant of San Jerónimo for so many years: a permanent and more comfortable chair by the grate. From here she could see the door to the churchyard and beyond it the road. How she dreamed about that road, imagining a life without rooms or bells or superiors.

"*Deus in adjutorium meum intende,*" she chanted, but in her mind she was already dissecting Padre Antonio's argument in the letter. It was his wish that she fast and contemplate her sins during Lent, but more than a simple purging, the purpose of her fast was to prepare herself for a general confession followed by a public display of penitence at Corpus Christi. What if, instead of the public penitence, she were to offer to write a public document, a chronicle of sins that could be distributed and posted throughout the realm. Would not that be a more effective and far-reaching humiliation than a single day's corporeal punishment? That logic alone would provide the intrigue necessary to get Melchora to return her pens and paper, which she hadn't seen in over a year, and surely Padre Antonio would not refuse the opportunity to display a chronicle of her sins written in her own hand. Maybe he would even be willing to intercede for her with the Archbishop, since it had been His Ilustrísima's decree that Juana's writing tools be confiscated. Another idea occurred to her. She could kill two birds with one stone by using this document as her confession, written during her forty days of silence. She knew well the confessional form that generations of nuns before her had perfected—the high art of self-abasement, the delicate balance between total disclosure and modest sincerity, the hungry eyes of the beholder.

She did not wait for Belilla at the close of the Office, and hurried, instead, to speak to Andrea about how best to fulfill her confessor's wishes.

"Good news, I hear, Juana," said Andrea, smiling openly. "Padre Antonio has agreed to resume his duties with you."

An arm's span behind them walked Agustina and María de San Diego, a new initiate of *las interesadas*, rumored to be Melchora's eyes and ears.

"Thank God he has decided to be charitable with me," said Juana, feeling her neck flush under the yoke of her habit. If anyone knew how little she trusted Padre Antonio it was Andrea. And yet Andrea had not ceased chastising Juana for succumbing to the temptations of the terrestrial sphere, such as smoking and talking.

"I would like to respond to Padre Antonio this afternoon, if possible, Juana," said Andrea. "Perhaps you wouldn't mind helping me. You know I have a torpid way with letters."

"In fact, that is precisely what I wanted to discuss with you," said Juana. "Would you care to walk in the orchard?" She turned to face the eavesdroppers, "By ourselves, for once."

Andrea cut a sidelong look at Juana and suppressed a smile. "Sor Agustina, Sor María, if you wouldn't mind, I promised Sor Carmela I would lecture to the novices today, but this letter to Padre Antonio is terribly important, and perhaps I could convince you to speak in my place."

The *vigilantas* stared at each other and then nodded curtly at their superior. "May I ask the topic of your lecture, Mother?" said Agustina through clenched teeth.

"Discipline, Sister, your specialty."

"Need I go, too, Mother. I mean, if the topic is—" began María.

"But, of course, Sister. Discipline is the domain of the *vigilantas*. The novices should hear your views on the subject as well. Thank you so much."

They walked off in the direction of the gardens, and Juana could not resist squeezing Andrea's arm in gratitude.

"What's going on, Juana?"

"Not yet. You know how even the trees have ears around here."

Juana led Andrea to the chapel in the cemetery, its cool, dusty shadows smelling of damp stone. Before speaking, she ascertained there was nobody lurking in the oleanders that surrounded the structure, then sat down next to Andrea on the only bench still in usable condition and launched into her appeal. "Andrea, you have to help me. This public penitence that Padre Antonio is suggesting will be the end of me, I know it. I'll never live down the indignity."

"What can I do, Juana? My hands are completely tied. You brought this on yourself."

Be calm, she told herself, *it won't help to antagonize your only friend.* "I'm not trying to shirk my responsibility, of course I brought this on myself, but that doesn't mean I want to be the laughingstock of New Spain. You know perfectly well that's what they mean to accomplish."

"At least they are willing to give you another chance, Juana. Any of the rest of us would be decorating the scaffold by now."

"If I can *write* my confession during Lent, Padre Antonio can take it to the Archbishop and they can have it published, for all I care, the way they published my critique of Vieyra. That would satisfy their ambition to see me publicly disgraced. And it would also give me a way in which to defend myself, without them knowing it, of course."

"This is not a defense, Juana. Nor a tournament. You're absolutely right. It is your public humiliation that they seek. It won't help to outwit them. Let yourself be chastened, and be thankful that's all they want."

Andrea was right, of course, but she could not tolerate the thought of such a spectacle. She, who had striven to cultivate the respect of her equals, who had proven her brilliance time and again to those who once judged their intellects superior to hers only by virtue of their gender; she who corresponded with viceroys and vicereines and bishops, who had three books published, and a reputation as the tenth muse and only poetess of América, Mexican scholar second only to Don Carlos de Sigüenza y Góngora, celebrated by court and clergy, how could she allow this defamation of her character?

"They can chasten me until kingdom come, but at least let me preserve my dignity, Andrea."

"Is that dignity or vanity that you wish to preserve?"

"For the love of Mary, now you sound just like Padre Antonio."

"You have been the toast of New Spain for nearly a quarter of a century, Juana. Now it's time to honor your veil and vows. You told me you would cooperate."

Juana stood up with clenched fists and began to pace, the hollow floorboards squeaking under her weight. On the other side of the convent wall she could hear the clatter and bustle of the street leading down to the Indian district. A woman was peddling sweetmeats and a man was calling out the names of the caged birds he was selling. For an instant, a conversation she had had long ago about the caged lot of womanhood filtered back to her. Whom had she been speaking to? Oh yes, Concepción. She felt herself blush in the shadows. *Destiny is the cage each woman is born with*, she had said, and here she was over a decade later, proving her own argument to herself.

"Do sit down, Juana, you're making me dizzy."

Juana arrested her pacing and leaned back against the stone altar, her eyes fixed upon Andrea, and attempted one final appeal to their friendship. "I remember at our veiling ceremony how we swore that we would always protect each other. Are you going to help me, Andrea, in the name of that promise, or are you just planning to watch me wither away in this cage of fools they're constructing for me?"

Andrea looked down at her hands and slipped the gold band on and off her finger. She spoke softly, staring at the ring. "At our veiling ceremony, I thought you my soul friend. Since you were the only one other than myself who had willingly professed, I thought you equally committed to serving Christ. I knew you had your vanities, even then, but I thought the life of prayer and devotion we had chosen would help you outgrow them, and so I never held anything against you. But then we went our own ways. While you held court in the locutory, I prayed novenas in my cell. While you wrote poems and *villancicos* and plays, I sewed mantillas with the others, taught classes, held vigils. While you garnered more and more political allies, I fasted and disciplined myself against envy and self-importance. I have been on the road to purification while you were perched on the ladder of prosperity. Now you have climbed as far as you can go, Juana. Your only choice if you wish to remain in this cloister is to submit to the Rule. Or will you be like Icarus and try to fashion waxen wings for yourself, for that is all that a written confession will be—a false escape, something that will only melt under the heat of their scrutiny."

Juana felt her stomach contracting. She wanted to weep with frustration. "I, too, have taught classes," she retorted, unable now to control her anger, "and every single piece of public writing I have done, every *villancico* and *loa* and play, the triumphal arch, the letter on the sermon, the *respuesta* to the bishop—all of it has been commissioned or motivated by others, and most of it has brought considerable money to the convent, if you recall."

"Your books have not brought anything to the convent but shame."

Juana swung her gaze away from Andrea and looked out over the orchard. She spotted a pair of maids in the citrus grove and knew she had better keep her voice down.

"What about prestige? What about the endowments we have received precisely because the families of our novices have seen my name and the name of this convent on the front leaf of those books? How else did we get patronage from the best families in Spain and Peru which helped us recover from the famine and the devastations? Were it not for the popularity of those books we'd still have our farms mortgaged and our roofs sagging! Purity and holiness are not the only attributes that enlighten an Order, Andrea. Or don't you realize that while you're holding your vigils and lashing yourself to perfection, Melchora and Agustina and Rafaela are spinning political traps for you *and* for me?"

Behind her, Andrea said, "It's true, Juana. Your fame has brought wealth to San Jerónimo in a short time. But what of the province of your soul? Have you no concern for your salvation? Does the world engulf you so entirely? These are the Archbishop's questions. You wear the habit of a religious, and yet there is no religious inclination in you. There is only the quest for fame and prestige."

"We live in different worlds, Andrea. I cannot hope to make you understand my position."

"Look at me, Juana."

She met Andrea's eyes and tried to hide the sudden fear that had welled up inside her. If she could pretend that Andrea was another enemy she would not lose her composure and break into sobs.

"What do you want me to do, Juana?"

Her eyes went blurry and she looked away again, shaking her head.

Andrea came up behind her, touched her shoulder. This, alone, was a transgression against the Rule, this touching of a sister in religion. "In spite of everything I've said, I still love you, Juana. I know how difficult these next months are going to be. Tell me what I can do to ease your burden."

Juana wanted to fling herself into Andrea's arms. She had not been held since la Condesa's last visit an eternity ago. But she could not display any more weakness. She gripped her arms under the scapular, and willed herself not to turn around. Andrea was demonstrating her capacity for mercy, and she needed to use that mercy to her advantage.

"Return my writing materials," she said. "That's all I ask."

Andrea removed her hand from Juana's shoulder. "I shall speak to Father Nazario and ask the Archbishop's permission," she said. "If he grants it, you shall have what you ask. In the meantime, I want you to come to my office after nones and help me draft a response to Padre Antonio. And don't forget that tomorrow is the feast day of Santa Paula. I would like you to sing in her honor at High Mass."

She tried to thank Andrea, but the lump in her throat made it difficult to breathe and Andrea was already leaving the chapel. She stayed behind and watched her friend disappear into the dappled shadows of the orchard. Now she could hear a muleteer cursing at his beasts on the other side of the wall. Just outside those *tezontle* walls, she thought, people were going about their business while in here her entire world was collapsing. Her eyes caught the orange flash of a monarch butterfly lifting itself out of the oleanders. It was almost time for the monarchs to leave Mexico, she realized. She had never written about this, never described the impossible beauty of a host of orange and black butterflies migrating north. For an instant she considered digging her writing box out of its hiding place— she had returned it there after Melchora's last inspection of her cell—but decided to wait until after compline when she was certain no one would see her.

Andrea was wise to ask for her help after nones, for it was during those four hours before vespers that it rained and the rain without her notebooks and her quills infused her with an unshakable melancholy. When Belilla returned from her lunch with Melchora she reported that the *vicaria* had wanted to discuss the new election year and was wondering if Belilla would be interested in being nominated for a post as assistant to the headmistress of novices.

"That's all she wanted to talk about? Election's a year away. Besides, I thought you were going to be our new infirmarian."

Belilla shrugged. "So did I, but it looks like she's got somebody else in mind for that."

"That's ridiculous! You've been training with Gabriela for years. Let *her* be the assistant to the headmistress! Did she ask you anything about me?"

"She did bring up the letter, Tía, but I told her I was not permitted to discuss it."

"Why did you say that?"

"Because that's what you told me."

"You were not meant to repeat that, Belilla. If you're to become involved in the political life of the convent, you must learn to keep things to yourself, particularly anything private that I've told you."

"Forgive me, Tía. I didn't realize—"

"What did she say about the letter?"

"Not much, Tía. Mainly she talked about Padre Antonio, and said that his eyesight must be worse than she thought."

Juana wanted to shake her niece. "Stop being such a dolt, Belilla, don't you see she's talking in riddles? She wasn't referring to Padre Antonio's health. She means his judgment, not his vision."

"Oh. Is she criticizing him, then, for agreeing to return as your confessor?"

Brilliant deduction, thought Juana. "You mustn't go over there again, dearest. You don't realize how dangerous and underhanded she is, and you're clearly not prepared to handle her innuendoes."

Belilla's chin trembled. She glanced down at the basket of embroidery she had brought from the sewing room and Juana saw that the corners of her blonde eyelashes had become wet. Juana rolled her eyes and went upstairs to rest.

"Don't forget to wash the dishes," she called down from the landing. More than anybody, today she missed Concepción, her good sense and ability to see through the hypocrisies of the nuns.

She was in a choleric humor when she entered Andrea's office later to dictate the letter to Padre Antonio, but managed to keep it under control when she saw that Andrea had no intention of composing the letter. She took her seat at the Mother Superior's desk and fondled the only pen. Though it was nothing but a plain turkey quill, the point brittle and badly cared for, she hadn't held a pen in over a year and it felt as though a part of herself had been returned, a missing appendage that fit perfectly in the crook of her hand. When the first drops of ink soaked into her finger she felt as if she were receiving a transfusion of her own blood.

"You must compose it as if it were in my own words," Andrea instructed.

"You have to copy it over," said Juana. "He knows my handwriting."

"Put tomorrow's date on it, Juana. Perhaps Santa Paula will intercede for you. You need all the help you can get."

Juana frowned but didn't say anything and gave herself over to the voice pounding inside her.

26 January 1693

Your Reverence,

It is with unprecedented humility that, on the feast day of Santa Paula, patroness of our Holy House of Saint Jerome, our errant sheep, Sor Juana Inés de la Cruz, acknowledges the extreme generosity of your decision to return as her confessor, though little she deserves it. Furthermore, she accepts your wise counsel, your exhortation to purge her mind and soul of all her sins. But since she thinks most clearly with pen in hand, and would like, in those forty days and forty nights of silent penance to narrate the chronicle of her sins, she begs me to request that her writing materials be restored for this purpose only. Therein, she will record every detail of her confession, discoursing not in the vague, though subjective, examples she provided in her most scurrilous response to the sage Sor Filotea, but in the objective scrutiny of an examined life; for, as Aristotle said, "an unexamined life is not worth living."

Indeed, you may decide upon completing this wretched chronicle, that life was wasted on her being, and it would be, she assures me, a charitable conclusion for one as repugnant as she. Yet, knowing it impossible to account for every infraction she has committed in the quarter century of her profession as a bride of Christ, and in the twenty years preceding it, she shall limit her examples only to the most flagrant occasions when that nefarious inclination, that passion for knowledge, made itself manifest upon the fate and character of one Juana Inés Ramírez de Asbaje, that she may forget that life forever and reenter her vocation as one who died and rose again in the purity of the Rule.

And so, my very dear Padre Miranda, by the grace of the Immaculate Conception, and under the guidance of our Fathers, Saint Jerome, Saint Joseph, and Saint Jude, Sor Juana awaits the commencement of Lent to begin the infamous fiction, cipher of her most sincere penitence. She shall not, of course, proceed with this humbling task until we receive the Archbishop's permission.

I remain your faithful follower,
Sor Andrea de la Encarnación, Prioress of San Jerónimo

On Ash Wednesday, it was Padre Antonio himself who drew the cross of ashes on Juana's forehead.

"Your Reverence," she said, forgetting the vow of silence he had enjoined her to take. She fell to her knees and reached for his hand between the bars of the choir grille. He had aged and thinned so much in the decade since she had seen him that he looked almost skeletal in his Jesuit habit. His knuckles jutted out like sharp pebbles, and the spotted skin of his hand felt like onion paper under her lips. A surprising tenderness stirred the liquid humor in her eyes. Why hadn't Andrea told her that he would be here?

"From ashes we come and unto ashes we shall return," was all he said, touching his sooty thumb to her forehead, down the bridge of her nose and across her closed eyelids.

She didn't see him again until Palm Sunday, when in his Paschal robes he said Mass in the church and then blessed the palm fronds of the entire congregation. On Maundy Thursday, with Father Nazario's assistance, he washed the feet of the nuns in the lower choir, and then Juana, with a devotion that surprised even her, removed his sandals and wiped the soles of his own feet with her tongue. They were dry and tasted of callous and limestone.

Her first confession with him since his withdrawal as her confessor came on Good Friday and she dutifully reported her infractions: vanity, impatience, melancholy. Padre Antonio absolved her with a light penance but said nothing about whether her chronicle had been allowed. The second confession was the same, and the third, and the fourth. Padre Antonio listened to her in absolute silence, administered her penitence, and said nothing about reinstating her writing privileges or returning her pens for the purpose of writing her general confession. Juana could not bring herself to ask him, as this would appear too much like begging. Andrea would reinstate nothing without the Archbishop's consent, but at times, inexplicably, she left her office while Juana was working on the accounts.

Juana wasted no time. She poured some ink into a vial she had taken from the infirmary, slipped a quill into her pocket, and pulled a clean sheet of vellum from the stack on Andrea's desk, hiding it in one of her books. Later, after compline, after the curfew bells, after she was certain that Belilla had fallen asleep, Juana would lock herself in the cold, dark study, illuminated only by a candle, and write. She had to be extremely frugal, make the briefest notations, abbreviate as many words as possible, but sometimes she gave in, surrendering to the implacable desire to let the pen glide over the page, the ink flowing like water or blood, without restriction. It was the closest she felt to being blessed.

Chapter 31

"But Tía," Belilla protested, "you've been forbidden to write!"

"I'm not writing anything. You are. This is the second letter from la Condesa that I've not been able to respond to. I have to tell her to stop writing me, that they're using her letters against me, and since I can't do it myself, I need you to write her for me. I have to thank her for the *Segundo volúmen*. As it is, she won't get this letter until Christmas."

"I will only do this once, Tía. Please don't ask me to compromise my vows again."

"Listen to me, *Sor* Isabel, you wouldn't have taken any vows were it not for my influence, so don't be righteous with me. I have matters to attend to in the world, whether you or Andrea or God Himself disapproves, and I need your help. When you needed me to arrange for your dowry and finance your veiling ceremony did I say 'only this once,' Belilla? Don't ask for my help again? Did I say '*hasta aquí*'? I will only love you up to this point?"

"If I had known that I would have to lie for you, that I would have to disobey for you, I would have gone to another convent, Tía."

"When have you lied for me? Just because I didn't let you watch me whipping myself. You were right outside the door, weren't you? You counted every lash out loud."

"I was ordered to watch you, I didn't want to do it."

"You didn't want to do it. I didn't want you to do it. The important thing is that you knew I was doing it and were able to give your little report every week."

"I was supposed to bear witness, Tía."

"Eyes are not the only things that bear witness, and who ever heard of a niece bearing witness against her own mother's sister? It was just another way of torturing me, another way of humiliating me. Is that what you wanted to do?"

"I took a vow of obedience, Tía. And so did you."

Before she knew it her hand had struck Belilla's face, not once, but twice. *Ingrate*, she had called her, *traitor*, *idiot*, *stupid idiot*. She had regretted it immediately, but the damage had been done and Belilla ran from the cell cradling her face in one hand. In her rage, Juana had crumpled la Condesa's note in her fist. She smoothed out the scented paper and let her eyes linger over the beloved handwriting.

Darling Juana,

Have not heard from you since you sent me those intrepid *villancicos* for Saint Catherine. Your courage never ceases to amaze me. Even in the midst of all that intrigue bubbling like water for chocolate all around you, you still manage to write carols and to make examples of historical figures like Catherine of Alexandria. I can see why you feel you have so much in common, but the irony, of course, is that she was prosecuted for being a Christian and you are persecuted by Christians. Write to me, Juana. I need to hear your opinion of *Segundo volúmen de las obras de Sor Juana*. It's a dry title, I know, compared to the title I gave your first book, but I think we've already established your reputation as Tenth Muse and Phoenix of Mexico, and the purpose of this second volume is to demonstrate the diversity of your talent and your wide-ranging intellect. It's more than just an anthology of poems, Juana; it is a collection of your finest scholastic works (dare I say *finezas* in honor of Vieyra?). I'm dying to know what you think. With Tomás gone (may he rest in peace) and José away at boarding school, I am ever so lonely for my Juana.

Impatiently yours,

María Luisa

28th of March 1693

A series of loud knocks pulled Juana out of her melancholia. She slipped la Condesa's note into her desk's secret niche, then hastened to the parlor to open the front door. She was taken aback to find Padre Antonio standing there, wearing the vestments of the Holy Office. On either side of him stood Andrea, looking forlorn, and Melchora with a Machiavellian grin on her face.

"Your Reverence," she said, genuflecting, her nerves rattled of a sudden. No priest had ever set foot in the cloister, as far as she knew. "Please, come in."

Padre Antonio stepped over the threshold and made the sign of the Cross over her face. "I have come in the name of the Holy Inquisition," he said, his voice raspier than ever. Through the wispy tufts of his white hair, she could see crusty chancres on his skull. His cassock gave off the odor of neftaline.

"How may I be of service, Father?" she asked.

"I have come to expurgate your library, Juana Inés de la Cruz, by orders of the Archbishop."

Juana clenched the fabric of her tunic, glancing quickly at Andrea, who stared at the floor of the parlor. Melchora crossed her arms under her scapular, eyes half-lidded like a lizard's.

She should have expected this. "Expurgate, Father? But why?"

"We have evidence to suggest that there are prohibited books in your possession."

"I told him that was a preposterous idea, Juana," said Andrea. "How could you own any prohibited books? Somebody has given you false information, Your Reverence."

"The Index changes so much anybody could own forbidden texts, Mother. If you own an early edition of *Don Quixote*, for example—"

"Surely Cervantes isn't banned?" interjected Andrea.

"Not the entire book, and certainly not the most recent editions, but in all editions prior to 1640, a sentence in a chapter of the second part has been excised. If I were to find an early edition in your library, Juana, I would be forced to report it."

"One sentence?" asked Juana. "Which one?" Her pulse was racing. Just in the other room, there was a pile of contraband books on her desk, compliments of Don Carlos. On top was Abelard's *Dialectica* on the nature of truth and reason, annotated thickly in the margins; under it, Plato's four dialogues on the trial and execution of Socrates; and for a bit of encouragement, Aristophanes' *Lysistrata*, to remind herself that victory over the ways of men was not just a hopeful figment of her imagination but actually had antecedents in the ancient world. She had been consulting these texts all week, trying to memorize the most significant passages, which she intended to use as marginal commentary in her chronicle of sins, if she ever received license to write it.

Melchora was peering over the arm of the settee into the brazier.

"Fourteen words, to be precise," Padre Antonio was saying. "Such is the rigor with which the Holy Inquisition performs its obligations. As Censor for the Office, of course, I have done my share of expurgations, but not for many years now, not since I became afflicted with this cataract condition."

"Is there anything I can do to assist you, Father?" asked Melchora.

Juana sneered at her.

"As a matter of fact, your assistance would be most welcome, Sister. I need someone to be my eyes and read aloud the titles of the books."

"I can do that, Father," said Juana.

"That isn't allowed, Juana. You must be removed from your cell while the expurgation is taking place. Sister Melchora will be my assistant."

"Where am I to go, Father? What about Belilla, I mean, Sor Isabel?"

"Your niece will remain here with us. Mother Andrea will keep you in a private cell until our work is finished."

"You mean a dungeon cell?"

"Of course not, Juana," said Andrea. "You shall stay in my own cell."

Padre Antonio frowned at Andrea. "What matters is that she be removed from here. Take her where you want, Mother, and beware, lest you become implicated in her sins."

"But what of my chronicle, Father?"

"The Archbishop has denied your request," he said.

Dread gathered in the pit of her stomach like a humor. "I don't understand," she said. "I can't even think without my writing instruments."

"You don't get to do any more writing," said Melchora. "Ever again!"

"But, Father—"

"After the expurgation, your confession will take place on Saint James's Day," he said. "In the chambers of the Inquisition. Open to the public."

"But, Father—"

"There is naught we can do, Juana, but submit to the Archbishop's will," said Padre Antonio.

"I don't understand," she said again, her voice breaking. "Why am I being persecuted like this, Father? Is this what it takes to renew my vows?"

"Hypocrite!" hissed Melchora. "Look at this!" She reached over into the brazier and removed the butt of a cigarillo. "See this, Your Reverence?" She held it out to him, but he did not reach over to take it. "On top of everything else, she smokes, too. Is that the behavior of a bride of Christ, Father?" The *vicaria* threw the butt back into the brazier.

Padre Antonio shook his head. "Everyone has a point, Juana. You have been most rebellious and remiss in your profession."

"I believe Juana is aware of how she has offended our profession, Your Reverence," Andrea stepped in, "and I also know that she is sincerely repentant—"

"Oh, very sincerely—" interrupted Melchora.

"Yes, Sister Vicaria, in my estimation, she is. For the last year we have all been witness to the progress of her purification. I have complete faith that she wants nothing more than to continue in the service of God and will do whatever it takes to earn that privilege."

"You're blessed with a devoted Superior, Juana," said Padre Antonio. "Between us we should be able to secure your salvation. What is an expurgation next to that?"

"Will you begin the expurgation today, Your Reverence?" asked Andrea.

"Unfortunately, no. It's almost time for vespers, and it will be too dark afterward. I will begin tomorrow after Mass. Mother, I need you to ask your archivist to join us. The Holy Office likes to keep meticulous notes on all of its proceedings. And we must also make an inventory of Juana's possessions."

Juana swallowed the bile stinging at the back of her throat. "Why are you doing this, Padre Antonio? Have you no charity toward me at all? You are proceeding as though I had already been condemned."

He narrowed his eyes at her. "We need a complete list of your books, Juana. The Inquisition has carefully examined each of your scribblings—none more egregious than that letter you wrote to Sor Filotea—and we conclude that you deserve no charity."

"This has gone beyond a Silver Jubilee, Your Reverence," said Andrea. "You did not tell me that the Inquisition was going to be involved."

"The Holy Office is always involved in matters of heterodoxy, Mother."

"Have you read my Respuesta yourself, Father? There is not a single reference to any banned source. All of my references are legitimate."

"You may not have referred to them in that letter, but your knowledge of heretical discourse is evident in everything you write."

"Not to mention that obscene correspondence with our former Vicereine," added Melchora.

Juana wanted to hit Melchora with her fist, feel her teeth loosen under the blow. Saliva gathered under Juana's tongue, like a poison that she wanted to spit at Padre Antonio's face. A sharp pain started at the base of her spine.

413

"Shall I be able to provide witnesses for my defense? Don Carlos, for example?"

"De Galve has dispatched Sigüenza to Florida," he said.

"But why?"

"He's mapping the area for settlement, I hear. I guess de Galve doesn't have better things to do with his Chief Cosmographer than use him to buttress the Crown's holdings against the French."

"I thought he was your assistant in the Holy Office? Was he not consulted for this examination?"

"This is not a trial, Juana."

"But someone accused of heresy is at least given the right to an advocate."

"This is a public confession on the occasion of your Silver Jubilee. It's a complete renunciation of your past that the Archbishop seeks, and unmitigated obeisance to the Church. It's the end of your worldliness, the end of your public life, the end of your rebellion, the end of your scribbling and publishing, nothing more and nothing less, Juana."

"Or else?"

"Or else the Tribunal shall declare you a heretic and rescind your petition to renew your vows."

"The Archbishop means to see me tortured, doesn't he? Maybe even hanged."

"You wouldn't be the first to die unjustly."

"Do you want that as well, Father? Is that why you agreed to return? To help them facilitate my demise?"

Padre Antonio shifted his feet. She heard his knees creak. "You are my daughter in Christ. If I must lose your life to gain the salvation of your soul, so be it."

She felt the sobs catch in her throat.

"Don't indulge in self-pity, Juana," he said. "The truth is your death would only increase your fame, and that is the opposite of what the Church wants."

"The Church or the Archbishop?"

"The Archbishop *is* the Church in New Spain."

"If it were up to him, I'm sure he would have me excommunicated, perhaps even exiled."

"Wouldn't you love that?" said Melchora. "Traipsing after Vicereines to your heart's content."

"Shut up, Melchora. Can't you get her out of here, Andrea?"

"Do you see how she talks to her superiors, Father?"

"It is time to go, Sister Vicaria," said Andrea. "Our business is finished here."

Melchora fell to her knees and kissed Padre Antonio's ring. "I shall do everything I can to help you remove this snake from our midst, Father."

Under her scapular, Juana dug her nails into her fists to keep from striking her.

"Get to your feet, Melchora," said Andrea, "this is not a chapel. Your Reverence, with your permission, we have matters to attend to before vespers."

"She's right, you know," said Padre Antonio when they were gone, his tone paternal of a sudden. "The Archbishop would not want you loose in the world. Though they don't admit it, both he and the Bishop of Puebla seem to fear the power of the word you have, Juana. They know you have powerful friends abroad who would facilitate your transition back into the world of the living. If the Tribunal declares you an outcast, Aguiar y Seijas will see you dead before he releases you from your vows. He can control you more effectively if you remain a *profesa*."

"Then I should make it possible for my renewal to be denied."

"And yet it is the one thing that protects you against the gibbet."

"So my vows make me both martyr and executioner," she quoted a line she had written in the Respuesta.

"It is the double bind of all religious. *El pescado muere por la boca*, Juana. Now come, walk me to the church. I promised to assist Father Nazario at the vespers Mass."

Installed in the choir, Juana paid no attention to the service. That phrase of Padre Antonio's kept echoing in her mind: a fish dies through its mouth. Was it a warning or a prediction of her own capitulation? *World, why do you insist on persecuting me?* she had written over a decade ago, bemoaning the incessant tirades she suffered from her sisters and superiors in religion against her penchant for learning. La Condesa had included it in the first volume of her writings, under the intrepid title: "She Complains of her Fate: insinuating her aversion to vice and justifying her devotion to the Muses."

World, why do you persist in persecuting me?
How do I offend you, when all I seek

is to place beauty in my mind
and not my mind on beauty?
   I do not value wealth nor treasures
and thus, it causes me more joy
to place riches in my thoughts
rather than my thoughts on riches.
   I love not loveliness which, despoiled
by time is vanquished,
nor does false finery deceive me,
    instead, my truth of truths
is to consume the vanities of life
rather than consume my life on vanities.

It chilled her to think that she had been predicting her own fate, for now her life was on the verge of being consumed by the flames of scandal and the perpetual purgatory into which she would be sentenced.

That evening between midnight and matins, she and Belilla hid the most condemned of her banned books: Abelard, Aristophanes, Bacon, Bocaccio, Descartes, Erasmus, Kircher, Luther, Machiavelli, Ovid, Petrarch, her beloved *Symposium*. She had so many. Like Hildegard von Bingen who had entombed an excommunicated soldier on hallowed ground, she buried her books under the floorboards in the *beatas'* chapel; that had been the best place for Pandora's Box and, though the damp ground would surely ruin the leaves and covers of the books, at least they would be safe from discovery.

Belilla did not object, said nothing at all when Juana woke her in the dead of night to help haul the books she had stacked in the water pails. "I want you to hurry, Belilla," she whispered. "And keep absolute silence. We don't want to wake anyone."

"Where are we going, Tía?"

"Follow me. And be quiet."

In the chapel, they pushed the bench aside and Juana pried up the rusty nails of the floorboards with a knife. Juana watched the girl carefully as she lowered the books into their hiding place, but could discern no sign of rebellion in her, no trace of resentment in her sleepy eyes. She sealed up the planking with a glue she had concocted of tree resin and flour, and then together they dragged the heavy iron carcass of the bench back over the boards, the short wick of their lantern flickering their shadows across the walls.

"Now go back to the cell," whispered Juana. "And I pity you, Belilla, if you're seen."

"Can't I wait for you, Tía? I'm afraid to walk through the orchard by myself."

Juana said a quick prayer to San Lorenzo, patron of librarians, to entreat his help in keeping her books safe from decay and discovery, then rushed with Belilla back across the garden and the cloister. They reached their cell just as the matins bells woke the convent. Andrea had revived the observance of the dark morning Office as part of their purification program. Not everyone was expected to turn up for the service, and Juana told her niece to sleep in, that she would make her excuses to the Mother Superior. Only she and *las santas* were moving at that hour. Juana stopped at the fountain to gaze up at the swarm of constellations in the black sky of Anáhuac, and suddenly a light streaked across the horizon, a shooting star. For a moment she thought of the comet, and of its undeniable portent in her life. Was this, then, another sign?

For the three weeks that it took Padre Antonio to finish the expurgation, Juana lived in Andrea's one-room cell. She slept on a *petate* on the floor and was allowed only a woolen sheet and a blanket for her bedding. Andrea drew up a schedule of obligations for her, beyond her teaching duties. On Mondays she worked in the sewing room. Tuesdays, she was required to scrub the floors of the priory with lye. Wednesdays, she helped in the laundry. Thursdays and Saturdays, she cooked in the refectory. Fridays, she balanced the accounts. Sundays, she fasted and held a vigil to Saint Jerome. There was no talking between them, not even at *recreo* time, for Andrea did not believe in recreation beyond that which would recreate her spirit in the image of perfection, and Juana preferred to help the novices harvest silkworms or pick peaches than be alone in that box of a cell with nothing but the drone of Andrea's prayers for company.

In a way it was a peaceful time, and she realized there was a certain serenity in not having to decide what to do, in having her actions and thoughts organized by the Rule of the Order. But the revery lasted only as long as she kept her emotions in check and didn't think about what was happening in her cell, for the very thought of Padre Antonio and Melchora invading her library, wasting her own materials to draw up their biblio-graphic evidence against her, filled her with anger and with an unmitigated yearning for escape. The only thing left of her life were her books, and now, even that had become a threat. The Index hung over her like a death wreath. At chapter or choir, Melchora and Rafaela gave her their haughti-est looks, tempting Juana to curse them under her breath, but always there was a *vigilanta* watching her, just waiting for her to do something they could report. It was then that Juana regretted her vocation. When even the re-pugnant thought of marriage seemed a better fate than this perpetual sub-jugation to fools.

And then, finally, the expurgation ended and Padre Antonio left San Jerónimo without bothering to say anything to Juana, though it was a Tues-day and she was on her knees scrubbing the planks of the priory when he passed. She followed him at a distance, and stood outside the Mother Su-perior's door as he informed Andrea that the confession would begin, as ordered by His Ilustrísima, on the day of Saint James, the following week. To Juana's benefit, he said, he had not found any banned texts in her pos-session, though he now had to investigate why his list differed so substan-tially from another list that had been submitted to the Holy Office. I knew it, thought Juana, and she knew also who was responsible for generating that list and who had submitted it to the Inquisition.

Her feet smelled. She could not remember how long it had been since her last bath. Since she had changed her coif and shift and undergarments. Since they had brought her the hair shirt and the bowl of ashes, which was all that was left of her burnt books. She could not remember how long she had been here in this cell of lunatic nuns who pulled at each other's naked breasts and urinated standing, but her fingernails had grown long, and she had used them to write letters on her flesh—on the tender, hairless flesh of her inner thighs. JIdl+, her initials on one leg, and MLMdL, María Luisa Manrique de Lara, on the other. When the crusts dried over the letters and her thighs itched, she would dig her nails under the crusts and scratch with abandon until the wounds reopened and the pain of it took her mind off the maddening itch around her breasts and waist. Only then could she sleep, feeling the blood trickle down into the lice-infested mat that was her bed.

She awakened from the dream in a cold sweat, her clammy face stuck to the wool of the sheet that she had bundled into a pillow. Panting for air, she pulled off the blanket. Groped for the tinderbox and lit the lamp. Oh God. She was safe. She was sleeping on the raw straw of her *petate* in Andrea's cell and that was Andrea under the sheet on that hard platform she called a bed.

In the name of the Father, the Son, and the Holy Ghost—she crossed herself and kissed her thumb—Amen. In the dream they had been asking her questions, unending questions about the intimacies she had shared with la Condesa and Concepción. They wanted detailed descriptions of what she had done, of the immodesties she had committed with her eyes and tongue. Did you delight in looking upon them? Did you touch them? Did you take carnal pleasure with them? Did you speak to them whilst you sinned? For every question they demanded she answer, she prayed a Hail Mary in her head. Question after question, Hail Mary full of grace, until she had enough for a full five decades of the rosary, pray for us sinners now and at the hour of our death, and even then they didn't stop. Have you indulged in self-corruption? Have you sought satisfaction outside of God? Do you confess to egregious acts of infidelity against your Spouse, to aberrations against your sex, to desecration of your sacred vows? The litany of questions went on for hours and she had borne it in silence, until at last, her inquisitors had resorted to speaking to each other:

But is her silence a denial or an acceptance?

And what is the penalty in either case?

A liar's tongue gets cut out, and yet we have no way of knowing if she lies or not. An insubordinate is sentenced to perpetual silence, and yet she already *is* silent. Do we remove the sacraments for holding her tongue? Or do we remove the tongue for blaspheming the sacraments?

Can silence be blasphemous, Brother?

At last, certain they could not break her out of that carapace of silence, they had thrown her into one of the secret jails of the Inquisition, in a cell of deranged nuns who wagged their ashen tongues at her in lascivious circles.

She rubbed her eyes until the pupils hurt. Modesty of the eyes, modesty of the tongue—the lessons of her novitiate days that she had never ever put into practice. Few of them did. Belilla, certainly. And Beatriz. And, of course, Andrea. She glanced over her shoulder at the bed; Andrea was buried under the sheet, head and all, for they were not supposed to leave any part of the body uncovered while they slept and they were to lie down fully dressed in a short veil and scapular, in stockings and cincture, as though they were dead. Juana looked down at her damp shift, her naked arms and calves, her bare feet, and shook her head. She had always been a very bad sister, the worst of sisters, the worst bride that Christ had ever taken, and for that, she was guilty of the sin of pride.

The burning sensation started again around her waist, and she took the lamp into the bath to examine her skin. She had been scratching herself desperately in the dream, the hair shirt and the lice, the perpetual prickling of her flesh, driving her insane as the other madwomen. The tile of the bathroom felt frigid under her feet. Nights had been cold this summer, and their firewood was still being rationed, so it was difficult to take hot baths these days or to keep the braziers stoked throughout the night. She set the lamp on the edge of the tub and pulled off the shift. Another sin, this revelation of one's body, for it led inevitably to a delectation of the eyes and a temptation of the hands that was difficult to govern. She shook her head again, thinking of all the times she had failed to govern that temptation.

At first she could see nothing unusual in the dim glow, but as the light took hold and illuminated the different colors of the tiles, she found them. Red welts the size of her hand all over her belly. Gouges on her thighs. Scratch marks on her breasts. A thin trail of blood down the inside of her legs. She had not menstruated regularly in two years and had not had to bother with the cumbersome ritual of sewing the linen swathing into her undergarments, but now, on the eve of her public confession when she most needed her rational faculties, she was bleeding again and tearing at her skin in her sleep.

At times like these she detested her female body. For what it did. For what it could not do. For the fact that her subjection was rooted in that body of mammary glands and bloody womb. Men had no monthly bleeding or colicking to disturb their sleep. No grotesque distentions of the belly in pregnancy, no painful racking of the innards and stretching of the hips at childbirth. No cutting of the nipples by hungry, suckling mouths. Men had nothing to bind them to the earth but the continual sowing of their seed which only led to the increased agony of women. And even if a woman bore no children, suckled no babes, and suffered not the impositions of the male member, she still had her monthly bleeding to remind her that pain was God's legacy to the daughters of Eve, for according to the Church, sin and death began with Woman, and for that Womankind would always be subject to pain and to the laws and the misogyny of men. She took a cloth and soaked it in the bucket of icy water standing in the tub and wiped the blood from between her legs, the cold shock on her sex sending a tendril of forbidden pleasure up her spine. After la Condesa had left, she had made a pact with herself not to indulge in any memories that would inflame her desire, not to surrender to that temptation of the hands ever again. It had been difficult at first, but as the years passed, and especially in the last year, after her pens were confiscated, she forgot her body altogether.

The wet cloth soothed the welts and gouges, and she imagined a cool tongue licking her flesh, loving her body with absolute devotion, the way she had loved la Condesa so many years ago. Her nipples stiffened. For an instant she was afraid of her own memory, a mind that could produce such vivid images. Go back to bed, she told herself. You need to sleep, clear your head, prepare for the confession tomorrow. But she had never been good at heeding anyone's advice.

She lifted a foot onto the tub and trailed her fingers over the moist folds of her sex, pretending it was María Luisa that she was touching as her fingertips rubbed the edges of that forbidden place, that swollen seed that contained the secrets of her own tree of knowledge. Her fingers were wet now with blood and other humors and she rubbed deeper into the furrows beneath the hair, remembering the sounds of María Luisa's pleasure, the soft arching of her feet. *If I could rub myself against your calf*, she remembered saying, *feel your knee break the waters of my shame*. Suddenly she felt the seed burst open and her jaws clenched as the climax shot through her. She wept, still standing there on the cold tiles.

When it passed she washed herself again, tucked a bandage of dry cloths into her undergarment, dressed in habit, scapular and veil, and returned to her bedding. Clearly, she would not be able to sleep. She had to think about how she wanted to appear to the Tribunal tomorrow. First impressions meant everything. Should she, as the dream had suggested, hold her tongue and keep silent, or would it be more effective to confess in the manner of a novice on the threshold of taking her permanent vows? Although the idea of silence, the idea of rebelling against this humiliating spectacle through silence, appealed to her, she decided that it would be more prudent to follow the other path and assume the posture and the rhetoric of the novice. She was renewing her vows, after all.

She reached over to the small chest beside Andrea's bed and removed her copy of the *Manual for Novices* from the drawer. She read until the bells struck for matins, and then she and Andrea joined *las santas* in chanting the first *alabanzas* of the day in honor of Saint James, persecutor of Moors and infidels.

Chapter 32

In the twenty-four years of her profession, this was only the second time that Juana had left the convent. The first time, she had gone to Panoayán to bury her mother. The entire world, she remembered, had collapsed into those channels of dirty water crisscrossing the valley of Anáhuac and those scrubby hills at the foot of the volcanoes; all that had mattered, then, was reaching her mother before she died, talking to her again, sitting with her through her final trial. This four-mile journey from the cloister to the Plaza of Santo Domingo where the offices of the Inquisition were located seemed infinitely more ominous. Not only was she the one on trial this time, but she knew that she was guilty of everything. She was not virgin, not *uxor*, not wife, not meek, obedient sister. She was truly the worst of women, as she had set out to be from the day her three-year-old self had followed her sisters to school and insisted she be taught to read to last evening when she had not so much succumbed to temptation as induced it.

She and Andrea sat in the back of Padre Antonio's rickety surrey with their black veils covering their faces and their arms crossed under their scapulars. As the prioress of the convent, Andrea had received a special dispensation from the Archbishop to accompany Juana. Andrea had insisted that they take their rosaries in hand and pray a decade of Hail Marys as they rode to commend the outcome of this confession to the Mother of God.

Juana muttered the prayer through her lips, but her mind was on the city around her. They were taking the long way, for the bridge that connected the southern districts to the *traza*, the once-lovely Santa Rosa with its stone columns and arched abutments, was having its rotting timbers replaced. South along the aqueduct of Chapultepec, then north around the back of Hospital del Amor de Dios, then west past the university and the Plaza Mayor—Juana absorbed the city with her eyes. She noticed the Indian women washing their clothes along the embankments of the canals, the long line of indigents waiting outside the hospital, the students in their robes and mortarboards shuffling past the gate of the university. Crowds surged all around them. Once, when they stopped to let a pack train by, a *mestiza* girl ran up to the cart with a basket of persimmons and prickly pears. How she would love to bite into the orange flesh of a persimmon, she thought, feel the red juice of the prickly pear running down her chin. But then, for some reason, the girl stopped in her tracks, her eyes wide with dread. Juana reached out her hand to her, and the girl made the sign of protection against the evil eye and took off running. Juana remembered where they were going, and that the mark of her disgrace was visible to sensitive eyes plunged her into a state between fury and melancholy.

Her depression deepened when she laid eyes on the Plaza Mayor. She caught her breath at the charred doors and balconies of the palace. The marketplace rang out with the noise of reconstruction. The *municipio* looked like a squalid colony of makeshift booths and stalls, with *castas* camped out under the arcade and a stench of urine that billowed out over the street. Only the Cathedral remained intact, and the scaffold, which had been re-built with two platforms rather than one, and which rose as high as the cupola of the archiepiscopal palace.

"Out of my way, Woman," bellowed Padre Antonio to an old *mulata* dragging a crate of empty bottles across the road. "All of you! Get off the street! Lazy good-for-nothings! Doesn't anybody work in this city?"

"Why are all those doors boarded shut, Padre?" Juana asked as they turned north again at the Calle de San Agustín.

"*Pulquerías*," said Padre Antonio, shaking his head. "It was in those dens of debauchery that the drunken Indians organized their attack last year. The Corregidor is turning them all into *viviendas*."

The riots seemed a decade back in time. She remembered how the flames in the Plaza tinged the dusk with an almost phosphorescent orange glow, how the somber bells of the Cathedral tolled day and night to warn the city of the Indian mutiny upon the palace and the government.

"This Galve has done nothing for the city," Padre Antonio grumbled over his shoulder. "If he would take his eyes out of his wife's bosom, maybe he could see the *inmundicia* that Mexico has become. But, of course, he can't even see the horns over his head, cuckolded fool."

"You can't blame the Viceroy for everything, Padre," said Juana. "The rains and the blight caused much of this damage."

"That man is an imbecile! He's been working the Indians to death in the mines and the causeways rather than returning them to the fields where they belong."

She noticed that the back of Padre Antonio's neck had turned red. Andrea pinched her to be quiet, but Juana would not let up. De Galve was not her favorite Viceroy, but it irked her that the priests, who had more influence over the masses anyway, were unwilling to share responsibility for the devastations.

"Can we hold the Viceroy responsible for the apocalyptic interpretations of the rains and the eclipse, Padre? The riots were but a manifestation of our own irrational fears."

Padre Antonio turned to glare at her. "Who do you think you're speaking to, Woman? How dare you address me as an equal! We're on our way to your public confession and you sit there contradicting the only supporter you have!"

Andrea pinched her again, harder, and told her under her breath to curb her tongue.

"Forgive me, Padre," she mumbled.

"You have no humility, Juana. That is why I fear for the outcome of this confession."

She tried not to listen to his words. They had just passed the street that led to the Alameda and she remembered those Sunday carriage rides with la Marquesa and the Marquis de Mancera in the verdant shade of the massive poplars, the royal coach followed by an escort of lords and ladies on horseback. Another memory of the Alameda made her shudder, for there was where the Quemadero was located. Now the surrey was pulling up between the monastery of San Francisco and the House of Tiles, as it was called. She had forgotten the name of the aristocrat who lived in this mansion, which was completely covered in blue and white tiles, a house she used to pass almost daily when she lived with the Matas and at the palace. The sight of it made her want to weep, but she gouged her own arm under the scapular.

Finally, they stopped in front of the Church of Santo Domingo. Directly across from it stood the massive building of the Inquisition. Two constables helped them down from the cart, Padre Antonio, first, followed by Juana, then Andrea, and led them away from the throng of beggars that had gathered around the surrey. They stepped into the dark foyer of the building. The iron-studded door echoed shut behind them. From the court-yard they proceeded up a granite staircase into one of the public chambers of the Tribunal. Andrea stayed behind. Padre Antonio took Juana to the front of the room and told her to get on her knees facing the Tribunal's bench. On the bench itself, she noticed, were the two editions of her first book, and a copy of the second volume.

From the corner of her eye she saw that in the first pew to her left sat the Archbishop, the Bishop of Puebla, and Padre Antonio, the trinity of her nemesis. Behind them sat a cluster of priests from every Order and of every rank. In the pew to her right sat Don Ignacio de Castorena y Ursúa, the Rector of the university, and beside him the priest who had delivered a homily in the church of Saint Jerome in support of Juana's views of Vieyra, one Father Xavier Palavicino. She could not turn around to see who was sitting in the pews behind them, but from the commotion of their voices she could tell the room was filled. The whole city had come to watch her demise, and it occurred to her that the Tribunal had become a *corral de comedias* and that she was the protagonist of the *empeños* of another house, the House of Saint Jerome. A shiver ran down her arms at the thought that, again, she had predicted her own fate.

Somebody from the balcony threw a kerchief down; she glanced up and caught a glimpse of Josefa and her nephew, Panchito, among the crowd. The one face she most wanted to see was Sigüenza's, but he had still not returned from his sojourn in Florida. He would be sitting by Castorena, she wanted to believe, on the side of her advocates.

For an instant it seemed to her that she had traveled backward in time and had walked into the east salon of the palace where the Marqués de Mancera had scheduled her tournament with the forty professors. She had been wearing black then, too, and had recently discovered a painful secret about herself that had tormented her for nights and threatened to pollute the clarity of her presentation (*always so many secrets, Juana,* she told herself). But she had prevailed, or, more accurately, the hemisphere of her intellect had prevailed, and she had, as the Viceroy predicted, astonished and out-witted them all. Even then, though, this same shadow of scandal had been hovering over her, and she remembered how she had shocked Padre An-tonio and a few of these same obstinate men with her talk of Mayan mythology, and how the Viceroy and Fray Payo had tried to dissuade Padre Antonio from hauling her away to a nunnery for the sake of her salvation.

426

The irony of her life almost made her grin behind the black gauze of her veil. A secretary stationed just beneath the bench called out the names of the officers of the Tribunal as they strode into the room and climbed the stairs to their broad-backed chairs. Anaya, the *fiscal*, was in charge of prosecutions, and sat in the middle. To his right sat Dorantes, to his left, Olmedo. It did not surprise her in the least that they were all Dominicans like the Archbishop. The *fiscal* began by invoking the name of the Pope and pleading the grace of the Virgin Mary with a Salve Regina.

"I, dispossessed daughter of Eve, summon thee, my advocate in this valley of tears," she prayed under her breath.

After the prayer, the secretary read from a scroll.

"Juana Inés de la Cruz, *monja profesa* of the convent of Santa Paula of the Order of Saint Jerome, you have been brought before this court today to render testimony of all your faults and imperfections before a board of inquisitors appointed to examine the state of your conscience and judge whether you are worthy of reentering religious life as a Hieronymite. Have you anything to say to your Superiors?"

As she had decided the night before, she drew on the prayers of the novitiate for her response. "Oh, most clement God, since Thou hast made known to me Thy will through my Superior, I firmly resolve to obey him as I would obey Thee, and on Thy account shall I submit myself wholly to him and with a good heart."

"I beg the indulgence of the court," said Castorena, getting to his feet.

"Announce your name and title before you speak, Sir," said the secretary.

Castorena complied. "Before we begin I would like it clarified for the sake of our royal audience—" He shifted his eyes to the left and Juana wondered if the Viceroy himself, or perhaps Doña Elvira and her retinue of ladies, had come to witness her decline. "—as well as for the sake of our records, whether this is a trial or a confession, and if the latter, to explain why it is that the confession is taking place in this public forum rather than in the privacy of the cloister. And if the former, to explain the charges against Sister Juana, and to appoint me the advocate in her case."

"There are no advocates or prosecutors here, Maestro Castorena," said the *fiscal*. "This is a nun's general confession on the occasion of her Silver Jubilee. Her superiors have mandated that it take place here for the purpose of increasing her penitence, at her confessor's behest."

"There are no charges against Sor Juana, then?" insisted Castorena.

"Only those that her own actions have brought upon her, and those that have been documented in the archives of the Order of Saint Jerome."

Castorena sat down and wrote furiously in a notebook. Thank the Virgin, she said to herself, that at least one of her friends was going to keep a record of the events.

"Ilustrísima," the *fiscal* directed his question at the Archbishop, "may we have license to begin?"

Her knees were starting to ache already, but she didn't move, didn't lift her eyes from the veined marble of the floor as the one named Dorantes approached her. A breathless silence pervaded the room.

"You will begin, Sor Juana, by saying an Act of Contrition and a Credo," said the inquisitor.

She obeyed, her breath moving the veil up and down in front of her mouth.

"You have been brought before this court to purge your conscience of every vile act you have committed against your profession," said the *fiscal*.

"I entreat this merciful court to hear my confession," she said, her voice a monotone, "that it may serve to illuminate the depth of my repentance and the vigor with which I hope to renew my life in religion."

"Are you content in your vocation?"

"I am very content."

"Why have you been disobedient to the laws that govern your vocation?"

"Because I am a sinner and the worst of women."

"What are the things that you love most, and pursue with the greatest ardor?"

"What I love most is Jesus Christ, my Lord and Divine Husband. And yet I confess that I have been unfaithful. That I have pursued learning with the greatest ardor, seeking to fill my mind with every form of knowledge available in books and in conversation with the learned. I confess that this ardent pursuit of knowledge has many times steered me away from the True Cause of my vows. That I have been disobedient. That I have been arrogant. That I have been proud. That I have given way to anger and vainglory."

Her knees were starting to go numb.

"What are the passions to which you are most inclined?"

"I am most easily inclined toward sadness, despair, and anger. Love, too, is a passion that I have not been able to govern. Love of learning. Love of comfort. Love of food and music and beauty. Love of the written word."

"Are you bound to anyone by a particular friendship?"

"I am no longer bound to anyone in this regard. It is true that I once was bound to our former Vicereine, la Condesa de Paredes, for in her I found a kindred spirit in matters of poetry and philosophy and science."

"I beg your pardon, Padre Anaya," the Bishop of Puebla addressed the *fiscal,* "but we have submitted evidence that Sor Juana's particular friendship to the Vicereine, as well as to the Viceroy, was not strictly on intellectual terms. She did, I believe, confirm their firstborn, establishing a *compadrazgo* with them that was entirely illicit for a religious of her gender."

"I beg *your* pardon, Señor Obispo," said Castorena, getting to his feet again, "but we were told this was a confession and not a trial. Since when does evidence get submitted for a confession?"

"Perhaps 'evidence' was too strong a word," said the Bishop, changing his tone. "Let it suffice to say that we heard other confessions from a great majority of *profesas* of the Order of Saint Jerome and were given to believe that Sor Juana's conduct with said Vicereine and Viceroy, and with several highly placed nobles and scholars, like yourself Maestro, as well as the favoritism displayed toward her by another Viceregal couple and our former Archbishop, Fray Payo, have induced in her sisters the vices of envy and anger, the passions of hatred and aversion, thereby compromising a great many of their virtues."

Juana heard a clatter of heels.

"It's all in her books, Maestro," the Bishop continued, "as surely you must know, since you are one of her more ardent admirers."

"I remember sharing many an evening with you, Your Grace, at Sor Juana's *locutorio,*" said Castorena. "You seemed particularly friendly with her confections and most amenable to her discourse."

She had lost feeling in her knees, but now a cramp had started in her hip.

"This is not the confession of *my* sinful inclinations, Señor," said the Bishop.

From the Tribunal's bench, the *fiscal* struck the triangle. "Gentlemen, if you wish to carry on a private conversation, you may step out into the foyer. Otherwise, be seated and we can continue. Fray Agustín, please take over the questioning."

"I repeat, Sir," Castorena said to the *fiscal*, "this public questioning is aberrant behavior for a nun's confession."

"There are many who denounce her of wrongdoing, Maestro Castorena," said Olmedo, his voice mellifluous as a choirboy's. "Accusations brought about by her own actions, as we said earlier. It is the nature of these proceedings to find out if the accusations are true, as this will come to bear upon our decision to allow her to renew her vows."

"Who denounces her, Your Honor?"

"You know very well that the Inquisition never reveals its sources," said Dorantes. "She may guess them if she's so inclined, and that is, in fact, the direction I want to steer this confession."

Dorantes took one of her books and held it between his hands as he talked.

"Can you recall, Sister, any action on your part which your accusers might interpret as errors in religion?"

The cramp in her hip arrowed down the back of her leg. "I have many enemies, Your Honor. No doubt most of my actions would appear faults in their eyes."

"With whom do you feud, Sister?"

"With the exception of two or three persons in this court, I should say I feud with everyone who finds fault with me."

"What is the cause of these feuds, pray tell?"

"That I write. That I publish. That I cultivate the fields of my mind with study. That I own real estate in the convent. That for twenty years I was the favorite of the court. That I have been favored by several prioresses. That I correspond with the world. Shall I continue?"

"Are you confessing to these sins, Sister?"

"If they be deemed as sins, Your Honor, then I confess them."

"Do you doubt that they are sins, Sister? For sins they most certainly are in the holy eyes of the Church; that you disbelieve they are sins is equal to disbelieving holy doctrine, and this, in turn, is equal to blasphemy, if not heresy."

She could not resist pointing out the flaw in his logic: "Are they sins, then, for the general population, for if so, we are surrounded by heretics. Indeed, the very Bible is a heretical text written by learned men."

A buzz went up in the back of the room.

"Do not intend to befuddle an inquisitor with tricky rhetoric, Sister. You know perfectly well that it is forbidden for religious women to engage in any activity that inflames the sin of pride. From all of the evidence we have assessed, it is quite clear that you excel at that sin."

The cramp made the muscles in her leg quiver. "I do not deny it, Your Honor."

Dorantes cleared his throat and started turning the pages of the book. He dog-eared a page and held it out over the bench. "Take this to Sister Juana," he said to a clerk sitting beside the secretary.

The clerk brought her the second edition of *Castalian Inundation*.

"Read the underlined passage out loud," said Dorantes.

Juana had to focus on keeping her leg still. She inhaled and exhaled quickly, but her hands shook as she read. "'Either her appreciation for being favored and celebrated, or her acquaintance with the illustrious gifts bestowed by Heaven on the Lady Vicereine, or that secret influence (which until today no one has been able to verify) of the humors or the stars, known as sympathy, or all of these together, generated in the poet a love utterly pure and ardent for her Excellency, as the reader will see in the whole of this book.'"

The Bishop jumped to his feet. "'secret influence of the humors or the stars'! Does *that*, Maestro Castorena, sound like a strictly intellectual relationship?"

Now her other leg was trembling. She didn't know how long she could kneel here without collapsing.

"Is she to be held responsible for how another interprets her character?" asked Castorena.

"You have a point, Maestro," said Dorantes. He rifled through a stack of pages. "Let us see how our Hieronymite postulant judges herself." He turned to face the Archbishop. "I beg your pardon if this causes offense, Ilustrísima."

"'If the moon represented passion rather than wisdom and the sun reason rather than power,'" his voice boomed over the chamber, "'it would make sense that the Sun God should triumph over the Moon Goddess, for she like a dark empress (or the Onyx Queen I gave to Concepción) tyrannizes my nights and I find relief from that tyranny only when the light of reason illuminates my heart. Otherwise I would go mad, and be plunged, like Phaëton or Lucifer from glorious heights to the cold currents of doom.'"

They had copied everything. Even the notes she had scribbled on the inside covers of her First Dream. The thoroughness of it angered her so much she forgot the ache in her knees for a moment.

"Are those your words, Sor Juana?" asked Dorantes.

"They were written on the evening of the eclipse," she answered.

"And who, pray tell, is the referent for this 'dark empress' who tyrannizes your nights?"

"It's a conceit, Your Reverence. A metaphor."

"And is the part about you plummeting to the cold currents of doom also a metaphor?"

"No, Sir, it's a simile."

"Likening yourself to Lucifer," said Dorantes.

"Not to Lucifer, per se, Your Reverence, nor to Phaëton; but to the act of becoming consumed by a passionate desire for clarity."

"Yes, that is our same desire on this Tribunal, Sor Juana."

Then you, too, are like Lucifer, she wanted to say, but bit the inside of her cheeks instead.

"There is still no evidence of any wrongdoing between Sor Juana and our former Vicereine," insisted Castorena.

The *fiscal* struck the triangle again. Dorantes took another piece of parchment from the bench.

"I have here, Maestro Castorena, a letter I would like to read. There are many like it, but this one, I trust, will clearly illuminate this court about the nature of the friendship between our former Vicereine and our good sister, so that the Maestro does not accuse us of hearsay."

"Proceed, then, Fray Agustín," said the *fiscal*.

"'Dearest Juana. Don't laugh. I found this letter tucked in an old reticule, the beaded one I used when we first arrived in New Spain (perhaps you don't remember it; you never seemed to pay attention to any of my fashionable accessories). Forgive me for not having shared these thoughts with you at the time, but I guess I could not bring myself to admit that there were several possible interpretations for that comet. My mind was set on convincing you rather than allowing myself to be convinced with your good logic. I remember the quarrels we had about this and all, ultimately—'" The inquisitor raised his voice several octaves. "'—all, ultimately to condone the views of some priest. How foolish of me to side with foolish men rather than with my own heart. But then, I, too, was foolish for your unmitigated devotion, Juana, and could not tolerate any differences between us.'"

Dorantes lowered the page and glared triumphantly at Castorena. I was right, thought Juana; Concepción did betray me, after all. She had never seen that letter and the girl had not destroyed it as Juana had instructed her. The bolt of anger she felt straightened her back and her leg stopped trembling.

"Is that the end of it?" prodded Castorena.

"The best part is yet to come, gentlemen, but I would like our jubilant Sor Juana to do us the honor of reading this lost letter of the Vicereine for us. It will, I think, make more impact if read in her voice."

"Sister," ordered the *fiscal*, "you will comply with Fray Agustín's request."

The clerk brought her the copy of the letter—it was Rafaela's handwriting, Juana noticed—and told her to lift her veil so that her voice would carry.

"Señor *Fiscal,* I protest!" interjected Padre Antonio. "A nun cannot show her face in public. The inquisitor knows that."

"She may read with the veil on," said Anaya.

Juana squeezed her eyes shut and took a deep breath.

"You're wasting the time of these good men, Sister," said Dorantes. "Read! And be sure not to skip anything. The secretary has it memorized."

At first her voice was tremulous, but it grew bolder as she got caught up in the beauty of the writing. "'Last night I sat for an hour on the terrace that overlooks the rose court and just stared at the comet, really looked at it and tried to see it as you might. In my fancy, I saw you standing behind your telescope, looking through the glass and then writing in that notebook you always carry with you. I made a miniature telescope with my cupped hand and focused only on that light, first a twinkle at the tip, growing wider and then blossoming into a white, refulgent star, behind which burned a haze of orange sparks, an arc of diaphanous light shooting out and then tapering like an evanescence into the star-filled night. I understand now that this is the symbol by which I will always remember you, Juana, our special friendship—'" Juana swallowed hard at what was next. "'—our evanescent and celestial love. Is there such a thing, Juana? A love as wide as the comet's light, as full of promise, and as unreal and frightening as that star which shoots across the sky when God wills it. You would probably say (in that way of yours that makes me feel as though I do not understand science): Señora, God does not determine the life of comets; rather, there are forces pulling at the earth, celestial bodies intersecting the earth's orbit. What would you say, I wonder, if I told you that for me, you are a comet and I am the planet whose orbit you have intersected?'"

A loud murmuring went up in the gallery. Juana wanted to weep. If only María Luisa were here, she would feel brave in the face of this humiliation; she would bear it proudly. Instead, she felt shamed and exposed and soiled.

433

"Do you admit, Juana Inés de la Cruz," said Dorantes, "to having transgressed in more than word and thought with la Condesa de Paredes?"

"We were intimate friends, Your Grace."

"Quite intimate, I gather. Isn't it true, Sister, that you had *physical* contact, with both la Condesa and her husband, the Count and our own Viceroy?"

"I could not prevent them from touching me," she said. "Fray Payo himself, during his term as Archbishop as well as Viceroy, often embraced me when he bid farewell after a visit."

"But an embrace is not the same as a kiss, now is it, Sister?"

"I don't know what you mean, Your Reverence."

"It was witnessed by one of your own sisters." Dorantes read from his notes: "La Condesa de Paredes kissed Sor Juana on the lips and Sor Juana kissed the same personage in return!"

A loud gasp echoed in the chamber.

Very clearly she heard Josefa's voice: "Oh, Juana!"

"And the Viceroy kissed your shoe, did he not?" interjected the other inquisitor.

Another gasp.

The quivering in her leg resumed. A spasm shot through her hip and hardened into a cramp at her coccyx. "Sir," she said, "you are proceeding under the assumption that I will deny your allegations, but the Tribunal has heard me say that I deny nothing. I confess to everything. I prostrate myself to your will and to the will of the Church. I ask only that I be allowed to live at the feet of Jesus the rest of my sinful life."

She took advantage of the opportunity to illustrate the sincerity of her statement and stretched herself out on the floor, biting her lip to keep from groaning as the cramp eased its pressure on her spine. The joints in her knees popped back into place. Through the thin fabric of the veil she felt the grittiness of the floor.

Padre Antonio came and stood above her, so close she could smell the horse dung on the soles of his shoes. "Save your hypocritical displays for the cloister," he said.

"This is not the choir of your convent, Sister," said one of the inquisitors. "Please get up."

"Get on your knees, Juana," Padre Antonio ordered.

"If you please, Ilustrísima." She turned her face sideways to speak to the Archbishop. "Allow me to demonstrate the sincerity of my penitence."

The gasping had turned into a loud buzz from the audience.

"Unchaste daughter of Judas!" hissed the Archbishop. "How dare you address me!"

"Get up at once!" ordered the *fiscal*.

She obeyed, pushing herself up with her palms and wincing as the cramp sliced through her left buttock. The inquisitors' questions continued. The one named Olmedo discoursed at length on her critique of Vieyra, on the mortal sin she had committed as a nun and a woman in attempting to defy the teachings of a holy father. Then he performed an exegesis on every single verse she had written for la Condesa, luxuriating in dissecting every metaphor and pun and allusion. He gave the same treatment to two poems for the Viceroy and to the requiems she'd written to commemorate the death of la Marquesa. He went on a tirade about the hypocrisies of wearing a veil to hide her face when she had so flagrantly made her name public currency in the world. The hourglass was tipped, and he rambled on for another hour about the dangerous rhetoric of her response to Sor Filotea.

Juana drifted in and out of awareness. She was reciting "Hombres necios" in her mind to keep from thinking about her knees or her back, knowing that eventually she would collapse again and not be able to lift herself. It would be the best thing, she decided, for her knees to buckle, for her to fall gracelessly onto that cold floor. *Stubborn men who accuse women without reason, dismissing yourselves as the occasion for the very wrongs you design . . .*

There was a respite from the questioning, and she realized that the *fiscal* had ordered a recess for the midday meal. The room cleared quickly. Juana was allowed to get up from her penitent's pose, though it took both Andrea and Castorena to lift her. Somewhere they found a stool for her, and Josefa came down from the balcony and got to work rubbing the blood back into her legs. It felt so good to be touched. Hands that cared for her. Hands that knew just what to do. Good, capable, loving, sisterly hands. None of them saw her tears under the veil.

"What's going on here, Padre Antonio?" asked Josefa, rubbing Juana's calf between her strong palms. "Is this a confession, or a circus?"

Padre Antonio was livid. "It's an obscenity," he said. "A mockery of a solemn occasion. I should have known that's what they wanted."

"Don't vex yourself, Your Reverence," said Andrea. "Juana's will is strong. She can take this."

"I can?" she mumbled, but no one heard her.

"It's not about having a strong will," snapped Josefa. "It's about being dragged through the mud-like a criminal—"

Juana held out her hand to still her sister. "Let it be," she said. "None of this surprises me. It will pass."

"It isn't passing soon enough for me," said Padre Antonio.

"Tía, I got you a sausage!" Panchito bolted in carrying a bundle of steaming sausages in a stack of thick tortillas.

"Offer one to the priest, first," said Josefa.

At first Padre Antonio refused, but Andrea insisted that he eat. Juana could eat nothing, and asked her nephew to bring her something to drink instead.

"There!" Josefa said, patting Juana's kneecap. "Is that better?"

Please don't stop, she wanted to say, but she only nodded. "I need to walk," she said.

Josefa supported her waist and Juana put an arm around her shoulder. Together they walked up and down in the aisle between the pews. Panchito rushed in again carrying a small, dark coconut with a rough hole chipped in the shell. Juana drank it so fast the sweet liquid oozed out the sides of her mouth and trickled down into her neckcloth.

"If you will forgive my intrusion, Sor Juana," said Father Xavier, standing beside Castorena, "I just wanted to say what a great admirer I am of your work and would deem it my most sincere honor to have you autograph my copy of *Segundo volúmen*."

"I don't think now is the time for that, Father," said Padre Antonio.

"I delivered the sermon in defense of your interpretation of Vieyra," he said.

"Yes, I heard it, Father Xavier," said Juana. "It was brought under examination, was it not?"

"The Holy Office found fault with it, yes. I was sentenced to a hundred lashes in the Plaza Mayor."

"You took one hundred lashes for defending me, Sir?"

Father Xavier glanced at Padre Antonio. "For attacking the so-called soldiers of the faith who thought your analysis bordered on heresy."

"Not bordered, Sir," interjected Padre Antonio. "They *were* heretical!"

"Vieyra is not Holy Writ, Padre Antonio," said the young priest, "but I know that the Archbishop esteems him greatly and considers him close to a prophet."

"After forty years that the Sermon on the Mandate has been circulating from the highest to the lowest offices in the Church," said Padre Antonio, his spittle gathering at the corners of his mouth, "to have a woman find his arguments invalid! Such a learned and Catholic man as Vieyra! You went too far, Juana!"

By the time the bells tolled for nones, everyone had gathered back in the chamber and the inquisitors had resumed their places. The constable took away her stool, but at least Juana felt strengthened by her sister's massage. She took a deep breath and held it, telling herself that it would only be a matter of hours for the ordeal to be over.

She was wrong. The confession took days, and Juana had to kneel through all of it. Her main fear was that they would keep her in one of the secret jails of the Inquisition, the customary practice for these proceedings, but the inquisitors seemed content with Andrea's promise that she would watch over Juana herself and make sure she did nothing foolish before the confession came to a close. Andrea stopped accompanying her after three days for she had duties to attend to at the convent. Belilla made her hot chocolate every morning into which she stirred a bit of laudanum to help ease the torture on her knees. Josefa brought her fruit and bread to keep her strength up, massaged her legs and lower back while she ate. Padre Antonio grew wan with fatigue, and the task of escorting her back and forth from the convent fell on Castorena, followed closely by a constable on horseback. It occurred to Juana that Castorena had to be trusted; she needed his help getting manuscripts off to la Condesa before the spies of the convent found them and submitted them to the Holy Office as more evidence. She had Belilla wrap what remained of her papers and notebooks in two bundles and one of the *beatas* took care of placing them quietly in his carriage.

At last, on the feast day of San Lorenzo, five days before the Feast of the Assumption, the confession came to a close. Juana had said next to nothing. It had been the inquisitor's performance completely.

"Juana Inés de la Cruz!" the *fiscal* called out as though she were not kneeling right under the bench. "Are you satisfied that every infraction you have committed against your profession has been disclosed before this Tribunal?"

"I am most satisfied, Your Honor."

"Have you nothing else to confess?"

"Only that I have grown weary of this protracted penitence that keeps me away from my sisters and my students and the work that God has given me. And also, that I have wished with all of my soul that leprosy afflict all of my enemies."

"How dare she?" shouted the Archbishop.

"I beg His Ilustrísima's forgiveness," said Juana, making sure not to address him directly. "I had to confess that last sin."

Out of the corner of her eye she spotted Castorena grinning at someone in the audience.

The inquisitors consulted each other for a time, and she could hear nothing but the scratch of the secretary's quill and the mumbling of the crowd. Finally, the *fiscal* got to his feet.

"The Tribunal has concluded its deliberations," announced the secretary.

Dorantes and Olmedo came down from their seats and, standing at either side of her, half-dragged her to the front of the Tribunal's bench. She felt a painful tingling in her legs as the blood rushed back into circulation.

The *fiscal* stood up and read from the parchment.

"We find Sor Juana Inés de la Cruz, *monja profesa* of San Jerónimo of the Imperial City of Mexico, guilty of the sins of pride and rebellion which have led her to transgress against the orthodox teachings of the Church in total disavowal of her sex and her vocation."

The Archbishop fixed her with the cobalt of his eyes.

"Because of your perpetual correspondence with the world," Anaya continued, "because of your worldly publications, because of your unchaste relationships with members of the court and your particular friendships with women and men outside religion, because of the infidelity of your devotion to books and for your immodest and incessant pursuit of secular learning, we declare you, Juana Inés de la Cruz, a blasphemer against the faith. Because of your heinous acts of rebellion we pronounce the last twenty-five years of your life an abomination against the laws of the Holy Catholic Church. You are, therefore, sentenced to a full Reconciliation with your faith and with the sacred vows of your vocation. If you wish to continue in the service of the Church, we deem it just and necessary for you to forswear all the trappings of that life, now and forever. All books and all instruments of your ungodly trade shall be confiscated. You shall write nothing save the documents required for your reconciliation. You shall never receive another guest or engage in any correspondence with the world whatsoever. On the feast day of the patron saint of your Order, the

Chief Vigilanta will administer one hundred and fifty lashes on your person in the presence of the entire community of your house. And, as a sign of your perpetual infamy, you will wear the *sanbenito* over your habit until such time as you are deemed worthy to renew your vows as a bride of the Incarnate Christ."

Dorantes forced her to her knees again.

As had happened during the examination with the forty scholars, Juana felt her mind cleave into its diametrically opposite halves. In this contest, however, it was not Reason or Memory that would prevail, but the abject surrender of her free will. In the logical hemisphere of her mind she heard echoes of the letter she had written Padre Antonio over a decade ago, when at last she had lost her patience with his censures and realized that it was in her power to dismiss him as her father confessor. She had had such clarity, then, such strength of will and purpose. She invoked the fragmented memory of that text to form the confutation the inquisitors would never hear, a rational counterpoint to the submissive replies they were seeking from the side in which logic had no roots.

"Do you, Juana Inés de la Cruz, renounce that life of sin and rebellion?"

"I renounce it."

Vexing me is not a good way to assure my submission, nor do I have so servile a nature that I do under threat what reason does not persuade me, nor out of respect for man what I do not do for God . . .

"Do you renounce the study of books?"

"I renounce it."

Did not Saint Catherine study, Saint Gertrude, my Mother Saint Paula, without harm to her exalted contemplation, and was her pious founding of convents impeded by her knowing even Greek? Or learning Hebrew? . . . Then why do you find wicked in me what in other women was good? Am I the only one whose salvation is impeded by books?

"Do you renounce all of your worldly associations?"

"I renounce them."

Did I solicit the applause and public celebration? And the private favors and honors bestowed upon me by the Viceroy and Vicereine . . . What fault was it of mine that Their Excellencies were pleased with me? And though there was no reason for their pleasure, could I deny such sovereign figures?

"Do you renounce the pursuit of secular knowledge?"

"I renounce it."

Your Reverence wishes that I be coerced into salvation while ignorant, but beloved Father, may I not be saved if I am learned? . . . Is not God, who is supreme goodness, also supreme wisdom? Then why would He find ignorance more acceptable than knowledge?

"Do you repent for your sins?"

"I repent, oh Lord, in heart and soul for having offended Thee," she prayed the Act of Contrition again.

Like men, do women not have a rational soul? Why then shall they not enjoy the privilege of the enlightenment of letters? Is a woman's soul not as receptive to God's grace and glory as a man's? Then why is she not as able to receive learning and knowledge, which are the lesser gifts?

"Do you wish to die and be reborn in religion?"

She drew on the *Manual for Novices*: "I desire to be conducted to this happy death, and to die to myself in order that by the destruction of my own life I may have the happiness of living for God."

I have this nature; if it is evil, I am the product of it; I was born with it and with it I shall die.

"Then shall you forsake everything which contaminated that life, for poison lurks in objects and persons and thoughts, and all of these must you repudiate as though they were the Serpent himself."

"I wish to know nothing, to love nothing, to desire nothing save God and the virtue of obedience."

Dorantes and Olmedo pulled her back to her feet. She felt like a puppet between them.

"Go, then, errant daughter of the Church, into your year of approbation, that God may find you worthy to continue wearing the habit of the Hieronymite Order."

"The constables of the Inquisition will call upon you to remove all traces of temptation from your life," said Dorantes. "And try to remember that we do have an inventory of your possessions, so do not attempt to remove anything or you shall face another year of approbation as your penalty."

"God's will be done," said Juana.

She genuflected, despite the pain in her knees, and managed not to fall over. She had withstood fifteen days of this torture to her body and spirit and knew that purgatory did, indeed, exist among the living. Before they released her, one of the clerks appeared and handed her the gray and yellow penitent's smock that she would have to wear for half a year. She slipped the *sanbenito* over her head, pulled the heavy sleeves of her habit through the sleeve holes of the smock, and hung the placard that read "reconciled" over her neck.

Outside in the small plaza of Santo Domingo, there was an air of rejoicing and she was surrounded by people whose names she no longer remembered except for those who had remained close. They bought flowers and pulque and sweetmeats and laughed and kissed and sang. They thought she had won against Aguiar y Seijas and Fernández de Santa Cruz, indeed, that she had vanquished the Inquisition itself, but in truth victory was not hers. They had just witnessed the last performance of the Tenth Muse. Didn't they realize that she had been condemned to death in life? Without the companionship of her books or the solace of the pen or friends to discourse with or letters to keep her connected to the world—this was not a life she wanted to live. They may as well have sentenced her to hang. At least her demise would have been quick, and so would the end to her disgrace.

The constables appeared with a long rope, and for an instant Juana thought they intended to flog her out here in front of the crowd. Instead they tied her wrists together and looped the rope to the back of their mule cart and were going to drag her through the streets of the *traza*, but an old friend of hers stepped in, the accountant, Don Fernando Deza, who tendered each constable a handful of coins to keep them from carrying out this final humiliation.

Padre Antonio stood beside Juana for a moment, as if he wanted to say something, but instead he raised his arm and made a blessing over her face, then retreated back into the shadows of the building. Castorena led her to his carriage. Josefa came along and sat with her arm around Juana's shoulders, kissing her sister's cheek over and over while Castorena maneuvered the horses out of the tangle of carriages in the square and down the street that led to the Plaza Mayor.

"May we stop at the Cathedral, Don Ignacio?" she asked.

"At your service, Sor Juana," he answered, and led his horses to the east entrance of the Metropolitan Church, the same door at which her triumphal arch had once stood.

"Shall I go with you, Juana?" asked Josefa.

"I'm not going in," said Juana. "I just wanted to look at the palace from here."

Juana stared at the burnt plank of the central balcony, where she had so often sat among the ladies-in-waiting imbibing la Marquesa with her eyes, and bid farewell to the girl-scholar who had once lived to please the court. From that day forward, she promised herself, she would do everything in her power to exorcise the memory of Juana Inés Ramírez de Asbaje.

Through the knot of her vocal chords she whispered a verse from her *villancico* to Saint Catherine, another girl-scholar, equally persecuted, equally reviled for having climbed the tree of knowledge: "Her sage syllogisms are lost to us, but those she did not leave with ink, she left written in her blood."

"Juana, are you talking to yourself, love?" asked Josefa, rubbing her back in soothing circles. "Aren't you happy? It's over. They've left you in peace at last."

But Juana was thinking of something else, imagining the convent's Book of Professions where she would renew her vows and sign her new testament of faith. *I, Juana Inés, the worst of the world*, she would sign it, and the quill would scratch her signature across the page in the red ink of her blood.

Tlilli, the Aztecs called it, the red ink of wisdom.

I die (who would believe it?) at the hands of what I love best. What is it puts me to death? The very love I profess.

Mate

1693–1695

Belilla's Notebook

Tía has given me this notebook in which to record important events that happen to her. It's like keeping a diary for someone else. It makes me uncomfortable because I don't know how to keep a diary. Tía says it's like talking to yourself and I ask her if that's allowed, for we are only supposed to talk to God through prayer, not indulge in private conversations. She says that if I love her I will do this. I asked Mother Andrea's permission, and she gave it, so there is no reason not to proceed.

30 of September of 1693, day of our father, Saint Jerome
Tía wrote a petition to the Tribunal today, stating in writing that she convicts herself of all the allegations made against her, and that in the tribunal of her own conscience she condemns herself to eternal death. She wrote that she has lived in religion without religion, as a pagan would live, but that it is still her will to take the habit and and be accepted back into the Order of Saint Jerome. I had to be a witness. Afterward, she received one hundred and fifty lashes in the chapter room, administered by the Sister Vicaria.

12 of November of 1693
Tía's birthday today, I think she's forty-five. We've been packing up all of her books for the Archbishop. He's convinced the Inquisition that he needs the money from Tía's library to rebuild the hospital of the poor. I wanted to ask her about the books we hid in the chapel in the cemetery, but she was already so upset that I hated to add to her burden. Watching her part with her books has been like watching a mother burying her children. She holds all of them tenderly before she lays them into the chest, but some she is closer to than others and these she opens and strokes their pages, taking time to reread any commentaries she may have written in their margins. I have even heard her speaking to some of them, as if those books were alive. Last night, she wept bitterly when she had to box up her in-

struments. I didn't realize how attached she'd become to those things, that magnifying glass, that pendulum clock, that telescope, that astrolabe by which she said she could chart the history of the Milky Way, that dusty, faded Indian headdress that used to hang over her desk. They're even taking her desks and her bookcases and her chess table. She sat up all night playing chess with herself, hugging her little aeolian harp to her chest. She isn't allowed to keep anything in her study. She isn't even allowed to have a study anymore. My conscience bothers me because I know about those books and that writing box buried under the floorboards in the chapel. Dare I say anything to Mother Andrea? Dare I tell her that Tía ordered me to take Abuelo's chess set and her mandolin and hide them behind the chest of linens in the parlor? That she gave me her jewelry and jade rosary to stash under my mattress?

"We can't be left in the street," she told me when I protested about the jewelry. "All we have is our annuity, Belilla, if the Archbishop doesn't take that as well. Don't be foolish. They'll eat us alive in here if they know we have nothing." So I hid her bracelets and rings, her jade rosary, and the ring that has la Condesa's tiny portrait on it, along with my copy of Tía's first book—all in a hole I cut out of the mattress, just in case anybody looks under my pillow and discovers that I'm abetting Tía in her disobedience. It's so hard to choose between my vows and my devotion to her, but I know that I am all she can rely on now, and that she needs me. She is utterly alone, she says. At times at night she holds long conversations with Don Carlos or la Condesa in her sleep.

8 of December of 1693, Day of the Immaculate Conception
Tía has been disciplining herself without remorse. Now that her study is empty, she's moved her bed and armchair to that room and at night I hear the scourge falling on her flesh. I try not to count the lashes, but she went to thirty last night and damaged herself so much she was barely able to get out of bed. It frightens me, this sudden passion for discipline. When I asked her about it this morning, she said she was remembering an old friend, her secretary, Concepción, whose birthday is today. She is not supposed to remember anything about her past life. I remember Concepción. She was always sitting at Tía's feet when Aunt Josefa and I came to visit and I remember feeling so jealous of their closeness. Padre Antonio spends hours with Tía in the confessional. He's happy, I think, that Tía is at last living by her vows. He told Mother Andrea to put her to work in the infirmary,

slopping chamber pots and scrubbing linen. Mother Andrea protested, saying that only Juana could manage the accounts. But she doesn't want to continue as treasurer. Holding a quill, she told me, even if just to write numbers, is too much of a torture for her to bear.

22 of December of 1693

I still don't know what to do about the books. I almost said something to Father Nazario at confession today, but I can't help feeling like such a traitor. She's my aunt, after all, my mother's sister. And yet, we're supposed to forget all of our attachments when we take our vows and I so much want to be a good nun. I hope the Christ Child forgives me for keeping this secret. Another secret I have to keep for my Tía. I can't even write about the other one. It would be a sin, I think, to describe what I saw. My poor Tía. She has so many secrets making holes in her heart. I wonder if she's written anything about it in that writing box under the floorboards.

26 of January of 1694, day of our mother, Saint Paula

I was helping Sor Clara roast pumpkin seeds for her parakeets, and when she asked me how Tía was holding up under the stress of her penitence, I told her about the books. I didn't tell her where they were, or that they were banned books, just that I had helped her hide them somewhere on the premises. Why did I do that? Sor Clara is the biggest gossip in the world. She's almost deaf. Maybe she didn't hear me. And if she did, at least it won't be me telling on my tía. Does this qualify as betrayal? Forgive me, Tía. I feel like such a Judas. Must hold a vigil to Saint Joseph tonight in repentance.

31 of January of 1694

I knew it. Mother Andrea called me to the priory yesterday to ask me about the books. I told her I would bring them to her, that I did not feel right about revealing their location, and she chastised me for having gossiped to Sor Clara. "You should have revealed this to your father confessor or to me," she said. "Don't you think your aunt has enough suffering?" As penitence for my infraction, Mother Andrea had me slap my mouth until I drew blood, and I am to wash the dishes in the refectory and to eat off the floor for a month. I am also to take her to where the books are hidden. I begged her to let me get them, but she didn't accede. I am to take her to the chapel this evening after vespers. I don't know what she intends to do, but I'm afraid for Tía's writing box. What if I dig it out and hide it in that dilapidated old shed where the gardening tools are kept? Sor Clara says a prisoner lived there once, daughter of a refugee slave whom Concepción helped to escape. I better hurry. Maybe I can dig a hole in the ground of the toolshed and hide the writing box there.

after matins, 1 of February of 1694

Found a loose adobe in the wall of the toolshed and when I pulled it out I discovered a good-sized niche with a broad-rimmed hat inside, the straw riddled with holes, and the hat was filled with dry red flowers, peach pits and mango pits, stiff orange rinds, and strands of hair wrapped around a piece of parchment, crisp with age, and nearly black down the creases. When I removed the hair and tried to unroll it, the parchment fell apart like a piece of dry earth, but there was something black and solid, like a dry black sponge, wrapped inside it. There was also a necklace of black and red beads. I wonder if these things belonged to that prisoner that Sor Clara told me about? There was something unholy about it all, so I took everything out of the niche, swept it out into the irrigation ditch, and left the niche clean and smooth. I saved the necklace, though. It's just a necklace and it would look pretty draped around the wrist of the Saint Joseph statue we have in the parlor. Tía's box fit inside the niche, but it sticks out and I can't replace the adobe. I've dragged a pile of pots in front of it. Hope nobody discovers what I've done. That's the problem with secrets. They multiply, like sins or fish.

11 of February of 1694

Trying to govern the temptation to read Tía's diary. That's what's in the box, and some old letters from la Marquesa and la Condesa. And a goose quill, yellow and brittle with age, and an owl-shaped inkwell with a dedication from the Virreyes of Mexico dated 1666, the ink dry as coal dust inside. I'm going to polish the inkwell for her and give it to her on the day she renews her vows.

17 of February of 1694

Under Padre Antonio's instruction, Tía wrote a short explication on the mystery of the Immaculate Conception of our Blessed Lady in the Book of Professions today (she was so happy to be writing again, it broke my heart). As prefect of the Brotherhood of the Immaculate Conception of Mary, Padre Antonio wanted her to leave evidence of her devotion to this mystery, which is evidence of her devotion to his own reverential person.

He's so old, but still has a vigorous light in his eyes when he gives Communion, though he can barely see what he's doing now and ends up dropping the host into our hands. I must admit I'm afraid of him. He's so strict with her, even though nobody could be doing better at perfecting herself through prayer and discipline. He still wants her to do more. She submits to anything he says, but I can see the look of resentment hardening in her eyes. Something in her face, maybe the resignation in it, reminds me of my grandmother. It seems so long ago that we went to Panoayán to bury her.

5 of March of 1694

Tía signed her *Protesta* today, reiterating her desire to renew her vows and serve God and the Holy Faith for the rest of her life. She wrote that she would be willing to shed blood in defense of her faith and her beliefs, and then, to the horror of the witnesses and to my own revulsion, Tía stabbed the quill into her wrist and gashed the vein and used the blood for ink to sign her name. *La peor*, she called herself, *la peor del mundo*. No one said anything, but I noticed that just before she crossed herself, Mother Andrea shook her head ever so slightly. I think I even saw tears in her eyes. She loves my *tía* more than I realized, which must be hard for her to admit as the Mother Superior of this house. Nothing more has ever been said about the secret books, so I don't know if she has unearthed them or if they're going to stay under the chapel forever. Tía wept when I gave her the inkwell, but then she gave it back to me and told me to use it for when I record these thoughts.

after curfew, Easter Sunday of 1694

Tía woke up screaming just now. She said she dreamt she was standing on the platform of the scaffold in the Plaza Mayor in front of thousands of people, and then she saw herself swinging from the gibbet, and a man's voice called out over the crowd that the famous Hieronymite nun, Sor Juana Inés de la Cruz, had been declared a heretic by the Inquisition. She has a fever, I think. Her eyes are glazed and her mouth smells like medicine. I wonder if she's caught anything at the infirmary. It wouldn't surprise me, the way Padre Antonio has been making her work.

18 of October of 1694

Have not been able to write in six months. A plague has fallen over us, an epidemic of some kind that produces ugly red spots all over the body and severe respiratory problems. The infirmary is overflowing with the sick. Mother Andrea has packed off all the boarders and quarantined this side of the cloister. No one is allowed on this side except the *beatas* and Sor Gabriela, and myself as her assistant, and of course, Tía is here, scrubbing and slopping like the lowliest of slaves. Padre Antonio and Father Nazario have begun administering last sacraments to the most critically ill. Tía says she doesn't want me in the infirmary, but I'm quarantined here, just like she is. I'm glad I brought the notebook with me. Even if I don't have time to write, thinking about what I would write helps take my mind off all those bodies writhing from the fever. And the smell! Like meat rotting on old bones.

another day

I've lost track of the date. There are no calendars in the infirmary. A new epidemic has hit. This one infects the bowels and makes everyone vomit a mixture of black blood and deep yellow bile. And it is so cold. There's barely enough wood to heat water, and there aren't enough blankets to keep everyone warm. Tía won't let me near the beds, won't even let me help her wash the linen or gather the chamber pots. Sor Gabriela has fallen ill, and so now it is just Tía and Mother Andrea and the *beatas* caring for the sick. My job is to peel the potatoes for the soup and soak the corn flour for the *atole*, which is all anyone can stomach, and even that, not for very long. Dear God, please help us. The death bells are tolling all over the city.

another day, morning

Sor Clara was found dead by the gate. They don't think she died of the disease, but of old age, but still they brought her in here and her body has been dragged out to the alley that runs behind the infirmary where the pestilent bodies are collected in the night. It rains all the time and the sound of teeth chattering and constant groaning is beginning to affect my nerves. Dear God, I miss Panoayán. I want my mother.

Tía is working too hard. Even Padre Antonio has asked that she take more care, for she holds the dying sisters in her arms and croons to them as though they were children. She's taken to wearing a hair shirt under her shift and doesn't eat and sleeps only two hours a day, between the nones and the vespers bells. Dear God, don't let her become infected. Please, God, make her stop punishing herself.

Sor Agustina was brought in ill last night and passed at sunrise.

Sor Melchora has the rest of the sisters walking around the cloister in the rain, the backs of their tunics torn to better administer discipline to their bodies. Even through the sound of the rain I can hear the bite of the scourge on bare flesh and the nearly demented cry of their prayers. I peer through the shutters of the infirmary and a terrible fear invades me as I watch them. Some walk on their knees and instead of whipping themselves, they lick the flagstones, their wet coifs plastered to their heads and their veils dragging heavily behind them.

Padre Antonio and Father Nazario brought the tabernacle and said a Mass in the infirmary and gave everyone Communion. I feel so much better now with the body of Christ inside me.

5 of February of 1695

Tía insisted that I find out the date today, and tears came to her eyes when I told her it was Saint Agatha's feast day. I can't believe it's already a new year and that we've been besieged by these epidemics for so long. Padre Antonio collapsed this morning on one of the *beatas* to whom he was giving extreme unction, and Tía's been attending exclusively to him all day.

"*Por favor*, Juana," I heard him telling her, "get yourself out of here. Don't let yourself die like this. I thought you were flying toward perfection, but I see that you're just indulging in revenge."

"Revenge against whom, Padre?"

"Against God, Juana. I know you. I know how you think."

"Quiet yourself, Padre. Here's Father Nazario to take you back to your house."

"If it isn't revenge then it's something worse," he said.

"Please, Padre. You mustn't distress yourself."

"Saint Peter won't let you into Heaven if you do that, Juana."

I wonder what he meant.

17 of February of 1695

Father Nazario came to tell us that Padre Antonio died today. Tía fell to her knees and started praying the rosary. Mother Andrea is worried. She says Tía looks deranged. Her cheeks are flushed and her eyes are always glazed. Mother Andrea says she looks like a sack of bones inside the habit.

6 of March of 1695

At last Tía is sleeping. For days she's been tossing violently in the bed, consumed with fever, her skin like an iron just lifted from the coals. She's lost control of her body functions, and I watch Mother Andrea tending to her, cleaning her, cooling her body with wet cloths. I rub eucalyptus oil into her feet and hands, which look awkwardly large compared to her meager body. Her skin has gone almost completely yellow from one day to the next. I sing her songs, snippets of her own *villancicos* that I remember. She won't eat a thing, and we've taken to giving her a wet sponge to suck on when her tongue hangs out of her mouth like a dry fish. I'm so afraid. I know she's dying. My *tía*'s dying. Only Mother Andrea's looks keep me in check.

23 of March of 1695

I've been bleeding Tía's arms to see if we can get the infection out of her body, but it doesn't seem to help. Each bleeding seems to have the opposite effect, seems to age her and make her even weaker. Father Nazario administered last rites yesterday, rubbed her eyelids and her forehead with that oil for the dead. Dear God! I'm so conflicted. I know it's selfish of me to want to keep her alive when her body is so diseased—her belly is one hard lump now—but I don't want her to leave me. I don't want her to die.

7 of April of 1695

Tía woke up at the sound of the prime bells looking alarmed.

"Concepción," she said to me. "You'll be late. They'll see you. Hurry up."

"Hush, Tía," I said. "Go back to sleep. There's no Concepción here. It's me, Belilla. Hush."

But she wouldn't be appeased. She kept rambling about money and pirates and going to Panoayán. "Stay with my mother," she said breathlessly, gripping my hands with a strength that I never would have expected from one as ill as she is. "Don't go anywhere with that prisoner, Concepción. Promise me you'll stay in Panoayán, you'll stay with my mother." And then she started stroking my face with those cold yellow hands of hers. "I need to know you're safe, *cariño*," she said. "Will you promise?"

452

"I promise," I said, and kissed her on the forehead, and she went back to sleep.

I remember Concepción's eyes. They were different colors, and I remember thinking how ugly she was, and I couldn't understand why Tía always let her join our visits. *Cariño*, she called her, and even in the grip of this disease she's worried about Concepción's safety. Why doesn't she talk to me that way? Doesn't she worry about me? Doesn't she realize she's leaving me all alone here? God forgive me. After all these years of prayer, I'm still jealous.

"Prayer won't take away your sins, Belilla," my *tía* told me when I first got here. "It just helps you forgive yourself for not being perfect." I remember thinking she was wrong, thinking I would be a better nun than she. How stupid I've been! She's been vomiting a green-black humor. I can tell by looking in her eyes that she's already left us. I pray to all of the saints to take her.

17 OF APRIL OF 1695, SUNDAY

QUERIDA MAMÁ,

I write to tell you that after months of battling the diseases that afflicted the House of San Jerónimo, Tía Juana succumbed to her destiny at four o'clock this morning. I stayed with her until she died, attending to her as she attended to the others before she became infected by the disease. She did not want me near her, afraid I, too, would grow ill, but I refused to leave her bedside. Mostly I rubbed her feet. She found great comfort in that, although toward the end she suffered severe pains in her womb and did not want to be touched. She had not eaten for five weeks and could barely suck water from the sponge. She was spewing a thick dark green liquid that reeked of spirits. Mother Andrea held her in her arms while she passed.

Mother Andrea will not let Tía's body be removed from the convent, like the others who have died of this same plague. She wants her buried in the crypt under the lower choir. The Mass is on Tuesday and she's going to ask Tía's friend, Don Carlos, to say the eulogy. Tía Josefa will be here. Won't you please come to see me? I feel so alone.

Your loving daughter,
Belilla (Sor Isabel María)
of the House of San Jerónimo

DEAR CONDESA DE PAREDES,

It is with deep sadness that I write to you today but I promised my *tía* that I would. A terrible illness infected her flesh and she left us in the early morning of the 17th of this month, though it wasn't until today that we lowered her body into the crypt. The bells tolled for two days and the church was filled with mourners. From the moment we laid her out, her friends and admirers came to pay their respects to our tenth muse. I hate to say this for fear of cursing her immortal soul, but I think she wanted to die. She said she had died already, the best part of her, and that her body was finally following her spirit to the grave. I can't believe I'll never see her again. That she lies under that heavy stone in the choir.

Instead of commending her soul to God, the last thing she said was your name, and she quoted a line from one of her poems: "Lovely illusion for whom I happily die, sweet fiction for whom I painfully live." She is buried with the ring you gave her, the one that opens like a locket with your portrait inside. Mother Andrea wanted me to include these letters of yours with my missive. They are unopened for Tía was not allowed to read any correspondence and Mother Andrea preferred to keep them sealed and under lock and key. I include also this sketch I found among Tía's papers; I believe it is a sketch of the volcanoes with something glowing above them very much like a moon but with long rays that seem to arc over the valley. I send it because it is labeled "the comet, la Condesa." I suppose you know what she means. On the back of the sketch you will find a poem written in my *tía*'s poor handwriting, "Litany in the Subjunctive," it's called. The writing has faded much over the years, but I hope you will still be able to discern the words which, I'm sure, were meant only for your eyes.

And now, Señora, I must leave you, for I have another promise to keep to my *tía* Juana.

I remain respectfully yours, and please give my regards to your son, whom I remember fondly,

Sor Isabel María (Belilla)

PS: Would you please send me copies of Tía's other books for my own collection? I have only *Castalian Inundation* and would like to have the others. Tía's copies were confiscated with the rest of her books.

twilight, day of my tía's burial

I've been sitting here in the damp shade of the toolshed for hours. The sun is going down so I can barely see what I'm writing. I came here right after the burial to exhume Pandora's Box from the niche. It's the last promise I made to my *tía*. I cannot believe that she's really gone and that all that's left of her are these scribblings from the silent depths of her heart, and the book she gave me of her writings, her firstborn, as she called it.

Our last conversation kept echoing in my mind as Don Carlos said the eulogy. It was just before she died and she was lucid enough to know that Mother Andrea was holding her, but I guess by then she was finished with secrets.

"You must do something for me, Belilla." She barely had the strength to speak, and I bent my head close to her mouth to hear her.

"Pandora's Box," she said. "You must burn Pandora's Box."

"Yes, Tía."

"Burn it. All of it. Promise me."

"I promise."

"My pocket," she said. "The key."

I didn't tell her that I had already found the key and transgressed upon her privacy. She was still for a few minutes, and then her fingers gripped my arm.

"Belilla?" she said

"I'm right here, Tía."

"If you read it, don't hate me. And don't tell your mother. Don't tell Josefa. They'd hate me if they knew."

"I could never hate you, Tía. How can you say that? I've always admired you. I wanted to be just like you."

She closed her eyes, but I could see the pupils shifting under the translucent skin of her eyelids, and she maintained her grip on my arm. Mother Andrea started to cry, her tears falling on Tía's hair. She had turned almost completely gray in the last months and yet her face had grown so small and thin she looked like a child wasting inside the habit.

"No, *cariño*," she said. "You don't know what you're saying. You can't be just like me. It's too heavy." She started to cough and a dark spittle stained the chapped flesh of her lips.

"Don't vex yourself, Juana," said Mother Andrea, stroking her forehead.

Her eyes opened again and her look was almost fierce. "Belilla?"

"Don't worry, Tía. I'm still here."

"You must write to la Condesa for me. After you burn Pandora's Box, you must write to her." She licked her lips, and I could tell that she was trying to remember something. "*Bella ilusión por quien alegre muero, dulce ficción por quien penosa vivo.* Tell María Luisa I said that."

"Yes, Tía."

She squeezed my arm again and I kissed her hand. And then the fierceness faded. The eyes closed again. The grip loosened. We sat with her for another hour listening to the waning of her breath. And then, very quietly, she was gone. Mother Andrea's sobs shook the cot.

I tore my scapular and tied up her chin so that her jaw wouldn't harden with her mouth open. She should not look undignified. We cleaned the body and embalmed it in bandages soaked in limewater to keep the infection, if there is one, from incubating down in the crypt. Then we laid her out in the white tunic and veil of a novice. She's entering a new novitiate now, said Mother Andrea. She wore a wreath of violets and roses and held the candle and the missal of the Order, her rosary draped around her wrists. Nobody saw, but after we took the body to be laid out in the choir, just before the sisters arrived for the wake, I tucked the ring with la Condesa's miniature portrait on it under her left hand, and under her right I placed a small feather, a dark blue one I found in the courtyard. She always said she felt incomplete without a quill.

The penumbra in the shed grows darker around this little pyre of twigs and leaves. I feed the pages of Tía's journal into the flames, one by one, and they curl and crackle and turn black. Tía's handwriting vanishes in the smoke. La Condesa's letters, la Marquesa's, everything must burn. That is what I promised. The bells are ringing for vespers, but I will not go until this task is done, until all that remains of Tía's secrets are the ashes that she, too, will become. The ashes from which she will rise like that mythical bird whose name graces the title of her first book: Phoenix of México.

Litany in the Subjunctive

If I could rub myself
along your calf,
feel your knee
break the waters of my shame;

if I could lay my cheek
against the tender sinews
of your thigh,
smell the damp
cotton that Athena
never wore, her blood
tracks steaming in the snow;

If I could forget
the devil and the priest
who guard my eyes   .
with pitchfork and with host;

If I could taste
the bread, the blood, the salt
between your legs
as I taste mine;

If I could turn myself
into a bee and free
this soul, those bars
webbed across your window
would be vain, that black
cloth, that rosary, that crucifix—
nothing could save you
from my sting.

Author's Postscript

Three hundred three years ago today, on 5 March 1694, Sor Juana Inés de la Cruz renewed her testament of faith to the Order of Saint Jerome by signing her name in blood. Today I finish the first English-language novel on her life,[1] a book that became my own life's blood for nearly a decade. I remember how the story was born, while sweeping my apartment in Boston and trying to imagine how to tell the story of this incredible woman, this first feminist of the Americas, tenth muse of Mexico, great-great-great, hundredfold-great-grandmother of my Mexican heritage. In one literally sweeping instant I conceived of the entire story, and it has taken me nine years to put flesh on that subject, to research her life, her times, her work. To learn her voice. To feel her words and understand her relationships.

Nearly all of the characters here are historically "true," that is, they lived under their own names and were related to each other as shown. Sor Juana, some of her sisters in religion, most of her family, the Viceroys and Vicereines, the Archbishops, the Bishop of Puebla, Sigüenza y Góngora, Belilla, even Jane—or rather, Juana de San José, Sor Juana's slave, whose name I anglicized to keep the reader from confusing her with the protagonist— all of them existed. Whether their characters were as I depicted is another story, as this is my interpretation of them, a writer's license into the realm of imagination and possibility. Whether Sor Juana had an assistant we will never know, although, again, it is historically "true" that she housed other servants and boarders in her cell. One of them may have been Concepción, though she is entirely fictional and the protagonist of her own story in a book to come.

Elsewhere I engage in a more direct argument with Octavio Paz about his interpretation of Sor Juana's "sapphic tendencies,"[2] but I do want to acknowledge the wealth of historical and political data about seventeenth-century Mexico that I gleaned from his book. His analysis of Sor Juana's poetry, particularly her love poetry to the Vicereines, I agreed with *not so much*, but Paz's work challenged me to delve deeper into the baroque structures of her verse, which, thanks to Margaret Sayers Peden's magnificent translations, facilitated my own translations and proved to me that, in fact, Sor Juana did leave us ample evidence of her desires, cloistered though they may have been, even to herself.

Although hailed as the "first feminist of America" as early as 1925 by Latin Americanist Dorothy Schons, the feminist label did not resurface in Sor Juana scholarship until 1974. To my delight, feminist translations of Sor Juana's writing, as well as critical readings of her texts rooted in feminist theory, surfaced in the course of writing this novel. Though they still shed little light on the matter of Sor Juana's sexuality, these books helped me to place her squarely within the theoretical and epistemological framework of contemporary feminist discourse. Two other texts about the documented existence of lesbian nuns prior to modernity—Judith Brown's *Immodest Acts* about a lesbian abbess in fifteenth-century Italy (Oxford: Oxford University Press, 1986) and Catalina de Erauso's memoirs published as *Lieutenant Nun: Memoir of a Transvestite in the New World* (New York: Beacon Press, 1996)—emboldened my conclusions about Sor Juana's "inclinations." Needless to say, my views are radically different from those of Octavio Paz and the homophobic "sorjuanistas" he represents, for I believe that Sor Juana not only refused to submit to the male construction of her gender, which would have women silent, ignorant, and pregnant, but also rejected what Adrienne Rich calls "compulsory heterosexuality" by joining a separatist community and cross-dressing as a nun.

I hope that Mexican readers will see that it is a patent homophobia, outweighed only by Mexican nationalism, that must deny or justify or pathologize this crucial aspect of Sor Juana's subjectivity. Perhaps, if they can overcome this, they will understand that it is not disrespect but a profound love and admiration for this Mexican cultural symbol second only to the Virgin of Guadalupe that leads me to disclose/dis-clothes what I see as her true inclinations.

There are many whom Sor Juana has visited in our time. Several of us, interestingly, are *fronterizas* from the El Paso-Juárez/Texas-Mexico border: the artist, Martha Arat; fellow writers, Estela Portilla-Trambley and Pat Mora, and me. Tell my story, Sor Juana says, you who can tell it in a language less veiled, you who have no Inquisition guarding your eyes and tongue. The late Argentine director María Luisa Bemberg made a sensitive and provocative film using Sor Juana's own epithet, *I, The Worst of All* (1990), as the title. In the compact disc *Sor Juana Hoy* (1995), Ofelia Medina, Mexican actress and performance artist, has set Sor Juana's poems to the contemporary rhythms of Mexican balladry, letting audiences hear the prescient feminism, pervasive eroticism, and postmodern ironies of this, our, Tenth Muse of Latin America.

I would like to thank my mother, Teyali Falcón, for the gift of this compact disc, and for the many other contributions to my research that she has provided in my nine-year dance with Sor Juana, and especially for the portrait of Juana Inés. Thanks to my buddy, Emma Pérez, for reading the even longer first draft and sending me daily email affirmations. Thanks to my "Honey," for her example of a dignified life. Thanks to las Madres, the goddesses and women of my altar who all these years have unfailingly responded to my diverse petitions for physical, mental, and spiritual stamina. Thanks to Emilie Bergmann for her stamp of approval. And thanks to my editor, Andrea Otañez, for finding as much spiritual nourishment in Sor Juana's story as I do.

Most important, I apologize and offer most sincere penitence to my *compañera*, Deena J. González, for my neglect of home and heart as I gave myself over to finishing this novel. Without her support, encouragement, inspiration, without those occasional letters she wrote me in the voice of la Condesa (and from which I borrowed at will, seeing them as the Vicereine's missives to her beloved, though distant and disembodied, Juana), without her patient ministrations to my writer's ego, I would still be sweeping the story back and forth in my mind.

Coatlicue, Aztec goddess of creation and destruction, was sweeping the temple one day and found a hummingbird feather. She put it into her bosom and continued sweeping, only to discover a few months later that she carried the war god in her womb. In many ways, Sor Juana has been my war god.

A.G.A.

5 March 1997

Claremont, California

NOTES

1. Though this is the first to be published, it is actually the second English-language novel on Sor Juana's life. The first is Dorothy Schons's "Sor Juana: A Chronicle of Old Mexico," which the author calls a "novelized" biography. The original manuscript is in

the Dorothy Schons Archives at the Benson Library's Latin American collection, University of Texas at Austin; this collection also houses the convent of San Jerónimo's *Book of Professions*, where Sor Juana signed her name in blood.

2. See my "The Politics of Location of the Tenth Muse of America: Interview with Sor Juana Inés de la Cruz," in *Living Chicana Theory*, ed. Carla Trujillo (Berkeley: Third Woman Press, 1998), 136–65.

Acknowledgments

Because this book would not have been possible without exhaustive research into the life and times of its protagonist, I want to acknowledge the many scholars whose work I devoured in my quest to know Sor Juana. Though they are too numerous to be named individually here, certain sources stand out as crucial to my investigation: Octavio Paz's *Sor Juana Inés de la Cruz, o, las trampas de la fe* (Barcelona: Editorial Seix Barral, 1982) as well as its translation by Margaret Sayers Peden (Cambridge, Mass.: Harvard University Press, 1988); Luis Harss's translation and critical analysis of "Primero Sueño," *Sor Juana's Dream* (New York: Lumen Books, 1986); Irving Leonard's *Baroque Times in Old Mexico* (Ann Arbor: University of Michigan Press, 1986); Alan Trueblood's *Sor Juana Anthology* (Cambridge, Mass.: Harvard University Press, 1988); *Feminist Perspectives on Sor Juana Inés de la Cruz*, edited by Stephanie Merrim (Detroit: Wayne State University Press, 1991); Amanda Powell and Electa Arenal's feminist translation of Sor Juana's Respuesta, *La Respuesta / The Answer* (New York: Feminist Press, 1994); Margarita López-Portillo's *Estampas de Sor Juana Inés de la Cruz* (México: Bruguera, 1979); and all of Margaret Sayers Peden's lucid and lyrical renditions of our "abuelita's" scribblings, now anthologized in *Poems, Protest, and a Dream* (New York: Penguin, 1997). The scholarly articles of Electa Arenal, Emilie Bergmann, Asunción Lavrin, Georgina Sabat-Rivers, Dorothy Schons, and Nina M. Scott also proved invaluable. Four other extremely important texts were R. Douglas Cope's *The Limits of Racial Domination* (Madison: Wisconsin University Press, 1994), *Two Hearts, One Soul: The Correspondence of the Condesa de Galve, 1688–96* (Albuquerque: University of New Mexico Press, 1993), the catalog to the exhibition, *Baroque Mystique: Women of Mexico-New Spain, Seventeenth and Eighteenth Centuries* (San Antonio, Texas: Instituto Cultural Mexicano, 1994), and the English translation of a sixteenth-century manual on the religious education of novices, *Instruction of Novices*, by the Ven. Fr. John of Jesus and Mary

Loughrea Co. Galway: (M. S. Kelly, 1920). The facsimiles of Sor Juana's signatures, her petition to sign her testament of faith, and the selections
from a legal document concerning the transfer of a slave to Sor Juana
were taken from *Testamento de Sor Juana Inés de la Cruz y otros documentos*,
published in Mexico in 1949. Finally, it is important to acknowledge the
Claustro de Sor Juana, a private university in Mexico City situated on the
grounds of the restored cloister of San Jerónimo, Sor Juana's convent,
which continues to keep alive the myth and memory of our tenth muse.
The Claustro recently published a fabulous tome entitled *Sor Juana y su
mundo,* edited by Sara Poot Herrera, to commemorate the three-hundredth
anniversary of Sor Juana's death (México, D.F.: Universidad del Claustro
de Sor Juana, 1995). The bookstore at the Claustro is still the best place to
find a variety of publications by and about Sor Juana, from a limited edition facsimile of the *Carta atenagórica* to a comic book version of her life.

Except for one poem, all the poetry cited in this book is Sor Juana's, as
are the excerpts from the "Respuesta a Sor Filotea" and from the letter she
wrote to her confessor in 1682, which appears in the appendix to Paz's biography. The translations of the excerpts and of those poems that I did not
translate myself are by Margaret Sayers Peden, Electa Arenal, Amanda
Powell, and Alan Trueblood.

Although attributed to Sor Juana in the text, all the journal entries and
personal letters that appear throughout the manuscript are my own creation. The final poem in the novel, "Litany in the Subjunctive," is also my
own, published under a different title in *Blue Mesa Review*, no. 2 (Spring
1990). Excerpts of the novel have been published in *Growing Up Chicano/a*
(New York: William Morrow, 1993) and *Tasting Life Twice: Lesbian Literary Fiction by New American Writers* (New York: Avon, 1995).